Who hasn't thought Pride and Prejudice could use more dragons?

Praise for Maria Grace

"Innovating and addictive ... this lady does know how to tell a story and how to invent an incredible new world ." *From Pemerley to Milton*

"Maria Grace did a wonderful job spinning a tale that's enjoyable for Austen lovers who do and who don't typically delve into the fantasy genre because she does a great job balancing the dragon world she has created alongside Austen's characters." *Just Jane 1813*

"Grace has quickly become one of my favorite authors of Austen-inspired fiction. Her love of Austen's characters and the Regency era shine through in all of her novels." *Diary of an Eccentric*

THE DRAGONS OF PEMBERLEY

Maria Grace

White Soup Press

Published by: White Soup Press

Dragons of Pemberley
Copyright © 2022 Maria Grace

For information, address
author.MariaGrace@gmail.com

ISBN-13: **978-0-9997984-7-8** (White Soup Press)

Author's Website: RandomBitsofFaascination.com
Email address: Author.MariaGrace@gmail.com

Dedication

For my husband and sons.
You have always believed in me.

1
Chapter

June 9, 1815 Derbyshire, England

PEMBERLEY!

Elizabeth swallowed back tears as the luxurious traveling coach, expertly driven by Alister Salt, crossed over that little, almost imperceptible bump in the road that meant home was around the next bend. Soon the steady clop of horses' hooves and the scratchy footfalls of the guard drakes Kingsley and Sergeant, running beside the carriage, would stop. No more road dust leaving her eyes gritty and her nose itching. No more watching the world go by as she sat and sat and sat.

They would be home.

She leaned back with the rock and sway of the carriage springs, melting into soft squabs. One could hardly object to traveling in a conveyance endowed with every possible comfort: from sleeping platforms to a tiny desk that dropped down from one wall. The Blue Order spared no expense in assuring their comfort and protection on the journey back home. The size of their party proved the only disadvantage— three ladies, three gentlemen, an infant, and seven minor dragons—and meant the men traveled in a lesser coach, separate from the ladies. It might be proper, but traveling at Darcy's side would have been far more agreeable.

Soon.

Soon that distance from him would no longer be nagging at the back of her mind. Soon this netherworld existence between here and there would be over, and life would begin again.

She drew a deep breath. There it was, a hint of peonies in the air. The bushes near the road that approached the house often bloomed earliest, in riots of pink and white, an exuberant greeting to Pemberley visitors.

Her nose wrinkled a bit. Anne's napkin needed to be changed soon. She opened one eye and glanced at May, the little black tatzelwurm curled up beside Anne in her sleeping basket. The way her decidedly cat-like nose twitched, the little dragon agreed.

Anne had grown so much since they had left Pemberley—it seemed like a lifetime ago. What would life be like now that she was in leading strings, able to move about and discover for herself? Mrs. Sharp, the new nurse, would no doubt have her hands full, especially with all the household dragons that would be spending time in the nursery with Anne. Elizabeth had warned her that managing those dragon interactions would be part of the nurse's duties, but it would not be surprising if Mrs. Sharp underestimated the sheer number of household dragons that would be involved. Babies did not usually receive so much company.

The manor house appeared as they rounded the final bend in the road, majestic, commanding, but most of all welcoming. The first time Elizabeth had seen the manor, it had intimidated her for so many reasons. She did not belong in such a fine place; she did not deserve such a home; she had no idea how to oversee such an establishment. So many tenants and servants depending on her to manage properly; an entire community looking to her for guidance and direction. Things Mama had never prepared her for.

But surrounded by people and dragons who wanted her to succeed, Elizabeth had found her place in the stately stone manor, serene and strong, as it looked out over fields and sheep. Oh, how she needed to be there once again.

They had definitely been gone too long.

"That is Pemberley?" Lydia squealed, face pressed against the side glass, eyes wide in little-girl wonder.

"No, my dear sister, that is the servants' quarters and the actual house is another mile ahead." Elizabeth quirked her eyebrow.

"You have become such a tease! Returning to Derbyshire is good for you." Lydia chuckled.

"Indeed, it is." Tiny fairy dragon April, in her turquoise-blue glory, hovered near the window with black- and-red Cosette beside her, her flight unhampered by her previous injuries. "You will like it here.

It is a proper dragon estate, with proper respect for the minor dragons who live here."

Truth and Mercy, Mrs. Sharp's pair of little green zaltys, slithered over Lydia's lap to the window to get a view as well, forked tongues flicking with excitement.

Mrs. Sharp tucked little Anne's blanket around her shoulders. "I wish the same could have been said for our last family. My little Friends were not welcome there."

"I wonder if it was for a general discomfort with dragons around children or it was something about snake-types in particular." Elizabeth studied the pretty little zaltys with noses pressed to the side glass. Sleek and emerald green, "dainty" captured them better than anything else. Big, dark eyes framed by long eyelashes spoke of their gentle dispositions and caring nature, while their yellow-and-red head crests resembled women's hats, giving them just a touch of whimsy. What was not endearing about the pair? "It seems that even people who are generally well disposed to dragons often have some discomfort when it comes to snake-type dragons, especially small ones."

The late-afternoon sun bathed Mrs. Sharp's deep-amber skin and shimmered off the soft grey curls peeking out from her cap. "It is not uncommon that people base their judgement on how one appears, Lady Sage. More than once, my Friends have been unwelcome in otherwise dragon-friendly company."

"Well, that shall not be a problem here. You should know, Mrs. Reynolds has mentioned that the dearth of snake-types at the manor was a true disadvantage."

"How extraordinary." Mrs. Sharp's eyebrows lifted so high they almost touched the silver curls on her forehead.

"You will find Mrs. Reynolds a remarkable woman for many reasons. I expect you will get on famously."

Mrs. Sharp's eyebrows rose even higher. Yes, it was a touch unusual to lavish such praise on one's servants, but letting someone know they were appreciated was hardly ever a mistake.

"How many minor dragons are there at Pemberley?" Lydia alternately stroked Truth and Mercy as Cosette came to rest on her shoulder.

"On the estate as a whole, I really cannot say at the moment. We will have to conduct a census of the wild dragons come summer. All the staff, inside and out, are dragon-hearers and their Friends are welcome. Most of the staff dragons have Friends among the warm-blooded staff, but a few are with us simply of their own accord. We have no dragon-deaf living at the manor house." A shudder slithered down Elizabeth's spine. How complicated life would be to have dragon-deaf in the household.

"Does that mean you will not invite Mama, Jane, or Kitty to stay with us?" Lydia asked, with no trace of the petulance that once would have dripped from those words.

"That is a good question, one to which I do not have a good answer. With us back in the neighborhood and the Bingleys not living far enough away to discourage travel between the households, it may be difficult to avoid."

"Cosette and I can easily persuade your mother that Pemberley is cold and drafty and she does not like such places." April suggested, landing on Elizabeth's knee, her head cocked just so.

"I do not think I will ask that of you just yet, but you can be sure it will be kept under consideration." Elizabeth scratched under April's chin. "We will have to see them soon in any case. Mama's last letter to Papa suggested that they need his approval of Kitty's beau soon."

Lydia sighed, wistfulness in her eyes. "Kitty is quite smitten with him."

"Has she been writing to you?" Elizabeth asked. "I thought she was quite put out at the idea that you were permitted to attend 'finishing school' and enjoy a ball for your come-out while she was not."

"She was at first, but once she discovered the joy of being Mama's only daughter at home, she quite forgave me." Lydia shrugged. "In any case, it seems she is anxious for approval so that the banns might be read. Mama delights in the notion of four daughters married."

"You do understand—"

"That my sisters are dragon-deaf and my own affiliation with the Order now makes things complex. Yes, Lizzy, even I am aware of the complications of the circumstance."

"I did not mean to imply … I do not think you are stupid. That is not what I meant." What a challenge, adjusting to this new Lydia.

"At Mrs. Fieldings' school, there was a lot of talk about the difficulty of 'half-Blue' families. Quite a number of the girls there came from such situations."

Perhaps she needed to take time to ask Lydia more about that. It was not something that Papa had ever talked about, but perhaps he should have. Were such families more apt to problems? It would stand to reason that they would be. Perhaps that was another topic she should write about. She needed to add that to her list.

"Oh, oh look! Is that the staff lining up to greet us? I had no idea our arrival would be so grand!"

Chapter 2

PEMBERLEY MANOR, THE core of hearth and home, the seat of the Darcy family, so dear it was almost a member of the family, revealed itself as they completed the last turn on the way home. Sturdy pale stone walls, strong and unchanging, surveyed its domain and declared it secure. Something tight released in Darcy's chest, and he leaned back into the carriage's stiff squabs. Perhaps, just perhaps, life as he knew it might begin again.

"One never grows tired of that sight." Richard Fitzwilliam chin-pointed out the smudgy side glass toward the manor. Sharp and rectangular like his father, Lord Chancellor Matlock, the lines beside his eyes spoke to the weariness the last few months had laid upon him. "Although that look of satisfaction you wear, Darcy, might become exhausting."

After all that they had been through whilst in London—so many impossible things had happened—somehow it was a relief to see the manor's classic lines and square countenance, still standing, overlooking well-groomed fields and flocks.

Better still to be standing on the doorsteps, not viewing it from a mile away, through the windows of a tired, dusty, sweat-stinking, coach. Soon, very soon.

"A man has a right to be satisfied at coming home." Darcy glanced across the coach at the Honorable Undersecretary of the Blue Order, Mr. Swinton St. John, who snored softly, slumped against the sidewall, as he had been for much of their time on the road. The man's hairline was receding, his belly paunchy, and his eyes close-set and squinty. Every time he spoke, his face screwed up like he had a bad smell under his nose, which entirely fit both his conversation and his personality.

Though being apart from Elizabeth was a form of torture unique unto itself, it was just as well that she had not been stuck in a carriage with the man. The years notwithstanding, she still bore him more than a passing resentment. Darcy was developing one of his own to match. St. John had been the one to conduct her testing for admission into the Order a dozen years or so ago. According to her and April, he had been insensitive, rude, and harsh throughout the whole matter. Though Darcy had thought their assessment might have been colored by the suffering experienced at his hand, after spending days with him on the road, he suspected they were actually gracious in their evaluation of him.

According to Castordale, Sir Edward Dressler's Pa Snake and one of Elizabeth's early champions among the Order officers, St. John disliked her father, resented that he held office as Historian, distrusted women, and did not believe that children should be able to hear dragons. So intent was he on proving his point, he engineered the entire experience to set Elizabeth up to fail.

Like many, he had been wrong, and not pleased to have been proven so—especially under circumstances so stacked against her. Circumstances he had conveniently arranged to deftly avoid criticism toward himself. What he lacked in character, he seemed to make up for in cleverness. Not the kind of man with whom Darcy wanted to have any dealings.

Neither his boorish manners nor his ignorant opinions on far too many matters seemed to have altered from Elizabeth's early descriptions of him. St. John still thought women had no place in the Order, considered Bennet an irritating old curmudgeon—on which point he might not be entirely in error—and disliked the entire notion of establishing any new Order office, especially that of the Dragon Sage. Why should the Order change when it had withstood the ravages of time better than any other governmental agency?

But he was sympathetic toward minor dragons — his one, lone virtue.

After their first day of travel, Richard had privately suggested St. John was still grieving the loss of his Friend, minor drake Rottenstone, and his abrasive personality could be the consequence of his grief. The dragon had died two years ago or so. Sir Edward, Lord Physician to Dragons, said it was from an incurable case of talon rot that got into the blood, a truly horrid way to go.

But, even if that were the case, Darcy was disinclined to consider that an adequate excuse for persistent oafish tendencies.

On the other hand, Richard had on more than one occasion suggested that Darcy himself was not entirely good company on this journey either—even more so than his usual failings in social settings. Richard was probably being gracious. Considering the dangers of traveling, especially in such a large party with ladies and a child included, sociability was a low priority.

Neither the four guard drakes—Brutus and Axel, who ran alongside the men's coach, and Alister Salt's Friends, who guarded the ladies—nor his faithful cockatrice Friend Walker, who flew with Earl above their party, could calm his anxieties. Only being back at home would achieve that. Perhaps it was a little irrational, but Pemberley felt safe—far safer than being exposed on the road.

And finally, it was in sight.

"I imagine you will want the rest of the day to become reacquainted with your estate." St. John muttered, his voice scratchy and irritating, as he righted his posture and straightened his brown coat. When had he woken up?

"It is customary. In fact, I think several days would be appropriate." Richard rolled his eyes a bit—that favorite Fitzwilliam expression he would likely never give up.

"I have been away some months, and I will need to meet with my steward, the head shepherd, and several of the major farmers."

"The local vicar, the magistrate, and the head of the parish council, as well, I imagine?" St. John all but sneered. "I find it telling where Order business falls in your priorities."

"Excuse me?" Darcy might finally succumb to his urge to pitch the man out of the carriage, something he had considered more than once over the last several days.

"You do understand the seriousness of the matters at hand?" Something about St. John's questions felt entirely insincere.

Why had Darcy agreed to have a man who was a clear opponent to his wife and her office as a guest in his home? Now that same man was questioning his loyalty to the Order? The irony. "No other estate employs as many dragon Friends, dragons, and hearers without Friends as Pemberley. I would say the business of Pemberley is the business of the Order."

"I am sure you would."

"What precisely is that supposed to mean?" Darcy's voice dropped in pitch as he pulled his shoulders back and expanded his chest.

"That you have an egotistical, self-serving estimation of what Order business entails." St. John huffed and folded his arms over his chest. "Yes, yes, I am aware that you have carried the Dragon Slayer and that, in popular opinion, makes you quite the hero of the Order. But such showy demonstrations are not what keep the Order running. A true hero of the Order—"

"A true hero? Have you any notion of what you are saying, man?" Richard brought his foot down heavily and leaned forward, just a hint of danger in his eyes. "I would not so freely insult one who has come face to face with not just one, but two angry firedrakes with blood in their eyes and lived to tell the tale. Can you say you have done as much for the Order?"

St. John had probably not even faced an angry puck.

His cheeks seemed to puff and his face colored. "That is exactly the trouble with men like you. You see the sword as the final, best answer to all the Order's problems, and it is not."

"Then what would you suggest is the final, best answer?" Once offended, Richard would not be easily called off, so Darcy leaned back into the squabs to let them fight it out.

"Have you never heard the pen is mightier than the sword?" Such a smug look St. John wore.

"You are going to prove your point with a cliché? You must be mad. I have never had a man try to kill me with his pen."

"You think not?"

"I am rather certain with what implements my life has been threatened." Richard also bore the scars left by a number of those implements, but it would not be proper to mention that.

"Have you ever considered the orders that sent you into those actions?"

"What do you mean?"

"The king's orders, the general's order, all of the like, those were formed by a pen."

Richard snorted, his upper lip curled back.

"You think that too literal? What about the Pendragon Treaty and Accords? Those came into being by an act of the pen, not the sword. They accomplished what the sword could not."

Though Darcy loathed to admit it, St. John did have a point.

St. John leaned in, eyes narrow. "And how do you think the provisions of those documents are managed? I will give you a hint, it is not by the sword even now. No, it is by the office of the Secretary of the Order. Through our enforcement of each and every provision, in every county, every parish, every village, every estate. The state of the Dragon State rises and falls on the oversight of the Secretary and his division. Not even the Chancellor has so much influence on the day-to-day lives of those in the Order as we do." The tight little smile that stretched his thin lips was nothing short of self-important. "And after the recent showing of the Derbyshire dragons, it is quite clear that the affairs of this county have not been properly managed for quite some time."

Darcy stepped on Richard's foot, hard; an unsubtle suggestion that he not comment on this new round of veiled insults. "Yes, that is quite obvious, and unfortunate, but I can assure you that Pemberley—"

"Did you not just say that you have been away for quite some time and are not even well-acquainted with the affairs of your own estate?" St. John settled his hands over his paunch, so pleased with himself.

"I said no such thing. I have left trusted men in charge of all aspects of the estate." Heat crept up from Darcy's neck to his ears.

"Who have run it in your stead, leaving you unaware of the specific details of the estate."

"That does not imply that the estate has been ill-managed."

"It does not imply that it has been well-managed."

"I have faith—"

"That is well and good for you, but the Order does not run on faith. It runs on facts and on adherence to the rule of law. If your estate is as well in hand as you suggest, then I am certain you will not object to me beginning my audit of the region with Pemberley."

Oh, how he enjoyed his show of power. Despicable creature. "Audit Pemberley?"

"Have you a problem with that?"

"It is a waste of your time! Pemberley has never warranted Order interference, and it does not now."

"Are you refusing the Secretary of the Order?"

Richard leaned back, arms folded in a casual posture that he assumed when restraining himself from throttling an imbecile. "Auditing Pemberley is as absurd as auditing Matlock!"

"That is an interesting notion." St. John rubbed his chin with his knuckles, eyes taking on a dangerous glint. "When was the last time that Matlock was audited?"

"Matlock? The seat of the Chancellor of the Order? You do realize what you are suggesting?" Richard bolted upright, barely choking out the words.

"I am well aware of the dragon and Keeper assigned to that territory."

"Cownt Matlock attends to those matters himself. He has always overseen all Order matters on the estate."

"As well he should, since he is the leading dragon of Derbyshire. His territory should be the exemplar of the region."

"I am certain that it is. There is no need—"

"I will be the one to determine what is needed." St. John drummed his fingers against his knee. "Now that you have suggested it, I think auditing Matlock is a good idea, a very good one. In fact, since it is the Chancellor's territory, it deserves my first attentions.

Then, no other Keeper can complain, with Matlock providing an example in all things."

Richard's features crumpled into a mix of dread, frustration, and rage.

"You will provide for me an introduction to your brother, the viscount, yes? As I understand, he is junior Keeper and running the estate while Chancellor and Cownt Matlock are in London."

"I will do so, Mr. St. John. You will, though, do Matlock the courtesy of permitting me to call upon my brother first and inform him of your plans." Richard muttered through clenched teeth. "I assure you, it is in the best interest of the Order to do so."

"I suppose a day or so of warning will not make a significant change in my findings. That will be acceptable."

3
Chapter

So, THIS WAS Pemberley.

This huge, imposing stone monolith of a house surrounded by a vast circular drive, which rose like an ancient henge, was Pemberley.

Lydia hesitated as the footman tried to hand her out of the plush traveling coach. Neatly lined-up staff waited to greet the master and mistress of Pemberley in front of a massive oak front door that stood open to welcome them inside. The ensemble felt only slightly less intimidating than the reception line of dragons she had faced at the Cotillion.

So many small dragons standing among the staff! All looking so excited, so pleased that the Darcys were come home.

But she was not a Darcy.

Breathe, she needed to remember to breathe. Swooning before she even set foot on Pemberley grounds would not set the right tone for her visit at all! She gripped the carriage doorframe a little more tightly.

Of all that Elizabeth had told her about the house, none of it prepared her for it to be so very, very grand. Mama had a great deal to say about Mr. Darcy's—no, it was Sir Fitzwilliam now—about his wealth and consequence, but it all had felt like the flavor of exaggeration Mama was prone to.

But it was not. Not at all. He really must be rich as an earl.

Lydia sucked in another unsteady breath.

If Mama had any idea how grand a place Pemberley truly was, it would be difficult to persuade her by any means that she did not want to visit—or better yet, take up residence there. No wonder Lizzy had become so pensive at the thought. Mama should definitely not be in a place with so many dragons. Not even for an afternoon tea.

Even when Mama was under the draconic persuasion that the dragons were mundane creatures, she was short and impatient with them. No, Mama was rude. That was the truth of it. They interfered with her notion of how things should be. That was enough to bring out a side of her that was not so genteel. And that was not a healthy attitude when surrounded by dragons.

Lydia and Cosette would have to give the matter a good hard think and see what they could come up with to help Lizzy manage Mama. Cosette was clever with such things, and extremely persuasive when she needed to be.

It was the least they could do, all things considered.

With the footman's help, Lydia, Cosette on her shoulder, stepped down and hurried along the crunchy gravel path to Lizzy's side at the front of the servants' receiving line.

April flittered toward them. "Come, Cosette, I will introduce you to the household fairy dragons and the other dragons of the staff."

Cosette rested her front foot on Lydia's ear, her way of asking for Lydia's opinion. "Yes. It is gracious of you to make introductions, April. Thank you."

Cosette zipped off behind April.

Just how many fairy dragons were in line among the staff? Three at least. And several little drakes, pucks—and was that a lesser cockatrix? Yes, it seemed so. And there must be wyrms in the gardens and woods, tatzelwurms in the barns, not to mention the shepherding drakes in the fields, and probably a few cockatrice who discreetly guarded the poultry. Heavens above, so many!

Was Pemberley like this before Elizabeth became mistress, or was this a change she had wrought?

Considering the number of older servants in line with their Friends nearby, at least some of them must have been with the house since Mr. Darcy was a boy. How utterly unlike Longbourn, where Papa assiduously avoided having minor dragons in the house, except of course for April, whose presence he actively resented. And the late addition of Rumblkins, who he did not seem to appreciate either.

Oh, this place was going to take some getting used to.

"Lydia," Elizabeth gestured toward a woman who could only be the housekeeper, with a brown-spotted drake trotting beside her. "This is Mrs. Reynolds, Pemberley's housekeeper."

The old woman curtsied, her expression entirely impossible to read. She was a small, compact woman, a little like Hill at Longbourn, who had been known to wear her authority like a military rank. Given the way the other servants looked at her, respect, not fear, ran her command. Wire-rimmed glasses perched on her thin nose, on an equally thin face. Grey hair, not a curl in sight, peeked from the edges of her plain, sturdy mobcap. Clearly this was not a woman to cross.

Oh, what must she have heard about Lydia being sent to Mrs. Fieldings'? What must she think of her? Lydia's face burned. Oh, what a bother it was to have an embarrassing episode in one's past and forever wonder at what people knew and thought of one for it.

Auntie said there was nothing to do for the past but acknowledge it happened and walk on. Probably good advice, but it might be far easier for a dragon to follow than a young lady.

"I have heard a great deal about your excellent service to Pemberley." Lydia nodded at Mrs. Reynolds.

"Thank you, Miss Bennet." She spoke Lydia's name gently. That must be a good thing, no? "May I introduce Dale." A light brown drake the size of a hunting dog, with large dark spots, rose up on its hind feet, as though to shake her hand, and bobbed his head. Unusual.

Cream-colored, pointy scales ran from his chin to his shoulders, giving the appearance of an odd, spiky beard. More such scales ran along the back of his head, rather like the ring of hair many bald men had around the back of their heads. What a funny little dragon he was.

"April said she would introduce my Friend Cosette to the house dragons. I know she will be pleased to make your acquaintance, as am I." Lydia curtsied to the dragon. Naturally, the proper sort of greeting to a minor drake had completely fallen out of her head.

Dale matched her movements—that was supposed to be a sign of respect, was it not? "I make it my business to run errands from one part of the house to another. Your maid will show you how to summon me should you be in need of my services."

"I had no idea the house was so very large."

"Dale's service is much appreciated." Lizzy scratched him under the chin and the tip of his tail flicked. "As is that of all our household dragons."

Mrs. Reynolds signaled to a young maid, probably near Lydia's own age. Slightly taller than either Lizzy or Lydia, her round face and red cheeks matched her generally plump figure. "This is Betsey. I have assigned her as your maid for as long as you are with us, Miss Bennet."

"A maid? Of my own?" Lydia gasped and turned to Lizzy.

"That is the common practice, as I understand." The quirk of Lizzy's brow—she was teasing again!

"Are you comfortable with fairy dragons?" Lydia beckoned toward April and Cosette, who were conversing with a green puck farther down the line.

Betsey curtsied again and clicked her tongue three times. An iridescent-green fairy dragon zipped over and landed on her shoulder. "This is my Friend, Juniper. She is the smallest fairy dragon in the household. I have heard that Cosette is quite small, too."

"Yes, yes I am." Cosette zoomed in to hover in front of Betsey and Juniper. "But that does not mean I am slow or stupid."

"Of course not," Juniper said. "No more than I am. It is my job to help you become established here at Pemberley. I will show you where the best nectar flowers may be found and the places to avoid because of the rats and stoats. Oh, and all the best places to take a lovely bath."

No doubt she would also help Cosette find all the best places to listen for gossip as well. "I am glad that Cosette will have a companion here at Pemberley."

"Betsey, show Lydia to her rooms, then give her a tour of the house. Her trunks will be sent up as soon as they are unloaded." Lizzy turned to Lydia. "Go get acquainted with your new home."

Her new home! Lydia swallowed hard, whispering, "I won't disappoint you."

"I know."

"This will be your room, Miss Bennet." Betsey opened the door to a spacious chamber, light and airy, with the prettiest oak furniture and flowery paper hangings on the walls.

The counterpane, and bed and window curtains added soothing green tones that kept the room from feeling too busy. Though Lydia might have preferred more pink bits and a few pretty, fluffy pillows, it was still the finest room she had ever stayed in. Cosette whirred in and flew three circuits around the room, racing Juniper on the last one.

"As I understand it, the Lady Sage chose this room particularly for the flying space it provided." Betsey seemed to struggle against her smile. Servants were not supposed to have an opinion on such matters.

Lydia pressed a hand to her mouth, but could not contain her giggles. "How many households consider flying space when assigning quarters? Certainly, none I have ever known."

"Pemberley is well known among Order folk in Derbyshire for its welcome to small dragons and their Friends."

"Do not think I am criticizing, for I am certainly not. I know the Darcys are the best sort of Dragon Keepers and Friends, to be sure. It just does take a little bit of getting used to when one did not grow up in such a home. I imagine it did for you, did it not?"

"My father is the lead shepherd here, so I grew up with the shepherding drakes and all the barn tatzelwurms. It all seems rather normal to me, Miss." Betsey shrugged and her eyebrows rose in what seemed to be surprise.

Oh bother, Lydia had probably said something rather stupid. "Then you are very fortunate, I think. I know Lizzy is always happiest around many dragons, so one must assume that it is the province of dragons to make those with them happy. I expect, then, I shall be incandescently happy here at Pemberley." Yes, she was talking mostly nonsense and Betsey's expression confirmed it, but these were the right things to say in order to make a good go of it. It was also rather exhausting. "Show me the rest of the house. I can only imagine what it must be like."

"Shall I give you the housekeeper's public tour first, then I can show you the family rooms? Or do you prefer something else, Miss?"

"Pray lead on." With fairy dragons on their shoulders, Lydia followed Betsey out. Having a maid assigned to her was a lovely and thoughtful thing indeed, and more than she could have asked for. But it was also a bit strange and would take some getting accustomed to.

Betsey took her down the grand marble stairs, lined with graceful wrought-iron railings, to the front hall. How odd that, other than the staff dragons, there were no dragons to be seen in the décor at all. Every Blue Order establishment Lydia had ever seen was covered in draconic images from the front door to the back and everywhere in between. Many of them quite ugly, but as long as there were dragons, it hardly seemed to matter.

"I can see what you are thinking, Miss, and it is strange. Even our cottage has a carved dragon on the banister and fairy dragons carved into the wood trim. I have heard it said that generations of Darcys have thought that the dragons in Pemberley should all be of the flesh and blood variety, so only a few decorative ones may be found in the house."

"Have you heard why the past generations of Darcys decided that?"

"As I understand, and it is only from what I have heard. I am by no means certain. It is said that the Darcys thought that it was cheap lip service to decorate with dragons if there were no hospitality shown to them otherwise. So, they were determined to do different."

"That is a lovely sentiment, to be sure. It sounds much like something my sister would say." Perhaps that was why Lizzy had found such happiness with Darcy—Sir Fitzwilliam—so many similarities in the way they saw the world.

Betsey stopped at the base of the grand stairs. "The front hall here is most impressive, the largest in the county, next to that found at Matlock House, of course. The marble for the floor and staircase was imported from Italy, though a local blacksmith did all the ironwork in the house. Those paintings, hung over the hall table with the peonies, they are of the east and west views of the estate from the attics, where one can see for miles. This right here," she pointed to a hill on the east-facing painting, "is where Pemberley's lair is located, under that hill. It is well away from the sheep and the rest of the livestock. They get nervous with a dragon about, you know. So, the fields nearby are not used for grazing. On the west you can see the fields for the flocks, the dairy barns, and the stable for the horses."

"Do they still look like that today?"

"Later I can take you to the attics to see for yourself. But the barns are all bigger, as are the fields. Pemberley has flourished under Darcy management. The drawing rooms are just beyond." Betsey walked off, clearly assuming that Lydia would follow.

Betsey flung open the door, "Wait here whilst I get the curtains." She hurried to the large windows. "This is called the Great Drawing Room, where guests wait for dinner to be served. The room next to it is the Lesser Drawing Room, which is used when there are fewer guests. But this wall here, it can be opened up for larger parties, and we call that making the Grand

Drawing room." Betsey pulled back the curtains with a flourish and light poured into the room.

Great, grand, whatever it was called, it was easily the finest room Lydia had ever seen. With eggshell-blue walls and white trims and moldings, she scarcely wanted to enter it, much less touch anything within, covered as she was with travel dust. The ivory upholstery and gilded wood seating would surely be sullied by her person. Perhaps she was being a mite hard on herself, but with so many mirrors reflecting light and opulence, it was difficult to ignore the abundant reminders of her disheveled state.

From there, Betsey led her to the dining rooms, several of them: the great dining hall, whose long mahogany table could accommodate an astonishing number of guests; the family dining room, whose white-linen-covered long table seated twelve comfortably; and the cozy little morning room. That room felt most like Lizzy, with warm peachy walls reflecting light from the east-facing windows. The round table would seat eight comfortably, with several smaller, chinoiserie sideboards between the windows, conveniently near the table, for food and drink.

The master's study, the mistress's study, and the library followed in rapid succession, each one every bit as grand, in its own way, as the large public rooms.

The long gallery, containing artworks collected over generations of the Darcy family, concluded the tour of the ground floor. Deep-red walls and heavy, lush, gold curtains accented the paintings, and marble statuary lined the walls of the room that ran at least half the length of the back side of the house. The ground floor of Pemberley alone was bigger than all of Longbourn put together, even including attics and cellars.

"As I understand, this space," Betsey pointed to an open place on the wall, "is to be filled by a portrait of Sir Fitzwilliam and the Lady Sage."

How strange it was to consider Lizzy being part of the company in this room.

"Now upstairs." Betsey described the paintings that lined the grand stairs. Darcy ancestors tracing back, she said, to the first Darcy to inhabit these halls. Supposedly there were paintings in the attic that dated back to before the Darcys took residence. It would be interesting to see those, someday.

The second floor boasted an ivory-walled music room with a huge bay window surrounding a dainty ivory-and-gold pianoforte, a harp, and an entire matching cabinet for sheet music. Perhaps a dozen wooden chairs, painted gold with plum cushions, made an arc in two rows around the piano.

"Such a shame that Miss Darcy is not here to enjoy it. The music room has long been her favorite," Betsey said. "She was an excellent musician, but I am sure you have heard her play and sing and know that quite well. Such a sweet girl—did you have the opportunity to know her well?"

Clearly Betsey, and perhaps the rest of the household, were ignorant of Miss Darcy's true nature. Perhaps they did not know she had been sent off to the same school Lydia had attended. No doubt they would find out soon enough, but not from Lydia. Cosette had probably already told Juniper by now. Fairy dragon gossip circulated very, very quickly.

How would the staff react to that news, though? Would they somehow hold that against Lydia? Perhaps it was a trifle farfetched, but people's feelings rarely made real sense if one looked at them too closely.

Betsey revealed three upstairs parlors, one favored by the Lady Sage and probably best left for her use alone, unless by invitation; one for the use of the family; and one for the comfort of house guests. Lydia, of course, would have the use of the family parlor.

Something in the way Betsey explained that—there was something unspoken there, but it was difficult to tell just what.

The guest bedrooms—or at least what she saw of them, as there were too many to visit them all—with their adjoining dressing rooms and sitting rooms, were grander than her own. A tiny pang of jealousy tried to spark its way to life.

But those rooms were in the guest wing. Her room was in the family wing and that was grander than any guest room could ever be.

4 Chapter

June 9, 1815 Matlock Estate

RICHARD DISMOUNTED AND handed his—or rather Darcy's—horse off to the waiting groom and sauntered toward Matlock's front door. The Palladian-style manor, with its towering columns and austere, classical exterior, frowned down upon him, as it always had. Some things would never change. That was comforting in an odd, uncomfortable way.

Aching back, hips, knees, and the makings of a capital headache, not to mention rapidly advancing afternoon sun, demanded that this be a brief visit. All told, he would have preferred to have cleaned up and settled into one of Pemberley's guest rooms rather than jump on a horse and head out to Matlock.

But the alternatives were far, far worse.

Father hardly welcomed surprises, and Andrew … detested was hardly a strong enough word to describe his reactions. Bad enough that Matlock was to be audited first—no Fitzwilliam alive would consider that anything but the gravest of insults. Allowing that to come unexpected to Andrew's doorstep? Unthinkable.

The tall, imposing butler, stone-faced as ever, showed him to the family parlor, where Andrew would deign to receive his company. Ivory-and-gold striped paper hangings somehow gave the room greater formality, not less. So did the just-barely casual furnishings with impractically pale upholstery. Heaven forfend one actually relax and feel comfortable in any public room of the manor. Or any private one, for that matter.

"You could have bothered to clean up before appearing for dinner. That is still considered decent, you know." Andrew stood from his uncomfortable chair, where he pretended to read a book, tugging his jacket straight. He sniffed through his thin, sharp nose, his pale-blue eyes vaguely watery. "I thought you were staying at Pemberley. Your room has not been made up."

"I am staying at Pemberley." Richard would sooner stay at the inn in Lambton than at Matlock. Even the barn might be preferable. "I am here as a courtesy to you."

"Courtesy? To me? Really? How might that be? It has never been your way before." Andrew flicked imaginary dust from his sleeves with long fingers that had never seen a day of work.

No, he was not resentful of his elder brother, not at all.

"I have news that you might consider important to act upon before it is too late."

"Too late? That does make it all sound rather urgent, does it not? Well, then, tell me of it, or do I need to beg you? Or is it a bribe you are looking for? Overspent your allowance, perhaps?"

"I am not dependent upon Matlock for my upkeep. Have you forgotten I have an estate and Keep of my own?" Damn! He had fallen for Andrew's bait—again.

"Oh yes, you have that foreign wyrm to manage, that is right, and the quaint little plot of nowhere they gave you to Keep him on. Is the estate supporting you in the manner to which you are accustomed?" Why did Andrew so resent the fact that Richard had become a gentleman? The elevation in status should have improved Andrew's opinion, not lowered it.

"Netherford and I are quite satisfied, thank you."

"A messenger brought word that Cownt Matlock would be back in his lair soon. Something about returning Pemberley to her estate, is that right?"

"As I understand it."

"I do not understand the interest he takes in that annoying little dragon of Darcy's. I do hope he does not plan to stay long. He is such a cross old lizard, complaining about everything whilst he is here." With Andrew's attitude, it was no wonder Matlock should be cross.

"I do not know of his plans, but I expect what I have to tell you will not make him any less cranky."

"What is it, man? Do stop holding this news of yours over my head. Out with it!"

"The Undersecretary of the Order, the Honorable Swinton St. John, is at Pemberley now and means to take a very close look at the Derbyshire Dragons."

"Are you suggesting I should invite him to tea? I will let Martha know directly. She is the one to manage social engagements. I expect he will be disagreeable company, though. Everyone in the Secretary's department seems to be rather boorish, what with all the rules and regulations they insist upon."

"I am sure he has no desire to have tea with your wife." No one did, actually, but that was another matter entirely. "He will be coming to call upon you."

"Me? Why? Surely it is Father he wants to talk to."

"No, it is you."

"For heaven's sake, whatever for?" Color rose along Andrew's pale jaw.

It probably was in no one's best interest to continue to plague him—though it jolly well felt deserved. "Not only are you junior Keeper here, but you have been managing the Keep whilst Father has been in London."

"What of it?"

"St. John has gotten it in his craw that the entire county has been mismanaged, hence the entire debacle prior to the Cotillion—"

"What debacle?"

"I have not had nearly enough brandy to discuss that. Nor do I intend to stay long enough for that to happen. It will have to wait until another day—or you can write to Father for the pertinent details. But the point is, the man is determined to get to the root of the problems in Derbyshire, and he means to start here."

"Start here? I do not understand." Andrew's eyes widened as bravado slowly drained from his face. He only ever wore a mask of courage, never had the substance.

"He means to audit the estate, every jot and tittle, to evaluate the nature of the Keeping here."

"He cannot do that. This is the Chancellor's estate. He has no place, no right to intrude—"

"I am afraid, dear brother, in that you are entirely and completely wrong. In matters of the Keep, the department of the Secretary outranks even the Chancellor."

"I will not have it." Andrew pounded his fist into his palm. "He cannot insert himself into my home—"

"Yes, he can. That is what I have come to warn you about. He will probably be here at dawn tomorrow, the next day if you are extremely lucky, with plans to audit the entire estate. Every clause of the charter will be examined, and evidence of compliance scrutinized. By the way, when was the last census of the dragons of Matlock territory?"

"Census? A census of dragons? I have no idea what you are talking of. That is the job of the steward, is it not?"

"That was what I was afraid of. You can find all the details of what will be required in two volumes kept alongside of the estate charter in Father's office. If I recall correctly, they have always been kept on the shelves behind his desk. Good day." Richard turned sharply and headed for the door.

"Wait! Wait! You cannot go. Clearly you understand what all this means. I insist you help—"

"No. As you made abundantly clear, I have my own estate to manage. Matlock is yours, all the privi-

leges and all the responsibilities. I wish you well in it."
He slipped through the door and shut it firmly behind
him.

5
Chapter

June 12, 1815

ELIZABETH ROCKED GENTLY in the old, white rocker, holding Anne close, drinking in that soft, sweet scent of baby. The one she had feared she might never experience again whilst locked in the dank, hopeless hold of the Sea Lion. The one she would never take for granted again.

Shutting her eyes, it was easy to pretend, for just a moment, that the rest of the world did not exist. Perhaps they could ride away on the old, white-washed rocking horse that stood in the corner—a toy Darcy remembered quite fondly. Or maybe build a tower of blocks, a castle retreat into their own private little world.

When Anne was first born, the attics seemed so far away, too far away for a nursery. Nanny and Anne had been established in a nearby room in the family wing. Only after Anne's constant sleeplessness emerged did Darcy insist on reopening the attic nursery suite. While Anne's sleep problems did not completely resolve until Nanny's dismissal, the quiet, soothing environs of the long, white room with windows that framed the picturesque Pemberley landscape improved her rest significantly.

Too much white in a room could feel cold and sterile, forgotten and ignored. But here, in the room where Darcy had spent his infancy, with its fresh, clean smell, simple white-painted furniture, and plain polished floor, white was calming, peaceful, an escape from the complicated, serious aspects of life that took place downstairs. A place Elizabeth relished escaping to as often as she could.

Anne wriggled and squirmed, so Elizabeth set her down on the faded rug—another one made by the late Lady Anne, for whom little Anne was named. Scraps of family clothing and household textiles braided into the rug told stories of the previous generation of Darcys. Perhaps one day Elizabeth would add her own rag rug to this room.

"Is there anything else you will need to fit up the nursery?" Elizabeth asked the quiet, patient figure, who sat reading in the far corner near the windows.

"No, madam, everything seems to be well in hand. My compliments to Mrs. Reynolds. There aren't many who can clean a nursery to suit me. She and I will get on famously, just as you said. Truth and Mercy are utterly smitten with Mrs. Reynolds' Friend, Dale. He took it upon himself to show them around and found just the right basket that would fit them and May all together." Mrs. Sharp gestured toward the knot of zaltys and tatzelwurm in a large willow basket by the painted fire screen that blocked the currently unused fireplace.

The fine lines of Mrs. Sharp's face were relaxed and her green eyes bright, radiating peace and contentment. Such a complete contrast from the nervous energy that had followed drake Nanny. With her white mobcap and apron over her dark dress, Mrs. Sharp seemed to fit into the nursery, as though it had been planned just for her. Yes, this was exactly the change the household needed.

"I am not surprised at Dale's solicitousness toward their comfort. He has taken it upon himself to be lead dragon in the household. He wears his dominance among the staff well."

"The dragons' house steward, as it were?"

"An apt description. Are you sure there is nothing else you need?" Elizabeth stood and stretched her shoulders forward. The tight, cramped feeling from the long journey had not yet faded.

"Are you certain you wish to have such elegant furnishings in my quarters? I hardly expected pieces that should belong in family rooms." Mrs. Sharp glanced toward the door at the far, narrow end of the room that led to her chambers.

"No, no, I am quite certain. It may not be the prevailing opinion, but it only seems appropriate to see to the comfort of the one who sees to my daughter's. Especially when your job has so many extra, unusual demands attached."

"I can hardly imagine accommodating the visits of the staff dragons will be taxing." Mrs. Sharp's eyes crinkled as she smiled. "We have not met a single one who is not amiable, nor failed to make Mercy and Truth feel quite welcome. We have already worked out a system, which, as I understand, Dale is explaining throughout the house, that when I have a ribbon hung from the doorknob, little Anne is not to be disturbed."

"That is very clever. Nanny was never welcoming toward the rest of the staff dragons. I have been concerned that they might make up for lost time a bit too energetically."

"I am sure May, Mercy, and Truth will all assist us in finding the right balance. It is such a remarkable thing, raising an infant with dragon companionship, Lady Sage. I am honored to be a part of the exercise." Everything in Mrs. Sharp's countenance suggested she spoke the truth.

With a delightful baby chortle, Anne crawled toward the basket where the three nursery dragons entwined. All three poked up their heads and looked at her. May purred loudly as Anne sat beside the basket and energetically patted the knot of dragons.

"Gentle, Anne. You must be gentle with your Friends." Elizabeth crouched beside her daughter. "Remember, it is a privilege to be Friends. You must always be kind. Mercy and Truth, I have told May already, but you must feel free to let her know if she has been too rough with you."

"Yesss, Lady Sage." Mercy, whose head crest had wide yellow stripes and red spots, rose up tall and reached for Elizabeth, who stroked under her chin.

Such soft, supple skin she had and such elegant eyelashes.

"No other human hatchling we have known has sssseemed to hear us so well as Miss Anne." Truth said, in her sweet, hissy-lispy, distinctly snake-type voice.

"I am pleased to know that." Elizabeth gave each dragon a scratch and her daughter a gentle hug, then stood. "I anticipate Mr. Darcy will be visiting the nursery quite regularly."

Mrs. Sharp raised an eyebrow—yes, it was odd for fathers to take interest in babies, especially daughters. "Very good, madam. Will he find the rocking chair comfortable, or should another chair better suited for him be found?"

"An excellent thought. I am not certain, but I will consult with him on the matter and make the necessary arrangements. And I will let him know about the ribbons myself. After so many months of sleeplessness, he will not want to awaken Anne accidentally. I shall return later this afternoon."

Anne pulled up on Elizabeth's skirt. She picked Anne up, cuddled her a moment more, and put her into Mrs. Sharp's waiting arms.

"Miss Anne usually naps until three o'clock, unless you wish me to try to alter her schedule."

"Oh, heavens no! It is quite a joy to know she has one at all! I will adjust myself accordingly."

Mrs. Sharp curtsied, and Elizabeth left the nursery.

The plain hallway seemed cold, dark, and empty as she shut the door behind her. If only she could spend the rest of the day in the nursery. After all the time lost to her encounter with the Movers and the recent crises of the Cotillion and Bolsover, her time with Anne had suffered. That would change now they were home, though. Still, she did not have to try to make up for all the loss in a single day.

Or so she would tell herself as often as necessary, until she believed it.

The narrow attic stairs ended in a landing that connected the family wing, the guest wing, and the grand stairs. A maid and her puck Friend, a feather duster carried in her jaws, bustled past. Her respite from the world was definitely over.

She would meet with Mrs. Reynolds after breakfast, as usual. Until then, her office called.

The final rays of sunrise poured through open curtains, lending a peach glow to everything they touched. Nearly everything seemed quite as she had left it before their sojourn in London. A pitcher of fennel water with a matching crystal tumbler waited on her desk. Mrs. Reynolds must have been there before her.

While sharing a working space with Darcy in London had its own charms, there was something soothing about being back in her own territory. Gracious, how draconic that sounded.

The wood-paneled room had once served as a steward's office, convenient to Darcy's study, with the library sandwiched between the two. But at Darcy's insistence, another space was made available to the steward. Ample bookcases, though a bit mismatched, had been procured from other rooms, now awaiting the books she had brought back from London. Wooden book crates were stacked before them. Her nose itched—someone had forgotten to dust the books before packing them. She sneezed. That would need attention soon.

So many things needed her attention.

A graceful writing desk and matching chair, all loops and swirls and feminine grace, stood near the windows—impractical as they were attractive. A squat, practical table sat beside to hold the reference books that would inevitably overflow the desk. A pair of comfortable chairs with a matching footstool had come from a dressing room in the guest wing. It was a shame to pilfer from their guests, but far better for the furniture to have regular use, than to stand collecting dust. Mrs. Reynolds insisted they would not be missed, and Elizabeth dare not argue with her.

An iron dragon perch that matched the heirloom one in Darcy's office stood between desk and windows. April needed only a small basket lined with "soft" to feel comfortable in the room, but with Walker's typical cockatrice dislike of perching on chairs, it was important to ensure he was as comfortable and welcome here as he was in Darcy's office.

She sank into the chair behind her desk. It was good to be home.

Opening the blue leather diary that sat atop a neat stack of journals on her desk, she found Mrs. Reynolds' list of staff dragon interviews for the day. No better way to become alert to any issues in the house than to hear it straight from the dragon's mouth. Next week she would have to—

No, next week was just that, next week.

Focus on today, lest the overwhelming number of tasks to be accomplished distract her from even managing even one. Breathe, just breathe.

She turned to a fresh page and retrieved her pencil from the desk drawer. Time for a list. Little settled the overtaxed soul like a proper list to order one's thoughts and quell the fear of forgetting something.

Except when the list grew to two pages and was far from finished.

She leaned back in her chair and squeezed her temples.

Her new secretary, a drake recommended by Papa's secretary Drew, should be arriving in a few days. Darcy insisted that she needed the help, but truly? What was a secretary going to do for her? It was not like Papa, who needed help fetching materials from the library and writing things down. He could barely walk or hold a pen these days. She was perfectly capable of both. How would she possibly find enough for a secretary to do? One more thing to add to her list.

Talons scratched at the door.

"Come in." And so it would begin.

Dale padded in on four feet, tail held slightly above the carpet so his scales would not catch. Among all the minor drakes she had known, he was unique for many reasons. With his unusual beard and dark spots on lighter hide, he was one of those drakes one could identify at a distance. Like his Friend Mrs. Reynolds, he considered the pride of Pemberley manor as dear to him as his own, perhaps a mite too serious about it at times. But even that was difficult to consider a true shortcoming in his character. Even if his sense of humor might be lacking, he was dependable and loyal and forthright, sometimes to a fault, making him the perfect dragon with whom to begin conversations.

He stood before her desk, extended his front feet and touched chin to the ground. "Good morning, Lady Sage."

She stood and tapped the back of his prickly head gently with two fingers. "Good morning, Dale. I look forward to what you have to tell me. Pray, take a seat." She pulled the worn wooden footstool near the desk.

He hopped up and sat down, a little like a dog might have. A touch informal, but the arrangement put him closer to eye level with her, which was always far more comfortable for her, and did not require him to fit himself into a chair that cramped his glorious tail. Dominance had been established and recognized, so there was little need to reinforce it by towering over him.

"With what shall I begin, Lady Sage?"

"I should like to know about the household, particularly regarding the dragons. There were several new servants and Friends added to the house shortly before we left for London. I did not see the hall boy and his little wyrm Friend in the reception line. Perhaps begin with him."

"Ah, yes, Oliver and Peat." Dale rasped his spikey chin against his forepaw. "There is a story to be told there. Oliver was a good enough lad, all told. Rather like most small boys, but he was trying hard enough that Mrs. Reynolds was willing to endure the vexations of having so young a person in service. But the wyrm was another matter."

"In what way?"

"In the way wyrms are apt to be, Lady Sage."

"I do not approve of judging a dragon by its type, and I will not tolerate that in the household management. I thought I made that clear." She almost swallowed back her snort, but that was the manner of posturing dragons best understood, so she indulged.

"Forgive me. You have. I only meant that this wyrm, in particular, proved unsuitable to the household in all the ways that one usually expects of a wyrm."

Hardly better, but at least he was trying. "And what ways would those be?"

"For one thing, he developed a disagreeable habit of burrowing under the carpets, pulling up the tacks and rumpling them. Molly, the scullery maid, nearly broke her ankle tripping in a room that the wyrm had plundered. She is well recovered now, though."

"I am pleased to hear that, but plundered? That is a very strong word."

"What else does one call it when the liquor cabinet is overturned, and the wyrm is found inebriated, asleep in the middle of a puddle of brandy? And before you ask, yes, the rules of the house were made clear to him, and there was a proper beer ration offered. He was neither hungry, nor thirsty, simply mischievous." Dale bared his teeth in an expression of draconic disapproval.

Elizabeth winced. Yes, that was cause for dismissal.

"The boy was given a letter of character and recommended to another house not too far from here, one that does not employ dragons among the staff. The Friendship did not seem secure in any case. I would not be surprised if Oliver and Peat part ways sooner rather than later."

"It does take a rather special character to befriend a wyrm. They do tend to prefer the company of other wyrms to warm-bloods." Who would have thought the Gardiners were that sort of people? But Indigo and Lapis were quite happy in their Friendship. Perhaps it was because the pair became Friends together rather than a single wyrm on its own.

"Indeed, Lady Sage. On a positive note, though, you might say we have learned a great deal from the experience and better know what to look for before accepting a wyrm on the staff in the future."

"An important lesson learnt, to be sure. Has this affected the garden wyrms at all?"

"I do not think so. It is my belief that they had some passing acquaintance with Peat and did not think he would adapt to life in the manor house well."

"Then, should the situation arise again, I will make a note that we consult the garden wyrms' opinions of future wyrm staff before making a decision to hire."

"I am sure they will be honored by such attentions." Only the tiny flick of the tip of his tail gave away Dale's hearty approval. "The new scullery maid, Agnes, and Fern, her puck Friend, though, have settled in quite well. She is a hard worker, even if Cook is still not satisfied with her attention to detail in some matters."

"She is still young. Hopefully, Cook will be able to assist her in rectifying those issues. And Fern?"

"Fern is an asset to the household, full stop. She is an older puck, who had been Friends with Agnes' grandmother, I think. Fern's character is quite steady and an excellent influence on the younger dragons in the household. Her hoarding instinct is quite well regulated."

Elizabeth winced at the word 'hoard.' Pray, let not hoarding issues plague Pemberley as well. "What does she hoard?"

"Bits of paper—not torn out of books, mind you, but bits otherwise destined for refuse. As I said, she has the urge under good regulation and does not meddle with books or correspondence. Mrs. Reynolds sets aside a few scraps for her quite regularly, and she appears entirely content with the situation. Fern particularly loves bits of old lists with handwriting upon them. Though she cannot read, she is entranced by the loops and swirls, as she calls them."

A well-regulated puck? Who had heard of such a thing? Perhaps there was a monograph to be written on the matter. "How do the older dragons of the household regard her?"

"Liked and well-trusted. More than once, I myself have observed her sort out issues of dominance and territory squabbles among our flying dragons. I could not have handled them better myself. If I may speak freely, Lady Sage, I think Agnes' shortcomings are more than made up for by the asset we have in Fern."

"Duly noted, Dale. I am pleased to hear it." She made a few notes in her household book. "Have you heard of any concerns among the staff? Anything which may need to be addressed?"

Dale shuffled uncomfortably. "Since you have asked, there is one matter, but I am afraid it is sensitive, and you might consider it insufferably rude."

That nagging little pain in her belly knotted again. "Is it perchance the matter of Miss Darcy?"

"Yes, yes, it is."

"What is the nature of the concern?"

"Well, it is rather complicated. I believe you know about her complicated relationship with the staff dragons here?"

"Complicated relationship. No, I do not think so. I do not recall you or anyone else discussing the matter with me."

His tail swept across the stool with a scratchy swish. "It is rather a sensitive matter, I am afraid. As the dominant female, it is your territory and your right to permit whichever others you wish in it."

"I see." Elizabeth sighed, mostly for Dale's benefit. "Am I to assume that she did not have a good working relationship among the staff dragons?"

"Most recently, Pax usually managed all matters between Miss Darcy and the staff, and did it most admirably …"

"I see. Should I assume that the staff wishes to know when to expect her return?"

"That, yes. And if Miss Bennet should be expected to be here under those same terms?"

A sharp rap at the door. Darcy.

"In brief, those answers would be, not soon, and no. I expect Miss Bennet to be quite appropriate in all her dealings with the staff. If that is not the case, alert me immediately." She stood. "Come in."

Darcy stepped in.

"I will call for you later to continue this interview." She nodded at Dale, and he scurried away, looking a little relieved.

6
Chapter

"AM I INTERRUPTING something?" Darcy stepped out of the way to allow Dale to scurry past. It still took him aback, seeing the old steward's office turning into something so entirely different and feminine. It was not that the room seemed untoward that way, but for nearly all his life it had been the plain, practical steward's office, and he simply expected it thus. The delicate desk with its loops and swirls and the bowls of dried lavender that perfumed the air changed the tone so dramatically, it still caused him a bit of a start.

"Nothing that cannot be postponed until later. Do come in." She gestured toward the overstuffed floral chairs that had come from the guestroom Aunt Catherine favored. She would probably complain about their absence, if she ever visited, which hardly seemed likely anytime soon, considering Cousin Anne's new-found interest in Mr. Rutledge.

At least he had not been identified among the "problematic" young men wearing snapdragons. That was something, but at some point, Darcy would be asked for his opinion on a match with that young man and investigations into financials would be required. But one problem at a time.

"We have only just come home, and already I miss our morning ritual from London." He chuckled as he sat down. Aunt Catherine's herb-and-rose perfume, which rather clashed with Elizabeth's lavender, still lingered on the cushions. How was that possible?

"I have been thinking something very similar." Everything in her posture screamed weariness as she sat.

"Then you will not mind that I have arranged to have a sitting room established for us upstairs, and have explained to Mrs. Reynolds the rules we established in London."

That put a smile in her eyes. "She was amused, no doubt."

"Quite. Though I like to think she approves of the notion. I expect it will be ready for us in just a day or two."

"Until then, perhaps you will join me in the nursery to see Anne in the mornings?"

"Indeed. How have Mrs. Sharp and her Friends found the nursery?"

"Quite to their liking. She assures me she welcomes the staff dragons' visits and has set up a system so they know Anne is napping if there is a ribbon on the door handle."

"Though we hardly expected less, it is still good to hear it. I imagine, though, that is a hint that I should follow the same protocol, I suppose?"

"Only if you do not wish to wake Anne."

"Heaven forfend! That would not do!" Darcy pressed his hand to his chest. Those many sleepless nights were not to be forgotten.

"I told her to expect your visits, and I confess, her response most pleased me."

"Do tell. What was it?"

"She wanted to know if the rocking chair would be comfortable for you or if another chair should be found."

"A profoundly wise woman!" He chuckled.

"You do not like the rocking chair?"

"Despise it, actually. Completely uncomfortable in every way." He laughed again. "I even know of a most comfortable chair that will not be too difficult to get up the attic stairs."

"I wonder how she knew."

"Few nursery rocking chairs accommodate tall men, my dear."

"Few men attend the nursery." Heavens, her satisfied smile brightened the room! "Have you had a report from Brutus yet?"

"Only to inform me that he and Axel will be touring the house and grounds today with Walker, who is most anxious to have them thoroughly acquainted with every nook and cranny of Pemberley, inside and out."

"I am anxious to know what they have to say about our situation here." Her voice became quite serious.

"We are not in London anymore. The countryside is a very different place. It has its own dangers, to be sure, but they are ones that we all understand better, I think." He leaned back a bit and allowed his gaze to wander to the windows.

"It seems like you have something more on your mind." She clasped her hands in her lap, stopping just shy of worrying them together.

"You always know. I do. What do you make of St. John?"

"You know what I think of him." She sniffed and rolled her eyes in the most Fitzwilliam family of ways. "I have never forgotten the trauma he caused both myself and my father, and the strife he instilled between us simply because of his ignorant, antiquated attitudes. I would not have the man in our home but for the will of the Order." A tight smile flashed to match her mild and indifferent opinion.

"I can make arrangements to move him to the Black Bull at Lambton, if you wish."

"I thought you said Chancellor Matlock was insistent he stay with us."

"It will facilitate St. John's work to be here, but—"

"The way you say 'work' … I do not like this. Be plain with me and tell me what is going on."

He flinched. "All I know with certainty is that he is here to examine what is going on in Derbyshire and to promote remedies for the problems he identifies."

"If that involves speaking with minor dragons near to Pemberley, then yes, that is better accomplished here. But somehow it does not seem that his efforts will be limited to that alone."

"No, they will not. And I suspect that was one reason Matlock insisted he stay with us. On the way here, St. John spoke of audits."

She dug her elbows into the chair's arms and leaned forward. "Audits? Those are only conducted when there has been an official complaint filed by an estate dragon."

"One might argue that the actions of the three Derbyshire complainants were sufficient to trigger audits of those estates."

"Let me guess. You believe that St. John is going to take that point and expand it as far as he possibly can so he can extend his authority beyond where it is welcome or even appropriate."

"Essentially. He has already stated as much." His tight smile matched hers.

Her eyes grew wide, and her jaw dropped. "No, he would not."

"Richard has already been to Matlock to warn his brother that St. John will be starting his audits at Matlock. The precise thing I think Uncle was hoping to discourage."

She sprang to her feet and paced between the chairs. "Great merciful heavens! There is little reason to expect that the viscount has ensured all the aspects of the charter have been upheld, much less the regular duties to the Order performed."

"Exactly what I anticipate, but my bigger concern is, what are the chances that Cownt Matlock himself has carried out his duties completely and to the letter of the Charter and Accords?"

"Dragon's fire! Excuse me, but St. John will be playing with dragon's fire if he tries to exert dominance over Cownt Matlock that way."

"Do you have any doubt that St. John will try?" He craned his neck to follow her pacing.

"I wish I did, but no. He's the type of man who will push and push and push, grabbing at any form of dominance, to take what he can until he is stopped by force. Perhaps I should write to Castordale for advice. It was he who put an end to the games Mr. St. John was playing with my father and me. I am not sure how he did it, but I can find out."

"I would just as soon not see you involved in these matters. But—"

"It is the role of the Dragon Sage to smooth such tensions between men and dragons. I see no way I can remain uninvolved for long. The only real question is whether I should attempt to insert myself preemptively." She fell back into her chair and squeezed her eyes shut. "There are times I wonder why I agreed to take this office."

"I suppose, then, it will be easier to manage those issues if he stays here and remains close at hand."

"My skin still crawls when I see him," she rubbed her hands along her arms, "but I cannot disagree. You expect Pemberley will be audited?"

Darcy laced his hands behind his neck and looked at the molded plaster ceiling roses. "It was his intention to begin at Pemberley."

"Lovely. So, in what ways do you anticipate St. John is going to find fault with Pemberley? I know your steward is an excellent man—"

"Excellent, but not perfect. I know you intended to manage the dragon census, but even if you were to have it done by the time an audit begins, St. John would be dissatisfied. It appears it has been overlooked since before Old Pemberley's death. With his death, the irregularities of Young Pemberley's hatching, and Anne's birth, there were more pressing matters at hand. Though I am sure no quarter will be given for those."

"What else? If the census were the only matter of concern, you would not be—"

"I had been quite certain that Pemberley was being run as a model estate. But ..." he caught her gaze, his stomach churning the way it did when he was a boy and fault was found with his lessons. "Where do I begin? To start, there is a stream that defines one of the far boundaries of the estate. But since the charter was drawn, the course of the waterway has shifted. I do not know what provisions are made for such a change, or if the Accords even address the possibility. I am left with the question, does it still mark the boundary? Or is the boundary now drawn outside the stream and if so, exactly what are the markers? I am not even sure whether that is a matter for the Ministry of Keeps or the Office of the Secretary. And that is just the simplest of the issues."

He would have felt better if she had not looked so surprised.

"I have only just begun to consider the infinite complexities of having an infant dragon in a Keep appropriate for a large firedrake. She is not even capable of many of the duties of the dragon to the territory."

"For example?"

"While Pemberley has enjoyed an extraordinary education, she is hardly capable of managing disputes among the wild minor dragons—debates of territory are only just the start. The issue of dragons preying upon smaller dragons is a perennial problem. You know that has been a contentious clause in the Accords from the beginning. The sheer number of dragons we have recognized as having protection under the Keep is well beyond what any other estate recognizes and is difficult to keep sorted. If I can barely keep it straight, then there is no way that Pemberley can."

"Certainly not."

"According to the charter, she is supposed to handle those matters independently and report the results to me regularly so that a report can be sent to the Order. I am sure you are not surprised that since well before Old Pemberley's death, none of those reports have been filed."

"Dragon's bones! It does put Bolsover's demands in a rather different light, does it not?" She squeezed her eyes shut and pressed her temples, rocking just the tiniest bit as she did.

"I hate to agree with anything that dragon said, and yet it is difficult not to. And that is hardly the end of it. Surveys and reports of the capacity of the land to support the dragons that inhabit it and its actual productivity in that regard also fall under Pemberley's duties. What does she know of such things at this point? I know she will be able to learn, but I am not sure I apprehend the matters well enough myself, yet. How can I teach her what I do not know?"

"At least that is clearly a question for the Ministry of Keeps. I am sure Sir Carew will offer us some form of assistance."

"I will be writing him directly. In fact, if you are agreeable, I will invite both him and Langham to stay with us and sort out exactly what Pemberley's responsibilities to the Keep are and how they may be accomplished. It is humiliating to have been so certain that Pemberley was in order, a model dragon estate in all ways, only to discover that I was entirely wrong." Darcy closed his eyes and shook his head. "St. John will not be impressed. I can only imagine his glee to find so much fault here."

"So, he will write a reprimand. That is embarrassing, but not unrecoverable."

"I could live with it, if that were the extent of matters, but you well know how he is. If he can find fault here, it is not impossible that he will try to use it as leverage to gain authority over Pemberley estate. 'Bring an estate under the stewardship of the Order' was what he called it during our most recent conversation."

"No!" She gasped and covered her mouth with her hand. "And once he has his hands in …"

"Precisely, the very thought makes me quite ill. No Darcy has ever lost control over Pemberley, and if it should happen now, there is no telling how or if we could get it back. Only your father would know the precedents of such things."

"Do you really think the Order would try to extend its reach so much? I did not think it your uncle's way."

"Uncle Matlock, no. He is a firm believer in the rights of a man to his own property. But, as St. John so forcefully reminded me, the Secretary's office is the one most involved in the day-to-day running of the Order, and if it begins a subtle grab for control, the Chancellor's office may not notice until it is too late."

"Then, I suppose it is a mercy that the first audit will be of Matlock. It is just possible St. John will be stopped there before he even begins."

"One might hope for that. But things never seem to work out so simply when dragons are involved. In the meantime, there is a great deal of work to be done here."

7
Chapter

June 12, 1815

LYDIA MADE HER way into the morning room half an hour later than she had expected to be there. She had taken the long route, stopping in the family sitting room, the parlor, and the gallery on her way there. No, those were hardly necessary stops, but it was pleasant to take a few minutes to remind herself that she would not get lost in the halls of Pemberley. Cosette had told her it was a silly worry altogether. She was perfectly able to help Lydia find her way about— fairy dragons had an uncanny sense of direction, after all. Though Lydia did not doubt it, one did not always want to rely upon someone else for such things. So, she endured a bit of fairy dragon scolding on her way to breakfast.

Whilst helping her dress and doing her hair, Betsey had also assured her that breakfast at Pemberley was a relaxed affair, where family and guests came and went as they pleased. At Longbourn, Mama had an unspoken expectation that all her girls would appear at the table together so that she could prepare them for the day, during which time Papa would keep his nose in his paper and make tart remarks. The tensions that often erupted there made for a less than agreeable start to the morning.

How much had life changed since then? How much she had changed since then! She hugged herself tightly. What was it all going to be like now she was to be established at Pemberley?

Cosette zipped into the morning room ahead of her. "It is true! It is true, just as Juniper said! There are fresh cut flowers on the sideboard near the window, the kinds with lovely nectar!" She flew two circuits around the room and hovered among the pink and white fluffy flowers, sampling each.

Lydia followed her into the airy, fresh room. The windows had been opened, just enough to fill the space with fresh morning air and the perfume of the abundant cut flowers on the round walnut table and chinoiserie sideboards. Morning sun poured in, painting the peach-colored walls in an extension of the glories of sunrise. A dragon perch had been added to the furniture since her brief glance at the room yesterday. Was it really only yesterday?

She closed her eyes and drew a deep breath. It was almost like being in Mama's little flower garden. Her eyes prickled just a mite.

For all Mama's faults, Lydia missed her. Things would never be as they once were and it still made her chest tight and stomach hurt. Auntie would probably scold her for it, but Mama's steadfast belief in her had been a pleasant thing. Lizzy could be lovely, but it was harder to have faith in her sister's regard when haunted by the ever-present fear of losing it.

She drew another deep breath. Hot tea, fresh breads, and was that a bit of ham? Perhaps some breakfast would help settle her mind and sort out what to do with the day.

"Good morning, Miss Bennet."

She jumped as Sir Richard sauntered through the door, his young cockatrice Friend, Earl, perched on his leather-gloved arm. He was one of those not exactly handsome men whose looks improved with acquaintance. Sharp and angular with a shock of nearly black hair that tended to fall into his hazel eyes, he resembled his father, the chancellor, but with the edges sanded off. His smile, though, was quite pleasing— she had never seen Chancellor Lord Matlock smile, ever—and his sense of humor was far better than Mr. Darcy's.

"I did not mean to startle you. Pray forgive me. Pemberley does take a bit of getting used to when one is accustomed to more ordinary surroundings, does it not?" He bowed from his shoulders, a genuine smile crinkling the edges of his eyes.

"But you grew up at Matlock. I would have thought this kind of house would be entirely normal to you."

"Grew up there, yes, but it has been quite a number of years since I have called it home." He gestured her toward the table. "Do you mind if Earl joins us this morning?"

"I thought dragons were always welcome at the tables of Pemberley. Cosette is here with me now." She pointed to the flowers near the window.

"Ah, yes, but fairy dragons are polite and dainty diners, who poetically sip flowers and drink honey. Earl is, shall we say, a rather more robust eater."

"He means I like meat, preferably raw." Earl grumbled and shook his wings. The young cockatrice had the gangly look of an adolescent boy who was tired of being neither child nor man. "Although I would not complain about having ham or kippers this morning, if that would be more agreeable to you." He bobbed slightly in what must be a form of bow from his kind.

"That is considerate of you." Especially considering how crusty Darcy's Friend Walker could be. "Having spent a great deal of time with Auntie and other drakes who were training as companions, I have had quite my fill of raw meat at the table. I am afraid it is not exactly to my taste, especially first thing in the morning."

"Then I shall request a plate of kippers be sent in for Earl." Sir Richard held out a chair for her and moved the dragon perch nearer the table.

Earl lit on the perch, rocking it only slightly as he found his balance. "That is most kind of you."

"Forgive me if it is too forward, but you said 'drakes.' Are there many dragons at Mrs. Fieldings' school? I know her reputation in the Order is impeccable, but I confess I know little of her methods." He sat beside her.

"I think many would be surprised at the true nature of her education." She quirked her brow and cocked her head. Did he dare ask the question?

"Yes, there are many dragons there." Cosette hovered over the table, a bit of yellow pollen coating her glistening black beaky nose and scarlet throat. "And there are lessons for Friends just as much as for warm-bloods."

"I had no idea." Sir Richard rang the bell for Mrs. Reynolds, who appeared almost at that moment, a young maid—Agnes, was it?— following behind with a bowl of kippers that she placed in front of Earl. How many housekeepers could have anticipated the request? "Do many of the students come to her with Friends?"

"Not so many. While I was there, it was just Cosette and one other, I think. And they were all fairy dragons. There was a prevailing notion that only fairy dragons were … tolerant, was the polite term. There were others far less … tolerant about befriending girls who might not be … ah … well-versed in the ways of the Order." She dodged his gaze and filled her plate.

Earl tossed a kipper into the air, caught it in his beak and swallowed it whole. Show-off.

"And the drakes you spoke of?" Apparently, he was one of the rare sorts not afraid of information that might challenge his view of the world.

"Many of them were students as well."

"Students? You must explain." He parked his elbow on the table and chin in his hand.

"Where do you think the dragon companions for young ladies, like Auntie, are trained?"

"I never gave the matter a thought, to be honest. It never dawned on me that it would require special training." His brow creased as though he were truly surprised.

"What of the apprentices to the Scribe, or any other dragon you have seen employed about the Order's establishments?"

"I had just assumed—"

"Assumed that they came by all that knowledge naturally? Or that perhaps their tasks were so unskilled as to require no training at all?" Lydia chuckled as embarrassment registered across his face. "I had never thought much about it, either. You might find it interesting that there are a number of schools for dragons who wish to have a trade of their own and to be gainfully employed. Not all minor dragons are so fortunate as to have a Friend able to support them, as your young Earl."

Did it hurt when Sir Richard's eyes went that wide? "I never considered the matter at all. Since so many minor dragons are not imprinted and live wild, I imagined that manner of life was the common choice."

"Mrs. Fieldings says that unless they employ minor dragons themselves, few among the Order give it any thought at all. But really, sir, is that the life you would choose for yourself, given any other options?"

"It will take me some time to become accustomed to that notion." He raked his hair back. Heavens, he seemed handsome when he did that. "So do these dragons attend classes with the girls sent to the school?"

"After a fashion, you could say that they do. Especially in matters like reading and history and mathematics. Those destined to be companions were considered advanced students, with proficiency in such subjects already. They were each assigned to a girl there as a final test of their abilities as a companion."

"So, you were their journeyman project, as it were?" His eyes twinkled with quiet laughter.

"You might say that. Bridges, a lovely white-and-cream colored drake, trained with me, with Auntie's full approval." Lydia spooned a large dab of jam on the side of her plate. "It is a very different thing to have a companion rather than a Friend, like Cosette. Cosette did not like her much at first."

Cosette landed on the table, near the jam on Lydia's plate "No. She was bossy and disagreeable and rather ill-tempered."

"I do not disagree, but we probably were not the easiest of students, either. And do not repeat that to Lizzy. I fear she would be rather insufferable to hear me admit such a thing."

Sir Richard laughed heartily. "Have no fear! Darcy can get that way himself! I have no wish to inflict that on another!"

"Did you spend a great deal of time together whilst you were children?"

"As much as I could, to be honest. Matlock was a—challenging place."

"You have met my father. And I have encountered yours. I have some notion of what challenging might mean." That was probably far too familiar a remark. She tried to conceal her cringe.

Thankfully, he laughed, that rueful kind of laugh one made around those who truly understood. "Yes, they are rather singular men, to be sure." He buttered a piece of toast and chewed it thoughtfully. "Are you still willing to do what my father has asked?"

"Asked? I rather thought it was more a demand."

"To me, it was a demand. Toward you, it was a request. You are under no obligation to serve the Order in such a capacity."

"I suppose it is nice to know that I do have a choice. But ..." she swallowed hard and glanced at Cosette, who bobbed her whole body in a decisive nod, "our decision is unchanged. I am honored that you would ask me to be a part of your efforts and astonished that Darcy and Lizzy would not object."

"Excellent. I hope that does not change."

"Perhaps this would be an appropriate time to instruct me in the details of the matter? You know, those things which might have changed our minds, had we known them at the beginning." She cocked her head in an expression she had seen Lizzy use so many times.

Sir Richard covered his mouth, probably to keep from spitting toast as he laughed. "Earl, would you ensure that there is no one listening to our conversation?"

Earl swallowed another kipper and winged several circuits around the room, inspecting it carefully. Finally, he screamed a small, terror-inducing screech and returned to his perch. "I detected no eavesdroppers."

Lydia covered her ears. Gracious, merciful heavens, what a sound! So much worse than his table manners.

"Then why did you screech?" Sir Richard rubbed his ears.

"It seemed an appropriate thing to do."

"I think you enjoyed it."

Earl shrugged and returned to his meal. "Walker uses that technique and recommended I do the same."

"I see. I shall make note of it. I will acquire cotton wool for my ears in the future and offer Miss Bennet a supply, as well."

She shook her head sharply to dismiss the shivers down the back of her neck. "It is a rather memorable sound."

"But not entirely unrelated to our task." He sipped his coffee as though trying to fortify himself.

"And exactly what would that task be? You must admit, to be of assistance in the defense of the Order is hardly a specific description. I suspect you gave Sir Fitzwilliam a more thorough account in order to obtain his permission to recruit me?"

Sir Richard sighed as though he wondered if her directness were a good thing. Best he know what he was dealing with now, though. She would never be the demure, ladylike joy that Jane was.

"I am charged with investigating the smuggling of dragon parts within the boundaries of the kingdom."

The blood drained from her cheeks. That such things might be happening was hardly surprising, but utterly mortifying when one considered them. "How does one investigate smugglers? Are you to be some sort of riding officer, here, so far away from the coast?"

"Not precisely, though at some point I would not be surprised if I would be charged with finding and confronting the smugglers myself. I promise, you will not be involved in such dangerous escapades."

That might be his intent, but those things could not be so easy to predict. That sounded awfully exciting, like a heroine in a novel, but was it the type of excitement she and Cosette desired? "I have seen accounts of riding officers killed in the execution of their duties."

"While that is sadly true, as I said, I have not taken the role of a riding officer. Moreover, I promised Darcy I would ensure your safety. I will ask nothing of you that I could imagine would endanger you or your Friend. And after facing the French on the continent, I have a rather vivid imagination as to what might endanger you."

"I mean no disrespect—"

"What I am asking you is definitely outside the bounds of a genteel young lady's normal realm. I take no offense. And if at any time you do not feel up to the task, then you are free to withdraw with no hard feelings. In fact, I suspect Darcy, and I know Elizabeth, would be relieved if you did."

How had Lizzy responded to the idea she might be engaged in such activities? "I understand. I am certain, though, it is time for you to tell me how Cosette and I might figure into your plans."

"Right, right." He licked his lips as though considering exactly what to say. How much she hated it when people chose to consider their words so carefully. "I need to conduct a ruse. We have some inkling of where the smugglers may be operating. In specific, there are apothecaries that we suspect of being knowingly, or perhaps even unknowingly, supplied by traders in dragon parts. Some of those parts are known to be used in potions favored by young ladies. There is also a possibility that dragon parts may be utilized in the making of colors, of paints. There are two painting masters we are suspicious of in that regard. To that end, it would be of great advantage to have a young lady for whom cosmetic potions and painting supplies might be acquired. That is where you come in, Miss Bennet."

"A role play, then? Who do you wish me to be, sir?"

He stroked his chin, thoughtfully, as though he had not yet considered the question. "Staying as close to the truth as possible would be the easiest thing, I think. A young cousin for whom I am acting as guardian seems the most appropriate fiction."

"Perhaps one recently placed in your care, through some unforeseen, unfortunate circumstance, whom you do not know well? You are trying to manage her only as long as you have to, until a proper companion might be found, and she may be set up in her own establishment, or, better still, until she can be married off and your hands washed of her?"

He nodded slowly. "That is an interesting thought. I think that might work."

"You will have to decide what sort of girl you wish me to be. What is my character: compliant, defiant, silly, or smart? Mrs. Fieldings was fond of using drama in her school—she said it was an excellent means of teaching us to understand the perspective of another. I expect you will find me a competent enough actress for your ruse."

"I will have to give that additional thought. I confess, I had been rather focused on other aspects of the effort. I see I have definitely found the right partner."

8
Chapter

June 13, 1815

RICHARD MOUNTED YET another horse borrowed from Darcy—a lively chestnut gelding with white blaze and socks—and urged it into motion across the lush clover field. Dew-laden green smells of morning swirled up from the horse's hooves, smells that reminded him of his boyhood, those moments of escape when responsibility did not weigh down on him, crushing the very will from his soul.

What a maudlin thought—but a bit closer to true than he would have preferred to admit.

Perhaps he should write his steward and have several of his own horses sent down from Netherford. If Earl took the message himself, he could have them by tomorrow, without too much wear on the horses.

Darcy would not balk at stabling them for him. Having his own mount would offer a much greater sense of freedom.

One that he needed right now.

Under the cloudless sky, fresh morning air was giving way to summer heat that threatened to turn oppressive by afternoon. Earl flew lazy circles overhead, cawing loudly, mostly because he could. With all the time spent in London told to be unobtrusive, the freedom to stretch his wings and voice was not to be wasted. Earl would probably enjoy the flight out to Netherford.

It was difficult not to envy the cockatrice his juvenile freedoms from worry and forethought, to just fly and dive, and screech for the joy of startling the stupid birds in the trees. Ah, for those halcyon days of youth.

He urged the horse into a faster gait, his heart pounding in time. The wind in his face, the power of the horse's muscles bunching beneath him, jolting across the land, matching his motion to the horse. There was a reason men loved horse racing.

Sweet wildflowers blurred past in a heady flash as the world around him lost focus and narrowed to contain only him and his mount. Perhaps just a little faster.

That was all the encouragement needed to send the animal into a full gallop. Perhaps it had been feeling as constrained as Richard and needed to be released.

Past the fingerpost at the crossroad, its directions distorted beyond reading at this pace. Across the little road that led back to Pemberley manor, dust and gravel kicked up by thundering hooves. To the large stream, now running beside it as though to catch the rapidly moving water. The burnt-out cottage ahead, a full mile from the clover fields.

Such a morning run! He sucked in deep, restorative breaths. It had been a long time since he had enjoyed such an indulgence.

Best not wear out the animal just for his own satisfaction, though. He reined the horse in and directed it toward the gentle bridle path that would provide an excellent means of cooling down.

Sweat trickled down the side of his face as his heart grudgingly slowed. Time for sensible thinking and attending to important things.

Important things like the notice that had arrived by Blue Order cockatrice messenger that morning. The fifth man with the snapdragon insignia from the Cotillion had been partially identified as a businessman, probably an apothecary, in Sheffield, which narrowed down the possibilities significantly, and yet not enough.

How galling, though. Yet another Derbyshire tie for the enemies of dragons.

Then again, perhaps, it was too soon to be making that determination. It was possible the snapdragon connection was a strange coincidence. It was possible that they had overestimated the danger to the dragons of England.

And it was possible that gnomes and fairies filled the forests.

The horse snorted and shook his head as though sensing Richard's thoughts. Clever creature.

Trusting his own instincts had kept Richard alive in France. This was no time to stop trusting them, regardless of what would have been convenient for

Father and those who wanted to ignore the dangers to the Order.

Oh, Father!

The horse snorted again.

Chancellor Lord Matlock was going to be thrilled when he found out what St. John was about. Tension between the Office of the Secretary and the Chancellor had been a long-standing problem, so it was hardly surprising that St. John should relish the opportunity to take the Chancellor down a notch or three.

It was probably wrong, but a part of him wanted to be there for the confrontation. It would be satisfying to see St. John put in his place. But another part of him would rather have avoided one more explosive conflict and drawing of battlelines.

The rapidly approaching conflict when Darcy discovered Richard's suspicions about St. John would be quite enough to manage.

He rubbed sweat away from his face with his sleeve. How had it come to this?

What were the chances Darcy was man enough to be able to understand the untenable position Richard had been put in and forgive him for it? Excuse Richard for convincing him to harbor St. John, a suspected smuggler, at Pemberley? Grant absolution for possibly endangering Darcy's wife and daughter?

Darcy-before-Elizabeth would cast him aside and never speak to him again. No doubt at all. But perhaps, just perhaps, the man Darcy had become since Elizabeth, since carrying the Dragon Slayer thrice, since becoming responsible for the safety of the Dragon State, perhaps that man could see past his own demands to forgive Richard for what he must do.

That was a hope worth clinging to.

He turned the horse toward the old Ring Pond, a swimming hole he and Darcy had frequented as boys. The horse was cooled down enough for water now.

How much should he tell Miss Bennet about his business, though? Would she go to her sister with all that she knew, chattery as a little fairy dragon, telling Elizabeth things the Chancellor did not want her to know?

It would be prudent to believe that and act accordingly.

Prudent indeed, but would it be wise?

Perhaps the real question was, what did Miss Bennet need to know in order to carry out her part in the mission without creating unnecessary risk for herself or their objectives? She was a clever little thing. In many ways as clever as her sister, though a great deal less serious. It would be a mistake to treat her as a shatter-brained little girl, just a prop in his own machinations.

All that she had said over breakfast, her immediate grasp of her role, and what she could do to be more effective—she was not a woman to be underestimated. Much like her sister.

If it became relevant for her to know the Order's suspicions regarding St. John, he would tell her. But not until then. And it might not be for some time, considering St. John's current occupation with Matlock.

What was going on in his father's house since St. John's arrival?

St. John would probably be enjoying himself mightily, taking apart Andrew's Dragon Keeping. A little seed of satisfaction planted itself in the back of

Richard's mind. He had warned Andrew often enough that the role of the junior Keeper should be taken seriously, only to be told that it was Richard's jealousy speaking.

There might have been jealousy from time to time, but it did not invalidate his concerns.

Which also meant he needed to meet with his own steward and with Netherford himself. Though small and insignificant by comparison, there was little hope Netherford would escape St. John's fervor for audits. He definitely needed to send Earl with a message.

He pulled his silver whistle from his pocket —a gift from Darcy to commemorate Earl's hatching and their Friendship—and blew the sharp, shrill notes that would beckon Earl to return. He stopped his horse and scanned the sky.

Wait, what was that circling over the trees, toward the pond, just off the bridle path? Those were not hawks, but cockatrice! Pendragon's Bones! He urged his horse into motion. When cockatrice gathered like that, it was usually to finish off an injured dragon.

The horse carried him just to the edge of the trees before it balked and refused to go any further. Not surprising. Horses had an instinctive fear of dragons, cockatrice in particular. He jumped off, looped the reins about a convenient bush, and peered into the woods.

If there were an injured dragon within, approaching with caution was the only option. Even a dragon imprinted upon men could be dangerous when wounded, and if this were a wild dragon, the hazards increased exponentially. Getting himself killed by a dragon during his first days at Pemberley would be a humiliating way to die.

He moved into the woods, slowly, carefully. Not as dark as typical dragon woods, with younger trees, not ancient hardwoods, one could easily forget that danger could lurk within. A few more crunching steps, and he peered around a broad tree trunk.

Hissing, growling, scrabbling of feet.

He brought his head up sharply. Sounds of thrashing and a struggle. The hissing came from wyrms, no doubt. They had a peculiar guttural sound that was impossible to mistake. But the growls were from something larger. Significantly larger. And there were words in dragon tongue! If only he could understand the language!

He advanced on the sounds, keeping cover behind the trees. Cries of pain and of fear grew louder, clearer. There! Some thirty feet ahead, a scuffle in a small clearing between tall trees. Blood stained the forest floor. Small, dark bodies swarmed over a much more substantial one.

A large cluster of forest wyrms, not the breed with the azure stripes that had been among the Movers who kidnapped Elizabeth, but the typical ones, with scruffy leonine manes, long, sharp fangs, and blood-lust in their eyes. Nasty band of creatures, like street thugs going after helpless old men. They wove a loose circle around a grey-brown four-legged dragon, the size of a small pony.

Not a familiar face from the denizens of Pemberley. Where had it come from?

What was it?

A drake? No, it was shaped wrong for that—too long, too slender— and it had a pair of odd wings on its back. A firedrake, then? A wild firedrake?

Pendragon's Bones! A wild firedrake had not been encountered for—

Wait, no, the wings were wrong for that. Long and narrow, delicate and without the proper skeletal structure for flight. That dragon would never be able to fly. It raised a forepaw to bat at its assailants to reveal bloodied, webbed toes.

Long, lithe body, webbed feet, fin-like wings—a knucker, a water dragon?

There was a knucker living on Pemberley? A battered, wounded creature who would not be alive for long, though, if the wyrms had their way. But if it were wild, then he had little ground to intrude.

The knucker caught his gaze with wide, terror-filled eyes. "Help!"

No wild dragon would call for help in such a manner. It might have been living without a Friend, but it definitely had imprinted upon men. This was officially a Blue Order matter that demanded his immediate intervention.

But with what? With only his small knife on his person, he lacked any useful weapon. There, several stones. He hurled them at the wyrms. "Away from there! Now! He is not prey and is protected by the Order."

The wyrms stopped and turned their collective, red, predatory eyes on him.

Like staring down the barrel of a rifle pointed at his heart.

Distant sounds of battle and gunfire played in his ears, threatening to paralyze him.

No! Not the time to succumb to those ghosts!

He scooped up a large fallen branch, with many smaller branches and dead leaves still attached, and swept the space ahead of him as he ran at them.

Wyrms were inherently cowardly when faced with a creature larger than themselves, even when hunting in a cluster. The branch made him very large. They hissed and spat, weaving before him, trying to distract, mesmerize, create an opening to attack.

A pale flash dove from the treetops, shrieking at the top of his lungs. The wyrms screamed and disappeared underground.

"Capital timing, my Friend!" Richard waved at Earl as he hurried for the wounded dragon, dragging the branch behind him, just in case. "Are there cockatrice still circling above?"

"I will dismiss them." Earl squawked and disappeared into the trees.

As a juvenile, he did not have the dominance to take on a pack of wild cockatrice, but with the authority of the Order behind him, it should come to naught. The urge to call him back was strong, but Earl was no longer an infant and needed to spread his wings, as it were.

Richard stopped two paces from the injured dragon.

What had happened? That was not wyrm-inflicted damage. Great swaths of scales had been scraped from its grey-brown back and paler belly. Every one of its black front talons had been lopped off down to the quick, leaving its feet bloody—the poor creature would barely be able to walk under such conditions. The knucker's legs slid out from beneath him, and he fell to his belly, legs splayed out in all directions.

Trails of blood leaked from both forelegs, but those were not bite wounds. At least one tooth in its long, narrow snout had been freshly jarred from its mouth and its bottom fangs were broken off close to the gumline. One of its short, round ears seemed nicked, possibly in the attempt to cut it off.

Not a single wound was technically fatal, but together they left the creature without the means of feeding or defending itself, and that was fatal for a creature living without a Friend.

Only one creature could have inflicted such wounds. A warm-blooded one.

"May I approach?" Richard set the branch down and extended open hands toward the dragon.

"Who are you?" Though weak, the dragon's voice had a vaguely watery quality.

"I am Richard Fitzwilliam, Keeper of Netherford, son of Matlock, knight of the Pendragon Order."

"You are not of Pemberley?"

"I am cousin to Pemberley's Keepers and a welcome guest on the estate."

The creature gave him the stare of one sizing up a potential enemy. Finally, he sighed, more in surrender than assent, and lowered his head to the ground. "Approach."

Slowly, carefully, Richard made his way to the dragon's side and crouched beside it as it panted and quivered. Such a great deal of pain it must be in. "Have you a name? What may I call you?"

The dragon managed a chuckle as it turned dark, liquid eyes on him. "I live in Ring Pond and have been known as the Ring Wyrm by Old Pemberley. I have not been introduced to Young Pemberley yet."

"Then you are a member of Pemberley Keep?"

"For all of my life."

"Then it is my privilege to extend to you the protection of the Keep."

"I fear it may be too late for that. The cockatrice are circling above. That is a sure sign that my time is nearly expired."

"My Friend has gone to warn them away." As if on cue, frustrated cockatrice screams echoed above. "They will be gone soon, as are the wryms."

"Despicable little scavengers." Ring hissed, his long, forked tongue extended and tickling the air.

"I heartily agree. With your permission, I will send Earl to the manor for a cart to bring you back so that we might care for you properly. The Dragon Sage is in residence. She will certainly know what might be done for you."

Ring nodded slowly. "I have never ridden on a cart. Will not the horses balk?"

"Pemberley has horses trained for working among dragons."

"Then I suppose it will be an interesting experience." Ring dropped his head to the ground again with a small thump.

Richard signaled to Earl, who squawked his understanding and winged away.

"I had heard tell of the Dragon Sage, that she was now part of the Keep. A Keeper here now."

"You have not been introduced?" Was it possible for a dragon to have hidden himself from her for so long?

"There are a number of us who tend to keep to ourselves, who have not made her acquaintance yet."

"I am surprised. I had thought Darcy quite attentive to such things."

The Ring Wyrm shrugged. "Perhaps things have changed since the last time I moved freely about the estate."

That sounded like a story that would have to be told later. "May I ask, what happened to you? How did you come to be in such a state?"

Ring groaned and his tail dragged back and forth through the fallen leaves. "I was captured in a net and dragged from my home. Plied with some awful-smelling substance and when I awoke, I found myself like this."

Dragon's blood! Richard rubbed down his raised hackles. "You were attacked? On Pemberley grounds?"

"I had thought Pemberley to be safe from such things, but perhaps the infant dragon is not sufficient to maintain the safety of her Keep."

9

Chapter

ELIZABETH DID NOT make it into her office until nearly two o'clock. Her meeting with Cook alone had taken a full hour, and another two hours were spent with Mrs. Reynolds going over the household books, and that was not including the quarter-of-an-hour distraction when Agnes barged in, her puck Friend Fern in tow, confused about her duty and disagreeing with her Friend as to how the upstairs sitting room should be cleaned. The dragon, clearly the one with more sense in their Friendship, was correct.

After that disruption, Mrs. Reynolds had most likely noticed Elizabeth's eyes glazing over and realized the remaining matters would have to wait until tomorrow at least. Elizabeth had tried to hide it as long as possible, but after Agnes and Fern's interruption, there was no more disguising her fatigue. All told, it might not have been a bad thing.

How welcome it had been to scurry to the peace and quiet of her office to clear her head just a bit. She sank into the floral-upholstered chair nearest the window to savor the warmth of a sunbeam, whiffs of lavender floating on the soft breeze through the window.

Had Pemberley been like this before they had left? Constant demands and lists and correspondence? It seemed so long ago; it was hard to remember. She hooked the footstool with her toes and dragged it close enough to prop up her feet. Merciful heavens, that felt good.

The squat table beside her writing desk had gained a new pile seemingly overnight. Her graceful, feminine desk overflowed with correspondence and invitations. And the crates of books by the shelves had not even been opened.

Was it possible the paneled walls were closing in on her? She closed her eyes. Yes, that was better, if only for a little while.

Where to begin? So much to be done. Household orders needed to be placed. Parties and dinners attended or invitations declined. Blue Order business was piling up—including the census. That was probably the most pleasant among the tasks. Who would not want to spend days just visiting with the local dragons?

Perhaps that was where she should start.

If only there were two, maybe three of her, then everything might get done. Perhaps Mama was right. She wasted too much time wool-gathering and daydreaming and would be far more efficient if she just got to the matters at hand. Mama never seemed to have trouble accomplishing all that she needed to do. Neither Jane nor Mary had ever written to her of these sorts of challenges managing a household. Perhaps it really was just her own shortcomings revealing themselves.

She opened her eyes and pushed herself up. Time to do what she always did, work harder, be diligent and determined. It would all come together. Somehow.

She sat down at the desk and opened the first letter on the pile. A dinner invitation for—

Mrs. Reynolds' knock nearly made her drop the letter. "Come in."

The door opened slowly, and Mrs. Reynolds appeared with a silver tray bearing a single missive, sealed with red-wax. Elizabeth took it without remark. Astute woman that she was, Mrs. Reynolds curtsied and left without a word. She had already learnt Mama's handwriting some time ago and what that meant. A hot pot of calming chamomile tea would soon appear, if past experience was any indicator. Mrs. Reynolds was truly a gem.

"Those scratches look familiar." April peeked her head out of her basket in the sunbeam and hopped across the desk to examine the letter, turning her head this way and that.

"Indeed, they are. Mama has written."

"What are you going to do with it?"

"It is customary to read such things."

"You should burn it and be done with it. It would save you the trouble of becoming upset. You always do." April tried to pick the letter up in her beaky mouth, but Elizabeth laid her hand across it.

"I expect it is more my fault than hers. I have been decidedly impatient with Mama in the past. She can be exasperating, but it is also true that I allow her to irritate me. I must, I will choose not to allow her to frustrate me so. Starting today." She traced the bloopy wax seal with her fingertips.

"Who has taught you such nonsense?"

"Several people, in fact. Aunt Gardiner, Lady Astrid, Lady Dressler. Women whom I admire and hope to be like some day. I am determined to listen to them and not allow Mama to disturb my equanimity."

"But is this how they told you to do it? I do not think they told you to waste your time this way. I am sure of it." April chittered, scratching her feet along the letter. "Very well, then. Go ahead, then, open it. See what new vexations she has to add to your life."

Mrs. Reynolds knocked and entered with a small tea tray. The flowery, fuzzy scent of chamomile wafted in with her. She placed it on Elizabeth's desk, curtsied and disappeared. Such a treasure!

"She brought honey!" April landed on the honey pot's lid and twittered happily.

Elizabeth poured a cup of tea and dropped a dollop of honey on the extra saucer. She wrapped her fingers around the warm china. Even the smell of chamomile was soothing. Oddly, it smelt better than it tasted, but the flavor was not objectionable, just a little disappointing somehow.

Eyes closed, she drank half the cup as April sang sweetly. Nothing like the song of a fairy dragon to drain one's tensions away.

The tick of the mantel clock broke through April's melody. Best not procrastinate any longer, though.

There were other things yet to be done today. She broke the wax seal and unfolded the letter.

My dear Lady Darcy

—oh, how well that sounds! I take such delight in writing that name! That my daughter should be a Lady! I could not have wanted more for you.

Mama's loopy, flourished handwriting somehow conveyed her vaguely histrionic tones to paper. How ironic that Mama could never know that Elizabeth was a Lady in her own right and was actually Lady Elizabeth, not Lady Darcy.

Best ignore the little pinch in her chest that thought brought.

I know you are come back to Pemberley finally. I hope that your ball was everything you hoped it to be. Lydia has written to me of the raptures of it all. I know her coming out was the high point of her life, and she will never forget it. You have been so kind to her.

I confess my surprise and delight that you should so favor her. It is rather irregular, though, that you should desire to sponsor your youngest sister when Kitty is older and in just as much need of your attentions. Ah well, I suppose your father had a hand in that. He never did see much to be admired in Kitty.

No, nothing Elizabeth did would ever be enough in Mama's eyes, would it?

Despite your neglect, I am pleased to say Jane has done her duty by Kitty.

How fortunate for everyone.

Whilst staying here at Ingleside, our dear Bingley introduced Kitty to his friend, who found her very agreeable. I expect your father has told you, we are all expecting a betrothal soon.

Did you know that your papa has charged your own Mr. Darcy—that is, Sir Fitzwilliam—(oh, how well that sounds, too!) to approve of Kitty's beau in his stead?

Yes, yes, she did. And though not surprised by it, she still rather chafed at the imposition upon them. But Mama definitely did not need to know that.

I know he claims that travel is difficult for him, but it is highly irregular that he cannot be bothered to make the journey to Derbyshire. Still, though, I know your husband is a kind and agreeable sort of man who will find no fault with the young man his own friend has brought into our little family circle.

Since you have only just arrived, it is understandable that you have not invited us to Pemberley yet. But Kitty is impatient, as is to be expected under the circumstances. A young lady always is when expecting a betrothal. I know I was, but that is neither here nor there, I suppose.

Your dear sister Jane, though, being all that is good and gracious, has taken it upon herself to plan a dinner for you to become acquainted with the man I hope to call my son erelong.

Interesting how she hoped to call Kitty's beau a son, but Mr. Darcy was still simply 'your husband' not 'my son. Yes she was being petty, and yes it was a problem that Mama brought that out in her.

I expect you will say that you are as busy as you were in London. I am sure that was true, and I do not begrudge your failure to host us at Darcy House. But this invitation is of vital import to your sister's happiness and to my own—although that is nothing to hers, to be sure. So, when Jane's invitation arrives, do pay proper attention to it. Surely you can manage to break away from whatever it is you are doing and attend.

    Your loving mother,

FB

Elizabeth set the letter aside and drew several deep breaths, struggling not to mutter. Was it possible Mama had become even more bold, to the point of brazen, now she was in Derbyshire? It was the kind of change Elizabeth might accuse a dragon of inspiring, but at Ingleside, that was simply impossible.

"You see, she has upset you, just like I said she would. I can take this to the kitchen fire and burn it for you if you would like." April had her own resentments toward Mama and probably wanted to burn the letter on her own account.

"I am quite well, thank you." Elizabeth clutched her teacup in trembling hands and raised it to her lips.

"You only breathe like that when you are upset."

"I am quite in control of my own reactions. Thank you. She merely writes to tell us that Jane will be hosting a dinner party soon, and she desires us to attend."

"I am sure that is part of what she said, but there is more you are not telling me. I know—"

The door burst open, and Mrs. Reynolds dashed in, her eyes wide and her face flushed. "Lady Sage, pray forgive the intrusion, but there is an emergency that requires your immediate attention."

Elizabeth jumped to her feet, nearly dropping the tea. "Has something happened with Anne?"

"No, no. Everything is well with the nursery. Pray come to the back near the kitchen. Sir Richard has found a wounded dragon—he says it is an old knucker who lives in Ring Pond— it is hurt something awful."

Unladylike though it might be, Elizabeth sprinted to the kitchen, leaving Mrs. Reynolds in her wake. April barely keeping up. Cook intercepted Elizabeth and directed her to the back door.

Three steps outside, she stopped and drew a deep, calming breath. Never surprise a dragon, especially one ill, irritated, or injured.

The creature was indeed a knucker, laid out on a farm cart, pulled by an old, gentle horse well accustomed to the local dragons. The cart stood in the shade of the manor, protecting the bloodied creature from the heat of the day. How had a large minor dragon come by such injuries?

Richard stood near the back of the cart, his hand resting lightly on the dragon's head as he whispered something to it. "Lady Sage, pray come."

The dragon looked at her and slowly blinked, probably as much of a welcome as the poor creature could manage.

She approached slowly and carefully. Large patches of hide were rubbed raw of scales, oozing clear liquid which was just beginning to crust over the wounds. How had it lost all its talons, and incurred the damage to its fangs? Just how many places were bleeding?

Her stomach clenched into a little icy knot that flipped end over end. Merciful heavens, no, it was not possible.

"May I present Ring, the knucker from Old Ring Pond."

"I have been known as the Ring Wyrm, Lady." For all his wounds, he twitched his eye in a wink.

So like his kind to find some form of humor even in such a desperate situation.

"Lizzy!" Lydia appeared at her elbow. "April came for me and Cosette. Tell me, what can we do?"

Her first instinct was to tell her to stay out of the way, but no, if April thought she might be helpful, then she should have the chance. "Get me warm water and clean linens to cleanse his wounds. We need styptic water. No. Bring agaric of oak to stop the bleeding. Once you have brought them, then I need common plasters made up for his skin. Oh, and bandages. Mrs. Reynolds will help you. She will know the tincture I need as well."

Lydia nodded and ran off.

"April, will you find—"

"I believe Dale has already been sent to find Darcy. I shall find Walker." April zipped away.

Dear, sensible little Friend.

She walked around the farm cart. The knucker's wounds became even more troubling with her inspection. "We must get you somewhere you might be cared for properly."

The Ring Wyrm craned his neck to look at her. "But it is so comfortable. I had thought perhaps to relocate from my knucker hole to a cart upon my recuperation."

"Your sense of humor does reassure one that you will recover." She patted an uninjured spot on his shoulder. "But I must insist upon your leaving the cart, if only to spare the horse, who should not spend the rest of his life hitched to the cart."

"When you put it that way, I suppose I cannot argue." The tip of Ring Wyrm's tail flicked with good humor.

"What arrangement would you consider most comfortable under the circumstances?"

"Such a shame I do not think I can manage stairs at this time. Otherwise, one of your guestrooms would suit rather well, indeed."

Richard snickered under his breath. Oh yes. He had been standing by all this time.

"Room might be made for you in the stillroom if the house would be best suited, or—" Elizabeth glanced over her shoulder toward the house. No, the stillroom really was the only possible place in the house that did not require stairs.

"He could easily take the place of the farm cart in the barn." Richard pointed to the smallest barn, the one nearest the house. "I expect it might be rather more comfortable for him, without the worry of damaging some bit of the house."

He made a good point.

"Such an embarrassment of riches to choose from." Ring nudged her hand with his nose. "I do not know the rules of a house and have always been outside, so, if it is no inconvenience, I would prefer the barn, if that—"

"Is no inconvenience at all." Elizabeth stroked Ring's soft, smooth snout and turned to find a stable hand and a young undergardener waiting on instructions. "Go make the barn ready. Sweep it well and pile fresh hay for a bed. Cover the hay with empty feed sacks so it will not irritate his skin. Quickly now."

The young men scampered off.

"May I examine your wounds more carefully now?"

"It is a shame that I must make your acquaintance in such dishabille." Delicate, fin-like wings fluttered.

Elizabeth stepped closer. "I am surprised not to have made your acquaintance before now. I thought I had met all the Pemberley dragons."

Large patches of hide on both his sides were missing scales, as though they had been scraped away. Little dots of blood welled along the raw skin. The meaty, metallic scent of dragon's blood threatened to turn her stomach.

"I have always been a rather reclusive sort, I am afraid. It is the way of one who dwells in deep, dark pools of water."

"It is such a shame, though, when you clearly have such a refined sense of the absurd. Such things must be shared with others who appreciate them." She lifted his front foot. The talons had not been broken, but cleanly cut, deep into the quick. How desperately that must hurt. She would send Lydia for yellow basilicum ointment from the stores to treat those.

"I confess, I do feel that loss rather powerfully. I have discovered that neither fish nor frogs have the capacity to laugh, nor the wherewithal to know what they should be laughing at." Ring laughed, a rather liquid, rippling sound.

"I can well imagine." Two puncture wounds, still trickling blood, marred his front limbs. Neat and regular. Those had been intentionally made. No natural hazard could have caused such injuries. "Are you aware of other dragons on the estate with whom I have not become acquainted?" A young groom ran toward them, waving. "May we take you to the barn now? Then I shall be able to clean and dress your wounds."

"Such an honor, Lady Sage. I am wholly undeserving of such attentions, but I shall enjoy them ever so much, I am sure. Your attentions will be the source of much notoriety for me on the estate. I do not know what I shall do with such popularity. The least I can do will be to acquaint you with the few Old Pemberley dragons whom you have not met." He lowered his chin to the cart once again, weariness in every move. How much was his good humor costing him?

"I would be most grateful." She signaled Richard to lead the horse on toward the cart barn.

Poor Ring winced at each bump of the cart.

Just how many dragons were there on Pemberley whom she did not know? Did Darcy know them? Why would there have been a cadre of dragons who had kept themselves secret, especially from her?

Whatever it meant, it was surely nothing good.

Which would probably delight Mr. St. John.

10
Chapter

SEVERAL HOURS LATER, the sun low in the sky, Darcy, Walker, and Richard stood in the small barn, watching Elizabeth, with Lydia's help, tend the knucker's injuries. With its low thatched roof and thick walls, the structure had been storing the farm cart and other equipment for as long as Darcy could remember. He sneezed in the dusty, slightly musty humid air, sweat trickling down the side of his face.

No horses or donkeys were stabled here. A few of the barnwurms made their nests under its shelter, especially to lay their eggs in a quiet place with little interference from the vermin that might otherwise prey upon their eggs and young. Exactly the sort of place for a recuperating dragon.

Vaguely herbal, medicinal scents hung in the air as Elizabeth cleansed and dressed Ring's wounds with the same calm assurance that Sir Edward managed. He would be proud to know how much she had learnt from him and how well it was being applied.

The Ring Wyrm received her ministrations with grace and good humor, which was, all told, rather remarkable. Few dragons naturally exhibited a sense of humor, and to demonstrate such when one was— uncomfortable—spoke a great deal for the knucker's character. Even Pemberley had been cross and cranky when Elizabeth had treated her tail blisters and other maladies so long ago.

Even more surprising, Lydia made a competent and steady nurse, not flinching at the rather more gruesome parts of her duties, the ones that brought bile into Darcy's throat. Her cheerful chatter seemed to distract their patient from his suffering and made the process easier on everyone. Embarrassing, really, how much Darcy had discounted the value of such a skill. Definitely not what he would have expected from the girl he had sent away to Mrs. Fieldings'.

Pray the same transformation might be worked in Georgiana.

"April, pray summon the barn tatzelwurms." Elizabeth stood and dusted her hands together.

"Come, Cosette, they need to understand your place of dominance as well." April flew a circle around Cosette and zipped away.

"Dominance of fairy dragons over tatzelwurms. That sounds rather unnatural," Richard muttered.

"After a fashion, that is true," Walker said. "Keepers receive their status from the major dragons they Keep, but dragon Friends receive their status from their warm-blooded Friends. In this case, that means the fairy dragons have rather substantially increased standing."

"And the minor dragons of Pemberley simply accept that as the way of things?" Richard's wrinkled face spoke his skepticism, or was it disapproval?

"Nothing is that simple with dragons. You know that. But the dynamic of Friendship is completely different from Keepership. The dragons understand it, though, and that seems key in making it all work. And, if you had not guessed, it is the reason cockatrice are quite particular about their Friends." Walker squawked a rather self-satisfied sound.

He was right. There was a certain honor in being accepted as the Friend of so dominant a cockatrice.

Elizabeth approached, her posture as expressive as a dragon's. "Once the tatzelwurms have ministered to his remaining wounds, I will ask that a pair stay with him in case there is some crisis during the night. After the meal I ordered arrives from the kitchen, I will return to the house, and we will discuss this matter further."

It would not be a pretty discussion.

Walker looked up at her and cocked his head. "I will see there is a cockatrice guard to stand watch on the roof whilst Ring recovers."

"I am sure we will all rest easier under their watch, thank you." Elizabeth's tone softened for Walker.

He spread his wings and launched, elegant in the economy of his movement.

With a sharp nod, she returned to the knucker, and Darcy headed toward the house, Richard close behind. Neither spoke until well out of earshot from of the barn.

"I will not ask if you are all right." Richard scanned the sky. Was he looking for Earl or Walker or just for anything unusual?

"Good. I would hate to have to state the obvious for you." Darcy clasped his hands behind his back.

"I suppose the problem of the dragon parts trade can no longer be a secret from Elizabeth, not now."

Little clouds of gnats rose up from the grass as they cut a path through the field.

"Under other circumstances, I would consider that a good thing. I never liked the notion of keeping secrets from her." No, it had been disturbing his sleep for weeks now. But such a revelation! "To have Pemberley so violated! I am sick at the very notion!" Blood pounded in his temples. It had been good he had heard the news on an empty stomach.

"I can imagine, better than you would expect, I am afraid." Something in Richard's tone made the claim believable.

"It is like reliving Elizabeth's kidnapping. Walker, as you saw, is taking this incident quite personally. He is already organizing the local cockatrice into a formal guard for the estate. And Brutus! There was bloodlust in his eyes at the news. He has already sent Axel to the Order office in Chesterfield to find more drakes for the estate guard and may yet go to Sheffield if our little market town cannot provide enough dragons. I cannot fathom how this has happened!" Darcy flexed his hands in and out of fists, forcing himself to breathe.

"I imagine she will be attended by a constant guard for the foreseeable future?"

"Absolutely. Alister Salt, with Kingsley and Sergeant, will be her driver everywhere now. She will not argue at the restrictions, I am sure, but to have Pemberley violated as Darcy House was … have you any idea of the trauma?"

Richard laid a hand on Darcy's arm, stopping him. "I understand more than you know. I learned a great deal on the continent, and little of it was about the art of war. When I say I am truly sorry for this, know that it comes from a deeper place of understanding than you can imagine."

They locked eyes. Somehow, yes, it really did seem he grasped the weight of it all.

"Was the Ring Wyrm able to give you any account of his attackers?" First, Darcy House and now Pemberley? How was it possible?

"Without any moon, he said he saw nothing, not even certain how many there were." Richard shrugged. "Though he might recognize their scent if he encountered them again."

"So helpful."

"I am afraid that is not the worst of it. The Ring Wyrm said that since the demise of Old Pemberley, the dragons of Pemberley have come to recognize the dangers of the new moon."

What could Darcy possibly say to that?

They continued in silence to the house and into Darcy's office. As his eyes adjusted to being out of the sun, the cooler air within eased the barest edge of Darcy's angst.

His well-ordered office with everything in its place welcomed them with somber dignity. Thank heavens something in his world still remained as expected. Traces of his father lingered here, his steadiness, his wisdom, even his stubbornness that could be so maddening. But his was the breed of stubbornness that would give way to reason—not like Matlock, who regularly refused to listen to reason—and it had made Darcy learn to support his arguments with reason. Darcy had learned to become a better man in this room and being here reminded him of all he could be. All he wanted to be.

He skirted around his father's massive dark oak desk, past the long wall of full bookshelves, and fell into one of the matching tawny leather wingchairs near the fireplace, the one whose lumps and divots matched his frame perfectly. The smell of books and leather, ink and order, filled him, braced him like his father's voice once had.

Life had only taken another unexpected turn. Not everything was crashing to an end. He needed to remember that.

Richard fell heavily into the matching chair, rubbing at a scar on his wrist. He pulled the stool from under the chair and propped up his feet, leaning his head into the soft leather. "The Ring Wyrm's equanimity throughout this has been surprising. I never knew knuckers to be so even-tempered. But then, this is the first knucker I have had the pleasure of knowing. Did you know about Ring prior to this?"

"I knew there were tales of a wyrm in Ring Pond, but no, I had never met him before now. I had thought them variants on the tale of the Lambton wyrm, which of course, was and is Pemberley, so I gave them little attention."

"Does it bother you—"

"That there are large minor dragons on the estate that I do not know?" Darcy slapped the chair's arms with both hands. "What do you think?"

"Forgive me." Richard blinked several times. "Why do you think they have chosen to remain unknown?"

"I can only imagine it was a precedent set by Old Pemberley. Why? I do not know. You recall how he was his last few years."

"Like an old man losing his grip on reality, little by little. One with long fangs and claws." Richard shuddered. "A senile dragon is not a creature to be meddled with."

"I do not know, but perhaps, he was apt to forget the dragons of his Keep just as he occasionally forgot who I was. I remember one particularly ugly incident—"

"I remember that well, or did you forget I was there with you?"

"I had. When one's estate dragon makes an earnest attempt to eat one, you try to put that out of your mind altogether. It was a vivid reminder of what the world looked like before the Pendragon Treaty."

"A world I would rather not see." Richard leaned close and clapped Darcy's shoulder as though to shake him from the reminiscence. "The question is, what to do to find those dragons? It seems likely that the censuses taken since Old Pemberley's decline likely reflect his loss of memory. I wonder if you were to go back to older censuses—"

"That is a good idea. Give me just a moment." Darcy stood and headed toward a bookcase on the other side of the room, lined with a shelf of green leather spines.

"And if I know Elizabeth, she has already secured the Ring Wyrm's promise to make us proper introductions."

"She probably has."

"I certainly have. He is quite an amiable creature." Elizabeth slipped into the office and shut the door behind her. She wore a gory apron over her gown and disheveled curls hung around her face. Weary creases lined her eyes. "I think your idea about looking to the much older census records an excellent one, thank you."

"Ring is resting comfortably?" Darcy pulled a soft upholstered chair from near the desk closer to them and held it for her, then seated himself.

"The tincture of dragon Sir Edward taught me to make has alleviated much of his discomfort."

"Tincture of dragon?" Richard cringed.

"What are you thinking? The herb! The French chef at Matlock might have called it tarragon."

"Oh, that is far better." Richard tried to laugh.

"Indeed, it is far better than a trade in dragon parts, which is no laughing matter." Elizabeth's lips pursed into an expression that did not bode well. "Neither of you seems as shocked at the attack on Ring as I would have expected you to be. I can only assume that it is because you have been aware of the possibility of smugglers in dragon parts in Derbyshire." She glowered first at Darcy, then at Richard.

Richard cast a warning glance at Darcy.

Perhaps Richard was right. It would be better to allow him to explain.

"Since your kidnapping, evidence has come to light suggesting there might be a far greater traffic in such … items … than we suspected. The Order has determined that investigation of the possibility should take high priority. However—and, my dear cousin, this is the thing you must understand—there has been no suspicion until this very day that there were active poachers or smugglers in this region. We acknowledged the possibility that there was traffic going through Derbyshire, but truly nothing more." Richard's voice rang with quiet authority.

"And this is the matter you seek to involve my sister in? And that you were aware of?" She pressed her elbows into the arms of the chair and stared straight at Darcy.

"Yes. It was thought, and I do still believe, that it would be easier to investigate those we think are making use of dragons in cosmetic and other preparations, if there were a young lady to appear to be seeking them. It is much more believable than a man sent alone on such an errand. I would never consider exposing any young lady, much less your sister, to the perpetrators of such heinous acts. I assured Darcy of as much before I sought his permission to approach your sister."

Elizabeth said nothing, but the lines on her forehead grew deeper. When they had discussed it before leaving London, she had assured Darcy of her trust in him regarding the matter. But perhaps she could not fathom something so heinous could be going on.

"If you wish her to be freed from her role in our investigations, say the word, and I shall do so without hesitation," Richard said.

She broke eye contact and looked at the ceiling roses. "I fear that after today, after seeing what happened to Ring, she will be all the more determined to be of whatever assistance she can be. There is an unsubtle stubbornness about her."

Darcy held his breath and clenched his jaw. She would indeed be the one able to identify unsubtle stubbornness.

Richard controlled his response much better. "She is a young lady of unusual courage, to be sure. But that will not sway me. I will submit to your decision."

"If I could, I would assist you myself," she said.

Darcy gasped, but her look silenced him.

"I am well aware that there are too many excellent reasons why I am the wrong person for the task. If my sister, knowing everything, still wishes to participate, I will not stop her. The cause is too important. Is my father aware?"

"Of the smugglers, yes. Of Lydia's connection to the investigation, no. I understood that you and Darcy have the responsibility for her now."

"We do. He still needs to be told, even if the responsibility lies with us."

Richard opened his mouth as if to speak, but shut it again.

"That is not negotiable, Richard. At the very least, it is disrespectful to the Historian of the Order to be kept unaware of matters affecting his family. I will write a letter to send by Blue Order messenger myself. And I expect you will provide me the necessary details."

Richard winced.

"Do not be mistaken, I consider it disrespectful to have been kept uninformed on this matter." She placed her hands on her hips, flared her elbows, and sat up straighter, filling her chest with a deep breath. "What was the argument for keeping the Dragon Sage unaware of matters that clearly are within the bounds of her authority?"

Richard leaned forward, elbows on his knees. "First, let me be clear, this was not my decision, and I argued most forcefully against it. Sometimes a soldier must follow orders he does not agree with. I pray you will forgive me for that."

Was it too much to hope her expression would soften at his request?

Apparently, it was.

"I grant that it is a reason and perhaps a reasonable one at that. A rational person might even accept it. I cannot grant that I am quite rational at the moment. Perhaps later, I will be moved to release my resentment, but for now, do not require that of me."

Richard put up a good face, but disappointment was still evident around his eyes. "If you wish me to repair to Matlock, you need only ask."

"I do not wish that on you. For the moment. Is it an incorrect assumption to think it was Lord Matlock who insisted that I not be privy to this information?"

"He and General Yates."

"I would expect that of a military man. I know that they see the world, even the dragon world, in different terms and do not accept women in roles such as mine." She looked at the ceiling and sighed. "And I have heard gossip about how Chancellor Matlock has spoken about me in my absence—"

Darcy winced. It was only a matter of time before that got back to her. Astonishing that it took her so long to mention it.

"—so I am not surprised. But I am … disappointed." The poignancy of her word stung. "I suppose it is to be expected, in an organization like the Blue Order. But that does not mean I like it." She looked directly at Richard with a piercing, even dangerous stare. "However, this is my home. There are to be no more secrets kept from me. I will not have it. I will insist on your immediate removal if I discover that you have been keeping anything else pertinent from me."

Richard nodded.

"Is there anything else you would like to tell me?"

"No."

"Is there anything that you are refraining from saying? Perhaps regarding Mr. St. John, whom I already loathe?"

Richard's jaw hardened and cold silence descended. If one could see a man think, that is what they were looking at now. And he continued to think. "I am not at liberty to say."

What?

Technically, he had said nothing, and yet Darcy's hands ached to throttle him. Dragon's blood! Richard! Bloody hell! How could he have kept that secret?

"I understand. Should there be any new matters of which you are not at liberty to speak, I expect you will let me know you cannot speak of them without delay."

The veins in Richard's temples throbbed. "Yes, Lady Sage."

Well done, Lady Sage!

She exhaled a little of her tension. "And in return, I shall remain observant for anything that might be of interest to you. The uninhibited chatter of many small dragons may yield something useful towards your goals. They will say things to me that you would never learn by your own efforts." She stood and smoothed her filthy apron. "Contrary to what our esteemed Chancellor seems to believe, I am neither flighty, nor out of control. I am as much invested in the security of the Order as he is. I am merely working from a place of different understanding, one which might actually prove useful to the cause. An end must be put to these atrocities. In this, I am your ally, not your enemy, and I expect—no, I demand to be treated as such. And yes, when Lord and Cownt Matlock come into the county, I will seek them out and tell them exactly that. But there is no need to give them forewarning."

"Of course not. I would never suspend any pleasure of yours." Richard bowed from his shoulders.

"In that case, I insist that you join us at the Bingleys' for dinner the day after tomorrow. My sister asked that our delightful and dashing cousin be included in our invitation."

Dinner with the dragon-deaf side of the family? Now? Why had he given Bennet that promise? He hardly had time to meet potential suitors now. Darcy fought to keep the creases out of his forehead.

Richard rolled his eyes. "I suppose my duties will permit me a modicum of time spent in agreeable company."

"I did not say it would be agreeable, just company." Elizabeth arched her brow, the tiniest part of her humor returning.

"Nonetheless, for you, I will endure the hardship. If you will excuse me." Richard stood and made a hasty retreat.

A deafening silence filled every corner of the room.

"How much did you know about all these matters?" She folded her arms across her chest and stared into Darcy's eyes, demanding.

He met her gaze steadily. No more secrets. "Less than Richard. I understood that there were concerns about the trade in dragon parts. That there is thought to be a trade connection to Chesterfield, but truly nothing more."

"That Richard would keep secrets from me, I do not like, but I can understand. But that you would? It is unconscionable. I cannot fathom how you justified it to yourself." The fury in her eyes said so much more.

"I was under orders from the Chancellor."

"And that is your excuse?"

"We are all under his authority."

"And you would have me keep secrets from you in the same way?" Her voice thinned, high and shrill, like an angry cockatrix.

He opened his mouth, but paused.

"Were you about to suggest that it is different because of the duty a wife owes her husband? Were you?"

It had crossed his mind, but he certainly was not about to admit that now.

"Am I to understand that you feel honesty, truthfulness is a one-sided endeavor? That it is owed to you, but not by you, in this marriage?"

He stood slowly, not breaking eye contact. "I never suggested such a thing."

"But your actions have implied it. Are we to be allies in this endeavor of Dragon Keeping, of service to the Order, of our very lives? Or unequal partners, as Matlock seems to insist?"

"Elizabeth, please—" He extended an open hand.

"No. That is not a rhetorical question. I will have an answer, but not now. Think on it, think hard, for I will only hear one answer on the matter, and be forever silenced on it." She stormed out of the room.

11
Chapter

June 15, 1815

AFTER A DAY and a half spent in a draconic sickroom, the thought of a day spent in other manners of useful employ was almost too much for Lydia to ask for. Not that tending the poor wounded dragon was an unworthy task. It was an honor to be permitted to do it, but perhaps, just perhaps, Lydia's calling was not the sickroom. As long as someone else was available to change dressings and cleanse his wounds, she would have been happy to visit and distract Ring from his woes. But the other, well, it just turned her stomach and gave her nightmares.

Poor Betsey, having to draw baths for her two days in a row. She would appreciate not having to do it a third day. Trying to be a proper lady's maid, she did not complain, but Juniper muttered and grumbled under her breath about how much work it was to prepare a bath and how tired her Friend had become from it. Finally, Cosette brought in April to scold Juniper for her attitude. Still, there was no other way to be rid of the peculiar odors of all the sticky-ooziness of Ring's wounds. Today, though, she would remain sweet-smelling and ooze-free.

Lydia slipped out of her room, closed the door softly behind her, and tiptoed down the hall. Yes, it probably was pointless, considering Lizzy's preternatural hearing, acute even among Blue Order folk. She would doubtless know Lydia had gone downstairs, but it made her feel just a bit safer to do it quietly. Lizzy was in a temper, and only a fool would not make a point of avoiding her right now.

Given how much Lizzy disapproved of so many of Mama's ways and prided herself on being controlled and rational like Papa, her resemblance to Mama when she was angry was nothing short of ironic. Lizzy did not take offense often, but when she did, she clung to it like a hoarding puck to its treasure. Worse, the level of her offense was not always well connected to the act that had offended her. It seemed like she bottled up all the things that bothered her until one final issue became the keystone that fixed her resentment into place. Just like Mama, except she did not tend to be quite so vocal about things. No, Lizzy tended to go silent, which was perhaps all the more unnerving.

Poor Mr. Darcy. He seemed to bear it well, stoic in his discomfiture, but the dragons of the house all knew the depth of his disquiet. And what the dragons knew, Lydia knew, thanks to Cosette, who was now quietly sitting on her shoulder, avoiding Lizzy and April, who was now rather short and snippy herself.

As much as any household's mistress being out of sorts upended a home, the presence of dragons only made it more pronounced, spreading word and rumors to the staff in a constant flow that non-Blue households would never experience. One of the unique joys of Pemberley.

With any luck, she would be able to enjoy a quiet breakfast, away from the cranky master and mistress of the house. But no, botheration! Shadows through the open morning room door promised her company.

She crept to the doorway and peeked in, ready to flee before being seen if necessary.

Relief!

Agnes the maid scurried past, leaving only Sir Richard to occupy the sunshiny, coffee-fragranced morning room. What was more, he had apparently ordered lovely crunchy toast and jam for her and her Friend. Earl gobbled kippers—not raw meat— from the dragon perch. So considerate.

Cockatrice could be rather disturbing to watch whilst they ate, especially when their meals were raw. Gobbets and bits of goo flying everywhere, littering the crisp white tablecloth. Mrs. Fieldings had tried to inure her students to the sight, but the lesson never quite took for Lydia.

Cosette zipped past her, diving for the bowl of fresh white peonies on the sideboard, bathed in the room's brightest sunbeam. There was little better than fresh nectar first thing in the morning, if Cosette were to be believed.

Sir Richard stood and pulled out the chair beside him. While he was not particularly handsome, his gentlemanly behavior certainly improved his looks in spades. "Good morning, Miss Bennet. You look well rested after all the excitement of the day before yesterday."

"Not quite as well as I might have hoped, I am afraid. Nursing does not seem my province, I think." She sat and pulled a fresh linen napkin into her lap.

His brow furrowed. "Are you still agreeable with our plans for the day? Or have ... recent events ... changed your mind?"

Lydia poured herself a cup of coffee—mostly because that was what Sir Richard was drinking, and it looked intriguing—and scooped jam onto a saucer for Cosette. "You mean the plans that we will go into Chesterfield, and you will buy me whatever I desire from the apothecaries and artists' shops?" She batted her eyes for the silliness of it all.

"And what will you desire?" He raised a brow, returning her good-natured flirt in kind.

"From the paint shops, anything that resembles April's blue color, for that is, at least for today, my very favorite of colors, and I am wild about painting something in that shade. Tomorrow, you may be certain, my favorite shall be a scandalous red, but today it is blue. And at the apothecary, there are any number of things that might appeal to my vanity. You may be assured, though, I have memorized the list of the preparations most likely to contain ... distasteful ingredients. Those shall be the items I most desire." She swallowed hard and hoped the churning in her stomach would settle soon.

"And that will not distress you?"

She huffed and snorted the way Cosette did when she was annoyed. "Of course, it distresses me! What do you take me for? The need for this entire adventure is disturbing in all its details. And what happened to Ring makes it even more so." She swallowed hard and exhaled slowly, with control. Yes, she needed control. "That is what makes our plans so necessary. I am not prepared to change my mind and leave you in need of finding an alternative approach."

Sir Richard sipped his coffee and hid behind his cup. A bit excessive, perhaps, but point made. "You are much like your sister, and I mean that in the best possible way."

"I will take that as more of a compliment when she has gotten over pique and begins acting more like herself again."

He smacked his lips and smiled. Clearly, he had been on the receiving end of her ire. "I have ordered the carriage be prepared to depart as soon as you are ready, perhaps as soon as we have completed breakfast."

They took the Darcys' oldest coach, one without any distinguishing mark to connect it with Pemberley. Though it best suited their purposes, it only served to remind Lydia just how easy it was to become accustomed to Mr. Salt's exceptional equipage. Not that she was ever likely to enjoy such luxury again, but it had been a most agreeable experience.

All things considered, though, even Mr. Darcy's oldest coach was nicer than anything Papa had ever kept and should be appreciated as such. That was what she needed to keep reminding herself. She pressed back into the soft-enough squabs and drew a deep breath filled with leather polish and the pleasant woody scent Sir Richard used.

Her pulse increased enough to feel it in her temples as the wheels crunched over the gravelly road to the steady beat of the horses' hooves. Cosette sidled along her shoulder to press into her neck, trilling softly. So very real it all had suddenly become. Not just a thrilling idea, but as real as the injured dragon in the barn, fraught with uncertainty and danger—

"There are two apothecaries currently in Chesterfield, Mr. Stanton Keats and Mr. Wilberforce Abrams—Miss Bennet? Are you well?"

She opened her eyes and shook her head, blinking. What was that he said? "Yes, forgive me, just a momentary distraction from the newness of it all. Two apothecaries, Keats and Abrams. Which one are you more concerned with?"

The vague look of alarm in his hazel eyes faded. "Forgive me if I do not wish to say until after we have visited them. I would like for you to view them both with untainted opinions."

"That seems fair enough. Your flighty young cousin, in search of fancy cosmetics with which her lady's maid might make her more beautiful and more likely to engage the attentions of potential suitors, will enjoy exploring what both shops might offer. If you are certain that your purse will accommodate." She pressed her hands to her cheeks, smiled and blinked coquettishly.

He nodded with the barest of winks. "The Order has supplied me with sufficient blunt for the purpose. I do not wish to carry over any accounts with anyone we visit today."

"Are any shops in Chesterfield owned by Order men?"

"The circulating library and the chandler, as I understand."

"Will we be calling upon them as well?"

"What do you have in mind?" He leaned a little closer, head cocked to listen.

Oh, that was a lovely thing indeed, to have someone taking her so seriously!

"If nothing else, Cosette can speak with any dragon Friends that they might have, or even the wild dragons in the area to see what they might know. Wild dragons are more apt to linger near dragon-hearers, even if they are not imprinted upon men."

The way Sir Richard's brows rose, it seemed he was unaware of that basic lesson drilled into her at school. Interesting.

"A circulating library might be a place to arrange meetings for dealing in goods as much as any public house, and perhaps even better because it is unusual. Those discussions could even be couched as the discussion of a mutually read book," she said.

"By Jove, I had not considered that! It is an excellent notion."

"And the chandler, assuming he deals in teas as well as candles, might well rub shoulders with dealers in 'specialized goods', shall we say. Both could easily have information that they do not even realize is pertinent to our needs." She shrugged carefully so as not to upset Cosette on her shoulder.

"Now that is another good thought." One he clearly found astonishing, coming from her. At least his tone was one of true respect. That made up for his surprise.

"I do not mean to step out of place, but having worked with April and the fairy dragon teams seeking information on Lizzy's whereabouts, I did learn a great deal about where information might be found—and who might be around to overhear it."

"I had not realized how helpful that experience might prove for our task at hand. Be encouraged to share your ideas and observations with me whenever you have them."

"Even the ones that seem silly?"

"Yes, most definitely. I promise not to dismiss your notions out of hand, Miss Bennet. There is a great deal more to you than many would recognize."

Heat crept from her shoulders all the way to her ears, leaving her eyes burning. Mrs. Fieldings had said that, too, when she was released from the schoolmistress' care, but it was difficult at the time to tell how to take such words. It was an extraordinary compliment to hear it from a man like Sir Richard.

The carriage trundled down one of the lesser streets of Chesterfield—a much larger market town than Meryton—and stopped at a modest storefront whose sign bore Mr. Abrams' name in small red print below a larger image of an apothecary's mortar and pestle. Sir Richard handed her out as Cosette and Earl flew off.

Theirs was the only carriage on the quiet, shady street. A weary-looking woman with three children in tow, a young man laden with packages, and an older couple lingering at the printshop window were the only others in view. Lydia exhaled heavily. This place seemed quite normal, even friendly. Yes, she could do this.

"Are you ready, cousin Liddie?" He straightened his coat and nodded at her, eyebrows lifted in query.

"Yes, cousin Matt." She slipped her hand in his arm and they entered the shop.

The herbal, dusty smell that all apothecary shops shared seemed intent upon smothering her as she stepped inside. Dimly lit and packed floor to ceiling with shelves and drawers and boxes, the shop all but screamed "I am full, I am full. Anything you need is here!"

She edged back half a step. That was no dragon voice, just her imagination having its way here. Best get that under better regulation before she said or did something entirely silly.

A door behind a long, wooden countertop squealed open and a short, bald man trundled out. Everything about him seemed round. His shiny head, his pronounced red cheeks, his bulging Adam's apple, his belly, even his hands seemed pudgy and round. Never before had she seen anyone so very … round. His brown suit, conveniently the color of dust, was covered with a leather apron.

That had to be Mr. Abrams.

Wiping his hands on his dusty apron, he said, "How might I be of service to you today, mister—"

"Locke." Sir Richard replied.

Lydia tittered under her breath. It really was a good joke. Matt Locke.

Sir Richard, quite in character, cast her a sharp look. "We are here for my dear sweet cousin, Liddie."

"I am to be married soon." Lydia minced forward and dropped a little curtsey, her voice pitched a little higher, and certainly sillier, than her usual tone.

"Congratulations, my dear girl." The apothecary smiled a huge, shopkeeper smile, the one intended to loosen both purses and tongues. "When is your wedding to be?"

"Oh, there is no day set, you see. Not even a young man right now. But I am actively seeking one, you see. I would like a very handsome one. And one with a good income. He does not have to be rich, you see, just comfortable. And in want of a wife. Do you know such a man?"

He leaned back a bit and blinked at her. Good. He did not know what to make of her. "It is not my business to be making matches."

"I thought as much, but it is always worth asking, you see." She slowly scanned the room, taking time to gaze at each display.

"Is there something else I might do for you?" He stepped a little closer.

"If I am to catch a good husband, then I must use all the assets the good Lord gave me, you see." She pressed her hands to her chest and tittered. "I have heard there are potions and lotions and such that can make a woman more attractive to young gentlemen."

"If you have receipts you wish ingredients for, then I may be able to help you, but I do not prepare such things myself."

"I do have such a list. Here, do tell me if you have everything I need." She fumbled with her reticule, finally removing a tattered list that she had made just yesterday, especially for the occasion.

He scanned it, tracing down with a thick sausage finger. "I have most of these ingredients. But these," he pointed to the most important items on the list, "I have not even heard of, much less carry them. I will prepare the others, if you would like." He glanced at

Richard, as if hoping to find some bastion of sound reasoning there.

"No, no need, you see. If I get some here and some elsewhere, I know I will become all muddled, not knowing what I have and what I do not. I will only make purchases at an establishment which can fully supply me. I am quite determined." She slipped her list from his hand.

Mr. Abrams turned aside slightly and rolled his eyes.

"There, there, my dear, there is no need to become petulant." Sir Richard patted her shoulder with appropriate condescension and turned to Mr. Abrams. "Have you any confits with fennel? I should like a packet of those for your trouble."

The apothecary snorted something vaguely approving and shuffled to a large jar on the counter. "Mr. Keats on Beetwell Street specializes in the sorts of products you require and often trades in exotic ingredients. Mayhap he can assist you." He handed the packet to Sir Richard. "Six pence, please."

Lydia flounced out the door, while Sir Richard finished the transaction.

Her heart had pounded so loud in her ears! She gulped air tinged with horse and dust. Perhaps that would settle the tumult within.

They had done it. She had done it! She had actually done it. Going into a shop and playing a theatrical role should not be so difficult. She had played many roles at school. But somehow, this was entirely unlike—

"Well done, Miss Bennet, well done!" he whispered.

She jumped and spun to face him. "Gracious, that was … exhilarating … yes, that seems the best word for it."

"It is quite the experience, is it not? Definitely not for the faint of heart! Shall we proceed to Beetwell Street?" He gestured toward the waiting carriage.

Their destination, Beetwell Street, home to the Chesterfield coaching station, the post office, and a large public house, boasted active traffic: carriages, carts, horses, peddlers, pedestrians. The energy of the bustling street did nothing to settle her heart back into proper regulation. Hopefully, the consequent flush in her cheeks added to her ingénue role.

Elaborate signage featuring a decorative urn with Keats' name beneath, and a fancy storefront window announced their next stop. Where Mr. Abrams' shop was modest and even understated, Mr. Keats' was arranged with ladies in mind! Sir Richard pulled back to allow her to gawk. It was keeping in character, after all.

So many pretty jars and bottles with lovely labels and dainty names in the window. Accents of ribbons and lace and buttons wove throughout the display. A small sign announced those as being from the haberdasher's shop down the street. Interesting to see the cooperation, there.

Meryton never enjoyed such lovely displays. Kitty would simply adore this and Lydia would tell her about it—assuming, of course, they did not find what they were looking for here.

Oh, merciful heavens, how had she gotten herself involved with such a ghastly business?

Ring, remember the Ring Wyrm. That was why.

Sir Richard finally ushered her inside the large, bright shop. Floral scents, not herbal ones, hung in the air, the kind that a woman might have in her parlor or maybe her dressing room. Though well stocked, it did not have the overwhelming, jammed-in feeling of Mr. Abrams' shop. Tall stools near a polished white counter invited her to sit down and be welcome among the pretty packages and tidy, dustless displays.

A large, effusive man approached. Tall and a little stout, the apothecary wore a warm, engaging smile, but no apron over his well-fitting suit. He bowed from his shoulders. "Stanton Keats at your service. How might I be of assistance to you?"

She and Sir Richard launched into their prattle about her quest for a husband, leaving Mr. Keats visibly amused.

"I see, I see. You have come to the right place. I believe I have the things you are seeking. Allow me to show you." He gestured toward one of the stools and ducked behind the counter to pull out a tray of bottles and jars from a shelf behind him. "These are my most popular products. Allow me to demonstrate." He began a well-practiced show of entirely mundane products, all of excellent quality, but none having any of the hallmark looks or smells of the dragon trade. "Do any of these meet your needs?"

Perhaps this shop really was as delightful as it appeared and she and Kitty and maybe Jane could enjoy it all together. It had been a long time since they had been able to indulge in that flavor of sisterly society.

Sir Richard grumbled under his breath as he scanned the shop. "These seem so ordinary, and the family is anxious to see our cousin in the best possible arrangement."

Lydia clasped her hands before her chest and bounced a little on the stool. "Yes, yes! You see, I have a great deal of competition in our neighborhood. So many girls out, you know, and so few young men whose eye we might catch."

"I see." Mr. Keats stroked his chin with a thoughtful expression. "I do have another line. However, they are rather more dear, you know. Not the sort of products that are in most young ladies' reach."

Sir Richard patted his pocket. "We are very anxious. Pray, show them to us."

Mr. Keats reached beneath the counter and pulled out a large apothecary box, plain, simple, and sturdy. "Perhaps some of what I have here will be more to your liking."

Sir Richard's eyes went wide as the box was opened. That was probably not a good sign at all.

Cut-crystal bottles on little shelves lined both sides of the open box front. The wide middle section held ceramic jars above three layers of daintily carved drawers. Every one of them so pretty and so tempting.

Lydia pointed to a clear bottle that glittered horribly, suspiciously, in a sunbeam. Pray Mr. Keats did not notice her hand shaking. "Oh, what is that? So sparkly and shiny! I am certain it must be especially special!"

"It is, dear lady. A special formula of facial lotion guaranteed to make your complexion the talk of your neighborhood and irresistible to any young gentleman."

"Pray show it to me!" She held out her hand despite the urge to slap the bottle away and flee.

He opened the flask and poured a few drops into her hand. She swirled it with her finger and closed her eyes to smell.

Oil of roses; that must be in the formulation. Another breath; muskiness. No, pray no. But it was there. Must not give way to the urge to cast up her accounts. No doubt at all. It contained dragon scales.

"Smell it, cousin!" She held her hand close to Sir Richard. "It is amazing. I must have some! And that!" She pointed to a jar with a particularly fancy label in some script she could not read; perhaps Latin? "You must tell me of that as well!"

"It is a lotion for a lady's hand. It will beautify your hands and nails beyond anything you can imagine." He offered her a little spoon of the creamy substance.

Pearlescent, probably from the shell of oysters, with a definite odor of fish. Pendragon's bones! That one contained dragon talons. "Pray, Cousin, I must have this as well!"

He also showed her a hair wash, which promised to brighten her lovely locks and make them softer than the finest wool. From the color and smell, it probably contained dragon's blood. That was by far the most difficult to insist upon.

Mr. Keats closed the apothecary box and returned it below the counter. "Before I prepare these for you, is there anything else with which I might help you?"

"I have a particular receipt handed down through the women of my family for many generations. It is said to be excellent for ..." she leaned in and cupped her hand near her mouth, "… for beautifying a lady's … ah …ah…"

"Unique assets?" Mr. Keats winked.

"Yes, that." She pressed her hands to her very warm cheeks and giggled. "But there are ingredients that I do not recognize. No apothecary we have seen has been able to help me. Perhaps you might?" She removed a worn scrap of paper from her reticule.

Mr. Keats took the paper and scanned it quickly. "I believe I might be of assistance. But pray, sir, may I examine your hands?"

"My hands? Why would you need to see my hands?" Sir Richard stepped back, confusion and a touch of offense in his tone.

"Over the years I have found that there are people who react rather violently to some of these ingredients. So much so, they cannot even tolerate being in proximity to them in their raw state. I can tell by the shape of your hands if you are one of them. My conscience prevents me from selling them to anyone who might be harmed by them."

"How interesting! I would never have conceived of such a thing. You must be very clever to have come to such an understanding." Lydia gushed, batting her eyes as she looked up at Mr. Keats.

Horrible, sickening, vile creature.

"I see." Sir Richard extended his hands for Mr. Keats' inspection, palms up, then palms down.

Mr. Keats took hold of his hands and brought them closer, examining the skin of his fingers closely. "Very good, sir. I see no reason not to make the sale you request. I will prepare the items for you directly." He trundled to the shop's back room, humming a little tune under his breath.

Lydia released the breath she had been holding. It had been a good thing that Sir Richard had removed his Order insignia before they left for Chesterfield.

12
Chapter

June 16, 1815

THE NEXT MORNING, an unceremonious thump on the bed post jarred Richard from a restless slumber. Earl's claws left faint marks on the polished wood.

"Dragon's fire! What is this?" Richard, tangled in his fine sheets and tumbled out of bed, instinctively searched for his sword.

But there was no sword, not in the refined, peaceful environs of his usual guest room at Pemberley, with the rosy rays of dawn painting the elegant furnishings with their blush. Birds and fairy dragons twittered beyond the window, just above the sounds of a bucolic country morning. Nothing hid in the depth of the oak paneling. No enemy lurked behind the chairs or beneath the press.

Take a deep breath, man! Guns were not about to start blazing. The enemy was not in the camp.

Earl squawked and cocked his head in that funny confusion he often expressed.

"Napoleon best be at the walls to justify that sort of entrance."

Earl spread his toes and picked at something between them. "Not Napoleon. Cownt Matlock."

Richard fought his way out of the bedclothes and fumbled for his garments. Calling his valet would take too long, given Earl's dramatic entrance. "He was due to arrive, with Pemberley, in the next day or so. What is the problem? Is there something amiss with Pemberley?"

"No, no. She has arrived and is waiting at Matlock. Dale has already been dispatched to meet them, and his Friend is making ready the cellar lair for her. Lady Sage and Darcy are also aware."

"Was Matlock not in readiness to receive the cownt?"

Earl snorted and flapped. "Matlock expected the cownt, but the cownt did not expect what he would find at Matlock. A local fairy dragon heard the commotion and alerted me."

"Damn and bloody hell and damn again!" Richard shoved his legs into his trousers and snatched up his riding boots. "Could you tell if Andrew was involved as well?"

"You know how fairy dragons, especially those without steady Friends, can be. It was lucky I could make that much sense out of what they were twittering on about. They were certain a great deal of shouting was going on, but as to who was involved …" He shrugged his wings.

"No doubt with St. John doing his share." Richard muttered invectives under his breath as he pulled his boots on. "Be a good fellow and find a groom to ready my horse. I ought to be off as soon as possible. Not that I have the first idea of what I can do to remedy anything."

"I am hungry." Earl, like every young male of any species, was always hungry.

"I will acquire something from the kitchen on the way to the barns."

"I should like something raw today. Cooked meat is off-putting." He preened the feather-scales on his shoulder.

"I will see what I can do, you greedy gullet. Now off!" He scratched under Earl's chin until the cockatrice crouched and extended his wings to launch through the open window.

Richard made his way to the press and liberated a clean shirt. He had hoped for a little more time before he had to deal with these matters that really did not concern him.

By the time all was said and done, it would probably require the Dragon Sage's intervention to manage the commotion. If it could be managed at all.

Though no further evidence against St. John had yet turned up, it was difficult not to wonder if this was a ploy to distract not only Keepers and dragons, but the Secretary's office as a whole, from further investigating the trade in dragon parts. It would be clever to create a diversion by using a real problem.

That was not the level of cleverness he had ascribed to St. John, but then again, the smartest men often hid in plain sight by playing the buffoon.

That would be the sort of thing Elizabeth would be able to see through, though. Assuming at least some of her equanimity were restored before setting her at Matlock and St. John. As she was now, peace-making would probably not be her long suit.

He shrugged his shirt over his head and reached for his cravat. Perhaps her new secretary's arrival would help ease her strain. Chisholm had reached Pemberley yesterday, just as he and Miss Bennet were leaving for Chesterfield. Since there was no general commotion among the household dragons when they returned, it was probably safe to assume that Elizabeth had not immediately rejected Chisholm on sight.

Under normal circumstances, that would have been unlikely. Elizabeth was far more sensible than that. But under current circumstances she seemed less open to assistance than she usually was—which was generally not much at all. Ironic that she would reject the thing she needed most.

Where was—oh, there, his waistcoat and coat. He scooped them up from the chair he had left them on and made his way to the mirror. He never quite managed to get the cravat right without being able to see what he was doing. Something Miss Bennet had picked up on immediately yesterday as she had insisted on tidying his knot.

A flush rose along his neck and tiny drops of sweat beaded along his brow. Miss Bennet.

What a conundrum she was! She had been an able ally in his endeavors yesterday, quick-thinking and courageous under the circumstances, with excellent insight and a good sense of humor, both valuable assets in this kind of work. And she was a well-looking, lively girl, who, interestingly enough, did not exercise her powers of flirtation, which was a touch unexpected.

And appealing.

Her dowry was modest, but now that he had his own estate, that was not such an issue—

Heaven forfend! What was he thinking?

He slipped on his coat. It was a lady's imagination that was rapid, jumping from admiration to love, from love to matrimony in a moment, not a man's! But yes, it did seem he was growing in admiration for the girl. But that was all.

It was all so complicated.

Gah! She was the sort of complication it was probably best to get away from for now. He left his room and headed toward the kitchen at a brisk march.

Darcy intercepted him at the landing of the grand stairs. "I imagine Earl informed you?"

"All but threw me out of bed." Richard chuckled as they walked in perfect step down the stairs. "I dread to think of the muddle that Andrew has probably created."

"It is hard to extend too much sympathy, when he has fought every measure of sound advice that has been directed his way." Darcy was not wrong.

"But it is difficult not to resent being the one charged with cleaning up the mess." Again. How long had Richard been cleaning up after his eldest brother's missteps? It should have stopped once Richard had his own estate to look after. It would stop.

"Our real worry is for Pemberley."

"I am not sure I understand."

"Chudleigh and Rosings have been her models in decorum, and we have instructed her diligently in the responsibilities we have to the Order and the Order has to us. A deliberate and careful choice on our part, and theirs."

"You are afraid that Matlock, St. John, and my brother will be a bad example to her?"

"Do you think otherwise? Pemberley is still so young and impressionable. To see the Grand Dug of the Order stomping and storming like Bolsover and his dupes—what will come of that?"

"I cannot fathom you and Elizabeth have so little influence over her—"

"It would be better not to be forced to exert that influence, would it not?" Darcy rubbed his chin. "The carriage is being readied for us."

"My horse should be saddled already. If you do not object, I shall ride over now. An advance guard, as it were."

In the midst of Matlock's best sheep pasture, two of the lower shepherding drakes intercepted him, and directed him to Matlock's lair. Somehow, they knew to expect intervention from Pemberley and were hopeful for a quick resolution to the matters at hand. Must be the fairy dragons.

He turned toward the lair, careful not to dash their hopes. It would not do to upset the Matlock staff more than they already were. Agitated dragons did not set the sheep at ease, and there was enough trouble for the day already.

A quarter mile through the sweet-smelling, lush clover field, under clear skies and morning sun, took him to the edges of the dragon wood, where his horse balked and refused to go another step closer. Even Pemberley's horses could only be trained to accept so much. Small dragons, even the occasional cockatrice, could be made acceptable. A creature that might eat them in a handful of bites, far less so.

He tied the reins to a fallen tree and took to the discreet path on foot.

Tall hardwoods flanked the barely discernible trail, their tall limbs weaving an eerie canopy overhead. There was something about dragon woods that set the hair on the back of his neck prickling. Was it the air of pungent dragon musk carried on every breeze, or the eerie quiet that lay like a smothering blanket over the terrain? Probably both. Every dragon wood he had known, even that at Netherford, had this same, unsettling quality.

The normalcy of it should have put him at greater ease. But it did not.

The path slowly grew firmer underfoot, littered with increasingly large rocks and the occasional bones of Matlock's larger meals. He usually crunched the bones like biscuits, but occasionally found one that, for some reason, was not to his taste and tossed it aside where vultures, deer, foxes, and the local rock and forest wyrms took advantage of chewing at them. One more disquieting bit of decoration, probably intended to keep visitors to a minimum.

Loud voices and growls echoed from just beyond his line of sight—perfect, exactly the breed of company he most wanted to walk in on first thing in the morning.

He forced himself the last hundred yards or so, across the rocky incline that ended in a small clearing and the entry to the lair. Dragon musk, tinged with the faint aura of smoke, assaulted him just before the clearing came into view.

Dragon's bones! That was one angry firedrake.

Matlock hunched like a cat watching for something interesting, rendering him as close to face to face as possible with the two livid men in his clearing. Filtered light through the dense tree canopy turned his normally blue-green hide a deeper forest-y shade and made his fiery orange eyes almost glow. His mouth was slightly open, displaying his fangs and the tip of his forked tongue, which quivered in time with his breath.

Did neither Andrew nor St. John realize just how agitated was the dragon in their midst?

Imbeciles, both of them.

Richard stood at the edge of the clearing, waiting between two thick tree trunks, to be acknowledged, or not. Preferably not. Then he could say he had tried, but had been refused.

"Approach." The ground rumbled with Matlock's command.

Damn.

Andrew and St. John stopped shouting and stared at him. Little red Pemberley peeked out around Matlock's haunch, wide-eyed, ears twitching, a pathetic and thoroughly miserable little firedrake.

He stepped forward and dropped low to touch the ground with arms overhead, in the proper firedrake greeting. Not the time to risk offense with inappropriate familiarity. "Greetings, Cownt Matlock."

"I do not welcome more company at my lair. Why are you here?"

Why indeed? "I thought to offer assistance—"

"Remove the interloper from my territory!" Matlock hissed in St. John's direction, causing him to edge back, wiping viscous spittle away from his face with both hands.

"I am not an interloper." St. John dragged his sleeve across his eyes.

"I did not invite you. Nor did—" Matlock flicked his tongue toward Andrew.

No title, no name, just a flick of the tongue? Was Andrew even aware of how deeply the cownt had just cut him?

"I have tried everything but having the footmen physically throw him out. Perhaps I should order that, too." Andrew tugged his sleeves a little straighter.

"I would not recommend that." Richard stepped a little closer. "With all due respect, Cownt, you understand the nature of St. John's office, yes?"

"He has no authority over my Keep." Matlock rose to his haunches and stomped his front foot.

Pemberley squeaked and trembled.

"Pray, Cownt, recall the company you are in. The vicontes is of a tender age." Pemberley had clearly shown that she was far hardier than the typical youngster, but for the moment, he could pretend that it was not so if it provided an advantage.

"No like shouting." Pemberley said softly. The look in her eye—clever creature, she understood. "Not civilized. Barwines Chudleigh say proper dragons not shout."

Matlock stretched his neck around to look at her. "Chudleigh is not always correct."

"You want I tell her that?" Pemberley crept closer to Richard.

"I will tell her myself … after this trespasser is removed from my territory."

"I am on Order business. You may contact Lord Dunbrook or your own Lord Matlock for confirmation." St. John crossed his arms over his chest and planted his heel hard. One had to give the man credit for courage—or perhaps it was simply stupidity.

"Just get him out of here, Richard. That is what you military types do, it is not? Enforce order here." Andrew clutched his temples and waved impotently Richard's way.

Blood roared in Richard's ears and his face burned. But Andrew's opinion of him was not new, just offensive. "You confuse the militia with the army, brother. And I am attached to neither. I have not the authority to remove Mr. St. John from his duly-appointed duties."

Unless St. John proved to be part of the dragon trade. Then he would happily remove the ill-mannered little man. But he could not act on that suspicion yet. Being pushy and disagreeable was hardly a crime in itself.

"As I have been saying all along. Now, about those records …"

Pemberley huffed and scratched at the ground. Richard beckoned her closer until she crept to his side. "Are you well, Vicontes?"

"Cownt Matlock talks much, says little." She shook her head gloomily.

Out of the mouths of babes. "Has Mr. St. John—"

"*Her* no like him. He mean to *her*. I no like him." The barest trickle of smoke drifted from her snout.

"I know *she* would say that is not cause for flame right now, no?"

"Yes, no flame." She dragged her front foot along the ground, talons scraping against the rocks, and her wings sagged.

"*She* will be proud of you."

Pemberley stretched her head toward him, as though asking for a scratch. He obliged.

"You will have to do without those records." Andrew's lip drew back in a sneer.

"You have a legal requirement to produce them," St. John said in a quiet, dangerous tone that made Andrew edge back.

"I cannot produce what does not exist."

"If they do not exist, then that is an even greater transgression, and action will have to be taken by the Order."

Matlock growled, gobbets of tawny yellow spittle hanging off his fangs. "With what do you threaten me?"

Pemberley squeaked and bumped Richard's chest with her head. "Look!"

Darcy and Elizabeth stood at the edge of the clearing!

"Cownt Matlock!" Elizabeth called. "May we approach?"

"Approach!"

Richard winced and covered his ears. If his hearing survived this—

"Both of you!" Matlock stomped hard enough that Richard felt it all the way through his knees. Pemberley pressed her head under his arm.

Darcy was right. She should not be exposed to such unseemly behavior by one she ought to respect.

Elizabeth and Darcy quickly advanced and made their greetings.

"We have come to offer assistance," Elizabeth said.

St. John turned on her. "This is no business of yours, Lady Sage."

Pemberley growled and landed at Elizabeth's side in a single flapping leap.

Darcy and Elizabeth closed ranks around the young dragon, arms across her shoulders. Thank heavens they could cooperate in that much!

"He means me no harm, dearling." Elizabeth stared at St. John as she spoke.

"No, he does not," Darcy all but snarled. "Sometimes one forgets one's manners whilst discussing important things."

Andrew and St. John snorted at the accusation. Wonder of wonders, they agreed upon something.

"Pemberley, as the issue at hand regards Cownt Matlock's territory, not yours," Darcy's eyes narrowed in a truly dangerous way, "it would be best for you to go back to stand with Richard. It is unseemly to impose oneself, uninvited, into the private affairs of others."

Pemberley glanced from man to man, then to Elizabeth, who nodded. "Yes, Keeper." She dragged her tail as she returned to Richard's side.

He scratched under her chin and behind her ears as she leaned into him, a little dejectedly.

"It is still not the concern of the Sage, either," St. John moderated his tone into something almost civil. "It is a matter for the office of the Secretary."

"There is a great deal of overlap in our duties, Mr. St. John, and I shall be the judge of what is in my purview, thank you." She parked her hands on her hips, like a cockatrix opening her wings.

"I would speak to you first, Sage." Matlock rumbled and thundered into his lair, tail lashing behind him.

"Excuse me, then," Elizabeth curtsied, though she clearly did not mean the courtesy, and followed Matlock into the lair.

Nerves of solid iron she had, following an angry dragon into the hillside like that.

"Mark my words, Viscount, you will regret this." St. John shook his finger under Andrew's chin.

"Regret what? Showing you your proper place? Do not expect to set foot in my house again, St. John. You have never been welcome, and if you return, I will instruct the gamekeeper that you are nothing but a poacher on the land and to handle you accordingly."

Richard grimaced. Stupid, stupid, stupid!

Pemberley ducked her head into his armpit.

"Be careful of your threats, sir," St. John spat the honorific. "You might recall that you are not even Keeper of the estate."

"In all but name, I am. Lord Matlock has not run the affairs here since his induction as Chancellor of the Order."

"And it shows, Viscount, it shows."

"What is that supposed to mean?"

"Had the Chancellor himself been directly responsible for the blatant violations of charter and Blue Order law I have found here, there would be no choice but to see him removed from office."

"Are you threatening my father? He will hear of this, I swear to you!"

"I am not threatening him, sir. I am threatening you."

"Threatening me? With what are you threatening me?" Andrew's face turned an unhealthy shade of red, a little like Pemberley's hide.

"You are an incompetent Keeper and should be replaced."

"And who would you replace me with? Him?" Andrew pointed at Richard. "I should have known this was another one of your schemes to have Matlock for your own."

No, not today! Richard clenched his fists. Was there nothing that would shake loose Andrew's insecure delusions?

"That was untoward, ungentlemanly, and inaccurate." Darcy stepped between Andrew and St. John. "Richard, pray would you do us all the favor of escorting Pemberley back to her lair in the manor's cellar?"

"There is nothing I would like more. Pray come with me, Vicontes. I have it on good authority that Dog and Puppy await your return." He gestured toward the path.

She took a few steps, paused, and looked over her shoulder. "I miss Dog and Puppy. I like see them."

"You will see them soon." With a hand on her shoulder, he guided her down the trail and onto an obscure footpath. One did not take the main road whilst walking with a major dragon, even a very young one, and the only nearby access to the dragon tunnels was through Matlock's lair.

She dragged along beside him, silent for the first mile. Finally, though, she stopped and bumped his chest with the top of her head. "I need know. You tell me."

"Tell you what?"

"What for Cownt and men angry?"

"It is complicated."

Pemberley extended her wings and lashed her tail, stirring up dirt and leaves. "I may be little, but I not dumb. I smart. I have territory. I need understand things! You tell things. All the things!"

She was right. She needed to know, and she would have to understand before St. John came knocking at Pemberley's door. "It is a matter of the Order's rules for dragon territories …"

Chapter 13

CANDLE IN HAND, Elizabeth led Pemberley through the dark, narrow dragon tunnel that connected Pemberley's cellar to the main dragon lair. Pemberley was still small enough to enjoy the nearness to the family in the house, and with the possibility of trespassers, both Elizabeth and Darcy felt better knowing she was safely under the watch of the house guard. Brutus and Axel would meet them at the tunnel exit nearest the small barn and escort them the rest of the way there.

A dank, earthy cellar-smell and an odd muffled quiet unlike any quiet above ground made the dragon tunnel a strange, otherworldly space, betwixt and between, neither here nor there. Just wide and tall enough that Darcy might have walked through without ducking and dodging, the low ceilings and tight walls squeezed in like a corset laced too tight, all but itching along Elizabeth's skin. Somehow the tunnel would have to be improved as Pemberley grew larger. She should always have access to the house, even when she grew large enough to stay in her lair.

Pemberley had so many questions after her encounter at Matlock's estate. It was not the way they had hoped to introduce her to the issues plaguing her own territory, but there was little to be done for that now. Richard had offered her good initial answers for her questions. Afterwards, Darcy had been extraordinarily patient, simplifying and explaining matters to her in a way that she might understand. He really was an excellent Dragon Keeper.

If only he had not kept the matter of the smugglers from her! How could he expect her to manage all that was on her shoulders when that information remained hidden? Did he think her too fragile to hear such things? Too flighty to keep such secrets to herself? He was acting just like Papa!

She sniffled and swallowed hard. Papa had never really credited her with good sense or competence in any Blue Order matter. Even now, his respect for her office was grudging at best. She had always thought Darcy to be different to him. Better, more respectful. But now—

Then again, just this morning he had consulted her regarding the house guard: how best to manage a dominance squabble between them and a team of Blue Order messengers who were sharing the same accommodations in the west attic gable. That should count for something, no? And yet—

"Cownt Matlock is all right now you talk him?" Pemberley leaned her chin on Elizabeth's shoulder, looking up at her with huge dark eyes. "You always know right thing say."

"I wish that were the case, dearling." Elizabeth scratched under Pemberley's chin. "It is a complicated thing, I am afraid."

"How is complicated? He upset, you make better, yes?"

"In this case, I am afraid I have probably made it worse. Sometimes that is the way of things before they can be made better. You recall Keeper telling you of the problems he found at Pemberley?"

"With boundaries and records and small dragons and land product ... productly... making enough so all eat well?"

"Yes, those. You recall how you were upset about them?"

"Yes, upset! My territory should be right. I angry that things not right and need make them right. But not know how. That make me angry, too!" Pemberley snuffled and snorted.

"Cownt Matlock is angry about those things, too. But the difference is that ..." How did one explain such a thing to a young mind? It would not do to be critical of the Grand Dug of the Order, but Pemberley did need to understand what was going on in a territory so near her own. "You are happy to know the problems can be fixed and how to fix them. Not everyone feels that same way."

Pemberley stopped walking and creased her brow in what was her thinking face. "He angry because must fix?"

"I think so. He may also be angry to be criticized by Mr. St. John."

"I no like Mr. St. John. He mean to you. But that not mean he not right about problems." What a surprisingly mature thought. "But Cownt dominant dragon in everywhere. He should want fix and make right. If he make right, then everyone make right. He not understand that?"

"Things are always more complicated than they seem to need to be, dearling."

"Well, I think he being stubborn dragon, and I no like."

"I feel much the same way. But telling him so will not help. Promise me that you will not interfere in this. What has Barwines Chudleigh taught you?"

"Know when let bigger dragons handle a matter." She scratched her forefoot in the dirt.

"Pray make sure you heed that advice now."

"I will. I want good territory. Want be good estate dragon. Rosings is good estate dragon. She say she teach me when I ready. I ready. You help send message Rosings?"

Just ahead, sunlight trickled through dense vines that hid a tunnel entrance. Elizabeth blew out her candle and tucked it into a shallow wall niche. She held the vines aside to allow Pemberley to scrape through.

"That is an excellent thought. We can do that soon. It is better for you to focus on the matters of your own estate now than the problems at Matlock." Elizabeth brushed leaves and dirt from her gown as their eyes adjusted to the sunshine filtering through the trees. They headed toward the little barn at the end of the lush field, just beyond the trees.

"Like Ring and how he hurt?" Pemberley whispered.

"That is certainly one of those matters. We will be at the barn soon. Are you prepared to greet him?"

"Yes, I am."

"And remember, Chisholm, whom you have already met, is there as well."

"Yes, I 'member. She is you secretary, you helper." Something in Pemberley's tone seemed off somehow.

"You make that sound as though it is not a good thing."

"I want help you." She bumped Elizabeth's shoulder with the top of her head. "Why you need 'nother dragon for that?"

Elizabeth stopped and slipped her arm around Pemberley's shoulders. "Oh, dearling, you are so generous to want to help me. And you and I, we are partners, along with Keeper, in managing the Pemberley territory. We help each other in that very big job."

"Then why …"

"I have another job, that of the Dragon Sage, which is entirely separate from the Pemberley Territory. And to do that, there is a great deal of reading and writing to be done. Lady Astrid has helped teach Chisholm how to be good at those things. She is here to help me with the things she is good at, so I will have more time to spend on, well, everything else."

"I not good at read or write, yet."

"Not yet, but you will be, I have no doubt. If you like, I can ask Chisholm to help you learn them well. She knows about how best a dragon should hold a pencil or a pen and how to most easily form letters with your sort of paw."

Pemberley bobbed her head slightly, several times, as though the thoughts were bouncing through her head. "I understand now. Is good to have Chisholm to help you. But why you have two jobs? That seems very much jobs for one person."

"I suppose sometimes it is."

"Then you need much helps, yes? You should have much helps. More than just Chisholm."

"I am afraid it is not as easy as that. Having help can be complicated."

"No is complicated. Perhaps you make complicated when it very easy. I tell Keeper you need helps."

"No, dearling, do not do that."

"Why? He already know you need helps?"

"Yes, yes, he knows." Had the fairy dragons told her of their extensive discussions of just that matter?

"Good, then you have helps soon." Pemberley trotted the rest of the way to the barn.

Clearly she had been under Rosings' influence. She was a dragon who had no trouble delegating her tasks to those around her. With Cait as her Lieutenant over the estate, the territory ran with remarkable efficiency. Even if Lady Catherine could be difficult, there was much to be admired at Rosings Park.

Elizabeth squeezed her eyes tight and rubbed her temples. Darcy regularly made note that she was trying to do too much. Could that be part of why he had kept the problem of the smugglers to himself? Was that his way of keeping yet more from her weary shoulders?

But if it was, he had no right to make choices about what burdens she should or should not carry. He owed her the courtesy of allowing her to make those decisions for herself. Besides which, the poachers had already made that decision, forcing her into the secret. Keeping that from her had only made things worse and not better. And now she had to go and deal with the results.

Pemberley waited at the barn until Elizabeth caught up. With thick stone walls and a thatched roof, nestled in the fields with the woods behind, the image would have made a picturesque watercolor, if not for the red firedrakeling standing at the barn door. That did set it apart, with a fairy story flavor that was rather endearing all on its own.

As long as one did not know who was waiting inside the barn and why.

Coming alongside Pemberley, Elizabeth knocked firmly and pushed open the heavy iron-bound wooden door. Fresh hay and water-dragon musk—distinct from terrestrial dragon, with its distinct notes of algae and a vague hint of fish—greeted her first as her eyes adjusted to the barn's shadows.

The smallest barn on Pemberley estate, it could hold two barn carts, like the one that had brought in Ring, side-by-side, and was half again as deep. A pile of garden tools occupied the corner nearest the cart. Open-shuttered windows situated on adjacent walls brought in sufficient sunlight to see comfortably; cozy and conducive to conversation.

Pemberley waddled in, with as much dignity as one might muster while waddling. Dear, sweet creature, trying so hard to play the part of a proper estate dragon in the face of such deplorable behavior from Matlock.

A mound of hay, covered with feed sacks for Ring's comfort, dominated the other half of the hard-packed dirt floor, along with an especially large tub of pond water. The grooms had found the tub and suggested Ring might be more comfortable if he could be able to have a bit of his home nearby. The grooms would have a gift from the kitchen sent home with them for their thoughtfulness.

Pemberley stood back, studying Ring and his wounds. Her wings lifted slightly, and she breathed rapidly through her mouth. Saliva dripped from her fangs as her front toes quivered. Elizabeth tensed to spring. Ring's wounds were pulling at Pemberley's pouncing instincts, urging her to take advantage of easy prey. But she fought them steadily, just like Chudleigh had taught her.

Such a good girl she was.

If only warm-blooded instincts were so easy to understand.

"Lady Sage." Ring stood on the mound of straw, poorly balanced as he fought to keep the weight off his injured feet.

"Greetings, Lady Sage." Chisholm rose to her back feet until she stood just above waist-high to Elizabeth. Neither large nor small for a minor drake, with smooth, glistening hide so black it was nearly blue, and glittering jet eyes, she could blend into shadows and nearly disappear on a dark night. A trait that, according to Lady Astrid, had caused some not to trust her and made her difficult to place as a secretary. Chisholm dipped in a draconic curtsey. A rather endearing obeisance, all told.

Elizabeth gestured toward Ring. "Pemberley, may I present the Ring Wyrm of Ring Pond."

Ring paused for a moment, as though fighting dominance instincts of his own. He was, for the moment, the larger dragon and technically allowed to attempt to assert dominance, though that would have been a shortsighted and dangerous approach to take.

Finally, he quelled his instincts and extended his grey-brown front legs and pressed his chin to the ground, tiny wings covering as much of his long neck as they could.

Pemberley hesitated a moment before she touched the back of his neck with her tongue, matching the timing of his initial hesitation. An appropriate way to express her dominance without becoming overbearing. Exactly the manner of quiet communication most suited to the situation and their continued ability to work together. Pemberley was a fast learner and had excellent role models in Rosings and Chudleigh.

"If I may be so bold, Lady Sage, Vicontes, might I make an introduction of my own?" Ring fluttered a wing.

A glossy-black lesser cockatrix with a brilliant purple 'collar' around her neck crept out of the shadows, wings, edged with purple feathers, spread, and head down. Her thick charcoal-grey serpentine tail extended out behind her, where it could not be used to propel a pounce.

"Vicontes, Lady Sage, I present Raven, a long-time inhabitant of the local countryside, but not yet known to the Pemberley family. I am pleased to call her my friend."

The cockatrix extended her wings and pressed her whole self to the ground.

Pemberley licked the back of her neck.

"Thank you, Vicontes, Lady Sage." Raven muttered into the ground and slowly rose.

She was a fine specimen of lesser cockatrix, who often looked rather well-worn. Her eyes flashed with intelligence, and she held herself with quiet dignity despite being the smallest dragon in the space.

"Raven is a storyteller, Lady Sage." Ring settled back as comfortably as his injuries would allow, crossing his front legs to rest his long snout upon them. "You have been asking about Pemberley's history, and the dragons of the region. She knows them much better than I. Not only does she tell tales for the entertainment of her audience, she is also something of a local historian for the region. If there is anything to be known about the dragons of the estate, she would be the one to know it."

Pemberley hopped and flapped in the most dignified way she knew. "You know all dragons of Pemberley?"

"I know about all the dragons of Pemberley, Vicontes." Raven flipped her wings into place and puffed her chest. "And I am formally acquainted with all the larger minor dragons."

"How many larger minor dragons make their home in Pemberley's territory?" Elizabeth asked.

"You know Ring. There is also a basilisk, a large forest wyrm, a water wyrm, and a large minor drake."

"I do not know a basilisk." Pemberley sat back on her haunches. "Or the forest wyrm, I think. Why they not come to be introduced me when I first arrive? All dragons invited to introduction." She seemed perplexed and a little offended.

"There is a story in that." Ring nudged Raven with the tip of his snout.

Raven hopped back and locked one taloned foot around his nose, patiently holding it there until he withdrew from her space. Only dragons on exceptionally good terms would engage in such banter. This was what Pemberley territory should be.

"This important. Chisholm help us remember what say, yes?" Pemberley asked.

No, Elizabeth never forgot dragon histories. There was no need for assistance on the matter. But all four dragons looked at her with such expectation, she could not dishonor Chisholm's role that way. Perhaps it would be a good way to assess Chisholm's abilities. "Yes, Chisholm, listen carefully and record what you have heard once we return to the house. We can go over your notes once you are finished and create a final version of the tale. Two copies should be made, one for Pemberley's library and a second to be sent to the Historian in London."

Gracious, that would be quite a bit of work. It would be helpful not to have to do it all herself.

"Yes, Lady Sage." Chisholm sat still and focused her gaze on the lesser cockatrix. Not a predatory gaze exactly, but an intense one that would not let a single detail escape. The kind of gaze that it would be easy for warm-bloods to misunderstand. Probably another reason Lady Astrid had found her difficult to place.

"Pray, tell us that story." Elizabeth pulled a dusty stool from the tangle of garden tools and sat down.

Pemberley edged in close and rested her head in Elizabeth's lap.

"It is not a pleasant tale, I am afraid." Raven extended her wings slightly and leaned back on her tail, in the way truly accomplished storytellers had of setting a mood for their listeners. "It was ten years ago, perhaps, while the young master was away at university. Old Pemberley was in his declining days. Those were dark days in Pemberley, to be sure. Dark with Old Mr. Darcy's grief for the loss of his wife. Dark with Old Pemberley's looming fate. He had grown old, nearly ancient, and had just begun to consider the need for progeny to take his place when his days were over."

"That me," Pemberley whispered.

"Old Pemberley was in his decline, though he refused to acknowledge it, and therein lies another layer of darkness. He acted as though all the work of the territory was being accomplished, when in fact much of it was forgotten, and the dragons of Pemberley were suffering. But it was not only the work of the territory that was being forgotten. You see, when a dragon, a firedrake like Old Pemberley, is very full in years, he or she may lose their memory, in bits and pieces over time, and the more of their memory they lose, the more of themselves they lose with it."

Pemberley shuddered.

"The darkness embraced not just Old Pemberley, but all his Keep as well." Raven extended her wings fully and walked a long, slow arc between Pemberley and Ring. "The Keep suffered as the tenets of the Accord were not fulfilled. Worst of all, Pemberley began forgetting the residents he permitted to share his territory. At the start, he would get confused in meetings and snap like a predator at the smaller dragons."

Pemberley and Chisholm gasped. A shiver slithered down Elizabeth's back. Loss of memory was difficult for elder warm-bloods and those who cared for them, but in a large dragon, the results could be disastrous.

"If it had stopped at that, the territory might have recovered. But Old Pemberley grew steadily worse, until, one day, while out surveying the territory, he encountered a drake whom he had given permission to live near the home farm's barns to control vermin there. Old Pemberley grew enraged at the trespass, as he perceived it, and killed the drake he had permitted to take residence here."

Elizabeth hugged Pemberley tightly as the little dragon trembled at the horror. Exactly as Elizabeth would have done had Pemberley not needed her to be strong.

"Not surprisingly, all the larger minor dragons of the estate grew fearful for their lives. The forest wyrm and the water wyrm were familiar with Old Mr. Darcy and informed him of the danger Old Pemberley presented to the territory. He intervened insofar as he was able, trying to manage matters of the large minor dragons himself. But, eventually he died without having sent to the Order, or even telling Young Mr. Darcy. So Old Pemberley continued unchecked. The only thing left for the larger minor dragons to do was leave their territory or to go into hiding and carefully avoid any encounters with Old Pemberley. Though Young Mr. Darcy mourned for Old Pemberley, many within the Keep were relieved when his time was over." Raven stepped back with a bit of a bow, covering her chest with her wings.

Pemberley pulled herself upright and peered into Raven's face. "So that why they not come see me. They think I like Old Pemberley?"

"It is so."

"Must fix, then! Ring, you know other dragons? You introduce them? Tell them I not like Old Pemberley. That I and Keepers need know them?" Pemberley hoped from right front foot to left.

Ring lifted his head. "I would be honored to be of service to you."

"Tell me who we need meet," Pemberley said, "tell me all dragons on the estate."

Elizabeth leaned close to Raven. "Pray come outside with me."

Raven followed her out and perched on the sill of an open window on the shaded side of the barn. "You have questions, Lady?"

"Yes, but not about your story. Those will come later. What happened to Ring—do you know? Has there been any talk? Even any who witnessed the assault?"

The feather-scales on the back of Raven's head lifted and her voice cracked slightly. "Aye, Lady Sage, there are stories."

"Pray would you tell me of them?"

Raven shook her head in broad emphatic sweeps. "They are not pretty tales, Lady, not at all, and would not be pleasing to your ears."

"All the more reason why I must know."

Raven paced along the windowsill, head bobbing back and forth as she walked. "From when do you want to hear the stories?"

"I do not know what you mean."

"Those sorts of things have been going on here for quite some time."

She gasped as though snow had slid off the roof and fallen down her neck. "During Old Pemberley's decline?"

"Certainly then. There have been poachers, dragon poachers, trespassing for quite some time. It started before his decline, but has been worse since then."

"How long before his decline?"

"I do not know first-hand myself, but it has been said—and this is only gossip, and I would thank you not to identify me as the one who has spread it to you— that it began when Cownt Matlock and his Keeper were made Chancellor and spent so much time away from the estate. The junior Keeper is a lazy placeholder and has done little to manage the dragon matters of the estate, so the strongest and the wiliest are free to do what they will as long as the Cownt is away. Old Pemberley did what he could when he was strong, but when he declined, things turned for the worse. Of course, you know how much a region needs its major dragons to keep order in the territories and keep us smaller dragons safe."

She should know, but it seemed as though there was a great deal more to be understood.

14 Chapter

June 19, 1815

DARCY RAKED HIS HAIR as Elizabeth stormed out of his office, ostensibly to get prepared for the first of the introductions Ring was arranging for them. Apparently, it had been a mistake to suggest that there may have been mitigating circumstances at the Matlock territory, influencing the problems there, just as much as there were at Pemberley.

Darcy leaned back in his father's desk chair and stared up at the ceiling roses. Father had them painted as a reminder that this study was a place where one could speak one's mind, without repercussions and with the assurance that those words would be considered private. Walker, who had left with Elizabeth, ensured their privacy against eavesdropping little dragons. But the issue of repercussions was up to Darcy.

Should he call her on her irrational anger or continue in patience, hoping she would see it for herself? Strong arguments could be made either way.

He rose, skirted around the large desk and Walker's iron perch, and paced the long, narrow room, arms crossed over his chest, exhaling a long breath through puffed cheeks.

Everything that usually calmed him in this space weighed down upon him: the books, the knowledge, the memories. All called for him to make good decisions, to do the right thing. Pendragon's Bones! What was he to do?

His feet shushed along the thick carpet Father had chosen deliberately to dull the noise of pacing, which he had done quite often. Probably where Darcy had acquired the habit.

Between St. John's and Raven's new revelations regarding the state of Matlock, Elizabeth had good reason to be upset. He was upset, too, and embarrassed over the actions of his family, who could hardly claim ignorance on any front. The Chancellor of the Order had a duty to provide an example to the whole of the Order. Specifically, a good example.

On that, Darcy and Elizabeth both agreed.

Unfortunately, she wanted to deal with it immediately. And rather publicly, calling Matlock—man and dragon—out to the Secretary, Minister of the Court, Minister of Keeps, and whomever else she could think of that who might have an interest in the matter.

But even she knew that was not the way to successfully confront a major dragon or its Keeper.

Dealing with creatures so steeped in pride meant that making them feel the weight of their error was not nearly so important as making sure that error was corrected in the future.

Despite her current frame of mind, Elizabeth would never forgive Darcy if he allowed her current, uncharacteristically poor judgement to go unchallenged. She was bigger than her not-so-petty resentments against Lord Matlock and would want support to behave accordingly, no matter how hot her feelings ran now.

Matlock had once asked him what it must be like to be married to a dragon. Right now, it was not an easy thing.

He paused at the wing chair nearest the bookcases and braced his elbows against the top edge. Huffing another deep breath, he leaned until his head rested between his arms. How had it come to this?

Elizabeth was usually so calm, so stable. But now, little things seemed to agitate her, things that would not have garnered any notice before. She had no tolerance for frustration, and heaven forfend anyone suggest that she or any of her efforts might be less than perfect. While he had seen her temper before, this aspect was unusual, and concerning. It was unlike her and, at least for now, she was unwilling to help him understand. Did she even understand herself?

He stood straight and raked his hair back as he turned to face a suddenly bright sunbeam pouring through the tall window.

There was nothing to be done for it now, but to be patient and wait for her to be willing to face whatever was truly bothering her. Patience might not have been his long suit, but that was changing.

He meandered back to his desk and fell into his seat, to return to what he had been doing before Elizabeth stalked in … and back out. What had he been doing? Oh yes, that.

He scanned the open page on the top of the neat pile, Pemberley census records. The last records of the two dragons Ring planned to introduce to them—a minor basilisk who lived in the Blackwoods and derived her name from it, and a forest wyrm calling himself Grove, who took it upon himself to control vermin in the fruit grove—it had been over twenty years since there was a census record of these dragons.

Twenty years since Old Pemberley's senile violence had driven them into hiding. He smacked his lips and swallowed hard.

Had Father any knowledge of what happened? He should have known. Should have, but how? Clearly, Old Pemberley would not have said anything, but the minor dragons—he sighed and braced his forehead in his hand. For all Father's otherwise excellent Dragon Keeping, he had little in the way of direct dealings with the small dragons of the estate. He had ensured they were welcome and managed properly—at least he thought that he did—but had not made them a part of running the estate.

Clearly, the role of minor dragons on an estate as vast as Pemberley was an issue for the Blue Order itself to address, one of several he would have to bring up with Sir Carew when the Minister of Keeps arrived from London. More and more it seemed that it was time to look at Dragon Keeping with an entirely new perspective. The whole relationship between major dragon, Keeper, and minor dragons might need to change. Drastically.

No one, least of all dragons, liked change. Dragons could be pragmatic, though, and that was to their advantage. With Elizabeth's help, it might be possible to convince them it was in their best interest to do differently. If the dragons were convinced, then they might drag their Keepers into a modern age of Dragon Keeping—quite possibly like medieval prisoners to the torturer ….Perhaps that was a touch dramatic.

Hopefully, she would be of a mind to discuss such things by the time Sir Carew arrived.

Had he written back with a date yet? It seemed as though Darcy should have heard from the Minister of Keeps by now. Perhaps the letter was somewhere in this stack. The mantel clock chimed softly, and he pushed the pile aside.

All of it would have to be dealt with later. It was time to meet with Pemberley's dragons.

Brutus and Axel, the guard drakes, ran alongside the coach on their way to the Blackwoods, on the far side of the estate. Late-morning sun warmed the coach sufficiently for comfort, encouraging Elizabeth's lavender perfume to linger in the air. She leaned back into the soft squabs, her eyes closed, clearly not desiring conversation. Just as well, nothing he thought to say right now would be conducive to the manner of pleasantries one expected on a morning drive. A few new ruts in the road jostled the carriage. One more issue he would need to add to the long list of maintenance issues to be managed.

Elizabeth stirred and gazed out the side glass. "Sometimes I forget how vast the lands around Pemberley are."

"Even growing up here, sometimes I forget, too. Especially out here, where only dragons and wildlife dwell."

"I shudder that Ring could have been so badly injured on the grounds of Pemberley, that its shades could be so polluted by such criminals."

"I suspect that it is the sort of thing to which all great estates might be vulnerable. Walker is already—"

"And it is appalling to think that Matlock has played a role in allowing it to take place."

"Yes, it is." He bit his tongue and forced a thin smile.

She glowered at him as though waiting for him to say more, to provoke her into further discussion of his uncle's very real failings.

Instead, he rapped on the carriage ceiling. "We will have to walk from here."

The basilisk had not been prepared to reveal her lair, just yet, despite the Charter's requirement that she do so. Once she trusted them and Pemberley, it should be less of an issue. For now, though, they had agreed to honor her sensitivities. Since she had not wanted to meet in the open, or anywhere near the house, they had settled on a unique limestone outcrop, near the base of several rocky hills, on the far eastern side of the estate. It was likely that this was actually close to her lair. Minor basilisks were not terribly clever about concealing such things. But they were fast and dangerous and not to be underestimated.

The carriage rolled to a stop and, a little surprisingly, Elizabeth allowed him to hand her down out of the carriage.

"I will go on ahead." Axel's newly-oiled brindled brown hide glinted in the sunshine. He trotted off down a footpath near a deep, muddy rut at the side of the narrow dirt road.

"The carriage should wait here, at the ready." Brutus glanced over his shoulder at the driver, nose high, sniffing the slightly dusty breeze. "We might follow Axel at a comfortable pace. He will alert us if there is anything untoward."

Darcy offered Elizabeth his arm.

She did not take it, but that was hardly surprising just now. Patience, that was the only choice right now. Pushing would only make things worse.

The footpath quickly disappeared into a lightly wooded forest. The rocky landmark they sought was not too far in, but out of view from the road. Pemberley and Ring planned to meet them in the woods, then, together, they would have their audience with the basilisk.

Axel yipped in the distance, their sign that all was well. Another, different quality of yip signaled that Ring and Pemberley awaited them. Hopefully those were positive signs for the introduction.

Darcy and Elizabeth joined Ring and Pemberley in the woods near three man-sized, grey-and-white limestone slabs jutting up at an angle as though they were bursting from the ground. A small clearing opened between the woods and the outcrop. The stony hillside rose about the same distance behind the limestone slabs.

"The Broken Tooth Rock is just as I remember it," Darcy whispered.

"I did not know this place had a name," Ring replied, eyes on the hillside, not Darcy.

"It was what Richard and I called it as boys."

"Good name. Looks like tooth." Pemberley nodded, looking up at Elizabeth and leaning into her.

She scratched behind Pemberley's ears as she scanned the hillside, probably looking for any dragon sign.

The birds and insects suddenly stopped their busy chatter, leaving the forest in ominous silence. A dragon approached. The back of Darcy's neck prickled. Elizabeth pulled back her shoulders straight and rigid.

"There," Ring whispered, pointing with his bandaged tail to the far-right side of the hill as the basilisk came into view.

She was a smaller one. Six, perhaps as much as eight feet long. A yellow-green head crest of long, feather-like scales created a crown-like head decoration. Her deep-brown-almost-black head and her body were snake-like and covered with smooth, glistening scales. Her four lizard-y legs that held her a handspan off the ground did not really seem to belong on the snake-body to which they were attached.

She approached slowly, with dignity and grace, stopping ten feet or so from Broken Tooth Rock. Basilisks did not enjoy proximity to warm-bloods. "Approach."

Together they crossed the clearing to Broken Tooth Rock. Axel and Brutus remained in the shadows of the woods, poised to spring if necessary, but they all knew, if the basilisk chose to attack, they would not be fast enough to stop her.

Ring rustled his wings toward the basilisk, and she nodded. "Vicontes Pemberley, Lady Sage, Sir Fitzwilliam, may I present Blackwood, guardian of these woods for nearly half a century."

Blackwood kept her distance and studied each one of them. Her head crest twitched as though she fought the urge to pounce on the still-weakened, wounded dragon and baby firedrake, both of whom she could probably best with ease. Prey and pouncing instincts never vanished. They could only be managed.

Too many heartbeats later, Blackwood dipped in the proper greeting, though, with her legs so short, it hardly appeared she moved at all as her chin touched the ground.

Pemberley, her hide dusky red in the shadow of the trees, moved forward and tapped the back of Blackwood's head with her long, forked tongue. "Am pleased to be acquainted."

"You are the New Pemberley?" Blackwood asked in an odd hissy-raspy voice.

"I wish know of your place in my territory." Pemberley pulled herself up tall and opened her wings. It was her territory, and she would be big.

Blackwood performed the required recitation of Old Pemberley's acceptance of her residence in his territory and the agreed-upon boundaries of her range. Interesting. She also noted that her duties to the Order had not been performed in quite some time, but, if Vicontes Pemberley would forgive her the transgressions, she would be honored to perform them going forward.

Pemberley glanced first at Elizabeth, then at Darcy, as though asking for advice as to what she should do. The basilisk's transgressions were, at least technically, sufficient to see her removed from the territory.

Elizabeth stepped forward carefully, just one step. "Since you have asked, Vicontes, it is the opinion of the Dragon Sage and Pemberley's Keeper,"—she caught Darcy's eyes for just a moment, and he nodded—"that the unusual situations which have brought us to this place are sufficient to permit absolution for what happened in the past, as long as future obligations are properly fulfilled."

"Is good advice. Stay. Do your duties." Pemberley settled her wings across her back.

Blackwood's tail swished across the gravelly ground. "That is acceptable."

Darcy stepped to Elizabeth's side. "There is one additional thing we would ask of you."

Blackwood's eyes narrowed, stopping at the point just before they became threatening. "What isss that?" The connotations of the hiss were not lost on him.

"The details are still being hashed out. New security measures will be put in place in the territory. Each minor dragon will be asked to keep watch over their portion of the estate and report to Pemberley or her Keepers any trespassing upon the territory."

"Yes," Pemberley firmly planted her front foot. "That what I want. Territory must be secure."

"There have been too many irregularitiesss on Pemberley territory. It is good to hear that thisss will be corrected." Blackwood pulled her head back into a slightly defensive hunch.

"What sorts of irregularities?" Elizabeth asked.

"Vagrantsss of the usual kind sleep rough here from time to time. Poachers of game are as troublesome as ever. More recently, though, in the last several years, there have been poachersss of another kind. The kind that tried to take Ring."

Pendragon's Bones! How was that possible?

Pemberley growled deep in her throat, a sound one felt more than heard. She had not made that sort of sound in Darcy's presence before.

"Without a proper essstate dragon to guard the territory here or in Matlock—nor Bolsover, come to think of it—the poachersss have run roughshod over the entire county."

"You mean to say what happened to Ring has become commonplace?" Elizabeth gasped and turned white.

"Not precisssely common." Blackwood shook her head, flipping her crest right and left. "I would sssay close to once a month, when there is no moon, there is sssomeone about the territory that shouldn't be. Eggsss have been taken, mostly from fairy dragons and wyrms, but some drakes as well. Barnwurms have turned up missing, and a few fairy dragons also. Wild drakes have been harassed. One of the young shepherding drakes last month said someone or something had tried to take him away. But he has always been the histrionic type, so not too much stock was put in that tale."

"Dragon's blood!" Darcy's fists trembled at his side. "And this has been a regular occurrence?"

"On moonless nights when the weather is fair. Maybe nine times out of the year?" Blackwood flipped her crest side to side, making a strange whisking noise.

"I not having this!" Pemberley stamped her front foot. "This my territory. I say who allowed here and who not. This must stop. You will help, yes?" She stretched out her long neck and stared eye to eye with Blackwood.

Blackwood flinched back just the barest bit and blinked. "Yes, Vicontes, I will help."

"Keep watch. Before next new moon will have instructions for what else do. Want a report each sevenday. Sooner, if you see anything." Pemberley snorted as she pulled herself upright and stormed back for the path, her tail lashing.

Blackwood's crest flared and her body expanded, matching Pemberley's display.

"A cockatrice messenger will visit regularly to receive your reports," Darcy added.

"As you sssay, … Keeper." Blackwood bowed, signaling her recognition of Darcy's dominance.

Excellent. Precisely what they had hoped for.

Darcy and Elizabeth took their leave and nearly ran to catch up with Pemberley.

"Will not have territory trespassed. Especially not by … by … them!" Pemberley growled, wings flapping, stomping her way through the trees.

"Certainly not, dearling. It is not to be borne." Elizabeth reached for her shoulder.

Pemberley stopped and stared at Elizabeth with a look Darcy had never seen before. "I not dear. I angry. Will protect territory."

"Most definitely, we will …"

"Not we, I. Is mine and I protect. Is my job."

"But you are fair young for such a task." Elizabeth glanced at Darcy, alarm such as he had never seen in her eyes.

"I dragon. I protect my territory or it not mine. That why I fight Bolsover, to prove mine. I will do what need done. You not stop me. Not you, not

Keeper. I must do." Pemberley stalked away, leaving Elizabeth staring slack-jawed.

"It seems Chudleigh and Rosings have taught her well. I certainly hear their influence in her words." Darcy stepped to Elizabeth's side, in the shadows of the Blackwoods.

"Her attitude is quite correct. But I did not expect her to express it quite so soon. Perhaps we should—"

"Should what? Try to talk her out of it?"

"She is very young." Elizabeth followed after Pemberley as though trying to disappear into the trees herself, mayhap to avoid a conversation. "I cannot help but worry that she will take on too much and—"

"Rather like she did when she challenged Bolsover?"

"She should never have—"

"I beg to differ." Darcy drew a long, slow breath, tinged with Pemberley's musk and Elizabeth's lavender, and held it until his control returned. "It was the best outcome possible for her and for her territory. Pemberley proved she could protect it and reestablished an important precedent for minor dragons."

"I would have advised against it."

Darcy took several longer strides to come alongside of her. "And I am sorry to say, you would have been wrong. Pemberley would have lost her territory, and we would be facing an entirely different situation."

"What are you implying?" Her voice took on a shrill edge.

"Nothing that you do not already know, but something I think you might be ignoring."

"What is that?"

"That the Dragon Sage, for all her knowledge, instinct, and wisdom, is not always right. And it would be appropriate for her to listen to other counsel from time to time."

The glare she turned on him could have rivaled basilisk Blackwood's. "It would be helpful if I had full knowledge given me by said counsel."

"You are still angry and resentful because I did not disobey Matlock and tell you of the smugglers."

"Angry barely begins to describe it."

One, two, three long paces to consider his response. Small sticks snapped underfoot. "You are right. I should have found a way to make sure you were informed. But, if you consider what you said to me this morning about Matlock, you will also agree that there is good reason why you were not informed."

"You are calling me rash, impulsive, and hot-headed?"

"You do not think suggesting public humiliation for the Grand Dug of the Order and his Keeper at an emergency Conclave is hot-headed? Really, if anyone else suggested that same action, you would do anything it took to prevent such an ill-advised maneuver."

"You sound just like my father! He never trusted me with important information and yet expected I would know and understand those very things when it was convenient for him, then blamed me for my ignorance! How can I manage in my Office without the necessary information?" She threw up open hands.

"How can you convince the holders of that information that you can be trusted?"

"They should know—"

"Does your behavior affirm that?"

"I have never—"

"Never acted rashly with respect to dragon matters? Like running into the woods in the middle of a ball after a wild-hatched dragon?"

"That saved Pemberley's life." She stepped back, against a large tree, and hugged her arms across her chest.

"For which we are all eminently grateful. Yet, at the same time, you now bear a reputation for acting on your best instinct, not on Blue Order rulings. Like it or not, there are repercussions to those choices. I cannot change that. Only you can."

"Do you suggest I ignore my best judgement in matters of life and death?" She rose on tiptoe.

"No, there is a time when swift action must be taken. But not every time. And even in those times of emergency, how it is handled afterwards can make all the difference." He met her gaze, holding it until she looked away. "I know you have heard this before and are loath to hear it again. But the Blue Order consists of both cold-blooded and warm-blooded members. You excel in managing one, but not so much the other. Just a little more consideration for the latter might make a significant difference in the information they are willing to share with you."

"But I have been right in every one of the circumstances of which you speak."

"No, dearest, you have not." How her face colored! "In your own words, you should not have allowed the situation when Netherfield took you and held you captive in his lair. Or have you forgotten?"

She opened her mouth to speak, but closed it quickly. He was right, and she well knew it. Turning aside, her voice dropped to nearly a whisper. "It was the only way to deal with my father. To do things as I saw fit without bringing him into the matter."

"I know."

She walked on, as though she could not keep still, silent for many steps, then whispered, "Do you trust me?"

"Even when I do not agree with you, I trust you."

"Lord Matlock does not trust me."

"He is a fool, and I have told him so. Have the fairy dragons not told you that?"

She turned and stared at him, head cocked, reminiscent of April. "They would rather talk about the things Matlock has said."

"Of course, they would. My defense of you is far less tantalizing."

Thoughts rippled across her face, intense and poignant, too quick to identify. "I am sorry I did not trust you."

He took her hand and drew her closer. "It is not an easy life that we have found ourselves in, is it? I should have tried harder with Matlock. I am sorry that I did not."

"How are we going to manage these grown-up dilemmas that face our not-so-grown-up dragon?" She leaned her head against his shoulder, melting his tension so quickly his knees threatened to waver.

"Together, my dear, together."

15
Chapter

June 21, 1815

LYDIA HURRIED DOWN the grand stairs as the long-case clock chimed its hourly reminder. She was not late by any standard, but her longstanding reputation for being late still followed her. Just how long did it take those things to change once one had truly improved?

At least Lizzy and Darcy had settled their matters, and Lizzy no longer stalked about in high dudgeon. It was a good thing that the pair did not argue often. The atmosphere of the estate had soured whilst they were at odds with one another and reverted back to its normal pastoral tranquility when they settled matters between them. Lydia even seemed to sleep better after that. How odd was that?

It was a shame, though, that Lizzy's mood had shifted from irritable to melancholy. At least Mr. Darcy was not at fault for that.

Mama's letters in anticipation of the dinner tonight had grown both more frequent and more demanding. All but insisting that Mr. Darcy issue his approval for Kitty's beau, sight unseen. How could he possibly take issue with a man Bingley and the rest of them liked so well? Lizzy was to see to it that permission was granted tonight. What was more, Mama expected Lizzy to offer Kitty a very pretty present in the form of a new silk gown for her wedding, to make up for not sponsoring a coming out for Kitty in London.

Had Mama really been so brazen all this time? Back in Meryton, when Lydia was still one of Mama's favorites, Lydia had not thought so. But now, knowing that she would never be the beneficiary of Mama's demands again, Mama seemed different. Uncomfortably different, not like the mother she thought she knew.

Best think on that later. Better to enjoy the opportunity to dress up and feel pretty for the dinner party whilst she had the opportunity. Betsey had done a capital job with her hair tonight! Tucked up in curls with pretty rose-headed pins and ribbons. A pretty rose-pink gown Aunt Gardiner had gifted her before they left London, one she had not had an opportunity to wear until now, and the company of a well-looking companion—Sir Richard was not exactly handsome, but his company was pleasing enough to make up for any deficiency in his appearance—was certainly the sort of thing to improve a girl's spirits.

After caring for Ring and bearing the burden of her work for the Order, Lydia needed it.

She paused in the doorway of the lesser drawing room. Done up in the same eggshell-blue and white as the great drawing room, this smaller sibling was somehow every bit as intimidating. Perhaps it was the ivory-and-gilt chairs that threatened a scolding if she sullied them. Or maybe that they were so stiff and straight and promised to be entirely uncomfortable. Or maybe it was the lingering traces of expensive perfume, now old and stale, that probably no one else noticed. Too many reminders of cross and disagreeable ladies she had encountered in far too many places.

Cosette, who had gone on ahead of her, perched on a small table between Lizzy and Sir Richard. Cosette caught Lydia's eye and waved her in.

Juniper had helped Cosette preen the feather-scales on the center of her back, where it was difficult for her to reach herself. The thought of her fairy dragon having a little dragon maid was rather adorable. Cosette did so hope to be able to join them at Ingleside tonight.

"I do not see why Walker and Earl will be allowed to attend you while Cosette and I must remain here." April hovered in front of Lizzy's face, so close Lizzy had almost gone cross-eyed. Her gown nearly matched April's turquoise-blue feather-scales.

"Because Walker and Earl can hide themselves amongst the trees and in the sky as birds of prey whom no one would ever notice as out of place. You and Cosette are far too lovely to be overlooked or considered ordinary in any way." Sir Richard offered a finger for Cosette to perch upon.

"I like your answer," April twittered, "but I still do not like staying away. It is not as though your mother and sisters do not already know me. And they have met Cosette as well."

Lizzy arranged her face into something far more patient than she probably felt. "You are entirely correct. And if it were only them, then I would welcome your company for the evening. But the Bingleys are another issue. Neither Mr. Bingley, nor his sister, who I am informed continues to live with them, hear dragons, nor are they fond of small birds or other creatures. It would be an imposition for us to bring what they perceive as our 'pets' to dinner with us. Especially considering the trials they have experienced with a rather ill-mannered, tassel-hoarding puck who caused damage at Ingleside."

"Your mother always did consider me a pet." April landed on Lizzy's knee. "So insulting. I am not a pet any more than she is the housekeeper."

"Indeed. Do you wish to be subjected to that once again?" Lizzy scratched under April's chin. "I thought not. I do not ask you to stay behind lightly, you know. There are few I would rather have with me." She cast a sidelong glance at Richard.

He winced and dipped his head, acknowledging both her meaning and the not-so-subtle barb. Darcy may have been forgiven, but Richard had not yet risen to the ranks of such complete absolution. Perhaps another day or two of penance. Lizzy was really being quite stubborn about that.

"I shall ask Mrs. Reynolds to prepare a warm bath with flowers for you and Cosette in the stillroom. I know it is not as pleasant as the bath in the garden, but without Walker and Earl to keep watch over you, I would hate for you to use the baths outside."

Cosette cheeped happily on Sir Richard's finger.

"I suppose that would be agreeable enough." April fluttered her wings, clearly unsatisfied, but without further recourse.

"I know our company will be poorer for your absence," Richard bowed from his shoulders to April, "but your Friend is wise and considerate."

"I know that." April dove at him and nipped his ear lightly, more a perfunctory act than a genuine one. "Come, Cosette."

The two fairy dragons zipped away.

"I am surprised you convinced her to stay behind so easily." Lydia sat near Sir Richard.

"Had she been determined, there would have been little with which I could have persuaded her, but April still does not particularly like the dragon-deaf members of the family." Lizzy shrugged.

"I think Walker might have been called upon to help convince her if necessary." Darcy quietly strode in.

Lizzy rose to meet him, slipping her hand in his arm. Gracious, that was a pleasant sight. "I suppose you are right. She thinks very highly of him."

"Thinks very highly?" Lydia laughed. "She utterly dotes on him. Hero worship would not be putting it too strongly. To be sure, Cosette feels quite the same about him. Earl, though, has become a favorite of hers as well. He tries so hard to keep up with Walker, despite the fact he is so much smaller and younger."

"His determination is difficult to overlook, is it not?" Sir Richard's eyes lit. He never failed to appreciate a compliment to his Friend.

"The carriage is ready." Darcy gestured toward the door.

Hopefully, with pleasant conversation and a comfortable journey, they would be a merry party indeed when they reached Ingleside.

Ingleside estate was just north and barely west of Chesterfield's town center, roughly seven miles from Pemberley, about an hour's ride by normal carriage. Alister Salt's team and his well-sprung coach, though, managed the distance in a quarter of an hour less. Kingsley and Sergeant, the intimidating guard drakes who ran alongside, seemed to enjoy the opportunity to stretch their legs and keep up the brisk pace through the peaceful countryside.

The plush upholstery smelt vaguely of leather polish and the small dragons who were smart at cleaning confined spaces and who helped young Leander Salt with the task. So luxurious! Even with four people inside, there was room for elbows and shoulders and knees aplenty.

Both Darcy and Lizzy seemed rather introspective on the journey, not offering much in the way of conversation. Lydia managed as best she could. It was not the first time she had attempted to render such service to otherwise silent companions. In fact, she had become rather good at it.

"Are we near Old Whittington?" Lydia all but pressed her face to the side glass, drawing up as much enthusiasm as she could.

"Closer to Barlow, I believe," Sir Richard said.

"The countryside seems so different here, Lizzy, does it not? So hilly. I do not think there were so many hills near Meryton. What do you think?"

"I had not considered it. We did not go into Chesterfield by this road when we were last at Pemberley."

Elizabeth seemed so distracted. Fretting over Mama, perhaps?

"The other road is far more direct into town," Darcy murmured.

"If you look that way, you can just make out the coal mines." Sir Richard pointed through the right-hand side glass. "Horrible, dangerous places. Not a place for a lady, but interesting to know where they are."

Darcy nodded in that somber, meaningful way he had. So serious about nearly everything. "As I understand, there is one mine that employs dragons—drakes and wyrms, I am told—to assist in the digging. If I recall correctly, theirs is a reputation for safety, though not the highest profit. But they only hire from among Order members, which limits the number they can employ. I have considered investing in their operations. We will look into that more soon, I think."

"Mining dragons! I would never have thought." Hopefully, Lydia managed to convey incredible interest in the matter, and they might be able to continue on the convenient subject for at least a little while longer. "It all sounds so exciting. I never thought about the employment of dragons in society before Mrs. Fieldings'."

"It is a thing too little understood among the Order, that there is actually a working class of dragons." Elizabeth huffed under her breath. "Rather like the warm-blooded working class, they are utterly ignored, beneath the notice of the upper classes. Apart from being Friends, what role do minor dragons serve? What use are they to anyone? Even the major dragons are apt to see things in that way."

"Unfortunately, that is the way of society." Darcy sighed, and the conversation died.

It was not an unpleasant silence, but to sit so stupidly while one was in company was truly irritating, as prickly as a cheap woolen blanket that rasped on the skin. "Do you think Mr. Bingley will have changed a great deal since we knew him in Meryton?"

"I have no reason to believe so," Darcy said. "His last letter to me was exactly as every letter to me has been, barely legible, with ideas that skipped along like a brook over a stream, sounding pleasant, but making little sense."

"He is a pleasant fellow." Sir Richard stretched his legs and crossed his ankles. "But one would never accuse him of wasting time in deep thought."

"No, his decision-making is rather rapid and influenced by the loudest voice nearby." Now Darcy was frowning.

Prickly, truly uncomfortable silence crowded the space.

"Do you think Mama has been very loud?" Yes, Lydia had just asked that. But someone needed to.

Lizzy cringed, winced, then sighed. "She is apt to be so."

"Bingley's letter did not speak of such, at least not directly."

"Yes, but what has he said indirectly?" Sir Richard cocked his head and lifted his brow.

"I am inclined to believe that he approves of Kitty's suitor because Mrs. Bennet is certain that he should, and that Mrs. Bingley is convinced that her mother is quite correct."

"Jane strives to be agreeable," Lydia said.

Lizzy's forced smile was actually painful to look at. "Papa's assured me that he expects our full scrutiny of this gentleman. Family connections outside the Blue Order must be examined even more carefully than those within. And I am afraid he is not wrong."

"I still do not like that he is putting the burden on you and Darcy." Lydia harrumphed. "It is lazy and unfair."

"You know how difficult it is for him to travel. You lived with him in London and could see how hard—"

"You are too easy on him, Lizzy. With him it is difficult to tell the difference between what is difficult and what is merely inconvenient."

"And you are too critical of him. I know he neglected you—"

"He neglected all of us. Even you, in many ways. But that is not the point. Papa is apt to do just as he pleases and create plausible excuses for what he is not pleased to do." Why did Lizzy persist in defending him?

"Even if that is the case," Sir Richard tossed a quick warning glance Lydia's direction, "it may be better this way. All of us together can certainly bring more to bear on investigating this chap than a single old man. I expect we can make quick work of the question and get on with more important things."

"Hear, hear! I am sure you are right. Since dragons are not involved in this matter, who is to say things will not be simple and straightforward?" Perhaps if Lydia smiled broadly enough, the attitude would be contagious.

Lydia hung back after Lizzy and Darcy left the carriage. Let them get some air and some distance from her. The whole discussion of Papa had turned Lizzy positively sullen and put Darcy on edge, killing any possibility of pleasant conversation.

Annoying as it was, it was difficult to blame either of them. Lydia might not know all the details, but she knew enough to agree. Both of them had good reason for wariness, even resentment toward Papa, and, by extension, Mama. Even Jane had grown distant as the demands of the Order and all its secrecy widened the gulf between the hearing and non-hearing members of the family.

No matter what, Lydia would not marry, not even consider, a dragon-deaf man. Not now, not ever. Spinsterhood would be better than to live under a divided roof again. Gracious, Mrs. Fieldings never thought she would be so changed on that matter! Lydia just might tell her so in her next letter for the sheer pleasure of shocking her.

Lydia accepted Mr. Salt's help down from the carriage and took in Jane's new home, Ingleside. The house stood, square and boxy, on the top of a little embankment with a dozen steps leading up to the front door. Half-windows peeked out at ground level, bringing light to the cellars below. Red and white brick walls contained two stories of full windows and little attic windows above those, finally topped by a cupola large enough to allow one or two people inside. To either side, small gardens were bordered by low decorative stone walls, gardens for proper ladies to walk through whilst sharing secrets. A small wilderness peeked out from behind the house, a place where Lydia would rather wander, if anyone asked her preferences.

Larger than Longbourn, but not half so grand as Pemberley, Ingleside seemed peaceful and content, rather like Jane and Bingley. No doubt, Mama would have preferred something grander, but it felt right for the Bingleys.

The white-paneled front door swung open, and Jane, definitely increasing, strolled out on Mr. Bingley's arm. Mama and Kitty followed. Kitty only paused to curtsey at Lizzy and Darcy, then bounded up to Lydia.

Perhaps it was true what they said about a woman in love. Kitty glowed with an energy, a vibrancy she never had before. Her dark blonde hair had been arranged much like Jane's, probably by Jane herself, giving her an air of maturity that contradicted the bounce in her step. Jane had once worn the gown Kitty wore now, a yellow sprigged muslin. But it had been altered and refreshed for Kitty, giving her an odd, grown-up-little-girl air.

"How well you look!" Kitty exclaimed, taking Lydia's hands.

"And you! Jane has dressed you herself, I am sure. You look so much like her now, which you know is the highest of compliments. She has always had the best taste. It seems life in Derbyshire is suiting you well."

"Oh, indeed it is! Come, come, walk with me in the garden before the rest of our guests arrive. Jane asked for you to come a full half hour early so she could have your party to herself for a bit." Kitty grabbed her hand and pulled her to the right-hand garden.

"I am sure you mean she wanted to have Lizzy and Darcy to herself." Lydia shrugged. No point in saying how Lizzy's importance as "Lady Darcy" had elevated her above both Lydia and Jane in Mama's esteem. Even though it was true.

Yes, it was still a bit of a sore point, but Lizzy and Darcy had done so much for her, she should not allow resentment to creep in. That would only make things difficult.

"Mama will be Mama. You can hardly expect that she has changed. And now that Jane is increasing, Mama is like a strutting hen, crowing about Jane's success even before the treasured heir is born." Kitty pulled her inside the garden wall. "Personally, I am convinced the baby will be a girl."

A polite stone path wound its way through equally polite groupings of well-behaved flowers—Lydia was not sure what those were called—that offered just a hint of sweet perfume to the cooling early-evening air. Hardly the sort of place to encourage the sharing of sisterly confidences. No, dignified conversations and sensible talk would be required here.

"You remember Mary is increasing, too. I am sure Mama is excited about that as well," Lydia said.

"Yes, I suppose. But really, you must agree, it is difficult to be excited about anything regarding Mary."

"She is mistress of Longbourn now. Surely that is worthy of note."

Kitty tossed her head and sniffed. "Through no effort on her part. She was Mr. Collins' second choice, and we all know that. It is a wonder that he chose her at all when Lizzy would not have him. I mean, really, if you think about it, you or I deserve to be mistress there much more."

"But Mary is the next oldest. It only makes sense …"

"But she put forth no effort to be worth looking at! She is dull and boring, and though she might be able to play pianoforte better than any of us, she is a bore to listen to."

"And you would want to be married to Mr. Collins? I grant you, he has improved under Mary's influence, but still!" Mama had probably put those ideas in Kitty's head, but did Jane agree?

"That is beside the point. I am talking about what I am persuaded that you and I have deserved, not that we would have wanted it." Kitty was making no sense.

But come to think of it, that probably was not unusual. "Who has convinced you of such things?"

"No one. Since I have been here, I have had time to think for myself, something which I clearly did not do enough of before. I have come into my own ideas, you see, now I have not had Lizzy and Papa telling me what I should think. And I am pleased for it."

Kitty thinking for herself? It was probably ungenerous, but that hardly seemed possible. And even if it were possible, the outcome hardly seemed pleasing. Perhaps Mr. Mothman was not a good influence on her.

Kitty slipped her arm in Lydia's and pulled her toward the far corner of the garden, where a fragrant orange trumpet vine tumbled over the wall and would obscure them from the casual observer. Its sweet perfume crept over them like a silk shawl. "I am not sure I have forgiven you for being presented at Mr. Darcy's and Papa's club—Blue's, is it called?—and no one has even thought to invite me. You are the youngest. I have just as much right and even more—"

Lydia extricated herself from Kitty's grasp. "Yet you are the one with the beau and on the cusp of something more. What could you possibly have to be jealous of? I am the one who should be put out, as you have not spoken a word of him to me. I must know everything before I am to meet him tonight." Hopefully, that would distract Kitty from her venture into dangerous territory. If only Cosette were here to persuade Kitty away from topics which should not be entertained. Fairy dragons were far more useful than they were given credit for being.

Mrs. Fieldings was right. Half-Blue families were very difficult, indeed.

"Oh, my Mr. Mothman!" Kitty sighed and giggled, a dreamy look coming over her.

What a name! Lydia bit her tongue. It was the kind of name that she and Kitty would have made sport of not so long ago, pitying the woman who would have to wear it the rest of her life for the privilege of being a missus. "Do tell me, is he handsome? Is he kind? Does he have a quick wit?"

"A quick wit? When has that even been a quality you sought in a man? No, I would not call him a wit at all."

Well, that was a shame. "Forgive me. I did not mean to offend. I just want to know everything there is to know about him."

"Well, he is very handsome. At least I find him so. You might not agree. Miss Bingley is less impressed with his looks, but I think that is because she is more interested in a fortune, which Mr. Mothman does not have. That is not to say he is not well off." She shook her finger as if to make the point clear. "He is not a gentleman like Papa or Mr. Bingley, to be sure. But he keeps a manservant who travels with him everywhere. Rather like the secretary Mama always wanted Papa to hire, and a valet, rolled into one. Clearly, that means he is doing well for himself. And Mr. Mothman inherited his father's house in the country and a very pretty one in Sheffield as well, where he lives above his shop. Or so I am told, as I have never been there myself. But I hope to be invited there soon. His wealth will never rival Mr. Darcy's, not even Mr. Bingley's, but he certainly has enough for a comfortable life, which is all I have ever hoped for."

No, that was wildly untrue. She had hoped for a man like Darcy, with a large estate and fortune to go with it, as much as any young woman might have. Not that any of them had actually expected it would happen for any of them, except for Jane, perhaps.

"Mr. Mothman is agreeable, and knowledgeable enough to rival Papa. I know you will think well of him. He is so smart in his trade." Something about the way Kitty said that …

Lydia's heart beat a little faster. "What business is he in?"

"He is an apothecary. A well-respected one. In Sheffield." Kitty folded her arms across her chest as though daring Lydia to disapprove.

Which, of course, she did. Simply because of the risk. Why did she have to like an apothecary? Lydia was quite sure she would never trust a strange apothecary again.

"You do not approve, I see. You think I am not clever enough to be an apothecary's wife?"

"No … no … whyever would I think such a thing?"

"Trust that I have heard it more than once. What is your problem with an apothecary?"

"I … it just seems … well, they do seem rather stuffy and dull, for the most part. And they always smell quite strange. I cannot imagine that suiting you at all." Pray Kitty was not as adept as Lizzy at spotting untruth.

"You think a man like that would not suit me?" Kitty glowered, then dissolved into giggles. "Well, you are right. They are dreadful dull as Papa. And if the full truth is known, Mr. Mothman is not an apothecary—not anymore. I was teasing you—seeing if you still know me as well as you did. And you do! Mr. Mothman was once in that profession, but has decided it was too limiting. And I completely agree. He is a forward-thinking businessman and wants to be more than a simple country apothecary. Many have tried to talk him out of leaving the trade he took time to learn, but he will not be moved. His ambitions for success in business will not be allayed by any manner of persuasion."

"What sort of business?" Lydia swallowed against the sudden dryness in her mouth.

"That is a little more difficult to say. He has in mind to create a new breed of warehouse, you see."

"What wares will he carry?"

Kitty giggled again. "Nothing like that, you silly twitterpate! No, he has had a thought to create a warehouse of ladies' wares. He wants to bring in a linen draper, a milliner, a haberdasher, possibly a modiste, maybe a jeweler, and yes, even a dull old apothecary shop to provide beautifying potions for ladies. I think it a quite brilliant notion, do you not?"

"It is interesting and different, to be sure."

"How grand it would be to make just a single stop to find everything one might need. I cannot stop thinking about it. He even let me add a suggestion that a table or two be provided for tea and biscuits to encourage ladies to linger over their purchases."

"It is very novel. How is he going about creating such a place?"

"How am I to know? That is his business, and I leave it to him." Kitty flicked her hand as though shooing away a troublesome insect.

What was one to say when she thought her sister not just foolish, but stupid? "You say his shop is in Sheffield, not Chesterfield?"

"Chesterfield is too small for the ideas Mr. Mothman has. A mere market town is not sufficient for him."

"That is wonderful." Wonderful that he was no longer an apothecary and thus not likely at all to be connected with any of the Blue Order's concerns. Thank heavens! She could breathe again!

"It truly is. I am so happy, and I do so want you to be happy for me as well." Kitty clasped Lydia's hands again.

Lydia fought the urge to pull away.

"But I am a selfish creature! I have been so caught up in my own happiness, I have not asked you if there is anyone special in your acquaintance."

Lydia dodged her seeking gaze. "No, there is not."

"Truly? I had thought that perhaps Mr. Darcy's dashing cousin might have caught your eye. He is well-enough looking, if not exactly handsome, and he is an earl's son."

"Yes, and a gentleman with his own estate as well. He is retired from the army as a colonel, and a knight, like Darcy—Sir Fitzwilliam. He is gentlemanly, in his own ways, but I am quite certain he would never be interested in a girl like me. He is far too worldly, and in need of a better fortune than my dowry could ever provide." Why did saying something so true leave a little ache in her chest?

"Then we must introduce him to Miss Bingley. He sounds like exactly the sort of man she would be most interested in." Kitty giggled.

"And is she agreeable?"

"She is not disagreeable."

"Is she a woman of good opinions and sound learning?"

"She attended a fine girls' seminary."

"What exactly is that supposed to reveal?"

"Why are you so concerned?" Kitty guffawed and rolled her eyes. "I think you like Sir Richard yourself."

Lydia's cheeks burned. "He is Darcy's cousin and therefore family to me. I have no greater interest in him than that."

"As you say." Kitty tossed her head and glanced around the vine toward the house. "Oh, look, Jane is waving at us through the drawing room window. She looks irritated that I have kept you to myself. Come." Kitty grabbed her elbow and hurried her to the house.

16
Chapter

BINGLEY, WELL-DRESSED, but still managing the look of a student who had not yet learned the finer aspects of dinner dress, strode toward them with all the puppy-like affability Richard remembered, leaving his gravid wife to the company of her mother and sister. Richard wanted to like Bingley. He knew he should like the man who had befriended Darcy—a man who was generally all nettles and briars when it came to people in general. That should have spoken well of Bingley.

But he was such a puppy—and not the useful type, like a faithful hunting dog. Rather more like a lady's pug, who snorted and snored and simpered in her lap and offered nothing useful, not even proper companionship. But maybe Richard was jaded. After having draconic companionship, puppies paled by comparison.

Then again, it behooved him to recall that Vicontes Pemberley liked puppies; loved dogs, really. Perhaps he needed to give Bingley another chance. There might be something redeemable about him yet.

Richard strode forward and bowed from his shoulders. "Good evening, Bingley. It has been quite some time."

"Indeed it has, indeed it has!" Bingley stuck his hand out for Darcy to shake—an overly familiar greeting for a gentleman.

Darcy shook Bingley's hand firmly, briefly. Could Bingley not see the excessive degree of familiarity made Darcy uncomfortable, and that he was just too polite to refuse? Perhaps not. Darcy was not always easy to read.

"And now you are here. You have finally made it to my home. Made possible by your steady assistance and guidance." Bingley gaped at the coach behind them. "I say, Darcy, that is a fine vehicle you have arrived in. May I have a look at it?" Without waiting for an answer, he strode past Darcy toward the coach.

Alister Salt, as though he was accustomed to such attentions, had already climbed down from the box and stood beside the vehicle, brindled drakes Kingsley and Sergeant pressed close on either side of him.

"Are those wheels iron-shod?" Bingley circled the coach, all but drooling. "How comfortably do they ride? And the grease axles! Are they as good as I have heard? Whip springs! You have spared no expense! And the dormeuse boot—I am sure that made your travels far more comfortable. I cannot believe it! You actually have a sword case! For Sir Richard, I am sure—tell me, did you actually keep a sword there?"

Richard rolled his eyes. Yes, he was supposed to stop doing that, but who could blame him after such an outburst?

"And very fine boarhounds to go with it. I have never seen any quite so large. Are they friendly?" Would Bingley have strode up so confidently if he had known the drakes' true nature?

"They be guard dogs, sir. They be friendly when they been told one is a friend, and not so much otherwise." Alister Salt tipped his hat as he blocked Bingley's path to the dragons.

"Of course, of course." Bingley edged back a step and looked over his shoulder at Darcy. "What possessed you to acquire such a vehicle? It is not like you to indulge in such extravagance. May I see inside?"

After a quick glance at Darcy, Alister Salt opened the door and let down the steps. Bingley climbed inside.

"Is he always so—" what was the word to describe him? "—distractable?" Richard asked.

"Always. He is generally a good fellow, but at times lacking in social graces, but somehow always manages to have that overlooked, is even considered humorous and endearing." Darcy shrugged, vague irritation in his eyes. "He has a way of making people rather comfortable, I think. He has always been well-liked."

"He does have that in his favor. You helped him establish himself at Ingleside?"

"I helped him identify eligible properties, but the rest was upon him."

"I have never seen such a comfortable equipage!" Bingley jumped down from the last step and sauntered toward them. "Best not allow Mrs. Bennet to see it, or she will be all agog and insist that my Jane needs something so fine. She deserves it, to be sure, but I doubt I could ever hire such a vehicle, much less own one. I am surprised at you, Darcy. You have never been one to show off such luxury. Taking a full traveling coach—not even reconfigured for town use—on a visit of less than ten miles seems unlike you. Has married life affected you so? Or perhaps it is your wife—has she insisted upon it?"

Kingsley and Sergeant both growled, curling their lips and exposing their teeth. Not loudly, but a sound one felt in the hair raised at the back of their neck and the prickly skin between their shoulders rather than heard.

Bingley scrubbed the back of his neck with his hand. "I am surprised, I admit. That was not the way Jane ever described Mrs. Darcy. And I would not have thought you so easily influenced from your sensible ways. Who would have thought Darcy might be so changed, eh?" He clapped Richard's shoulder. Altogether too friendly, too familiar.

"The coach is too dear even for the likes of Darcy." Richard forced a laugh into his voice, even as he flashed an eyebrow at the drakes. "It is a loan, from Matlock. A gesture of thanks for favors done for my father, Earl Matlock, whilst in London."

Not entirely the truth, but close enough to be supportable. The loan was from the Blue Order and as Lord Matlock was the head of the Order, it could be said to be from him.

Bingley whistled under his breath. "What favors could have brought you such thanks? And this on top of a knighthood!"

"Darcy is a fine friend and deserving of the honor," Kingsley whispered in his raspy, irritating persuasive voice.

"You are glad for him. He is deserving. There is no need for jealousy. No need for questions to know more. You are glad for your friend's good fortune," Sergeant added, staring directly at Bingley.

He blinked several times and scratched his temple. "Well, I am glad for you. For all the good turns you have done me, I cannot imagine such favor going to a more deserving person. I would not mind taking a turn in it, though."

"Why not now, then? Salt, take us down to the carriage house. We will walk back." Darcy beckoned Bingley into the carriage.

What did he have in mind that would warrant more time spent alone with Bingley's prattle?

"Very good, sir," Salt mumbled as he mounted the box. It did not appear he approved much of Mr. Bingley.

Richard followed them in and settled back, legs extended in what his Friend Earl would call a subtle show of dominance.

"While we have a private moment, I do have a question for you," Darcy said. "I need your opinion on a matter."

"My opinion? I am honored. But I can hardly fathom what matter you might seek my advice on instead of the other way around. I say, those whip springs offer a very nice ride. I hardly felt that rut that usually threatens to knock the teeth from my mouth!"

"It is a matter you have far more acquaintance with than I." Darcy rubbed his hands together lightly. "But I need your complete honesty with me. Yes?"

"Of course. This sounds important. What does your man polish these seats with? They are so supple."

"I want your honest opinion on Miss Kitty's suitor."

Bingley cocked his head like a man confused. "Oh! You mean Buzby?"

"Buzby?" Richard all but choked on the absurdity of the name.

"I know. It is a rather unfortunate nickname from our school days, before university, where I met Darcy. I cannot recall now how exactly he came by it, though. I do recall it made sense at the time."

Thank goodness they would be spared some old, and probably dull, school-days story.

"I say, is there a platform to make a bed for traveling stored in the dormeuse boot? How does one of those work in a carriage fitted to accommodate four, no, six, I would say?" Bingley scrutinized the interior.

Darcy shut his eyes and pinched the bridge of his nose. "About your friend, Buzby?"

"Ah, yes. Well, we were school chums, you see, but lost touch with each other after I went on to university. Imagine my surprise when I ran into him on the streets of Chesterfield! It was as though we had never parted ways, picking back up as though it had been only yesterday that we had seen each other. He was interested to know of my sisters; pleased for Louisa's marriage; terribly sorry over the loss of Father; all the usual social courtesies."

"I am glad to know he is a man of good manners," Richard said. Best not force Darcy to field this all on his own, although his impatience was rather amusing to watch.

"Absolutely the best. Quite gentlemanly. And he was so excited to hear I had purchased Ingleside. Overjoyed for us, and could not wait to come and visit."

"It is a lovely property." Darcy forced a smile.

"Yes, yes. And you see that field, that is the one I told you about that has had drainage problems. There is standing water there even now."

"I can see that. May I suggest…"

"Buzby saw that, too. Right away, as a matter of fact. Very clever of him."

Very clever to notice a field swimming knee-deep in water after a rain? Very clever, indeed.

"He did not agree with your suggestion about the drainage, though. He thinks it money ill-spent to bother with such things when the next spring's rains should come and sort it all out on its own."

This time Darcy really did slap his forehead. Poor man was in agony. Even Richard, still learning the fine points of land management, could see it was a stupid recommendation.

"It seems that you do not agree, Darcy." Brilliant of Bingley to notice.

"No, I do not."

"But Buzby says—"

"Is Buzby a farmer?"

"No, he is not."

"Does he possess an estate?"

"No, he does not."

"Is he the younger son of an estate?"

"I do not believe so."

"Is he perhaps a steward to an estate and thus versed in land management?"

"Most certainly not! He is a respectable—"

"Does he keep a garden, perhaps? Grow a few herbs or flowers?"

"Yes, I believe he does, near his houses."

Darcy drew a deep, slow breath as though carefully organizing his thoughts before he spoke too rashly. "So, he owns houses, but not land. Keeps a small garden, but not a farm? And this then qualifies him to advise you on the best options for a water-logged field?"

"Well, he seemed so certain on the matter, so persuasive." Bingley's forehead knit and his gaze turned introspective.

Persuasive? "What makes him so persuasive?" Richard barely stopped himself from asking if he kept a pet of some kind. That would be just too odd a question.

"You should hear him when he speaks, so confident and assured of himself. He is quite certain that he is correct in all his opinions."

"Confidence in what one says does not make one right. One might be quite confidently wrong." Darcy stopped just shy of lecturing.

"I suppose you have a point. I had not considered that. Well, no, that is not true, either. I had considered it. But I thought there were better uses for the money I would have spent on drainage."

"Dare I ask what uses?"

"Buzby has a small trading company. Rather, he is establishing one, and planning to open an innovative, new kind of shop. The investment potential seems quite sound."

"Not supplied by free-trading, I hope. The last thing you need is trouble with the tax man." Darcy rubbed his temples. A headache would be entirely appropriate right now.

"No, nothing of the sort. He's shown me the paperwork, and it is on the right side of the law, as I understand it."

"And you think that a better return than draining the field?"

"Yes, I do. I have studied the numbers in depth, and I am convinced. Perhaps you might be interested in the investments yourself. I am sure he would be happy to tell you about them. Oh look, there is the carriage house. Is it not a fine one? I had it repainted just last month." Bingley pointed through the side glass. "Whilst we are there, I should like to show you the carriage I just had refitted. I would value your opinion."

Did Darcy just roll his eyes? The Fitzwilliam family expression he prided himself on avoiding! But then again, who could blame him?

They stopped, and Bingley dragged Darcy off to examine his vehicle. Richard ducked around behind the carriage house and whistled. It sounded enough like a birdcall not to draw too much notice, but it was not a birdcall, but rather a signal to Earl, who was supposed to be nearby. One devised by Earl himself, that he was quite proud of.

There! Silvery-grey Earl swooped low over the field, the picture of predatory grace, and landed with slightly less grace at Richard's feet. "You did the call rather well this time. Much improved from the last time, when you sounded like a dying dove."

Richard snorted softly and scratched Earl under the chin. "Did you or Walker notice anything of concern on the way here?"

Earl settled his wings and bobbed his head. "Nothing of note. It was lovely to get to stretch my wings a bit, though."

"Good. Excellent."

"You are not pleased." Earl shifted his weight from foot to foot, the tip of his serpentine tail flicking, and studied Richard's face.

"No, I suppose not."

"Why?"

"It may be nothing at all. But something does not feel right." Richard scratched the back of his head. "But then I suppose nothing ever feels right when you're searching for poachers and concerned you are sharing a roof with a smuggler."

Earl chittered, shaking his head. "You are listening to your instincts. That is good. I always listen to mine. You should listen to yours. What do they say?"

"That I would like to double the watch and sleep with a sword at my side. But there is no clear reason for it."

"It would not be instinct if the reason were clear. It is enough. I will tell Walker. He will know best what to do." Earl launched and disappeared into the first rays of sunset.

It was good to have someone who did not think him daft for his instincts.

17

Chapter

ELIZABETH FOLLOWED AS Jane showed them through the public rooms of Ingleside. Though the generous draping of her demure, pale-blue gown hid her state well, it did not disguise the tell-tale waddle of a woman nearing her confinement. Jane's face glowed with healthy color, though, and her voice—when Mama was not speaking over her—betrayed no distress as she described the house. Both good signs, indeed.

Ingleside was not a grand manor house whose housekeeper would be called upon by random visitors to give tours of the property—only houses far greater than Ingleside attracted that kind of visitor. And while such intrusions might have satisfied Mama's pride, Jane would probably be driven to distraction by a desire to please people she did not even know. She would not be able to bear turning curious gawkers away, as Mrs. Reynolds often did. So, it was all for the best.

That notwithstanding, Ingleside was a fine house and not deserving of the criticisms that Mama had heaped upon it in her letters. Truth be told, it was every bit as fine as Longbourn, and in some ways nicer. How could she be less than delighted that Jane was mistress of such a lovely home?

It did seem Mama's way, though. One of those things, like her dragon-deafness, that would never change.

They entered into the main hall, having just left the dining room and a pretty little parlor. Jane called it the garden parlor for the way it looked out over a flower garden that would have drawn every fairy dragon on the estate, if it were a dragon estate. As it was, the bees were still busy among the blossoms, with the occasional small bird nipping in for a visit. Elizabeth would have liked to linger, even though Mama declared it rather in need of improvement.

The hall, a bit dim as hallways often were, was lit by a large window at the far side. Sunlight gleamed off the polished wooden floor that Mama thought should be marble tile, and illuminated paintings that had been acquired with the house. No one currently living there actually knew anyone in the paintings. Mama thought they should be replaced as soon as a painter might be hired to craft replacements. Jane had hinted that such a thing was not in their budget and would not likely be for some time, so she amused herself by crafting pleasant stories of who those people might have been, jotting them in a notebook to share with the children as they grew.

Such a very Jane thing to do. It must be nice to have sweetness come so easily. No wonder she was such a favorite with Mama.

Elizabeth had already rehung portraits no one recognized in guest rooms that were little used. Only people they could identify deserved to look out onto the current residents of Pemberley. Neither Darcy nor Mrs. Reynolds objected to the sentiment. Naturally, Georgiana preferred the entire Darcy line looking down upon them in the hallways.

No, those thoughts were neither conducive to a good-humored evening nor helpful to her general mood. Best put a stop to those.

Mr. Bingley, Darcy and Richard on his heels, burst in with all the enthusiasm of a well-trained cocker spaniel. With his shock of curly blonde hair and his wide, happy eyes, he resembled a cocker spaniel just a bit. "You will forgive me. I could not resist a closer look at the fine carriage you arrived in. You are most fortunate to have such favor with the Earl of Matlock."

Favor with the earl? Oh, he must have been persuaded to believe that. Best make sure to remember it.

"Such favor, Sir Fitzwilliam! Oh, how well that sounds! Our Lizzy is indeed fortunate to have found herself such a distinguished husband!" Mama clasped her hands close to her bosom. "And a very handsome one."

By handsome, she meant wealthy.

"It is I who am fortunate to have found such a wife." Darcy flashed his brows at Elizabeth as a blush crept up her cheeks. Such a look in his eyes!

"You are far too good to our Lizzy." The sweetness in Mama's voice did not completely obscure the barb within.

"Not at all, madam." Darcy tucked Elizabeth's hand in the crook of his arm and drew her close enough to feel his warmth. "This is a most pleasant establishment, Mrs. Bingley."

"What do you think, Lizzy, have we your approval?" Jane asked, her big blue eyes shining, pleading for approbation. Her face glowed in the special way that increasing women had of looking, just this side of angelic and, of course, beautiful.

"How could I not endorse any place that has made you so happy?"

"You think she would not be happy? Why would anyone not be happy in so lovely a spot as Ingleside?" Mama snapped.

And so, it would begin. Elizabeth had not mourned the loss of living with Mama's abrupt shifts of mood and all that ensued from them.

"That is not what she was saying, Mama, not at all. Pray do not think Lizzy is criticizing anything." Jane all but pleaded.

"Well, it would be the sort of thing a *Lady* with such a grand place as I hear Pemberley to be, though I have never been invited—"

"It has been quite some time since I have been to Pemberley, come to think of it, eh, Darcy." Bingley winked.

Pendragon's bones! April would have been so helpful right now. Perhaps some evening she and Cosette could be sent—under Walker's watchful eye—to sing Mama into contentment and convince her that Pemberley would not suit her at all.

"We have not seen Miss Bingley, yet." Elizabeth peeked down the hall toward the part of the house she had not yet seen. "Will she be joining us tonight?" Not that she really wanted Miss Bingley's company, only a fitting change of subject.

"As a matter of fact, she is waiting for us in the drawing room. She did not wish to intrude upon what little time I might have with you, Lizzy. So thoughtful and solicitous to me! We are happy to have her with us." Jane slipped her hand in Bingley's arm as though the action would conceal the great lie she had just told.

"Perhaps it would be best not to keep her waiting any longer. Come, she will be glad to see all of you once again." Bingley led them down the hall, his entire posture shouting how much he did not really want to keep company with his sister.

If they disliked her company so, why was she still living with them? Surely, she could stay with Mrs. Hurst, or easily afford her own establishment? Odd.

"Perhaps soon, you might come ride the property with me, Darcy. I would like to have your opinion on it." Bingley glanced back over his shoulder.

"I would consider it an honor." Darcy's shoulder flinched. He was lying, too. That was not like him. What had transpired while they were outside?

"And our drawing room—" Jane gestured to the open door.

Oh! Miss Bingley must have had the arranging of this room. The dining room and parlor clearly bore Jane's touch, but this room? Heavens, was pretentious too strong a word? The space tried to boast all the trappings of an elegant sitting room in a home like Rosings Park—without the excessive draconic motifs— or Pemberley, which was not in and of itself bad, but it fit neither the house, the neighborhood, nor the mistress of the estate, which turned everything rather garish, even gaudy.

Ormolu covered every frame, every candlestick. Patterns and colors clashed so loudly one could almost hear them. For every two decorative items, a third should have been removed to give space to breathe.

A maid was trying to light candles whilst being as invisible as possible, while Miss Bingley's glare followed her around the room, rather like a disapproving cockatrix. But a lesser cockatrix, not a greater one. Even with her fine silk gown and turban decorated with ostrich plumes, she lacked the true superiority of a greater cockatrix. And she knew it, too. Why else would she put on such airs, dressing far more lavishly than the mistress of the house, and decorating what was effectively her lair in pure, unadulterated ostentation?

"How do you like it, Lizzy? Is not Miss Bingley's taste very fine? What a help she has been to Jane. Is it not a remarkable example of a drawing room? I am sure it is as fine as any Pemberley might boast." Was that a note of jealousy or bitterness in Mama's voice?

Elizabeth tried to force out words, but her mind had gone blank.

Lydia and Kitty flounced in, pausing at the door as though to take in the amazing sights. Thank heavens! A broad smile spread across Lydia's face, but did not reach her wide, and possibly overwhelmed, eyes.

"And here is the drawing room!" Kitty declared, waving expansively as though the room were hers to present. "Has not Miss Bingley done a masterful job with it?"

"It is like nothing I have ever seen." Lydia barely tripped over the words. If one did not know her well, it would have been unnoticeable.

All told, it was an honest response, but did not likely mean what Mama hoped it might.

Miss Bingley's glower implied she did not appreciate Lydia's answer. Perhaps she was more perceptive than Elizabeth had given her credit for being.

"And you, Sir Richard," Mama all but cooed the title. "Do you think it compares favorably to Matlock?"

Richard moved a little closer to Lydia and Kitty, adjusting his cravat. "Matlock has never seen the likes of such a chamber." He bowed to Mama and Jane. "Pray, I have not had the pleasure of the acquaintance of your daughter and Mr. Bingley's sister."

Clever way to change the subject.

"Forgive me," Jane said. "We are such a happy company. I had forgotten you had not been introduced. Miss Bingley, Kitty, may I present Sir Richard Fitzwilliam, son of the Earl of Matlock and cousin to Mr. Darcy."

It was probably for Mama's sake that she recited his connections. The ladies curtsied, Richard bowed, and Jane directed them to sit upon the tightly stuffed, slippery chairs and couch.

Elizabeth pushed her toes hard into the slightly faded carpet to ensure she did not slide straight onto the floor. She would have to discover what this fabric was called and make certain never to use it in her own home.

An awkward silence descended, the kind that prevailed when one had two distinct groups of company who had very little in common, but were forced into the same social gathering. Miss Bingley made several attempts to raise a conversation in the way accomplished ladies were instructed to do, but after three failures declared she had an abominable headache and excused herself from their party.

Interesting. Jane's reaction suggested she might not regard that as a loss.

"You have seen Papa recently?" Jane asked, watching Miss Bingley depart. "How does he fare?"

"He is in good spirits with ready access to the library at Blue's," Elizabeth said. "But he is definitely not able to travel to Derbyshire. Whatever he might have written to you of is real, perhaps even underrepresenting, his condition. Though Middle Set House is not far from his club, he has needed the use of a sedan chair to get there recently."

Lydia glowered at Elizabeth, subtly, but it was a glower nonetheless.

"A sedan chair? He is taking a sedan chair?" Mama fanned her coloring face with her handkerchief. "I do not understand why that might be necessary at all. He would never permit such expense whilst we were living in London with him."

"Pray, Madam," Darcy's tone, smooth and conciliatory, betrayed his discomfort. It would not be surprising if he were wishing for April and Cosette's presence as much as Elizabeth. "I have observed him myself. Movement is difficult for him. Recently, as I understand, the house was rearranged to accommodate his bedchamber on the ground floor so that he might not have to use the stairs."

"He rearranged the house in my absence?" Mama's voice turned shrill as she stood, gesticulating broadly.

"How could he do such a thing without even consulting me? He has no notion of how a house should be set up. A bedroom on the ground level?"

"Oh, Mama, do not become angry. I have had to help Papa manage the stairs, and it is altogether better that he should sleep on the ground floor." Lydia stood, matching Mama's posture, and stared directly into her eyes, almost draconic in her posturing.

Such strength of purpose from Lydia!

"He allowed you to assist him?" Jane covered her mouth with her hand.

Her face the embodiment of sincerity, Lydia nodded.

"Oh, very well, then!" Mama pouted and dropped back into her seat. "I suppose it is just as well, then, that he sent dear Sir Fitzwilliam in his place to approve Kitty's suitor."

Kitty tittered. "I am sure you will be far more understanding than Papa, and probably better mannered. He never has much patience for those who are not especially scholarly."

"Your friend is not a man of learning?" Darcy asked.

"Not at a university like you. But do not think him ignorant! He is very, very smart." Kitty clasped her hands before her chest and sighed.

Something in Darcy's expression suggested he doubted that.

"Certainly, you will find no fault in Kitty's friend." Mama fluttered her eyes at Darcy, then turned her gaze on Lydia, hand pressed to her chest. "And once all matters are agreeably settled, then we can turn our attentions to you, Lydia. It will be such a peace to my heart to have all of you girls well established."

Did she just bat her eyes at Richard?

Lydia and Richard exchanged awkward glances. Not embarrassed or horrified, but awkward. Surely that was meaningful.

The housekeeper arrived in the doorway. "Mr. Mothman, madam." She stepped away to reveal their final guest.

Tall and well-formed, if anything, he was more butterfly than moth, though his heavy, barely-not-red mutton chops did give him a slightly fuzzy appearance, like a moth's body. Not dandyish, but his dress was fashionable. His tousled, almost-ginger hair, though, was a mite less so. He carried himself well, with an air of assured dominance. Not arrogance, but definitely dominance. His eyes immediately went to Darcy, the most dominant man in the room, clearly sizing him up and considering his next move.

Elizabeth bristled, but perhaps that was not fair. Many of the dragon-deaf responded to dominance, even if they had no way of understanding what it was. But was he truly dragon-deaf? Dragon bones! Why had she insisted April stay behind? She would have been able to tell.

Jane, with Bingley's assistance, stood. "Lady Darcy, Sir Fitzwilliam, Sir Richard, Miss Lydia Bennet, may I present Mr. Edgar Mothman of Sheffield."

He bowed with a gracious confidence that Kitty would have found appealing. "I am pleased to make your acquaintance."

"Do sit down and join us." Jane gestured to an empty chair beside Kitty.

Mama all but quivered with approval, but somehow managed not to gush.

Kitty sat up straight and seemed prettier, the way one did when they were the center of attention. "My sisters and the gentlemen have just lately returned from London."

"You left the season a touch early, then." Mr. Mothman sat beside Kitty. "Are the charms of the season less than I have heard them to be?" The question seemed good-natured.

"We generally prefer the quiet of the countryside to the bustle of town," Elizabeth said with a quick glance at Darcy.

"Derbyshire is such a pleasant place. It is easy to understand its draw. Was it something special that drew you to London this year?"

"Indeed, it was!" Mama gestured toward Lydia. "Lydia was presented at a ball held by Sir Fitzwilliam and Mr. Bennet's social club."

Kitty looked as though she would have preferred Lydia's presentation not be mentioned.

"Presentation at a social club? That is an exciting event. Congratulations to you, Miss Lydia. Was it a very grand affair?" Mr. Mothman asked, though his expression suggested it was more politeness than interest that prompted the inquiry. Polite was not a bad quality in a man.

"It was the grandest affair I have ever attended. Quite possibly the grandest one I shall ever attend." Poor girl was suffering not to be able to share the intimate details of the Cotillion with those who could never know the truth of it all.

"You cannot leave us with only that, child!"

Lydia flashed a panicked glance at Elizabeth. "I do not know where to begin. Aunt Gardiner helped us with our gowns. They were magnificent, but I am sure the gentlemen do not care for the details of ribbon and lace. Did you know the London scandal sheets are just awful? Dreadful, terrible things that can leave one with nightmares!"

"I had no idea. How so?" Mr. Mothman actually seemed interested.

"One poor girl—I did not know her, mind you, but I saw it happen—she stumbled during a dance and tore the hem of her gown. It was difficult enough to watch, but not so remarkable a thing. We have all seen it happen at one assembly or another. But it was reported in the scandal sheet as though—as though she had done something far worse altogether. Like it was something entirely unforgivable, not just a little accident. It was mortifying to read! I can only imagine how the poor girl must have felt." Lydia pressed her hand to her cheeks.

"I have heard the society in London can be quite brutal." Mr. Mothman glanced sympathetically at Kitty. "Perhaps it is no real loss staying away from it."

"I cannot disagree. One tires quickly of the business." Richard leaned forward, elbows on his knees. "Bingley boasts of your reputation within your trade, but failed to mention exactly what that was. Do tell, if you will, what is the nature of your business?" To his credit, Richard managed to present the question without the note of superiority that the rest of his family would have attached to such an inquiry.

"I am an entrepreneur, sir."

"An entrepreneur! Is that not a fine thing to be able to claim for oneself?" Kitty batted her eyes at him.

"You are too kind, Miss Bennet, but your flattery may be too much. It is not the sort of thing one claims for oneself in refined society. The taint of trade, you know."

No wonder Miss Bingley left. Why would she want to spend time in the company of anyone who reminded her how close her own situation was to that "taint"?

"Mr. Bingley, was not your own family—" Lydia asked.

Mama cut her off with as violent a glance as might be mustered in a reasonably polite drawing room. Bordering on draconic, really.

Lydia coughed violently enough to redden her face.

"Here, here." Mr. Mothman pressed an embroidered handkerchief into her hand.

Lydia pressed it to her face, and her spell eased.

"Do not be so modest. Your ideas are so novel and unique. I am sure once you are established, the concept will spread through England as well." Kitty clasped her hands in her lap, a look of reverence on her face.

"That is fascinating." Richard regarded him with narrowed eyes. "You must tell us, what is this idea of yours that threatens to transform the whole of the kingdom?"

Mr. Mothman settled back, his posture and his voice shifting almost like a dragon's did when about to use persuasive voice. Perhaps this was the human equivalent of that. "Have you not been struck by how inconvenient shopping can be, especially for ladies? They must visit so many different shops and specialties. How pleasing it would be to bring all those goods into a single place where she could visit and find everything that she would need. Linens, haberdashery, hats and gloves! Perhaps a modiste, a shelf of books on housekeeping and deportment alongside of *A Lady's Magazine* and *La Belle Assemblée* and *Ackermann's Repository*! A table to enjoy tea and biscuits," he smiled broadly at Kitty, who simply beamed, "whilst being shown the finest in ladies' perfumes and beautifying products!"

"I think it a fine idea, do you not, Lizzy?" Jane was politely making it clear that no debate of business models or other such uncongenial talk should follow.

"That is interesting." Richard leaned back in his seat, a thoughtful cock to his head. "Have you been introduced to Miss Bennet's uncle, Mr. Gardiner? He imports fabrics and the like from the east. His information and connections might be useful to you. He eschews all the free-traders and may help you do the same."

"I would covet an introduction. For the most part, I plan to source my supplies from our fair land and avoid the whole trial of importing goods. If nothing else, it avoids the tax man." He shrugged. "Forgive me, but I dread the whole business of smugglers."

"Oh, pray, do not go into all the unpleasant discussions of taxation and money and criminals." Mama fanned her face with her handkerchief. "We are here for an evening of pleasure, not business."

"You are so very right, madam. Forgive me."

The full moon shone nearly as bright as daylight when Darcy handed Elizabeth back into the carriage. An ideal evening for traveling. Guard drakes Kingsley and Sergeant took their places beside the coach, while Walker and Earl cawed and flew lazy circles overhead.

Heavens, it felt good to be surrounded with dragons once again.

Fresh night air cleared the cobwebs from Elizabeth's mind that Kitty's and Mama's prattling had woven there. Even the slight chill was welcome for shaking off the lingering heaviness that spending time with Mama always left behind.

Lydia slid into the soft seat beside her. "Oh, I am so fagged!"

"Since when has a dinner party ever been hard work for you?" Elizabeth chuckled as Darcy and Richard settled into the seat across from them. "I know it has been some time since you have had the …" —she was going to say privilege, but that was an unnecessary reminder that Lydia did not deserve— "opportunity to socialize, but I would not have thought you to be out of practice."

Lydia leaned back and closed her eyes. "I suppose I have become used to company with whom one does not need to be so entirely guarded."

"Watching one's conversation can be wearying." Richard stretched his long legs and crossed his ankles. "But one does become accustomed to it after leaving the rarefied company that Blue Order events offer."

"It is not just London, though," Lydia sat up a little straighter. "Even Pemberley is quite different to Ingleside. And I do not mean simply in grandeur. Ingleside is quite as pleasant as Longbourn. There is a different feel to Ingleside, a place that has no idea of the Blue Order and its denizens. Hard to describe; rather like a child who does not understand the business of the adults that is going on in the floors beneath the nursery."

"What an interesting way to conceive of it. I take that to mean that you would require any beau of yours to be a member of the Order?" Richard asked.

Darcy caught Elizabeth's eye with a raised eyebrow. It was an interesting question for Richard to ask.

"Having a half-Blue family is every bit as much a trial as Mrs. Fieldings taught. I would not choose that for myself." Lydia shuddered just a bit.

"Speaking of choices, what was your impression of Kitty's Mr. Mothman?" Darcy's words hung in the air between them.

"I can see why Mama likes him so well. He seems quite solicitous of her. And he seems rather more well-informed than I would have expected for a man attracted to Kitty. He was rather interested in the connections he might gain through us, though." Elizabeth crossed her arms over her chest and rubbed her shoulders. She should have brought a shawl. "I do not know what to make of it. I suppose it is only natural for one in business to think in such a way. Though I have not heard the same … mercenary, is that the right word? … tone when Uncle Gardiner speaks of such matters."

"I confess, I was quite prepared to dislike him." Richard tapped one foot against the other. "Tradesmen can be quite as disagreeable as the *ton*."

Darcy chuckled and Lydia guffawed outright.

"I do wonder if he is truly dragon-deaf, though." Suddenly all eyes were on Elizabeth. "I wish I had Lady Anne Elliot's knack for identifying dragon-hearers. April and Cosette will have to help us to determine the truth of the matter. And we should check with the Order to see what they know of him."

"That being said, he does not seem like an entirely bad fellow. Perhaps I was too rash in my initial judgement." Richard shrugged in the moonlight. "His new concept is quite intriguing. What say you about that, Darcy?"

"He is very sure of himself, though his manners are lacking. He had no hesitation asking if I would be interested in investing in the enterprise. But such men usually are quite bold."

"What did you tell him?"

Darcy shrugged. "If he connects himself with your sister, then I will certainly offer some support his way. How much will depend upon the soundness of his business plans, which, you can be certain, I will study carefully. If they are unsound, I will find him mentors who can help and if he refuses, then any investment will only be a token amount. I do not wish to be unsupportive of family connections."

"That does seem prudent. I suppose a token cannot be harmful." Elizabeth pressed the side of her foot to his, and he leaned into her.

"I would beg to disagree." Lydia's voice was so low it was almost impossible to hear above the sounds of the road.

Chills raced along Elizabeth's scalp. "Pray tell us what you mean."

Lydia fumbled with her reticule and removed a white cloth. "You recall when he gave this to me? Yes, I know, I should have returned it. But when I looked closely at it, I knew you would have to see it, too." She spread the bright white linen open in a moonbeam, revealing the embroidery.

"Dragon's blood!" Richard took it from her.

"Is that what I think it is?" Darcy leaned closer to Richard.

Elizabeth clutched the edge of the seat. "What are you talking about?"

Richard swallowed audibly as he licked his lips. "My investigations in London found a symbol associated with traders in dragon parts. We are not certain, yet, but we think it is used as a way of identifying themselves to each other."

Dragons' bones! "But he is not an apothecary! Surely, he cannot be associated with such ... such business!" Elizabeth pressed her hand to her mouth.

"I do not know." Richard blew out a long breath through full cheeks. "Though it is possible it is all a coincidence. I hope it is all a coincidence. But prudence requires we take its presence seriously."

"Pray tell me what about that handkerchief has you so concerned?"

Richard pointed to the red snapdragons dancing along the edge of the handkerchief.

18
Chapter

DARCY SWALLOWED HARD as he stared at the edge of the handkerchief. Surely it must be some manner of coincidence. It had to be.

Even in the bright moonlight, the darkness inside the coach became oppressive as Elizabeth turned quiet, frighteningly quiet. Darcy slipped his arm around her shoulders, but she barely seemed to notice. Was she ignoring him or lost in her own thoughts? Or perhaps a bit of both. So difficult to tell.

During the rest of the journey back to Pemberley, Lydia made a valiant effort to maintain a light and pleasant conversation, but even she faded after a time. Even Richard, who was never without a quip or pleasing tale, found nothing to say. Who knew silence could be so loud?

Once the coach stopped, Alister Salt handed Elizabeth down, and she disappeared into the house with nary a word.

"It is never a good thing when Lizzy gets that quiet," Lydia whispered as she exited the coach. "I would not intrude upon her privacy right now. But you should." She hurried away before Darcy could comment.

She was impertinent, but right. This was not the sort of conversation that would benefit from waiting until morning.

"Wait." Richard's hand stayed Darcy's shoulder. "We should hear from Earl and Walker first. I asked them to investigate whilst you were admiring Bingley's carriage."

"Why?"

"Earl called it instinct." Richard shrugged as the two cockatrice flew in through the still-open door. He pulled the door shut behind them. "Were you able to learn anything?"

"That wyrms have a reputation for idiocy for a reason," Walker snarled.

"It helps when you talk to them in pairs." Earl pulled himself up straight, his head above Walker's.

Walker spread his wings and snarled, triggering an immediate lowering of Earl's entire being. Cocky young buck should never forget who was the dominant dragon. He was lucky his youthful oversight did not get him killed.

On the other hand, Walker's response lacked his usual level-headed restraint. A bad sign. "Fairy dragons are far more sensible creatures."

"You are right. It was a mistake leaving Cosette and April behind. Their help would have been useful." Earl's agreement might be a little too emphatic, but who could blame him?

"I agree. They are essential to our efforts. At the very least, they might have been able to help us get straight answers out of the few wild dragons we were able to locate." Walker squawked. "Matters were made even more difficult as we were trying to garner intelligence on a man who does not even live at the estate."

"So, you learned nothing?" Richard ground the heels of his hands into his eyes.

"I did not say that. Only that it came it in bits and pieces and required a great deal of high-level extrapolation to make some sense out of it all."

"It was good that we, not the drakes, were sent. The ground-based are not good at puzzling bits together." Earl preened the back of Walker's neck as though hoping to be admitted back into his good graces.

Darcy cleared his throat. "Pray forgive me, but the Lady Sage has need of me and should not be kept waiting," Thankfully, that seemed to get their attention. "Pray, tell us what you discovered."

Earl bowed to Walker and edged a step back.

Walker lifted his wings slightly. "While Mr. Mothman does not live at Ingleside, he does have a habit of visiting frequently and regularly. His visits are most common around the new moon. The wyrms tell us that a man, who does not live at the estate, is often seen skulking about the grounds during the new moon. Not infrequently, this person meets with other interlopers and exchanges occur between them."

"Dragon's blood!" Richard slammed his fist into his palm.

"Wait, what you have not said is as significant as what you have." Darcy held up an open hand. "Has this man been identified? Do his appearances coincide only with Mothman's visits? Have the goods exchanged been identified?"

"And there you have the rub," Walker swung his head to and fro. "The wyrms were not able to answer any of those questions. Which, all things considered, they cannot be faulted for when their bigger concerns are defending their territory against other local wyrms."

Earl hunched lower. Just how vigorously had he interrogated those wyrms? "Wyrms are always clashing over territory. One would think they would be used to it and pay it little mind."

Walker snorted. Clearly, he was losing patience with his offspring. "Strange dragons in their territory will always be a priority over strange men."

"It does suggest that someone at Ingleside is behaving suspiciously, at the time most likely for smugglers to be operating." Darcy worried his hands together.

"You do not suppose Bingley could be involved in any of that? The man can barely hold a thought in his head long enough to successfully arrive at the chamber pot! I can scarcely imagine him gallivanting about in the dark without forgetting what he was about!"

"I grant you that. It could easily be a servant selling purloined food or liquor from Ingleside stocks," Darcy said. "Frankly, that is exactly the sort of thing that would be likely in Bingley's home."

"You may be right. It might even be the most likely explanation," Walker said, "but we should not take a chance. I propose that Earl and I should make a clandestine visit to Ingleside at the next new moon and see for ourselves what transpires there."

"That means I shall have to delay my judgement on Mothman a fortnight," Darcy clasped his hands behind his neck. "Unavoidable, but unfortunate."

"Your mother-in-law is most anxious to have an answer sooner than that. I do not relish having to fend her off. Perhaps the excuse of needing to study the investment potential of his business might provide enough excuse to quell her enthusiasm, at least for a time? I expect to be visiting his shop soon in any case," Richard said.

"That might work, yes. Mrs. Bennet wants us to support his new venture, so that seems an ideal way to hold her at bay. Thank you."

"What will you tell Elizabeth?" Richard asked.

Walker and Earl fixed shining eyes on him.

"Tonight, nothing. Tomorrow, everything. Good night." Darcy left the carriage as the cockatrice chirruped.

After a few minutes, Darcy found her in their private sitting room. As with its twin in London, only Mrs. Reynolds was permitted to intrude on their privacy. It was the one place in the house that was theirs alone. Somehow it was comforting that this was where she chose to retreat.

Just large enough for two comfortable chairs, a tea table, and a small writing desk, the room had once served as a storage space. Hence the walls were still white, with no pictures hung to decorate them. Only the plainest of curtains hung over the narrow window, and a vaguely musty scent clung to the corners. However, the company he kept there more than made up for the simplicity that Mrs. Reynolds seemed determined to correct.

Elizabeth stood in the window, silhouetted in the moonlight, glistening trails down her cheeks.

"May I come in?" He stood in the doorway, waiting.

She sniffled and nodded without looking toward him. The woolen shawl he had given her when she was carrying Anne was pulled tightly around her shoulders, warding against a cold not in the air but somewhere within herself. He slipped in behind her and wrapped his arms around her waist, cradling the top of her head under his chin. Hopefully that would comfort her, too.

For several minutes she held herself stiff and straight, but finally melted back against him, nestling her cheek into his shoulder. "How am I going to tell him?"

"Tell who, what?"

"Papa. How can I tell him that we think Kitty's suitor might be so much worse than we could have imagined? He has not even responded to the letter telling him about Lydia's work with Richard, yet. I can only imagine what he will say."

"He put the burden on me. I will tell him."

"Even if you do, it will not stop the blame from settling on my shoulders. "

"What do you mean?"

"Do you not see? No matter what happens here, I will be at fault. I will be to blame. If we question Mr. Mothman, Ingleside will declare it is because I am not disposed to like anyone that I consider beneath me. Jane will be kind, of course, but she already thinks I am now above her station and does not know how to deal with me."

"She said as much to you?"

"In a Jane sort of way, she did." Elizabeth sniffled softly. "All those questions at dinner of what should be served, and how she should dress. If the house was comfortable. All of those questions were to see if she measured up to some standard she thinks I now have. It all seemed most unlike her, but it is not difficult to imagine that marriage and living with Mama have changed her."

"I did not hear that so much from Jane, but from your Mother ..." Perhaps he should not have said that.

"Merciful heavens! I do not want to think about Mama!" She rocked against him, trembling until the welling sob subsided. "Have you any idea of how insufferable she will become because of this?"

Yes, he did and was sorely tempted to give voice to just how much he understood. But that was for tomorrow. "Tell me of your concerns."

"It is silly and stupid and temperamental and should not be a concern."

"I know you are trying to be what you think is sensible and strong, my dear. But that is not the side of you I asked to hear. You know April will tell me straight away if I ask. I would much rather hear it from you."

She laughed, without mirth. "You know April's opinion of my mother. Sometimes I wonder if she is right, though. There is nothing I will ever do that will please Mama."

"Are you trying to please her?"

"Not especially, not anymore. I suppose it would be nice if it could happen. But it will not. She was so disappointed to learn of Anne's birth, you know. I failed you. I failed Pemberley. I did not give you a son and heir. Perhaps I might get that right the next time."

Darcy held her a little tighter. He had suspected Mrs. Bennet would say something like that, but hoped he was wrong. Horrid, insensitive—

"Whilst she is happy for my success in the marriage mart—you are quite the catch, Mr. Darcy—pray excuse me, Sir Fitzwilliam—she would far rather have seen Jane win such a prize."

Restraint. She did not need to hear his opinion on being valued like a stallion. There would be time enough for that another day. Restraint. "Bingley is not good enough for her?"

"In pounds and pence, you are far worth more, of which Jane, of course, is more deserving."

"Rubbish."

"Be that as it may, it is the way with her."

"I am so sorry, my dearest."

Her shoulders shuddered with silent sobs, shaking her to her core.

If only there were something more he could offer than to merely hold her and allow her the shelter of this space to give voice to those violent feelings. "It would be a simple thing to have nothing more to do with her, or even the Bingleys, if you like. There need be no obvious cut, but with the help of a little persuasion, we might avoid dealing with them in the future. I dare say April and Cosette would be more than happy to oblige, perhaps even a little relieved."

"I suppose. Maybe. If it is entirely necessary." She dabbed her face with the edge of her shawl. "But that does nothing to manage the current issue. Mama has all but begun picking out wedding clothes for Kitty! She has given her approbation and is certain that will be enough for Papa, and by extension, it must be enough for you. No matter what you may say, she will insist—and make Jane and Kitty believe—that any hesitation you have is because of me." She turned to face him, looking up into his eyes. "You know I am jealous, selfish, cruel, and self-centered! I do not wish to see my sister happy. I see myself as too good to have relations in trade—and will soon throw off the Gardiners as well. And Papa will do nothing to support me. He will be happy to have her ire directed at someone else. He has done that often enough before."

What was worse, hearing her say those words or knowing that she probably well understood her mother's attitude? "I wish there were some other way. But you cannot intend—"

"That we should give in to what they want because Mama, in her own way, is as ruthless as scandal-writer Mrs. Pendragon? No. No, I do not. But it does not mean I am easy about having my hand forced." She stepped back, scrubbing her hands over her face. "Have you any idea how angry I am? That by their thoughtlessness they could bring us into connection with someone so truly horrible, is unthinkable. And we will be left to manage this entirely on our own. Papa will be little or no help. That was why he laid the responsibility on your shoulders, taking the easy route again. Yes, he couched it in terms of his business with the Order, but had it been important, he would have found a way. If only we could have refused him this favor. I know it was not possible, but I wish …"

"I regret, I truly regret, that this could cost you your relationship with your family. We will not be alone, if it comes to that, though. I am sure of Richard's support."

"Of course you are right. Even if I am still a bit put out with him, he has always been and will always be our most faithful friend. But his father, the Chancellor? I can only imagine what his response to such a scandal might be. Neither Lord Dunbrook nor Lord Chudleigh will be quiet about it, either. It could even cost Papa his office! That would kill him."

He gently placed his hands on her shoulders. "It is not a crime to have foolish, troublesome relatives."

"It might as well be."

"Then we are both equally criminal. Or have you forgotten, a large part of the blame for the trade in dragon parts has recently been laid squarely at Matlock's feet? That should give the Order pause before it condemns your father." He opened his arms and drew her close.

Head pressed into his shoulder, she sagged against him like a wrung-out rag. He led her to the large, overstuffed chair across from the window and pulled her, fragile and weary, into his lap.

She sniffled and swallowed hard. "Is it so much to hope …"

"That your mother will ever change? That your dragon-deaf sisters will ever escape her influence and appreciate you as you deserve?"

She nodded.

"Yes, honestly, I think it is. I know it sounds cruel to say, but that level of change seems like far too much to hope for. Sometimes, the bravest thing to do is to acknowledge some causes are indeed lost and to pour oneself into those which are not."

"I suppose it is petty of me to sulk over having lost Jane when I have actually gained Mary and Lydia."

"Not petty. The disappointment is real. But pray, dearest, do not get so lost in it that you forget you are surrounded with love and respect and are not alone, no matter what your mother or sisters may say."

"I know you are right." The words were tight and forced, but at least she agreed, even if only in principle.

Chapter 19

June 22, 1815

MORNING SUNLIGHT PAINTED the flowery paper hangings of Lydia's room as tiny dust motes played on the beams. Sachets of orange blossoms perfumed the space. According to Betsey, it was the only room so perfumed, chosen specifically by Lady Elizabeth for her sister's pleasure. Lizzy had been right. It was a curiously pleasing scent and somehow made the room feel like her own. Perhaps she would acquire some orange blossom perfume and make the fragrance her own, just as lavender was Lizzy's.

Did Sir Richard like orange blossoms? Heavens! That was not the sort of thing she should be thinking right now. Lydia pressed her hands to her cheeks and settled her mind with several deep breaths.

So quiet and peaceful here at Pemberley, nothing like the chaos that seemed to follow Mama from room to room at Longbourn. How odd it was to be able to write a letter in peace and quiet, in her own space, without Mama or Kitty barging in to check on what she was doing, distracting her from finishing it altogether.

Strange, she had never noticed that before. The disorder of Longbourn had seemed so normal at the time. Come to think of it, Ingleside had a bit of that same feel to it. Should she tell Lizzy of Kitty's invitation to stay at Ingleside? Lizzy was upset enough from that visit. Perhaps she would keep it to herself as long as Kitty graciously accepted her refusal.

Lydia carefully folded her letter and dropped a blob of sealing wax on it, taking extra care to make the pool of red wax as round and regular as possible. Mrs. Fieldings thought it an extra measure of care and consideration that conveyed to the sender the value placed upon the missive. Whether that was widely true or not, she did value Mrs. Fieldings' opinion, so it was worth the effort.

Cosette, standing on the writing desk beside her, raised her front foot. "Please?"

The little dear had a strange affinity for sealing wax. "It would be an honor to have your seal on my letter."

Cosette hovered over the letter and pressed her foot, toes neatly spread, into the wax, then rose up a little higher to admire her work. "Yes, that is good. I like that very well indeed. It is too bad it does not stay warm longer. It feels nice between my toes."

"I am sure it does." Lydia tried not to laugh. Cosette did not like to be laughed at.

Mrs. Fieldings would probably enjoy Cosette's mark on the letter. While she could not tell the headmistress of her work with Sir Richard and the Blue Order, it was enough to be able to share her observations about life among the dragons of Pemberley.

She had enclosed a short note to Miss Darcy, as well. Hopefully, she would enjoy a bit of news from Pemberley. Assuming, of course, that Mrs. Fieldings approved it for Miss Darcy to read.

Mrs. Fieldings had an uncanny sense of what a girl needed to hear at a particular time and what might be less advantageous. She often held back letters until they would be of the greatest use to her pupils. At the time, Lydia had resented the invasion of privacy. But now, it seemed far more prudent and sensible. Hopefully, Mrs. Fieldings would deem her words useful.

How lovely it would be if Miss Darcy profited from Mrs. Fieldings' ways and was able to return to Pemberley. With all that was happening, the extra help could be truly appreciated.

Letter in hand and Cosette on her shoulder, Lydia picked up her bonnet and reticule. First to find Betsey to post the letter, then to the morning room.

"Good morning, Miss Bennet," Sir Richard rose and bowed from his shoulders, as Agnes the maid scurried from the sunny morning room, an empty bowl, the type Earl often used, clutched to her chest.

Smells of fresh breads and ham and stewed fruit wafted over the undercurrents of something raw and not to warm-blooded tastes.

Earl looked up from his perch across the table over his bowl of—no, never mind, she did not want to know what that was— and chirruped. Cosette zipped past to the fresh pink hydrangeas waiting in the window, twittering to Earl and Sir Richard as she flew. She plunged into the great mound of little flowers, disappearing into them. She did not particularly approve of Earl's choice of repast, either.

"I hope Earl's … ah … table manners will not put you off breakfast." He shrugged with a little-boy-in-trouble expression that was nothing short of endearing.

"I am sure he will not take offense if I look the other way." Lydia chose a seat that allowed her to angle away from the hungry cockatrice.

"Not at all." Earl muttered through a mouthful.

"I doubt there is much that could put him off his feed." Sir Richard chuckled and placed a bowl of stewed plums near her plate.

Had he noticed how much she enjoyed them? She fought the urge to smile too much, rather unsuccessfully.

It did not seem to bother him, though. "I gather from your bonnet and reticule that you have decided to join my errand this morning?"

"I am not a woman to resist the opportunity to go shopping."

"Of course, you are not. I would hardly dare suggest such a thing." He pressed a hand to his chest, feigning a look of horror.

"What do you expect us to be interested in on this trip?"

"That is the problem. I do not exactly know. As I understand it, Mr. Mothman currently runs a form of haberdashery. I am not certain in what way the trade in dragon parts might appear there. But he might have a few lotions and potions about in anticipation of the new shop concept he wishes to attempt."

"So, I shall discreetly ask for such things as I peruse his goods. Have you ever heard of dragon scales used in jewelry or as spangles on gowns? I have heard of beetle shell used in that way and was just wondering."

"No, I have not, but it is a good idea … yes, a very good one. We should add that to the list of items to watch for. What about feather-scales? Might those find their way into finery as well?"

"Yes, that is a good thought. I will watch for those as well. We both should be adept at spotting those." She chuckled. "Have you heard back yet from Sir Edward? It has been more than a week now since you sent the messenger to London with samples from Mr. Keats' shop."

"Not yet. I suppose it takes time to identify all the materials we sent him. I do not know how it is done, but perhaps it is a time-consuming process. I will be sending another messenger today after our foray into Sheffield and will inquire of Sir Edward then."

"I do not mean to sound impatient …"

"But when there are matters of such importance afoot, it is prudent to follow up." He refilled his coffee cup and filled one for her, looking just a little smug that he had made her like his beverage of choice. "What do you think of Chisholm?"

"Lizzy's secretary? Once one gets accustomed to her seeming to appear out of nowhere, she is quite like Elizabeth—though it might not be good to be heard saying that too loudly."

"It is rather alarming to find Chisholm suddenly at one's elbow without ever seeing her approach."

"As I understand, that is why she did not have a placement until now—she frightened people too often. But Lizzy always expects dragons in the shadows, so Chisholm causes her no alarm. The rest of us will simply have to get accustomed to her—and that laugh! I have never heard a dragon laugh so much! It is quite endearing, though, as I love nothing so well as a good laugh."

"None in my acquaintance have ever laughed so readily, but truth be told, I think it is probably a good thing for our Lady Sage to have a good measure of laughter around her." He raised his mug toward Lydia and sipped.

"I believe it is good for everyone."

Half an hour later, Sir Richard helped Lydia into the Darcy coach, and they set off for Sheffield, Cosette tucked in amongst the flowers trimming her bonnet. After all that had happened at Ingleside, neither of them wanted to be without the help of a fairy dragon. Earl flew overhead, eyes open for hazards, especially any that might endanger Cosette. Such good friends they had become, nearly as close as April and Walker. It would be a shame to see them part when Sir Richard had to return to his duties at Netherford.

Now was not the time to dwell on such things. Focus on the pleasantness in life.

How clever Sir Richard was in his conversation. Always with a witty story or interesting fact to share. But he did not gossip. That was perhaps the most notable aspect of his conversation. Where most of his class were gossipmongers at heart, his religion seemed to be to avoid talking of others simply for sport. A trait the girl she had once been had not valued enough, but the girl she was now truly appreciated.

She had been spending a great deal of time with him lately. This was the second time she had been permitted to ride in the carriage alone with him. He was family to Sir Fitzwilliam, so that made it all right, but it was still a little thrilling, nonetheless. His eyes crinkled up at the sides when he smiled or laughed— which he did rather more than was strictly proper. A fact she was not about to criticize. Even more appealing was the way he sought her opinion and listened to her thoughts. Few had ever taken her so seriously. Lizzy would probably tell her that his attentions to her were the reason why she had begun to notice the little ways in which Sir Richard was truly handsome.

But that could hardly be true. Lydia had just not taken the time to notice before.

"What was your impression of Mr. Mothman? Is he a man you would want for a brother?" Sir Richard's long legs stretched across the carriage, his ankles crossed. Funny how he tended to slouch when Darcy and Lizzy were not about.

"There was a time when I was not sure I wanted Sir Fitzwilliam as a brother. You should take that into account when asking my opinion."

"Do you feel the same about Darcy now?"

"Hardly."

"Then I see fit to trust your judgement."

"Well, in that case," she sighed and chewed her lower lip. "I have rather mixed feelings about him."

"I am intrigued. Tell me more." He folded his hands across his lap and looked as though he expected her to say something sensible.

How few had ever looked at her that way. "I can see why Kitty likes him so much. He is bold and confident and pays her a great deal of attention. He is ambitious, which my father was not. I think she likes that, too. She has always secretly resented the way Papa failed to do anything to make us more marriageable. Perhaps she thinks he will be a better provider than Papa."

"I sense there is more."

"I confess I do not know much about such things, but it seemed odd and uncomfortable to me that Mr. Mothman should be so forward about his business and investing in it at a dinner party. I have always been taught that the topic was not considered polite conversation, particularly at a mixed table of ladies and gentlemen. Those are the kinds of things gentlemen talk about in a more private way. I have never heard my Uncle Gardiner bring up such things at a dinner, and he is quite successful in his business. I am quite certain he would never approach a man he has only barely been introduced to with requests for his money."

"He was rather forward, and I agree, it was not appropriate to the situation. A gentlemanly man does not discuss business in polite company."

"But I do not know what to make of it. I have heard some say one cannot expect good breeding from those 'in the lower orders.' But neither of my uncles are gentlemen, and they have much better manners than Mr. Mothman. I know they are always concerned for their businesses but not so much so as to declare it to a dinner party. Has Mr. Mothman simply not been taught, or does he know better but allow his ambition to get the better of him? And if so, what does that mean for his character?"

"Good questions. I have seen men like him before, and in general, I have no good opinion of them. Those who cannot control their impulses, their conversation, often show the same trait in other areas of their lives. I wonder to what he would stoop when trying to make a profit." His shoulders twitched as though he smelled something distasteful.

"When you put it in those terms, that is rather alarming."

"But then again, it could all be nothing. His is not the kind of business that is apt to trade in dragons. I could be just an alarmist, trained by Napoleon to see danger in every shadow."

"Who has accused you of that?"

A dark shadow crossed his face.

Lydia winced. "Siblings can be the least understanding, can they not?"

"I suppose a woman with four sisters, even ones as grand as Elizabeth and Mrs. Collins, would know."

"Are all your siblings older than you?"

"How could you tell?"

"There is something about being the youngest in a family that manages to make one particularly identifiable. I imagine Sir Fitzwilliam drives you to distraction at times, playing the role of the family eldest?"

Sir Richard choked back a laugh, coughing into his fist. How his hazel eyes twinkled.

"Offering you direction and advice which obviously you are far too silly or naïve to have been able to see for yourself."

"So, you are implying that Elizabeth is well matched with her husband?" He flashed his brows.

"It is good for them, I suppose. But I should not like to be with someone so … in charge, as it were. I may have learnt sobriety with Mrs. Fieldings, but I dearly love to laugh and even she could not change that."

"I would not have it any other way. I cannot imagine you without laughter." Gracious, that look!

Butterflies tickled her chest. She clasped her hands in her lap to not press them away and look silly and coy. Pray she might not giggle like a feather-pate!

"There, I think I see the shop." Sir Richard pointed through the side glass. "Near the corner of Windermere Road."

"Is that the River Sheaf?" Lydia pointed out the other side of the carriage, where a waterway more stream than river trundled past.

"I believe so. What are you thinking?"

"I am not sure yet. It just seems the sort of thing that could be useful to know. It is quite a good means of moving things from here to there, is it not? Especially at hours of day that 'good people' do not ordinarily travel."

"You impress me, Miss Bennet." He winked in a way that would have been considered flirtatious had anyone else done so.

Still, her cheeks burned, and she lowered her gaze a moment.

The carriage rolled to a stop, and he helped her down, giving the driver instructions to wait at the pub on the corner of the next street.

"Heavens, look at that sign!" Sir Richard chuckled and pointed with his chin at a man perched on a ladder, hanging a sign near the haberdasher's window.

A large green moth upon a pile of yellow fabric, with the name "Buzby's" in fancy red letters underneath.

"Bingley said that was Mothman's schoolboy nickname."

Lydia giggled through her fingers. "Perhaps it would have been better had it stayed so. But then again, Mothman is hardly a name that engenders a great deal of warmth and respect. At least Buzby is amusing."

"And it suggests he has a sense of humor, or at least of the absurd. It is not a bad thing if a man can laugh at himself."

Cosette landed on her shoulder. "Why would a man want to portray himself as a bug? Bugs are prey to those willing to eat them. They are fuzzy-tasting, nasty things. He must not be dominant."

"Your Friend makes a good point." Sir Richard scratched under Cosette's chin, barely brushing Lydia's cheek as he did.

Her cheeks burned—pray they did not color, too. Such a flirt he would think her if he noticed.

"Do you think you will be able to tell if he can hear dragons?" He leaned back into his own space once more.

"I am not as good at it as some, but I will try." Cosette hopped back onto Lydia's bonnet and tucked herself in amongst the flowers and ribbons, in a spot Lydia had designed specifically to conceal her. Sometimes it was quite convenient to be a particularly small fairy dragon.

"Whilst we are inside, Earl will chat with the local small dragons to see what he can learn."

Interesting, how much Elizabeth's travails had raised the status of fairy dragons. Sometimes good things could come out of very bad ones.

Sir Richard gestured toward the door. "Shall we?"

Lydia dipped in a tiny curtsey, and he opened the door for her, carefully avoiding the man hanging the sign. A bell on the door chimed merrily, announcing them.

Sunbeams poured through the large front window, bathing the generous room in warmth and light. How could she contain her smile? This was her favorite sort of shop: one with so many things to explore. So many bits and bobs she could use to create pretty things with what she could afford with her pocket money. In Meryton, new dresses were often out of the question. But with a clever turn of ribbon and trim, Jane's, Elizabeth's, Mary's, and Kitty's old things could be changed into something quite different.

Lydia closed her eyes a moment and drew in a deep breath. Hints of chemical smells, typical of dyes and sizing and starch; warm dust and dried flowers; a hint of perfumed soaps. Most of the smells she associated with her favorite haberdasheries. All her questions about Mr. Mothman aside, this was the kind of place she could feel exceedingly happy in.

"Sir Richard! Miss Lydia Bennet!"

Lydia jumped and opened her eyes to Mr. Mothman's exuberant approach.

"I am honored by your visit!" He approached them with extended open hands, something warm and expressive in his eyes.

"After you described your shop the other night, I could hardly wait to see it." Lydia clapped and squealed, just a little, mostly for the show of it. Mostly.

"That is quite the sign you have hanging outside." Sir Richard jerked his head toward it.

"You like it? My man just finished painting it. That is him hanging it."

"Is that not a task for a shop assistant?"

"I suppose, but Caney is clever with all manner of things. Quite an asset, really. I set him at any number of tasks and he seems to manage every one." Mr. Mothman seemed to watch Caney through the window as he took down the ladder and left with it tucked under his arm.

"Did your man have the painting of your sign as well?" Sir Richard asked.

"He did and designed it, too. I grant the image is a touch odd, but I find that a bit of humor intrigues customers and encourages them to visit." Mothman chuckled as if to prove his point. "Your sisters will be most jealous of you, you know. Neither of them has been to visit, yet. The Bingleys only rarely drive to Sheffield."

"Perhaps I will not tell her, then. I should not like her put out with me. It will be our secret for now."

Mr. Mothman's wink was a little dismissive, but hardly unexpected, given the circumstances. "Of course. My lips are sealed."

Did Sir Richard just roll his eyes?

"Is there anything particular you would like to see today?"

"Everything. Show me everything. Gloves and feathers and handkerchiefs!" She twirled about to take it all in. "I do not know if Kitty has told you that I am ever so clever with ribbons and lace. I always trimmed her bonnets for her and helped her remake gowns. It has been some time since I have had a new project, and I cannot wait to see what your wares inspire!"

"Lace, she would first like to see lace." Cosette's persuasive voice was definitely less raspy and irritating than that of larger dragons. Is that why fairy dragons were more persuasive?

Mr. Mothman cocked his head and narrowed his eyes, as though listening for something. He blinked, but did not fix his eyes on Lydia's bonnet. "I have a lovely selection of lace. It just came in but is not yet on display. Perhaps you would like to be the first to see it."

"I was only just thinking how much I hoped you had some pretty lace!" Lydia clasped her hands in front of her chest and bounced on her toes.

"Come along, then." He led them to a counter at the back of the store. Boxes and wrapped packages filled the shelves on the wall behind the counter. Below sat drawers of varying sizes and depths.

"I cannot wait to see. Have you buttons and beads in those drawers?"

"More than you can imagine."

"Oh, how I love buttons! My sisters think me silly, but I think buttons and beads are jewelry a dress wears. How dull and drab they can be without them."

"What a clever turn of phrase, Miss Bennet. I may use it myself. It will take me a moment to fetch the lace, so perhaps you might like to look at my button sampler whilst you wait." He reached below the counter and pulled out a board covered in padded linen, with various buttons sewn in columns and rows with tiny numbers embroidered below them. "I will be right back."

"Who would have imagined so many kinds of buttons?" Sir Richard peered over her shoulder.

"I have rarely seen a selection so broad! Even when Aunt Gardiner was helping us to trim our Cotillion gowns, I never saw a selection like this!" Lydia ran her hand over the board, relishing the feel of each button beneath her fingers.

Those were bone, carved in clever shapes and dyed. But there would hardly be a call to use dragon bone for that. It was too hard and difficult to carve and did not take dye well, according to —who had told her that? Perhaps it was Uncle or Aunt Gardiner. Maybe Sir Edward? "These are horn, I think. Well carved, very regular." Round and slightly translucent in various shades of brown. "These round, faceted black ones are jet—very fashionable for mourning wear."

"What of these?" Sir Richard pointed to several sizes of thin, shimmery buttons. "Could they be …"

"No, these are shell, probably oyster, maybe mussel."

"These?" He hesitated to touch the swirled blue-green-and-gold disks.

"Abalone shell."

"You are certain?"

"I know buttons, sir." She glared, albeit playfully. "There is nothing of questionable origin among these. And more than a few that I would enjoy having myself."

"Ah, did I hear the sound of someone pleased with my wares?" Mr. Mothman trundled toward them with a large box in his arms.

"You have a fine collection of buttons. Probably the best I have ever seen."

"How many will you need for the gown you were talking about?" Richard asked, catching her eyes directly.

"Give me a moment to think." Why would he want to buy buttons when she was certain they had nothing to do with the dragon trade? Could he tell her heart was beating faster? "The sleeves will need six of this size and the bodice will require perhaps a dozen of these."

"I shall wrap them up for you while you have a look at the lace." He opened the box, revealing so many lengths of lace. So many varieties and sizes. Handmade crochet lace. French Chantilly bobbin lace, Belgian Point de Gaze. What would it be like to be able to afford such things? One should not drool over such goods, should one?

Certainly, no dragons would have been involved in the making of the lace, which was a good thing. But dragon smuggling was not the only sort going on in England, and the Order did not look kindly on its members being connected to anything nefarious.

20
Chapter

June 23, 1815

RICHARD SAT AT the writing desk in his guest room and stared at the blank piece of paper. Still blank. No words had suddenly appeared since he had last checked. Just the scent of fresh paper and an old bottle of ink.

Blast and botheration!

Three candles lit the room, though one might argue whether it was actually dark enough to warrant candles. Darcy was a generous man, though. He would not begrudge Richard the candles. Besides, the extra light helped him think, or at least it usually did.

Somehow today, though, the flickering shadows against the oak-paneled walls of the room he always used at Pemberley danced and darted and dithered about, demanding he not look away. They ducked around the press and behind the oak bed posts, under the comfortable chair near the fireplace, only to appear again on the floor. Fickle, like little flittering fairies. The soft evening breeze, with traces of sheep and grass, laughed at him as it carried about its business of stirring the flames.

It was not as though he were an illiterate man. It was not as though he were unable to write a simple report. It was not as though he were writing a letter of condolence that he dreaded writing. It was just a bloody simple report to the Blue Order.

And still, the words would not come.

Damn, he hated being so distracted.

He pushed away from the desk and stretched his arms wide, expanding his chest and taking a deep breath. A little like Earl when getting ready for flight. Focus, he simply needed to focus.

But how was he to do that?

If only he knew what to make of her. But how did one understand a woman like Lydia Bennet?

At the haberdashery she was all intolerable, silly little girl, bouncing and cooing over fripperies, the epitome of the feather-pated female that he dreaded. But as soon as they were away in the carriage, a transformation of truly mythic proportions took place. She became all sober intelligence and good sense. Granted, she claimed theatrical experience from her time at Mrs. Fieldings', but one did not expect so dramatic an alteration in the very fabric of her being.

Perhaps that was being overdramatic, but somehow it felt quite true. And quite unnerving.

Who was this young woman? Was she the woman he sat with in the carriage, sensibly discussing the dreadful possibility that Mothman could be a trader in dragon parts? With her deftly arguing both sides of the matter, playing devil's advocate, as it were, and with great skill as well. Helping him see the matter more broadly and come to much more reliable conclusions. Absolutely uncanny in her instincts for identifying what was important.

Or was she the silly, simpering girl, ridiculously excited for a packet of buttons that he had bought her?

He shook his head and dragged his hand down his face. Yes, he had bought them for her. Not with the Blue Order's money, but with his own. They had not actually had to buy anything on their visit to Mothman, but from the look in her eyes when she saw those buttons, he had to.

Why did he have to?

Because he recognized that look of longing in a youngest child who would be forgotten in favor of the elder, more important ones. And the pure joy in her eyes when he handed them to her touched a place within he had forgotten was even there.

But why did he care in the first place? What was she to him?

What indeed?

She was sister to his cousin's wife. Not exactly family, but perhaps uncomfortably close. Close enough that Darcy and Elizabeth's opinions would matter in whatever course he took.

Perhaps he needed to talk to them.

But what would he tell Darcy? Elizabeth? "I fancy your sister. What do you think of that?"

He cringed as he scrubbed his stubbled cheeks with his palms. No, he would never say that to either of them. How ghastly.

And it was not precisely that he fancied her anyway. Not in the sense it was usually meant.

She was not the sort of woman one "fancied". The silly, button-loving girl might be fancied, but not the woman he conferred with regarding their mission. She was smart, and sensible, and wickedly funny at times. She did not look at him as the 'younger brother' with only his connections to offer. In her eyes, he was a gentleman in his own right, with a fine estate and a dragon she actually wanted to know better—and apologize to for her own foolishness back in Hertfordshire.

She wanted to know Netherford! That should not be as important to him as it was. Then again, he was a Keeper and his dragon's opinion mattered. And if she wanted Netherford's good opinion, that could hardly be a bad thing.

What was more, Earl liked her and her Friend very well. Since Cosette offered Earl the same hero worship April gave to Walker, who could blame him? But it still felt significant that they should be so amiable with one another.

Yet, she did not come from Richard's class of people. Her dowry was well below what he should even consider. And her family—it was half-Blue at best. Her father, despite being a Blue Order officer, was neither an excellent Keeper nor good manager of his family. Those were considerations, too.

But should they be? Especially when in nearly all other aspects, she was a desirable prospect ... if she would even consider him in the first place. Her connection to Darcy and Elizabeth alone was enough to garner her a reasonable amount of attention in the

Blue Order marriage mart, where there were gentlemen with a good deal more to offer than he.

Enough! Enough!

He had to get a message written and into the claws of a messenger tonight. It would never happen if he did not focus.

He returned to the desk, dipped his pen, and dashed words onto the page as fast as he could. It might not be the most literary of creations, but it would do for his purposes well enough.

A fist pounded his door.

He jumped and left a large blot on the bottom of the page. "Come in!" He slammed his pen down on the blotter and stomped to the door. "What do you want?"

The door swung open to reveal Mr. St. John in all his squinty, paunchy glory.

Dragons' blood!

"What do you need?" He probably should not have snarled. That was not good form.

St. John glowered, but held his tongue a moment, as though carefully composing his answer. Candlelight glinted off his high forehead as he peered into the room. "Your brother the viscount has denied me access to the estate records at Matlock. Threatened me with bodily harm should I set foot on the estate again."

Bloody hell—then again, St. John probably deserved it.

Richard trudged to the fireplace and fell into a generously stuffed chair. "Sit." He pointed vaguely at the chair behind the writing desk in the far corner of the room.

St. John dragged the chair a polite distance from Richard's and sat. The wooden chair groaned beneath him. "What are you going to do about this?"

"Me? What do you expect me to do? You seem to be carrying the illusion that I have some connection, some authority with Matlock."

"You are one of Matlock's sons." The edge of St. John's nose pulled back in what was most certainly a sneer.

Richard leaned back and crossed his arms. "The youngest son. There has never been a day that my brother recognized me as anything but a 'spare' in the family line. A spare among other spares."

"You do realize the damage he is doing to Matlock's reputation? Not to mention, he is in violation of the Accords."

"I fully recognize all of that."

"And yet you do nothing." Such condemnation in his rather piggy eyes.

"What would you have me do?" Richard pounded his chair's arms with his fists.

"Talk some sense into—"

"If I had that power, do you think Matlock would be in the situation it is in now?"

That seemed to give St. John pause. "Have you tried—"

Richard brought his foot down hard on the wooden floor. "Before your first meeting with him, I tried. Every year when I make my regular pilgrimage to the family seat, I have tried. Darcy has tried. He will not see reason."

"And Chancellor Matlock? Why has he not taken oversight—"

"That is a question you will have to ask my father. I am not about to insert myself into the middle of that."

"Why not?"

"Because my family seems to think my aim is to replace my brother as junior Keeper and to get Matlock territory for myself! I am tired of trying to prove myself innocent of that allegation, and nothing you can say will cause me to ask for those accusations again."

St. John scratched behind his ear, rather like a fat lap dog. "That is absurd. You have a Keep of your own. You could not become Keeper to another dragon."

"You noticed? How good of you. Perhaps you would be a good chap and explain the matter to my insecure older brother."

"So, you really have no sway there?"

"Get out. If that is all you have to say, get out." Richard pointed to the door.

"Do you understand the depth of the problem at Matlock?"

"I can make a good guess, and beyond that I do not want to know."

"You are comfortable with the ignominy about to befall your family?"

"No, I am not. And frankly, I think you should think very carefully if you intend to bring down the Chancellor of the Order." Richard clenched his fists.

"You would protect your father, under these circumstances?"

"I would protect the Order and, to the degree protecting the Order means protecting him, yes, I would. For all his vast faults, my father is a good administrator and has served as one of the best Chancellors the Order has ever seen. Imperfect, to be sure, and we often knock heads, but I would be a shortsighted fool if I failed to recognize how he has advanced the Order and made it stronger than it was when he took office."

St. John broke eye contact and stared at one of the flickering candles.

"Have you conveniently forgotten those facts? Why are you so hell-bent on destabilizing the heart of the draconic world?"

"If all estates were run as Matlock—do you understand the danger to the Kingdom?"

Richard sprang to his feet but forced himself to turn away from St. John. "Do you know how many estates are run worse than Matlock, and yet, the Order stands?"

"You suggest, then, we should simply disregard the charters and the treaty? They are unimportant and optional?"

"Do not put words in my mouth! It is a travesty that Derbyshire has been allowed—" No, he should not mention the smugglers to this man, of all people! "—estates in Derbyshire have been managed poorly, and that must be rectified. But that can, it should, take place without precipitating the fall of the Order entirely."

"You think that is my goal?"

"Your actions have made it easy to believe that to be the case."

St. John rose to pace the window-side wall, his heavy footfalls echoing off the paneling. "My goal is to preserve the Order, in whatever way necessary.

Whether you believe that or not is hardly my concern. My loyalty is to the Order, and it always has been."

The man protested too much.

St. John turned and caught Richard's gaze. "At the least, you must stop interfering with the messengers I send to the Order."

Richard's feet turned leaden, and he rooted in place, cold prickles cascading along the back of his neck. "What are you talking about?"

"I received word from Secretary Lord Chudleigh today, demanding updates. It seems none of the messengers I have sent have made it through to London."

"Pendragon's bones! What exactly did Chudleigh have to say?"

"That I was derelict in my duties, not having communicated my findings over the last several weeks. And your precious father was quite put out." St. John's eyes narrowed, which hardly seemed possible. "I must say it seems clever of you not to have sent any messages yourself, either, making this appear to be a problem in Derbyshire, not your own work of sabotage."

Richard leapt toward him, stopping an arm's length away. "How dare you! I may dislike you and your methods, but I would not stoop to sabotaging my own people! I can only imagine the messages I have sent to London myself have gone missing, too. I have been awaiting important replies for days now!"

"What message would you be sending to the Order?" St. John's eyes narrowed, and he folded his arms over his chest.

"None of your bloody business." The implication of this news! "There is clearly nothing I can do for you on the matter of Matlock, so it is best you leave now. There is work I need to accomplish." He pushed St. John out and strode straight to Darcy's office.

Richard flung open the door so hard it hit the wall behind it. Walker squawked and flapped hard enough to rock the old iron dragon perch near Darcy's enormous desk.

Early-evening sun poured through the west-facing windows and bathed the room in a warm glow that should have been soothing, especially in the well-ordered space. But little, except perhaps throttling St. John, would ease his nerves.

"Richard!" Darcy jumped up from his desk, knocking an open book onto the floor. "You look a fright! What happened?"

"The problem is what has not happened. I just had a most illuminating talk with St. John."

Walker warbled a sour note.

"Sit. Sit." Darcy pointed at a padded wooden chair near the enormous desk. "What are you talking about?"

Richard stood behind the chair, hands clutching its back. "Apparently Undersecretary St. John has gotten word from London that none of the anticipated correspondence from Pemberley or Matlock has reached the Order."

"None of it?" Darcy's eyes widened as his jaw dropped, and he took on that faraway look that meant he was thinking rapidly. "That would explain why I have not yet heard back from the Minister of Keeps. The situation at Pemberley is the very thing that should have moved him to quick action."

"Apparently St. John has been scolded soundly for not making timely reports to the Secretary. He accused me of tampering with the messages—to protect Matlock's reputation, of all things! After insisting I should be able to go there and make all things right, but that is another matter entirely."

"Dragons' blood!" Darcy slammed his fist on the desktop. "What do you make of this, Walker?"

Walker paced along the dragon perch, bobbing his head with each step, wings spread and tail held slightly elevated, so as not to overbalance the ironwork. "Troubling, deeply troubling. Such a thing could not happen easily. Those messengers are carefully vetted. I know each one of them personally, and approved them myself. It is unthinkable that they could all have abandoned their duties. Nor could all of them have fallen to natural hazards—it takes a great deal to bring down a determined cockatrice. I fear the worst. They have been intentionally targeted." He jumped from the perch to the desktop and flipped open a book, scratching at the pages with his talons.

Walker could read? Why had he never known that before?

"What manner of operation could manage that? What would it take to interfere with messengers of the caliber of the Blue Order's?" Richard's knuckles turned white.

"Bowmen of some form—rifles are too loud, too likely to attract attention. But they would have to know where the messengers were launching from and keep an active watch for them. I think it unlikely that warm-bloods are the ones to have brought them down. With the heightened security at Pemberley, I do not see how warm-bloods could have remained hidden here. Matlock is a different matter." Walker stared at the page he had opened.

"Could there be two groups—" Darcy ran his knuckles along his chin.

"No, I think not. But there must be dragons involved, winged ones— cockatrice I expect— perhaps working with drakes or wyrms on the ground," Richard said.

"Is this related to the trade in dragon parts?" Darcy eased back into his seat.

"It is difficult to say. I am still trying to wrap my head around why the messengers from Matlock and Pemberley would be stopped." Richard dropped down into the chair.

Walker turned to Richard. "It may not be nearly that complicated. The discovery of the Ring Wyrm's injuries may have something to do with it, though. Earl stopped a band of wild-born cockatrice from finishing off the knucker, yes?"

"He did. Quite smartly."

"Then that would be the simplest answer. That band was recorded in this old census, but not since. I expect they have been avoiding notice since Old Pemberley's dotage. In the intervening years, they have gotten accustomed to having their way and now they are taking revenge for Earl's interfering with an especially hearty meal. They cannot directly act against the estate, but taking down other cockatrice in their territory is not entirely illegal. Especially if they claim to be protecting their territory against intruders."

"You do not think this is related to the trade in dragon parts?" Darcy asked.

"I do not know. I only suggest that the simplest explanation is that it is not." Walker squawked as though he were not entirely happy with the answer.

"Even if you are correct, then does this not indicate another new problem to manage? Wild-born cockatrice skirting the rule of law as though it does not apply to them?" Richard asked.

"The Blue Order has been dancing around that issue for decades. It is nothing new, just something ignored as much as possible for its inconvenience." Walker growled softly. "Our best hope is in trying to find those messengers or their remains. If it was wild dragons, I doubt their messages will have been disturbed in any meaningful way. If they have been …"

"Those messages you sent—" Darcy asked the rest of the question with his eyes wide and face pale.

"Breathe easy. They were all in cipher. Old habits die hard. I think it unlikely anyone would be able to break the cipher in a timely fashion. Sir Edward is the only one with the patience to decipher them."

"Even if it is just as you said, security needs to be improved," Darcy replied "The band may be emboldened by their success and begin to interfere with the livestock and the farms as well. This could get worse quickly. Vicontes Pemberley must be informed."

The young dragon would be none too happy and might be tempted to take matters into her own talons. That would surely make matters worse. Lovely, just bloody lovely.

Darcy stood. "Walker, gather Pemberley's dragons. There is a great deal to be done."

21
Chapter

June 26, 1815

ELIZABETH SAT IN the nursery rocking chair, Anne dozing on her shoulder and tatzelwurm May curled in her lap, purring. Was there anything more delightful than the scent of a sleeping baby? Soft sunlight and a comfortably warm breeze filled the white attic with a peace no other room in Pemberley possessed. The steady, gentle creak of the rocker eased her soul, a wordless lullaby sung only here, only now. If only she could only spend the rest of the day here, drifting in this soporific space, between waking and dreaming, where the world did not otherwise exist.

How she wished the world did not exist.

She and Darcy were still debating the merits of moving the nursery downstairs to a suite in the family wing. With the wall of windows and the distance from the rest of the goings-on, the nursery felt somehow less secure than the rest of the house, even with Axel stationed inside the door and another guard drake in the corridor just beyond. Elizabeth vacillated between concerns that it was too much and not enough. So did Darcy.

Pemberley estate had seemed so much safer than London, offering a panacea for all that was wrong in the Blue Order world. How incredibly naïve, even foolish she had been.

Walker had stationed a pair of cockatrice guards on the roof near the nursery. He seemed satisfied that four guard dragons, plus the three nursery dragons inside, would suffice to keep little Anne safe. Mrs. Sharp agreed, insisting that Mercy and Truth were far more formidable protectors than they might appear to be. Zaltys had a fierce bite when provoked and their bites were laden with a paralyzing venom that would subdue anything smaller than a wyvern.

A fact that ought to be added to the new bestiary, and perhaps a monograph on the species. Perhaps Chisholm could help her get that written.

Anne stirred and sighed in her sleep. Only in the last week or so had her schedule and her sleep finally settled into a calm and predictable pattern that rendered her happy and content most of the time. Perhaps, on the strength of Walker's recommendations, they should leave the nursery as it was. At least for today.

Elizabeth laid Anne in her crib and May spring-hopped up to join her, soothing the transition with her purrs. Such a dear and loyal Friend she was.

Elizabeth closed the nursery door behind her and tapped Mrs. Sharp's door to let her know she was leaving.

April, turquoise-blue feather-scales glinting in the sunbeam, met her in the corridor. "Is all well?"

"Yes, it is. I suppose I did linger a little longer than usual."

"Pemberley wants to talk to you. She is not happy."

Elizabeth rubbed her temples as she trudged toward the stairs. "I imagine not."

"More than not happy, she is angry. Very angry. Working herself into a temper. You should be prepared." April landed on Elizabeth's shoulder and nuzzled her neck.

"I suppose it is not surprising. This is a great deal to try to manage. None of us really considered all the ramifications of a baby dragon holding this kind of territory."

"It is unprecedented. Raven is already working on how to tell the story far and wide. She said there is none like it in the kingdom. It is good she is favorably disposed toward Pemberley. Such harm an alarming rendering of the story could do." April shuddered.

"I imagine so." Elizabeth swallowed hard. Was it too much to hope that Raven's story would have a happy ending, and not be some horrid fairy story where the hero and the dragon meet some dreadful end?

"Dearling, may I come down and see you?" Elizabeth asked from the top of the narrow wooden stairs, over the barking alerts from Puppy. The scent of dragon fire lingered near the cellar door, mingling with the faint smoke from Elizabeth's burning candle. Apparently, April had not exaggerated Pemberley's distress.

The candlelight faded as it trickled down the stairs, leaving the cellar a large, black void beyond. Pemberley poked her head into the candlelight. "Why you take so long? I need talk you."

"I told you she was angry." April twittered and zipped down ahead of Elizabeth.

"I am here now. I was putting Anne down for her nap." Elizabeth hurried down the stairs, the light slowly enveloping Pemberley.

Merciful heavens! Tendrils of smoke floated from Pemberley's nostrils, leaving the cellar air hazy with her rage.

"Pray tell me what is wrong."

"You not know? How can you not know?" Pemberley flapped hard enough to send April off course and retreating to the safety of Elizabeth's shoulder.

"I know generally the problem, but I need for you to tell me precisely what is troubling you right now." Elizabeth stopped at the base of the stairs. Best give Pemberley space to express herself.

"Everything wrong with my territory! I not know how fix. How keep my dragons safe?"

"We do not yet know that the messengers were hurt in your territory."

Pemberley turned aside and belched an angry spurt of flame, tail slapping the hard-packed dirt floor. Puppy yipped and skittered out of her way. "Do not plac …placatate … just try make me feel better."

"I am not placating you. It is true. Ask Walker."

"But it could have happened here, and I not know it. That problem. You know it true. I never knowed danger of wild dragons. Why not told?"

"Honestly, it is because we never considered the issue ourselves."

"But you Keepers!"

"Yes, we are Keepers, but our situation is so different to other Keepers. There is no other hatchling in England with a full territory. And my father has found nothing of it in the histories, either. We are quite literally writing an entirely new book of Dragon Keeping together, as exciting and frightening as that is. There are certain to be things that we do not anticipate. Like the wild cockatrice."

"I no like." Pemberley stomped. "I want know what to do. I want be good dragon. Have good territory. Is important."

"Of course, it is. Tremendously important."

"Then how do it?" Pemberley stomped with both front feet.

"We are learning as we go. We are reading, and seeking help from the Ministry of Keeps. We will figure this out."

"Seek help! That is good. I know how do that. Rosings will help. Matlock will help! Matlock is close. I talk Matlock."

Oh, merciful heavens! "He is busy with matters of his own territory right now. It might not be the appropriate time—"

"Is right time for me. I need help. I talk Matlock. I go Matlock now."

"Wait, no! Pray wait for one of us to take you. Tomorrow, perhaps. I will send word to Matlock and ask the cownt if he might see us then."

"No, too long. Too long. Need talk now. I go now. You not stop me. I go myself. Know the way. Know better than fly there. Can walk. You not stop me." She thumped her tail hard on the packed dirt floor.

"You will not be able to stop her," April whispered. "I can go through the tunnels with her. Let me bring Cosette as well. She can fly back to let you know of our safe arrival."

"I accept. Fairy dragons can come with. You stay, work on your workings here. I need be dragon of Pemberley. I will be. Quick, April. I want go now." Pemberley settled her wings across her back, peaceful in the wake of a settled decision.

April zipped off before Elizabeth could stop her.

"I still do not like it. You know Cownt Matlock can be cross and cranky and sharp with everyone, even with you. You do not like it when he scolds and growls."

"No, I no like. But I can growl too. I will growl if he mean to me. I walk from London with him. I know Cownt. He not hurt me." She bumped her head against Elizabeth's hand. "If he scold, he scold. Not new. But he knows what I need know and will tell it me."

Elizabeth hugged Pemberley to her, "But you are such a young dragon for such a big responsibility."

"Not matter my size, territory need what territory need. If I not hold it properly, it need dragon who can. I will be that dragon. That why I fight Bolsover."

Elizabeth's eyes prickled and burned, not just from the smoke. "You are every bit as stubborn as Keeper, you know that?"

"Am proud of stubborn. It good for dragon be stubborn when dragon right. I right. You know I right."

Elizabeth rested her chin on the top of Pemberley's head. "Yes, I know you are."

April and Cosette buzzed in, Lydia trailing down the stairs behind them.

"We are ready." April hovered beside Pemberley, Cosette just behind her.

"I go now. Will stay tunnels. April and Cosette will help, make you feel better. I return when I know what I need know." Pemberley bumped Elizabeth once more and waddled regally toward the dragon tunnel, fairy dragons in her wake.

There were moments, like now, where there was no doubt at all that Rosings was Pemberley's brood mother and Chudleigh her mentor. How formidable she was becoming! Elizabeth dragged her sleeve across her eyes.

Lydia watched from the base of the stairs. "You must be proud of her. She is a fine dragon, even if she is so young."

"I am proud, to be sure. But I am also afraid. Matlock will be in no humor for company. He is hardly personable on the best of days, and when I saw him most recently, he was—high dudgeon does not begin to describe it."

"It will ease his pride to have her seeking his advice. That will improve his mood considerably."

"I had not thought of that, but you do have a point. Who does not like to be turned to as a source of wisdom and counsel?" The tightness in Elizabeth's chest eased a bit. "I appreciate Cosette helping Pemberley."

"She takes after April a great deal. But she is learning some self-control. Did I tell you? When Sir Richard and I went to Sheffield, she managed to keep herself concealed in my bonnet the entire time. Mr. Mothman never noticed her."

Elizabeth's lungs clenched at the name. "He was susceptible to persuasion, yes? That is what you told me."

"Yes, and he gave no sign that he suspected her suggestions were anything but his own thoughts. Never even looked at my hat a second time. We are as certain as we can be that he is dragon-deaf, and there was nothing draconic anywhere in his shop, not even the cosmetics."

"Thank heavens." Elizabeth stepped back and leaned against the stair rail. "I cannot say I particularly like the man, but I would be happy not to have a reason to forbid Kitty's betrothal. I do not think Mama could tolerate that."

Lydia laughed even as she grimaced. "I do not even want to imagine how she would react to that. She was hardly subtle in telling Mr. Darcy that he should approve very quickly and how she would never see him again should he disapprove."

Elizabeth pressed her cool palms to burning cheeks. "I know we might have been the only other ones to hear her say that, but it was mortifying nonetheless. To think of trying to manipulate him so—and with such a thing as the pleasure of her company! I have never been so embarrassed."

"Oh, I think perhaps you have been. When Mama suggested a lovely wedding gift would be for Mr. Darcy to invest in Mr. Mothman's business venture?"

Elizabeth covered her face with her hand. "You are right. I had put that out of my mind. It was dreadful. I am thankful that my husband is a patient, gracious man."

Lydia giggled. "I think even he would be surprised to hear that description applied to himself."

"It is true, nonetheless."

"Oh, I almost forgot. I am such a goose! Raven came in a few minutes ago. Unfortunately, she was reporting that there was no news from the northwest side of the estate, where Brutus and his team are searching. She said she was going to check on Kingsley's team on the northeast side next."

"She has been such a help, with such a phenomenal memory for details." Elizabeth closed her eyes and pinched her temples.

"I know it is difficult waiting here, feeling like we are doing nothing. It is so much like the feelings in London when we were trying to find you. I cannot say it was something I expected to experience again, much less here." Lydia laid her hand on Elizabeth's arm. "Perhaps messengers from Earl's or Walker's teams on the south side will bring news soon. You know they are doing all they can."

"I know. Just the thought of a vindictive band of wild cockatrice is so distressing."

"You are not used to dragons being dangerous and frightening, are you?" Lydia's brow lifted in an uncomfortably knowing expression.

Elizabeth pressed her knuckles to her lips and shook her head. "Not usually, no."

"I hope you will forgive me for saying the sort of thing you would tell me: perhaps this is not such a bad thing."

"I should recall what this feels like and use the experience to better understand how the typical dragon-hearer experiences dragons," Elizabeth said in her best imitation of Lydia's voice, and rolled her eyes just a bit. "You are right, I do not like it, and I would like to snipe at you and tell you that you are insensitive and wrong. But you are not. I suppose it is something I need to remember more. Even if I do not like it."

At least Lydia did not gloat. "What can be done about the wild dragons? I do not quite understand how the Order interacts with those dragons who are not—"

Taloned feet scrambled down the wooden cellar steps.

"Lady Sage! Lady Sage!" Chisholm jumped down the last three steps and landed at Elizabeth's feet. The small bag on her back bearing her notebook and pencil flew open, nearly spilling its contents.

A green puck followed, almost knocking Chisholm over as she landed. Who … wait, yes, that was Fern, the young maid's Friend. Slightly larger—the size of a hunting dog—and more dominant than the other pucks of the household, Fern had taken the role of lead puck in the manor. Steady and sensible, her presence made the household much better.

"Pray forgive the intrusion, but this is important. At least, I think it is. No, I am sure of it." Poor, chattering Chisholm! Something must have disturbed her routine. That always sent her into a tumult.

Elizabeth crouched and extended her hand toward the agitated dragons. Both turned their heads, presenting their cheeks for a calming scratch. "Take a deep breath and tell me the situation."

"I was working on the notes for the *Household Dragon Hierarchy* monograph." Chisholm stood on her back legs, worrying her front paws together. "And I went to consult with Fern on a hoarding matter when she showed me something I was certain you must see."

"Do not be angry with me, Lady Sage. It is my right to take papers that are tossed into a cold fireplace. I did not violate any household agreement." Fern's frill lifted, gossamer pale-green lace spread open behind her head, rather like a fancy mobcap. "I found it in the fireplace, all crumples and wrinkles, in a little ball."

"What did you find?"

"I unfolded it and smoothed it, and then I found it."

"What did you find?"

"I showed it to Chisholm, and she said you needed to see it."

"What is it? You must tell me."

Chisholm fumbled in her bag and produced a ragged piece of paper. "See what is written here."

Elizabeth peered closely at the spidery marks on the paper. What had probably been words were scratched out and beyond reading. But at the bottom corner, a mark of loops and scrolls. "Lydia, is this what I think it is?"

"Dragons' bones! That is a snapdragon!"

Elizabeth stood slowly, head spinning, hands shaking, and dragged in several deep breaths. "From which fireplace did you retrieve this piece of paper?" There had to be a rational explanation for this. Richard, it must be Richard, from some of his work. Yes, it had to be.

"Please, Lady, I did not cross the house rules. You must believe me." Fern's hood colored to a reddish-brown.

"You have done well, Fern. I am not in any way angry with you. I am proud of your help, but I must know, in which fireplace did you find this?"

"In the guest rooms, Lady."

Yes, that must mean it was from Richard—

"The one the man you do not like stays in."

Pendragon's bones! The cellar spun around her. She braced her palm on the cold, packed dirt lest she fall.

"You have both done well. Lydia, would you take them to the stillroom where Uncle Gardiner's special dragon-favorite beetles are kept and see they both have a share. And pray tell Mrs. Reynolds and Agnes that Fern is excused from her duties the rest of the day as well. I know it is not much, but I want you to be certain of my appreciation of your efforts today. Pray excuse me. I must see my husband immediately."

Chapter 22

THE AIR IN Darcy's office all but crackled with tension. Even the temperature seemed to climb. It was a good thing that Father's solid desk stood between Darcy and Undersecretary St. John and that Richard stood by as a sober reminder that Darcy needed to keep his temper in check.

It might have been even better to have Walker in attendance as well, but then again, St. John's current attitude might have strained the cockatrice's patience to the breaking point. Perhaps it was just as well Walker was on patrol.

"I demand to speak with Pemberley. It is my right in the fulfillment of my duty." St. John slapped the desktop, his face turning red.

"I am not stopping you from doing so. You will recall that Mrs. Reynolds' Friend Dale looked for her and discovered she has gone to Matlock to speak with the cownt regarding managing her territory. She is simply not here for you to speak to." Darcy held his ground behind his desk. He would not be driven to untoward outbursts by this man. Not today.

St. John parked his hands on the desk and leaned toward Darcy. "You sent her away so that I would not be able to speak to her. You are willfully interfering with my duties."

"I have done no such thing." Deep breath. Control. "You can ask the Dragon Sage—"

"Who I find to be as adversarial toward me as you are!"

"You can hardly blame her for that." Richard snorted, lip curled back.

St. John whirled to face Richard. "I most certainly can hold her accountable—"

"Will you be accountable, then, for your wrongs against her?" Darcy asked. "If you will, then perhaps we might have a profitable discussion."

"I do not apologize for my reasonable attempts to protect the Order from—"

The door flew open. Elizabeth burst in with the fury of an angry firedrake, a faint odor of smoke lingering over her. How did she do that?

"What is the meaning of this?" She slammed a dirty, crumpled piece of paper on the desk.

"My privacy has been violated! Who stole this from my chambers?" St. John tried to snatch the paper off the desk.

Darcy slammed his hand on it, possibly growling as he did.

"A staff dragon, who has permission to take discarded papers, found it. The evidence was gathered legally. Do not pretend otherwise." Elizabeth looked ready to tear his throat out with her teeth.

"Evidence of what?" Darcy studied the ragged document. "Pendragon's bones!" He came around the desk and handed it to Richard, well out of St. John's reach.

"Bloody hell! What are you doing with a snapdragon on your correspondence?" Richard pushed it back at Darcy as he advanced on St. John.

St. John backed away, toward the door. "It is none of your concern. I will not have my privacy violated. My bags will be packed within the hour and I will be away from here quite gladly. That does not change the fact that I must speak to Pemberley and—"

Elizabeth sidestepped to block the door.

Richard grabbed St. John by the lapels and shoved him against the wall beside her. "You are not going anywhere until you explain the bloody snapdragon on your correspondence."

"It is a not a matter that relates to you."

"By decree of the Chancellor himself, yes, it is. And if you do not explain yourself immediately, I will slap you in irons and drag you before him myself."

Richard had brought irons with him. Interesting, and just within the realm of possibility.

St. John's jaw dropped, and with it, his bravado. "What does the Chancellor know of snapdragons?"

"What do you know of them?" Richard forced St. John back into a chair near the desk.

St. John glanced from Richard to Darcy, carefully avoiding meeting Elizabeth's eyes. "It is a private matter that I have been investigating."

"Investigating? You are investigating it? Why?"

"It is a private matter. I have no wish to discuss it with you. Any of you." St. John gazed at the floor.

Spongy, smothering silence expanded to fill the office with thick, heavy air.

Elizabeth moved behind the desk and leaned over it, speaking close to St. John's face. "Might it have something to do with Rottenstone? Perhaps something following his demise?"

What was she thinking?

St. John's head snapped up, and he gaped at Elizabeth. "What would you know of that?"

"Nothing, exactly. I am just hypothesizing. If the matter has something to do with Richard's commission from the Chancellor, then perhaps you might have gotten involved because of Rottenstone."

"I am not involved. I am investigating."

"Investigating? I find that an interesting choice of words. One which needs, nay, demands, immediate explanation." Darcy edged over to press his shoulder to Elizabeth's.

"You had best tell us what happened, Mr. St. John, lest Richard act on his instincts and haul you before the Minister of the Court on charges you would not want even mentioned in the same sentence as your name." Elizabeth's voice was so soft and calm. Few knew that it was her most dangerous tone.

"I have done nothing wrong."

"What precisely have you not done?" Richard towered over him.

"Shortly after Rottenstone's passing," St. John swallowed hard as he looked away, blinking hard, "after he passed, I had to make arrangements for his earthly remains. I was approached—"

Elizabeth gasped, fist pressed to her mouth. "No, it cannot …"

"A man came to my residence, ostensibly to offer condolences over the loss of my Friend. My very good Friend." St. John lifted his eyes, briefly glaring at each in turn. "But I had never met him before. He asked impertinent questions, including where and when and how my Friend might be interred."

Elizabeth, rapidly losing color, grabbed the edge of the desk. Darcy gently maneuvered her into his chair.

"He sounded every inch like a despicable resurrectionist, and I told him as much. He denied it, naturally, insisting that he only wanted to pay his respects. However, he was interested in researching the properties of dragon scales and the like. Perhaps there might be some remnant of Rottenstone left that he might have towards that purpose. I refused, of course, and directed him to Sir Edward, through whom all such research must pass. The man backed off, but gave me his calling card in case I should change my mind. And made some mention that funds might be offered in exchange for my help." Sweat trickled down the side of St. John's face. He dabbed it away with his shoulder.

"Have you that card?" Richard seemed poised to declare him a liar.

St. John fumbled with his pocket and placed the worn, dog-eared card on the desk. It bore the mark of the snapdragon. "It will come as no surprise to you that the name is false and the address is that of an abandoned cottage between Sheffield and Chesterfield. But the post office has recently told me that occasional missives and packages are left at that address and appear to be retrieved rather promptly." St.

John folded his arms across his chest. "What interest is the sign of the snapdragon to you?"

The Royal Mail? Could the smugglers really be that bold?

A conversation of looks and postures passed between Darcy, Richard, and Elizabeth.

"Does anyone in the Order know of your investigations?" Richard pulled a chair close and sat.

"No."

"Why did you not report your suspicions to the Chancellor or the Minister of the Court, or even to the Secretary?"

St. John's eyes narrowed. "Perhaps you are not aware. Neither the Chancellor nor the Minister of the Court are apt to listen to me. And with so little evidence, there was little chance Secretary Chudleigh would pay a great deal of attention, either."

It should have been more satisfying to learn how widely St. John was disliked.

"Thus, I decided to pursue the matter myself and approach them when I had further information. I have spent the better part of the last two years in that effort. I ask you again, of what interest is this to you?"

Elizabeth and Richard looked at Darcy, who slowly nodded.

"Since the Lady Sage's rescue from the Sea Lion brought the problem to light, the Order has been investigating the smuggling of dragons and traffic in their parts. The sign of the snapdragon has been associated with those activities," Richard said.

"The Order is already investigating this? Why was I not informed?"

"Why would you have been informed?"

St. John glowered, his face coloring. "What have you learned?"

Richard chewed the inside of his cheek, thinking, then nodded. "One of the men lost aboard the Sea Lion, Ayles, had ties to the snapdragon group. At the Cotillion, Misters Oakley, Munro, Fifett, and Dodge were seen wearing the insignia. In addition to yourself, of course." Richard allowed that vague accusation to hang in the air a moment. "Oakley was detained and remains under custody, his Keepership has been terminated, and his estate is being transferred into more capable, loyal hands. We have also identified a Chesterfield apothecary, Mr. Stanton Keats, as another affiliate. I sent samples of his wares to London in the hopes that Sir Edward would be able to identify if they had draconic origins."

"That message that never made it to London, I imagine?" St. John fiddled with his cravat. "It would seem that we have been working separately on the same matter for quite some time."

"Perhaps," Elizabeth said softly, "it is time for us all to set aside our differences in service of the greater good."

St. John sighed heavily as though weighing alternatives. "I have a portfolio of notes upstairs. Perhaps we might have the use of the guest sitting room to combine our insights?"

"That would seem the best course." Richard rose and gestured for St. John to precede him through the door. It closed behind them with a resounding thud.

Darcy sat back on the desk and slowly exhaled some of the tension still holding him together. "It would appear we have sorely misjudged St. John."

"Only, perhaps, in terms of his allegiances." Nothing about her, not her shoulders, not her eyes, not her face, seemed pleased about it. "The fact that he is loyal to the Order and has been investigating the same issues as Richard does not change his character one whit. He is rude, condescending, and insensitive."

He took her hand and squeezed gently. "And a new ally in our efforts."

"I suppose one does not have to like every one of their allies. I am sorry, though, to hear of how he was approached after Rottenstone passed. It seems he was far a better Friend than I gave him credit for."

23
Chapter

June 27, 1815

LYDIA STOOD AT the window of her chambers. The ones in the family wing of the Pemberley manor. She swallowed hard and dabbed her eyes with her sleeve. Fluffy white sheep dotted the distant fields. Songbirds chirped and twittered and all seemed right with the world.

More or less.

She turned away, hugging her shoulders, and wandered a circuit around her room, lingering in the warm morning sunbeams. Her feet scuffed across the dark-green carpet which softened each step she took, almost as though it were trying to diminish her presence there.

How strange last night had been. Darcy and Lizzy were in an uproar. Sir Richard and the awful Mr. St.

John were in conference in the guest sitting room. Cosette was away with April and Pemberley. Everyone took dinner on a tray in their own rooms.

And no one spoke a word to Lydia.

Not to check on her. Not to tell her what was going on. Only Betsey came in to inform her of the startling great change to dinner plans and to bring her a tray. It was not strange feeling alone and left out. No, that was very familiar; unpleasant, but familiar. It had not been happening so much recently, though. The change felt strange and all the more cutting.

What had she done to put them all out so?

It was tempting to barge into the sitting room and demand her share of the conversation. There was a time when she might have done just that. But Mrs. Fieldings' rules of conduct had been serving her well enough that it seemed reasonable to take the opportunity to apply them again. So, she spent her evening replacing the buttons on her striped walking gown with the new carved-horn buttons from Buzby's Haberdashery.

Why had Sir Richard insisted on purchasing them? He did not have to. Something in his eyes and his tone suggested he was pleased to give her something she liked. But that was probably assuming too much. Why would a man like him be bothered with her feelings?

Lydia pulled the olive-green-and-rust-striped gown out of the closet and adjusted the cheval mirror to catch a bit of the morning light. Pressing the gown to her chest, she turned this way and that. It was a fetching gown, even if two of her sisters had worn it before her. The fresh ribbons, fashionable new sleeves, and now new buttons made it something uniquely her own that suited her well. But would she ever have occasion to wear it now that things seemed so different?

She sighed as she tossed it on the rumpled, unmade bed and flopped into the chair near the window and the writing desk. The scent of orange blossom sachets mixed with the fresh-field scent on the breeze that rustled the green curtains, friendly and calm. The same as the room had smelt yesterday and the day before.

The beginnings of a headache intruded at the edges of her temples. Maybe, just maybe, everything had not suddenly changed, and she was not outcast. Perhaps there were good reasons for her sudden invisibility to her friends and family and all would sort itself out soon. Unlikely things seemed to happen here at Pemberley. Maybe it could work out that way.

A soft knock sounded at the door and it opened to admit Betsey, little green fairy dragon Juniper on her shoulder.

Gracious, she missed Cosette.

"The post just come, Miss. A letter for you." Betsey curtsied and handed Lydia a letter sealed with an irregular blob of red wax, Kitty's handwriting on the direction.

Lydia's heart tripped over its next several beats. "I will read this before breakfast."

"Shall I press your walking dress?"

Lydia hesitated a moment. There was no immediate need, but it could not hurt, either. Just yesterday Mrs. Reynolds had scolded Betsey for idleness ... "Yes, do that."

Betsey picked up the gown, curtsied again and ducked out.

It was odd, not having Cosette here to remark on the irregularity of the sealing wax. Or her disappointment that it was no longer warm and soft for her toes. Perhaps when she returned, Lydia would heat some wax just for the fairy dragon's enjoyment.

Kitty rarely wrote letters. Was it wrong to anticipate bad things because of that? Mrs. Fieldings' had cautioned her not to jump to conclusions. Lydia's fingers trembled just a mite as she broke the seal and unfolded the crisp paper, smoothing it against the writing desk. Faint, scratchy letters, such a difficult-to-read hand—that did not make her feel any better. Lydia turned so a sunbeam fell across the page.

My dear Lydia,

You know me too well to insist I dither about with pleasant nothings rather than come directly to my point. I am sure you can imagine how impatient I am to have approbation for Mr. Mothman. I cannot imagine why Mr. Darcy has not yet given us his approval. Perhaps he may have spoken on the matter in your hearing at Pemberley? I simply must know what he is thinking!

I am sure you think I am impatient, for it has been but a week since you were to Ingleside for dinner. But what might be expected from a woman so enamored of her beau? I am simply wretched.

Mr. Mothman told me of your visit to his shop, and with Sir Richard, no less! How could you?

I am jealous and put out and demand that you tell me everything of your visit. I have never been there myself and think it perfectly horrid that you should have gone without me. Why did you not invite me to go with you? You know how much I wanted to go. Cruel, simply cruel!

One might think you are beginning to take after our Lady Lizzy who seems determined to cast off her family because of her fine new connections. Pray, promise me that you are not becoming like her.

Dragon's bones! What a horrible thing to say! No wonder Lizzy had been so tense at dinner that night. Mama and Kitty, and even Jane would never understand the true situation. Not that they understood Lydia's or Mary's any better, but for some reason, they were not awful to anyone but Lizzy. What could have made Kitty so hostile? Perhaps it was that Papa made Lizzy a favorite that provoked them so.

I cannot imagine what the Pemberley family has against Ingleside, but it is unfair, and I am tired of it. I have taken it into my own hands, and I have written to Papa on the matter myself. Mr. Mothman took the letter to London and placed it in Papa's hands himself. He is as impatient as I and said he would wait until Papa responded and carry the response back to us. Is that not wonderful?

I expect him back in the next few days, with the approval we need, so Sir Fitzwilliam need not trouble himself on our account. If the opportunity arises, you may tell him that, and I do not even care if you do so politely.

How charming.

I cannot tell you how excited I am. Mama has already begun her letter to Uncle and Aunt Gardiner regarding the wedding clothes I shall need. I do not know how much Papa shall give me to buy them, but he should offer at least as much as he gave Jane or Mary. I cannot hope for as much as Lizzy surely got. Perhaps we will visit their warehouse in Cheapside, for Mama does not believe there are any as good in Sheffield.

Ironic that it was Lizzy who got nothing from Papa on her wedding. All her wedding clothes were from Mr. Darcy. At first Lydia had been sure Lizzy was lying about that—how could Papa be so unfeeling? But April confirmed it. Something about the irregularity of it all and that Papa never reconciled himself to Lizzy not marrying Mr. Collins.

You may tell Lizzy about my plans, or not, as you wish. I do not care. She might be a lady now, but that does not give her the right to spoil my hopes and dreams to show off how fine she is.

I do want you to stand up with me at the wedding, though. Pray tell me that you will do that!

Excited and awaiting news!
Yours
KB

Stand up with Kitty? As the only unmarried sister, she had to do that. But did she even want to? It should have been a pleasing thought, but no, it really was not. So many things simply felt off.

Mr. Mothman had gone to London to see Papa? In one way it seemed rather romantical that he would be so impatient to be married. It meant he would be away from his shop and no shopkeeper ever liked that. The sacrifice was a real one.

But it was probably something Lizzy would want to know about. Was it important enough—

A sharp knock at the door made her jump. "Yes? Come in."

The door swung open, and Sir Richard stood in the doorway, rumpled around the edges, dark circles under his eyes. "Good morning, Miss Bennet. Forgive me, I know it is early, but might you be interested in a walk before breakfast?"

She slipped the letter into the writing desk drawer, heart pounding so hard she could barely hear over it. "A walk sounds quite pleasant. In a quarter of an hour, perhaps?"

Some of his weariness seemed to fall away. "I will meet you in the front hall, then." He bowed and closed the door.

He sought her out! He wanted to walk with her! Fairy dragon feathers! What were the chances that Betsey would be done with her dress?

A quarter of an hour later, more or less, her walking dress freshly pressed and sporting its new buttons, Sir Richard offered her his arm and escorted her outside.

A guard drake she could barely make out in the front lawn paused and stared at them, then yipped like a dog, probably alerting the other guard drakes that the family was outside.

Earl landed, rather dramatically, in the shadow of the house, perhaps six feet from them, showing off his excellent wingspan. "Cosette remains with April and Pemberley at Matlock. Cosette asked me to tell you she is well, but they have not been welcomed to the house at all. She thinks the Keeper there is rude. Pemberley, though, has been considerate and made sure that Cownt Matlock has treated them well."

"Thank you for bringing her message. It was kind of you." Lydia curtsied. It was right to be polite to a dragon doing one a favor.

"I shall be about my rounds, then." Earl chirruped and disappeared into the sky.

"He is an excellent fellow. You must be proud of your Friend."

"I think the responsibility Walker has charged him with has done him well." Sir Richard shaded his eyes to watch Earl's departure. "Do you fancy the gardens or the wilderness this morning?"

"I think it a wilderness sort of day." It had certainly started that way, but now it was difficult to say.

"I think you are right; definitely a wilderness sort of day. And before I forget, the new buttons look very well on your gown. That has not escaped my notice." Did he just wink?

Just in case he did, she blushed. "I am glad you approve."

They set off toward the west side of the house. Lizzy never said it outright, but she was proud of the informal grove of trees and shrubberies where one could lose oneself in thought. Several new iron benches with scrolling branch motifs had been installed there, just for that purpose. Eventually a little folly for the fairy dragons to play in, and a bridge over the streamlet that crossed the path, might be added as well. Although Lydia did not agree with all of Lizzy's tastes, she had to agree on the appeal of the grassy, mossy paths that wound their way through the trees, unbounded by wall or hedge.

Light shade embraced them as they crossed onto the grassy pathway. "Pray forgive me if this is one of my moments of being too bold, but it sounds like you mean something more than you are saying."

Sir Richard chuckled. "Have I become so transparent during our acquaintance?"

"Hardly transparent, sir. I have merely grown accustomed to you. Not a bad thing, I should think. Do you wish to talk about the 'wilderness sort of thing' that weighs upon you?"

"Are all Bennet women so direct?"

"After a fashion, I suppose we are. Except for Jane, of course, who puts all of us to shame with her ladylike manners and mildness."

"I found her dreadfully dull. Like every other woman of her class. So mild as to be unmemorable. So accommodating, there was nothing to set her apart from a hundred others."

"You know so many ladies, sir?" Her throat grew tight with the words, although there was no good reason for it.

"Know? I would not say so. But when one is a younger son of an earl, there are many who have crossed my path, though not a one whom I could recall with any clarity."

"Except for Bennet women?" She leaned into his shoulder just a little. "What drives you to the wilderness today?"

"A great deal happened yesterday, and I am struggling to make sense of it all."

"I suspected as much. When Lizzy outright canceled dinner and sent up a tray to my room, I had a few suspicions that something might be going wrong. But perhaps I was overreacting."

He laughed aloud. "That was just a wee hint, was it not? I am sorry that I was unable to speak to you directly last night. I would have much preferred to do so."

She nearly stumbled and caught herself against his arm. "Indeed? Forgive me for asking, but you mean that? You are not just saying it because it is a polite sentiment?"

He stopped to face her, catching her eyes in a serious gaze. "Yes, I do mean exactly that. I have become accustomed to your ready help—and wit. I found myself missing both last night."

Her breath hitched and cheeks burned. How did one respond to such a compliment?

He took her arm again, and they walked deeper into wilderness, so entirely different in nature and character from the foreboding dragon woods nearby. "Things took a strange turn yesterday."

"I had imagined that, with little Pemberley going to Matlock with her fairy dragon escort. And without Elizabeth—that was a strange thing. I am surprised Elizabeth permitted it."

"Oddly enough, that was not even the strangest part."

Shivers coursed down the back of her neck. "I am agog. What happened?"

"You are familiar with Fern?"

"The maid's puck? Yes, she loves paper so. I have left her several scraps drawn with squiggles and curlicues—she takes such delight in them. Funny little dragon, with a great deal more sense than her Friend, I think."

"Fern, I understand, has been given leave to hoard whatever discarded paper she finds. Yesterday she brought a scrap to Elizabeth."

"Pray do not tell me …" Lydia's feet rooted in place.

"Another snapdragon."

"From where could it have come?"

"I can hardly believe it myself. It came from St. John, but it is not what you think." He gestured to one of Lizzy's new benches, and they sat amidst the iron leaves and branches. "It seems he has been investigating the snapdragons on his own for nearly two years now, having been approached by them upon the death of his Friend."

"Dragon Fire! Who would have thought? He is such a dreadful, disagreeable person. But I suppose that alone would not make him wicked."

"I spent the better part of the evening with him, and eventually Darcy and Elizabeth, understanding the intelligence he had gathered, and sharing our findings with him."

"Oh, I see." She pulled away from him, but he leaned into her shoulder.

"I became so distracted by the information he was sharing that, by the time I realized that you were not already with us, it was very late. Your maid said you were already asleep and Elizabeth did not think it appropriate to awaken you."

He had sought her? She gulped back the knot in her throat and blinked her burning eyes. "I am honored that you would have thought of me, but Betsey was in error. I was not asleep at all. I fear she was being lazy and did not want to be bothered with preparing me for company so late in the evening. She is still new to her position, I think. I will make sure it does not happen again." Betsey would soon learn how much angst her poor choice had caused her mistress!

"I feel the fool for not having called for you sooner. I was just so stunned by the turn of events. I had taken St. John for a possible player among the snapdragons, not one who would have had the wherewithal to conduct an investigation of his own."

"I imagine you did not share your suspicions with me—"

"Not because I did not trust you, but because I wanted your fresh perspective. I should have paid more attention to the fact that you did not suspect anything about him." His mouth wrinkled into that funny annoyed-with-himself frown she had come to recognize.

"I am honored that you should value my opinion."

"I hope it is not unwelcome if I say I value many things about you, Miss Bennet."

It took longer than it should have to find words. "Not unwelcome at all, Sir Richard."

"When we return to the house, would you join us in further discussions with Mr. St. John? If we return now, we can talk of last night's revelations over breakfast. I know it is an imposition, but would you consider it?"

What was there to consider? "I am anxious to hear what you have learned."

24
Chapter

June 29, 1815

RICHARD STALKED INTO the guest sitting room, now turned into their planning headquarters, and allowed his mask of calm and reason to shatter on the polished wood floor.

It was utterly foolish to work himself up into such a lather over Miss Bennet's simple trip to Chesterfield. After all, it had been his suggestion that she travel to Ingleside to learn more about Mothman's application to Bennet. Mothman's impatience might simply be impatience to wed, but Miss Kitty, with her limited dowry and, to be honest, limited sense, was hardly such a prize that a man could not wait to go through the proper channels established by her family. Something felt off.

It was hard to anticipate how Bennet would react to such a direct application, but Miss Bennet would be able to manage the situation. If necessary. If it was not simply a case of seeing villainy where there was none.

But the damage done from being too careful was far easier to repair than that from too little caution. So, that was the better mistake to make in a situation where it was guaranteed they would be making at least one mistake.

He huffed and raked his hair out of his face. The sitting room couches had been moved out, replaced by several large tables, now piled with maps, correspondence, notes and journals, and a handful of wooden chairs to fit around them. One large comfortable chair remained facing the far window. According to Elizabeth, that one was for thinking. An odd feminine touch, considering the room's current purpose, but she had been right. A spot with one's back turned to the chaos spread out on the tables, was conducive to thought, and Richard needed to think.

He fell into the chair with little dignity and no grace. The chair still smelt of the orange blossom scent that followed Miss Bennet.

Stupid, lazy maid. He was still angry about that. They could have used Miss Bennet's insights the night they had discovered St. John's investigations. But no, that ridiculous girl—Betsey, was that her name?—was too lazy to be bothered to tend her mistress. Mrs. Reynolds should have sacked her immediately upon finding out. That is what would have happened at Matlock.

But there were the dragons to be considered. Apparently, Juniper had become essential to Cosette. A dragon with a maid of her own—nowhere else but Pemberley would that ever, ever happen.

Could he tolerate such things at Netherford? Would Netherford?

Where had that thought come from?

Earl swooped in and landed on one of the two iron dragon perches that had been brought into the sitting room, one near the tables, the other near the window. "They are safely arrived at Ingleside."

In just these few weeks at Pemberley, Earl had grown larger and sleeker, starting to lose a bit of his adolescent awkwardness. Flakey patches on his grey tail hide and a few ratty silvery feathers near his shoulders suggested he was about to shed or molt or whatever it was called when he seemed to change his clothes, leaving bits of himself wherever he perched. Earl chewed at his shoulder, plucking out a tattered feather as though to prove Richard right.

"Good. And there is a guard …"

"A pair." Earl attacked another mangy feather. "If anything goes awry, one will return with word, while the other manages the situation. They will be unnecessary, though. I am convinced there is little danger to her and Cosette."

"And yet you insisted on that pair of guards." Richard would have insisted himself if Earl had not.

"Walker says prudence is better than regret."

"Walker is a wise dragon."

Walker winged in, a daunting black shadow sweeping across the room, and landed on the perch near the table. It rocked just a bit as he adjusted his weight to counter the momentum. "Yes, I am."

Earl flew to the table. Richard rose and settled Earl's perch near Walker's—too many papers scattered about for the table to be a pleasing perch, and the chairs were too unstable for cockatrice. "There is news?"

"Yes, and it is not all bad."

Richard winced.

"The remains of two messengers have been found, still carrying their messages." Walker glanced over his shoulder at the bag strapped between his wings. "Take them and ensure they have not been tampered with."

Richard unfastened the satchel. "And the other two?"

"Injured. Badly, as you can imagine. Darcy is leading a team to retrieve them now. Elizabeth is preparing to receive them at the barn where Ring continues his convalescence."

"Dragon's blood and bones, this place is becoming a dragons' hospital." Richard pried open the buckles and removed the still-sealed letters. What was worse, tending injured dragons or the need for it in the first place?

"Hopefully, the messengers will be able to help us understand if the wild cockatrice were, in fact, responsible for the attacks, and, if so, whether they were acting on their own."

"It is hard to know what option to prefer in this case." St. John lumbered in and dropped into a chair across the table from Walker, almost as though he knew the Pemberley dragons did not like him, and it was best to keep his distance.

"If the poachers are organized enough to target the messengers, it would suggest that things are even worse than we feared. That these remain sealed suggests that is not the case." Richard pointed to the letters on the table, nearly lost amidst the other clutter.

"That is true," Earl said, with an unsubtle glare at St. John.

"I am going to join Darcy. You will be kept apprised of what we learn." Walker bobbed his head once and disappeared through the window. Was he in that much of a hurry to escape St. John's company? Probably. Walker did not suffer fools gladly.

"We should be off soon as well." St. John looked toward Richard, carefully avoiding eye contact with Earl. "I have ordered the horses prepared."

"We will be ready in a quarter of an hour."

As much as Richard would have preferred her company, it was just as well that Miss Bennet was occupied with an errand of her own. Courage and boldness were admirable traits in a lady, but the journey today threatened too much danger for her to participate. Persuading her of that would have been difficult.

St. John had learnt the way to the abandoned cottage from the snapdragon calling card. There was no telling what or whom they would find there. Perhaps absolutely nothing. Perhaps it would be a den of thieves. One could not tell. But one could go into it well-armed, with two guard drakes and a pistol. Hopefully, that would be enough. But certainly, no place for a lady, even a bold, courageous one.

Two and a half hours over clear roads, in fair weather, was not exactly an arduous ride, but the company of a man one did not like, who lacked the skill of making conversation, made it so. With luck, the gathering clouds that kept the sun off their backs would not dump rain on them later in the day. That would make for a long ride home.

They approached the turn off the main road that, according to St. John's intelligence, would eventually lead to the old cottage. From the low branches tangling overhead, to the overgrown path, everything about the little lane discouraged one from taking it. Rather like a dragon woods, which was entirely ironic, considering what they were seeking.

There were no major dragons in this territory, but perhaps—that was an interesting thought. "Have you made any inquiry—do you know if there are any known dragons in these woods?"

St. John guided his horse a little nearer. "I had a look at the copy of the official reports before I left Pemberley—"

"You made a copy of the dragon census?"

"Only the most recent one. I could not risk removing the original from the Order offices. I only copied the Derbyshire records, though."

"Still, that is a significant task." A dull, fiddly, repetitive task Richard would have avoided at almost any cost.

"How could I do my job without it?" St. John shrugged. "There were no large minor dragons recorded here in the last census. The records of small wyrms and fairy dragons are always a bit questionable, of course. And it is possible there is a wild-hatched dragon or two about that did not submit themselves to be counted at the last census. Lands like these that are not administered by a major dragon are always a bit uncertain."

Just how much territory was not administered by a major dragon? How many dragons wandered about, unaccounted for, throughout England? Not something Richard had ever considered before. It was a rather unsettling thought, all told.

Fallen leaves and sticks crunched under the horses' hooves as they pressed deeper into the young woods. From within, it was less like an ancient dragon wood than Richard had expected. Probably a good thing, all told. "Neither Netherford nor I were properly educated in the true role a major dragon has in its territory, when we were assigned a Keep. We were given a list of responsibilities, to be sure, and have been regularly harassed to get them accomplished. But it would have been helpful to have been shown the larger perspective on the matter, how our estate might fit into the security of the kingdom as a whole."

"Few Keepers seem to know or care about such matters. The requirements of the Order are treated as irritating matters of form. Those who insist upon them are stodgy bureaucrats, insisting on their pound of flesh, as you yourself noted." No, St. John did not sound bitter at all. Not a little bit.

"Perhaps that is a conversation to have with the Sage. It seems the sort of thing that would fall under her purview."

St. John snorted and his horse aped the gesture.

"You do not approve of her, do you?"

"Accepting a child into the Order ..."

"Who knew her dragons and treaty better than most Keepers ..."

"Who actually spat at the dragons during our testing ..."

That would have been something to see! "Testing which you made up as you went along, which conformed to no particular rule but your own preference. And, I might add, I understand spitting was the appropriate etiquette for a dragon in that situation."

"A dragon, not a woman! With a father like Bennet, there was every reason to expect she would have inadequate supervision and run amok."

"I suppose I do have to give you that. But can you imagine what would have happened had she been kept from the Order? Pemberley—"

St. John glared over his shoulder at Richard. "The territory would now be in the talons of a proper dragon who could hold and protect the territory. Probably Bolsover, whose own territory—"

"Is now under proper stewardship and will be substantially improved for it. The Order would have been deprived of a significant and much-needed new officer."

"That is one man's opinion." St. John turned his face back to the trail.

"That is not yours?"

"What has she done but disrupt the Order? Yes, the dragons installed her, but what has she done since? Produced a whelp—a girl, no less—one who will likely make issues of inheritance of Pemberley a bloody nightmare. Your Lady Sage offended Cornwall, got herself kidnapped, and turned the Order inside out. Offended Bolsover, left Haddon and Renishaw feeling duped out of their rights of challenge. I hardly see the benefits of the office."

"And the books she has written? They have had no value?"

"The value of those will only be proved in time, if anyone bothers to read books penned by a woman. Women are only fit for writing domestic management guides and novels, and even those are questionable at best."

"Have you read any of her writings?"

St. John grunted.

"I have, and they are without a doubt the most practical works ever produced by the Order. Everything in Netherford's library is antiquated and cryptic. At least her works offer practical advice that can actually be followed by Keepers, not scholars."

"That seems faint praise to me. Encouraging Keepers to leave behind the tried-and-true ways—"

Pigheaded, short-sighted, irritating— "There, is that the cottage?" Richard pointed to a ragged structure tucked inside a stand of young trees.

"Cottage-in-the-Stand is the name of the place. Seems like that should be it." St. John stopped his horse, dismounted, and indicated Richard should do the same.

They tied the horses to a nearby tree.

Richard checked his pistol as Earl lit on the ground beside him. "I will check the house first." He must have learned that not-to-be-denied tone from Walker.

St. John waved him onward as he, Richard, and the guard drakes circled around the dilapidated structure. One story, a thatched roof that appeared to be falling in over one room. Not likely more than three, four rooms inside at the most. Shutters hung askew over the windows, barely hanging on by fingernails, it seemed. The only door, of worn and weathered, roughhewn wood, had lost its top hinges and draped drunkenly across the doorway. The broken daub of the daub-and-wattle walls revealed the structure underneath. If it were not abandoned, it gave every impression that it should be.

A light breeze rattled the limbs around them. What was that? Hints of dragon musk, small dragons though; wyrms, fairy dragons perhaps. But nothing larger. Birds twittered high in the trees, confirming that there no larger dragons were about.

Earl landed on the edge of the roof. "I neither hear, nor smell anyone within."

"You first," St. John pointed at Richard's pistol. He was probably right, though the temptation to judge him cowardly called. Loudly.

Richard approached the door slowly, listening, watching, skin prickling with anticipation. Exactly what he had hoped to leave behind when he traded the title "Colonel" for "Keeper." The door resisted as he wrestled it back enough to edge inside.

Blinded momentarily, he listened and smelled and felt. Still air. Old sweat. Stale foodstuffs. Was that dog dung? And traces of little dragon musk. His eyes adjusted, making out an old mattress on the floor, a chair with a barrel-turned-table nearby. The remains of a fireplace held burnt wood probably only days old.

Detritus blown in through open windows and door, and the hole in the roof, littered the floor. He crunched across it, peering into the two small rooms along the back wall. Both barren but for the leaf litter and what might have been a stoat's nest at one time.

"It is clear. Come in." Richard called, making his way out to the main room.

St. John wrestled the door open farther and forced his way inside.

"There is no sign of any use of the other rooms."

St. John turned his attention to the meager signs of occupancy, poking at the mattress, finally turning it over and poking it again, then subjecting the barrel to similar treatment. "Place seems a bloody waste of time." He stood, dusted his hands on his pants, and wandered to the fireplace. With a nearby stick, he poked and prodded at it. "Interesting. That annoying little puck was good for something, after all."

Richard crossed the room to stare over St. John's shoulder. "What's that?"

Gingerly holding the edges of his coat back with one hand, St. John reached into the back of the fireplace and pulled out a half-burnt scrap of paper. "Let us see, shall we?"

Richard rolled the empty barrel near, and they spread out what was left of the paper.

A list perhaps? Names? Items? It was difficult to tell. But at the bottom right corner …

"These here," St. John pointed to the corner. "I cannot be sure, but they seem to be—"

"—part of the snapdragon sigil."

Earl flew in and landed on the mattress. "I just spoke to a pair of forest wyrms and the local fairy dragon harem. They said packages are left on the doorstep sometimes. Within a day or so, a man comes to pick them up. They opened one, once, but only found papers inside, so they do not bother them anymore. Sometimes the man meets others here. That is when he sleeps here and makes a fire."

Was it good or bad that they had missed seeing this mystery man? "Do you think they could describe the man?"

"I doubt it. The little dragons kept their distance. According to them, those were not the kind of warm-bloods it seemed wise to meddle with."

25
Chapter

June 30, 1815

ELIZABETH TROTTED DOWN the cellar stairs, candle in hand. Pemberley should be here soon and she should not wander into a cold, dark, empty cellar all alone. That probably bothered Elizabeth more than it would Pemberley, but still, she had just done a very grown-up thing and deserved to be greeted appropriately upon her return.

The flickering candlelight kissed one wall, then another, with a warm glow that made what could have been an eerie space almost whimsical. Somehow it chased away the perpetual smell of damp and dirt, emphasizing the fresh hay that had been piled high for Pemberley's nest near the center of the room, with the soft, stuffed ottoman for company, usually Elizabeth, to sit nearby. Someday little Anne would come down here to visit with Pemberley as well. What a gift to be able to give both of them.

Pemberley trudged in through the dragon tunnels, head low, feet scraping the hard-packed dirt floor. Thank heavens April had flown on ahead to warn her of the little firedrake's exhaustion, else she would have been terrified by Pemberley's state.

"The maids have finished sewing your pillows, just as Mrs. Reynolds promised." Elizabeth stood at Pemberley's nest, a bed of fresh hay now topped by several dragon-sized canvas pillows. Though Pemberley coveted Barwines Chudleigh's silk pillows, Chudleigh had no talons to catch on the fine fabric. Pemberley had accidentally torn several of Chudleigh's pillows, so she had reluctantly agreed that canvas was a better choice, at least until she grew into her feet.

"Pillows! I like pillows. I need pillows! So tired." Pemberley tumbled headlong into the pile, burying her face in the softness.

"Are you hungry? I am certain it would be best for you to eat first."

"No eat. I sleep. So tired." The pillows muffled Pemberley's voice.

"Did you eat at Matlock?"

"Food yes. So much talk. So so so much talk. Ears tired. I tired. No talk now. Sleep now." Pemberley tumped over onto her side, curled her tail over her nose, and began to snore.

Elizabeth never advocated waking a sleeping baby; waking a sleeping dragon was never a good idea, either. The conversation would have to wait, whether she liked it or not. At least Pemberley's color was good. She usually took on a decidedly grey cast if she went too long without eating.

Not quite the reunion she had been hoping for.

April buzzed down the stairs and landed on Elizabeth's shoulder. "There is no need for you to worry. She did well for herself."

Elizabeth turned to the stairs. "Then perhaps you will enlighten me as to the nature of the conversations at Matlock."

"No, that is for Pemberley to say, not me." April nipped her ear lightly.

"She asked you not to tell me?"

"She has the right to tell her own stories. But there is nothing for you to worry about, and every reason to be proud of her. I certainly am."

"That is high praise, coming from you." Elizabeth climbed the stairs slowly. Having Pemberley and April finally home was a relief, but one cruelly tempered. "Will you be needing to sleep, as well?"

"Soon enough, but I am hungry, even if Pemberley is not. While Matlock might provide meals for one of his kind, he knows nothing of fairy dragons or what we eat. Cosette and I were left to forage on our own. We were too far from the gardens to find sufficient sweet, and if I eat one more insect, I shall certainly be quite ill. Nasty, crunchy, pokey-wriggly little things." She smacked her beak and shook herself fluffy, almost falling off Elizabeth's shoulder.

"That is truly a hardship. Matlock was entirely discourteous to you. He should know better. Come with me to the kitchen, and we shall find you a pot of honey, or jam, if you prefer."

"I want both."

Of course she did.

In the kitchen, Mrs. Reynolds oversaw Agnes and Cook as they assembled a tray, probably to be taken to the sitting-room-cum-office. Elizabeth requested jam and honey be added to the tray, and she and April headed upstairs.

Neither of the wounded cockatrice messengers had regained sufficient consciousness to speak, so there was nothing for her to report on that front. With their survival still uncertain, Elizabeth was reluctant to force the issue, so they would have to make do with what Mr. St. John and Richard may have learnt.

She shook away a shudder at the thought of that odious man. She did not want to like him. She could not like him. The only redeeming thing about him was his loyalty to the Order and to his late Friend. For that, she would tolerate him in her home.

The sentiment appeared mutual. Although he kept his opinions mostly to himself in her presence, the little household dragons made sure she was entirely aware of what he thought and said about her and the office of Dragon Sage. None of it complimentary. It should not bother her so that he disliked her.

But it did.

The Order was her place, the one where she belonged and was accepted. The place where the world actually made sense, at least after a fashion, and she did not have to pretend to be something that she was not. But, between Chancellor Lord Matlock and St. John, her security in the Order had been undermined. To what degree, though? It was difficult to tell, especially with so many crises on all sides.

What did the packages at the abandoned cottage mean? Who had been there? Was the mark on the paper even the snapdragon sigil, or just some random scribble on a page filled with scraps of words, scarred by burns and tears, that Richard could not even make out? Did they know any more now than they had before their reconnaissance? It was all so vexing.

Cosette met them at the top of the broad marble stairs, bobbing in a midair hover. "We have returned, and it is a good thing that you sent me to Ingleside with her! There is news. She would speak with you, Lady Sage."

At last! "Is she in the sitting room?"

"No, a private interview, please." Cosette hovered near Elizabeth's face.

"Certainly, then. A tray with honey and jam is being brought to the sitting room. Perhaps you should tell the gentlemen what you can whilst I speak with Lydia."

"Yes," April hopped off Elizabeth's shoulder to hover near Cosette. "And if they do not allow us to speak, I will nip their ears until they listen."

They buzzed away.

Perhaps she should not encourage, or in this case, permit, April to be so bold. But really, by now, if any of the gentlemen did not know better than to ignore fairy dragons, it was their own fault, and they should expect nothing less.

Elizabeth turned down the family wing, with its large window at the end of the corridor. The dark carpet sprigged with burgundy flowers softened her steps to a whisper. Portraits of Darcy ancestors observed her as she walked past, each with a peculiar, individual personality. Some approving, some disdainful, but they all tolerated her well enough that she had not felt the need to relegate them to the guest wing.

Lydia's paneled-oak door was open, so she rapped on the doorframe and peeked inside.

Lydia caught her eye and turned to Betsey. "You may finish unpacking later. I need to speak with Lady Elizabeth."

The girl briefly looked like she might argue, but quickly brought herself under better regulation. Good. Betsey seemed a good enough girl, but if she hoped to continue in service, she needed to understand what was appropriate for her station.

Betsey curtsied, "Juniper, too, Miss?"

"Yes. I will send for you when you are needed." Lydia gestured toward the door and Betsey and her Friend scurried away, closing the door behind them.

From the look of Lydia's half-unpacked trunk, she really had only just got back. Dresses were draped on the chair near the desk. Still-folded body linen was piled on the floor near the trunk. A pair of shoes peeked out from under the bed and a bonnet perched precariously on the corner of the press. Were those traces of Mama's perfume in the air?

"I am so fagged." Lydia dropped down on the bed and fell onto her back.

"There seems to be a great deal of that at Pemberley today." Elizabeth sat on the edge of Lydia's bed. "Dare I ask how things were at Ingleside?"

Lydia threw an arm over her eyes and heaved a rather dramatic sigh. "Far, far too much like Longbourn, if I am to be entirely honest."

"There are a great many things that could mean. Would you care to be a bit more specific?"

"Mama is as she has ever been, though perhaps a bit more so, if that makes sense. Mr. Bingley tends to be a great deal like Papa, giving way to Mama as often as he can to avoid the histrionics that come with displeasing her. Jane is as she has always been, eager to please and see Mama happy and satisfied, which I will tell you is not what a woman who is increasing should be doing." Lydia propped up on her elbows and let her head fall back. "Have you any idea what Mama thinks an increasing woman should be eating?"

"I do recall her describing it in several letters she sent whilst I was in that condition." Needless to say, that advice had been quickly ignored.

"Think of what it would be like having her overseeing the kitchen to ensure her wishes were carried out."

"I would prefer not."

"Mama is interviewing the local midwives and threating to have a man-midwife brought from London, if no one nearby suits her."

"A man-midwife? Merciful heavens! It may be fashionable, but I hardly think it a good idea." Elizabeth pinched her temples. "I almost feel guilty for suggesting to Papa that he should send her and Kitty to Jane."

"I tell you this, it does not matter what you say, I will never go there without Cosette—if I ever visit again. I do not know what I would have done without her. She is the only reason Mama ever gave me a moment's peace."

"Dare I ask what Mama demanded of you?"

"Everything and more. She wanted to know how much pocket money you and Sir Fitzwilliam were giving me, and if perhaps I might be willing to share that with Kitty, as Papa still had not told her how much she might have for wedding clothes. And that was only the beginning."

"Oh, merciful heavens!" This was forward, even for Mama!

"Then she insisted on hearing all the details of Pemberley and how you were managing Mr. Darcy—which I neatly avoided answering. Instead, I talked of what was served at the tables and what variety of candles were used. Happily, I did not know how much pin money you had, or if you might be willing to invest in Kitty's wedding clothes. I could, however, expound upon the details of your wardrobe, and how it compared to Jane's … oh, I could go on! It was just awful. At first, Cosette could redirect the conversation to something less personal. By the end of our visit, though, she had to persuade Mama she had a terrible headache and needed to lie down. I hated for her to do that, but what choice was there?"

"I am so sorry. I will have April speak to her about some of the methods she used to manage Mama back at Longbourn, without resorting to persuading her into a headache." Which had also occurred from time to time.

"I should like not to have to visit there again anytime soon. Maybe not ever again." Lydia sat up and dropped her head into her hands.

What a strong statement, coming from Lydia! "I had no idea it would be so difficult for you."

Lydia rocked back and forth. "They make me want to be as I once was, and I do not like that."

Elizabeth slipped her arm over Lydia's shoulder. "I well know that sort of unpleasantness."

"I really do not understand what Kitty sees in Mr. Mothman. I know he is not a gentleman, but he is hardly gentlemanly, either. It seems like his entire being is consumed with his new shop and the various lines of goods he wishes to carry. Maybe she likes him because he asks her opinion of his different ideas, as though Kitty really knew anything about what he was asking her. But she does not. She only says what he wants to hear, even if it is very stupid."

No doubt Mama encouraged that as well.

"Kitty never really had an opinion of her own, and now even less so. Whatever he says must be right, of course. And if not him, then the loudest voice in the room will do. I know I am not being charitable and I must sound utterly horrid. How do you stand it, Lizzy? You must tell me. How do you manage?"

She leaned her head against Lydia's. "I would give you a simple answer if I had one, but I do not. It seems the truth is that I do not think I handle it well at all."

"And the way that Mr. Mothman gloated over his success in London. It was truly repulsive, making himself out to have bested Sir Fitzwilliam's attempts to thwart their betrothal. As if that somehow made him superior to a man to whom he might never compare. I am not even certain Mr. Mothman delivered the letter himself. I think he sent his man to do the deed whilst he pursued business contacts in London. Utterly disgusting."

"Vulgar would be the word I would choose for such reprehensible behavior." Elizabeth laughed softly.

"He read Papa's letter aloud, which congratulated Mr. Mothman on his boldness and determination to marry Kitty. And of course, offered hearty approbation for a man so ambitious and strongminded. Supposedly, Papa could never deny such a man his fondest desires. Ugh! It sounded nothing like Papa.

You know he is not prone to such speeches. He never uses one word more than necessary."

"I do not like the sound of that." Elizabeth wrapped her arms over her chest and held her shoulders.

"Neither did I. I hope you will approve of what I did, for it did not cast Sir Fitzwilliam in entirely the best light, but it was all I could think to do."

Elizabeth dug her nails into her palm. "I am certain it could not have been so bad."

"I asked Cosette to persuade them that Sir Fitzwilliam was proud and controlling and would insist upon seeing Papa's letter for himself. He might even be offended that Papa would have the audacity to make an answer himself. I know it sounds rather awful, but it came to good use, I think. Mr. Mothman gave me the letter to bring back and show to Sir Fitzwilliam myself."

"That is good thinking. I do not mind it in the least. I am sure he will not, either. Pray, will you show me? There is no telling what might be learnt from it."

Lydia found her reticule, retrieved the letter, and handed it to Elizabeth. "I have read it, and it says exactly what he claims it did. I am not sure what you can learn from it, but I do hope you can learn something."

Elizabeth moved to the writing desk near the window for better light and smoothed the letter over the desk. Lydia was right, it sounded nothing like Papa, but there was something more. She held it up in the sunbeams and studied the pen strokes. Wait! "Lydia, you are nothing less than a genius."

"What do you mean? What do you see there?"

"You recall, Papa no longer writes his own correspondence, yes?"

"Now that you mention it, I do. But what of it?"

"Drew writes nearly all his letters for him now. Because of the shape of his paw, he usually writes with a pencil, and when he does write with a pen, he regularly smudges the descenders of letters." Elizabeth pointed at several lines. "Not only is there not a single smudge on this letter, I am quite certain this is not even Drew's handwriting."

"Are you saying that this letter is not from Papa?" Lydia blinked rapidly, as though trying to make sense of the new information.

"You said yourself, it sounded nothing like him, and now this? What else can we conclude? We must show Darcy and Richard."

26
Chapter

DARCY SQUEEZED HIS eyes shut and took a deep breath. Patience, the situation warranted patience.

Maps and notes and journals covered the guest sitting room's large table from edge to edge, with articles threatening to fall off on all sides. Why was it impossible for Richard to think in orderly environs? Such a wonder that St. John did not threaten mutiny for being forced to endure such disorder.

For all his other many and varied flaws, he was an orderly man. One had to focus on the few virtues one could find when dealing with St. John.

"I know I saw that list a moment ago." Richard pawed through the stack nearest him.

Walker, on an iron dragon perch near the table, peered over Richard's shoulder, as though his far superior eyesight might be of use. But it was not. Not unless he could see through the piles to reveal what lay beneath.

Pendragon's bones! Now was not the time to suggest tidiness and order, though the temptation was stronger than Darcy cared to admit. Patience.

Elizabeth slipped in, her face drawn and tight. Lydia edged in behind her, her mien little different. That Elizabeth should wear that expression was one thing; that her ever-gay sister followed suit suggested something serious. The fairy dragons, still guzzling honey at the pot in the windowsill, paused to look at their Friends. They chirruped but Lydia waved them back to their meal.

"Elizabeth?" Darcy hurried to take her arm.

Richard jumped up and pulled two chairs closer to the table as St. John briefly glanced up, then returned his attention to the map he studied.

"You have news? The messengers?" Darcy escorted Elizabeth to the chair next to him.

"Not that. I am cautiously hopeful they will survive, though I fear it could be some days before they are able to speak with us." She sat down and laid a paper on the table. "Something else has come to light which may or may not be related to these matters. It is difficult to tell."

"Then perhaps it should wait until we have finished discussing—" St. John muttered under his breath.

"No." Richard banged the heel of his hand against the edge of the table. "Clearly both of you think it significant, and that is enough for me." He pushed Lydia's chair in for her as she sat beside him.

Interesting, the look that they just exchanged. Darcy chewed his cheek. It was not the sort of look that Richard was apt to share with a woman. One of respect, but was there a bit of warmth as well? Interesting. But now was not the time to ponder that.

"What concerns you?" Darcy pointed at the paper Elizabeth had laid before him, eyebrow raised.

"I just arrived back from Ingleside," Lydia said. "You recall, Mr. Mothman wrote directly to Papa seeking his approbation to marry Kitty?"

That did sound vaguely familiar.

"Mama and Kitty are certain that Papa has written back to them giving them exactly that."

Darcy began counting the number of troubling things about that statement, but stopped, taking note of Elizabeth's knotted forehead and narrowed eyes. "You have a specific concern?"

Elizabeth unfolded the paper and pointed at several spots. "This is most certainly not Papa's handwriting, and I am convinced it is not Drew's, either."

"I suppose you know his secretary's hand—excuse me, paw—quite well, then?" St. John's upper lip curled back just the barest bit.

April dove for his ears. "You will watch your tone when speaking with her!"

He covered his ears and leaned back from the table. "It is a legitimate question. How many ladies know the hand of their father's secretary?"

"More than you might imagine." April hovered just out of his arm's reach.

"Mr. Darcy," Elizabeth said through gritted teeth, "you are quite familiar with Drew's hand. What say you on the matter?"

He had no need to verify her assertion, but since she asked, he glanced over the page. "No smudges on the descenders nor scuffs on the paper from the rough hide on his front paws. And the letter forms are all wrong. Definitely not Drew."

St. John snorted.

"I imagine the letter paints Miss Kitty's betrothal to Mr. Mothman in glowing terms?" Richard glanced at Lydia with a little eye roll.

"Disgustingly so. The letter even goes so far as to suggest Papa insists both you and Mr. Bingley should invest in his ventures." Lydia's eye roll matched Richard's. Clearly, they had been spending a lot of time together.

"That most definitely does not sound like your father." Darcy held the letter up closer to the light.

Elizabeth extended her hand as a perch for April. "Absolutely not. He barely talks of money at all, and when he does, it is restricted to the company of other men."

April chittered at St. John and lit upon Elizabeth's finger, accepting a scratch under the chin and soothing strokes to her ruffled feather-scales.

"I do not see why this family matter should interfere with the work of the Order." St. John scanned the room, as though hoping someone was paying attention to him.

Walker squawked and flapped a wing at him.

"This handwriting, it seems familiar." Darcy patted his pocket. "Yes, I think this is it." He placed the letter on a clear spot in front of him and retrieved a folded sheet from his pocket, carefully placing it alongside the other. He beckoned Elizabeth closer, and they studied the two pieces of paper.

"The writing, it must have been done by the same person." She tapped nearly identical words on both papers. "Such a distinct form to the capital 'B'."

"Not just the same person, but the same pen, I would wager. It seems the tip was cut a bit irregularly. I received this letter from Mothman just yesterday, hoping to encourage my investment in his business."

"One must give him credit for tenacity," Richard said. "And duplicity, I suppose, if both letters were indeed written by him."

"I have no reason to doubt the one sent to me is from him, so it seems he is willing to go to underhanded lengths to secure your sister's hand," Darcy passed the letters to Richard.

"I hardly know what to make of it." Elizabeth chewed her lower lip and shook her head.

"That cunning napper. There is no doubt." Richard pressed the papers toward Lydia, pointing at a particular line. "And you see the capital 'B'. Does it not remind you of a certain shopkeeper's sign?"

"Heaven forfend!" Lydia gasped.

"But to what point?" St. John trundled around the table to look over Richard's shoulder. "None of this has anything to do with the important … wait!" He reached around Richard and traced something on Darcy's letter. "Dragon's blood and bones! Where did that go?"

St. John rifled through a stack and set it aside. Four, five, six times the process repeated, St. John muttering under his breath and glaring at Richard as he completed each pile of papers. "Yes, here it is." With thumb and forefinger, he extracted a tattered, burnt slip of paper.

"You must be joking!" Richard cleared the table in front of him and laid out the two letters, with a wide space between them.

St. John crowded in, between Richard and Lydia, and laid the scrap on the table. "If you would stop blocking the light, Miss Bennet."

Lydia slipped from her chair and stood behind Richard's other shoulder. The narrowing of her eyes suggested she had no few opinions on St. John, but had mustered the fortitude to keep them to herself for now. April and Cosette landed on her shoulders as though to offer their support. Or be at the ready to nip ears. The latter was more likely.

"Dragon fire! Look, here and here, and possibly here." St. John pointed at the scrap.

The invectives Richard followed with were hardly fit for the current company, but it was difficult to blame him.

Lydia leaned into Richard's shoulder. "Lizzy, the list is from the cottage. It is Mr. Mothman's handwriting. I am sure of it."

"Pendragon's bones!" Elizabeth lost all color in her face.

"This does put a different light on the matter." St. John scuttled back to his seat and furiously scribbled into a nearby journal.

"Very different, indeed." Darcy ran his knuckles along the side of his jaw.

"How do you propose to stop the betrothal and bring him in for examination?" Walker squawked and flapped hard enough to scatter papers on the desk. "We cannot apprehend him from Ingleside, nor from any public venue."

The fairy dragons hovered over the letters, chittering among themselves, finally landing on either side of the tattered list.

"Get away from there," St. John waved at them. "You will ruin—"

Walker screeched just enough to raise the hair on the back of Darcy's neck. St. John shuddered.

April pecked at a spot near the bottom of the paper. "These look like numbers, like a date is written here."

"Look, look and see." Cosette hovered in front of Richard's face.

"By Jove, they are right, it is a date. July 5, if I am making that out correctly."

"What significance could that have?" Lydia asked.

"It is the day before the new moon." Elizabeth paused, blinking rapidly. "Raven, the local cockatrix, told me that poachers were most likely to come to Pemberley during the new moon."

"That is the answer." Walker hopped to the middle of the table.

"Of course!" Richard slapped the letters. "If the man is associated with the poachers, how could he resist an invitation to Pemberley at the new moon?"

"Invite him to Pemberley?" Invite a potential poacher to have access to his family? Pemberley's territory? Darcy's skin crawled as though dozens of spiders danced along his arms.

"Not just him, I fear," Elizabeth pressed her hands to her face. "Depending on the outcome, a great deal of persuasion may be needed to conceal the truth. It would best be done quickly and for all the parties involved. The best way for that to happen is to have all of the Ingleside party here. Including Miss Bingley."

"But what of the staff at Ingleside?" Lydia asked. "Surely, they will take notice if things suddenly … change …"

"While that is true, since they are less directly related to matters, far less persuasion will be needed," April said, "Cosette and I can take Pemberley's household fairy dragons to Ingleside to manage what is necessary."

"What precisely are you planning? I insist—" St. John's round face colored as though his authority had been usurped.

"Pemberley must host a brief house party to celebrate the couple, at the new moon. In case that is not enticement enough, Darcy and I will ask to know more of the investment opportunities Mothman proposes. He will not be able to resist that. Over the course of several nights, several moonless nights, Mothman will have opportunity for an assignation with the poachers, whom we will be ready to apprehend." Richard gave a quick nod toward Elizabeth, who responded in kind.

"I will oversee the security teams," Walker squawked. "If so much as an unfamiliar rat moves on the estate, we will know of it."

"We should decide ahead of time what persuasions will be used should Mr. Mothman be taken into Blue Order custody." Lydia said. "I shall work with Cosette and Fern to prepare the household dragons, should that be necessary."

"If it becomes necessary to hold prisoners, it should not be at Pemberley." Elizabeth said. "Shall I speak to Cownt Matlock on the matter?"

"No, let me. My brother Andrew will also have to be apprised of the situation. There is no need to subject yourself to his stupidity."

"What shall I do?" St. John asked. Did that mean he might actually make himself useful in the matter? How singular.

"Help me identify the most likely locations for clandestine meetings to occur and plan appropriate surveillance around those places," Darcy said.

"Well, then I suppose that leaves me to plan a house party. I will speak with Mrs. Reynolds immediately." Elizabeth sighed heavily and hurried off.

Hours later, she returned with dinner on trays. How had it gotten so late? Elizabeth slipped into the chair beside Darcy and quietly ate her dinner, studying the, as yet, incomplete plans laid out on the table. She quietly pointed out a few concerns—she was right, of course, but in his defense, they had not yet finished their discussions, either. Even St. John agreed with her, which, all things considered, was rather remarkable.

The mantel clock struck eleven, and Lydia declared herself "fagged", scooped up an already-sleeping Cosette from the back of the soft chair near the window, and dragged herself from the room.

"She is right. This will all be here in the morning." Richard stood, stretched, and clapped St. John's shoulder. "You, too. We will all be smarter then."

Surprisingly enough, St. John grunted something vaguely polite-sounding and trudged after Richard.

Elizabeth laced her hands behind her neck and leaned back. "I suppose Lydia is right."

Darcy tucked her hand in his arm and escorted her to their private sitting room, shutting the door against the rest of the world. He placed the candle he carried on the mantel, the flickering light insufficient to push back all of the darkness, but just enough to make a refuge of brightness for him and Elizabeth.

"Do you really think Mr. Mothman is caught up in all of this?" Elizabeth stood in the middle of the room, back turned, shoulders bowed under the weight of it all.

"As inspired by profit as he appears to be, it seems more likely than I would prefer." He stood behind her, hands on her shoulders.

She leaned into him. "Of all people, how is it possible Kitty should attach herself to such a man?"

"Many a man has played with a young woman's affections in order to obtain her fortune or connections. You know that is a common enough thing, reprehensible as it is."

"I am so conflicted. I almost wish to find him part of the snapdragons."

What an odd sentiment, coming from her.

"If he is, the Order will take him into custody, the fairy dragons will persuade Ingleside he has died or disappeared, and we will be done with him. That would be so much easier." She scrubbed her face with her hands

Darcy pulled her in and tucked the top of her head under his chin as he wrapped his arms around her waist. "Easier than calling him out on his blatant lies and denying permission for the betrothal in front of our friends and family?"

She shuddered against him. "I would like, even just this once, not to be at the center of making my family unhappy."

"Take heart, my dear. If it comes to that, I shall happily shoulder all the blame and allow them to be angry at me. I do not take kindly to being lied to. You may insist and try to change my mind however you can, but to no avail. What kind of man would I be if I allowed my wife to talk me out of such well-earned resentment? No, in this case I will be quite unmovable. Mothman will be no relation of mine."

Chapter 27

July 2, 1815

LYDIA MADE HER way to the morning room, a weary Cosette on her shoulder. Such a flurry the last few days had been! Planning a house party—perhaps it was just *this* house party—boasted far more complications than Lydia could ever have imagined. With only six guests, it had not seemed it should be so complex. But when the men's servants, the ladies' maids, and the coachmen were all added in, the party more than doubled in size, and the necessary considerations tripled.

At least tripled.

So many details! Had there not been dragons to consider, the list would have been extensive, but with the additional intricacies of hosting the dragon-deaf at an estate teeming with dragons—oh, the headaches!

So many of the chores, done by the staff dragons, would have to be assumed by the human staff. Persuasion could hardly be relied upon when pucks were openly dusting and drakes running about the halls carrying bundles.

Temporary staff had to be brought on to manage the work, and the poor dragons! So hurt and offended that their efforts were not sufficient for this particular set of guests. Thankfully, Lydia and Richard had been able to add them to the security efforts. Every guest room now had little dragons watching and listening at all times.

No wonder even Mrs. Reynolds had been seen sipping willow bark tea! A pot of the stuff had been appearing regularly on the breakfast table, in the sitting-room-cum-planning-room, and the dining room. At this rate, Lydia just might be developing a taste for the ginger and sugar combination that made the bitter brew palatable.

Chisholm, the glossy black secretary drake, who had become Lizzy's shadow recently, a stuffed satchel on her back, nearly ran into Lydia at the head of the grand stairs.

"The sitting room is being restored to its original purpose now?" Lydia asked.

"Yes. The disagreeable one has just taken several armloads of material back to his rooms." Chisholm smacked her jaws, like a fairy dragon chittering under her breath.

"There are two piles of which I am to take charge, but I have an errand for the Lady Sage this morning—"

"You would like help seeing them to your rooms?"

"I can manage that for you, right now." Sir Richard appeared over Chisholm's shoulder.

"Very good." Chisholm scampered down the wide marble stairs without waiting for a response, and disappeared into the shadows.

"I am sure you have more important things to do." Poor man looked utterly exhausted.

"I have just finishing shifting several baskets of detritus, as Darcy calls it, to my own chambers. It is no trouble. Just show me exactly which ones you need moved." Sir Richard beckoned her back to the sitting room. "What errand has Elizabeth for you this morning?"

"I am to introduce Mr. St. John to Ring. He has asked to interview Ring himself, regarding his recent … experiences … and Lizzy could find no grounds upon which to refuse. I offered to make the introduction for her since she has to visit Blackwood and Grove today to go over their instructions for the new moon."

"Probably best to keep Elizabeth and St. John apart at the moment."

"How could you think that my motive?" She batted her eyes as she lifted her brows and pressed a hand to her chest. "I simply suggested it because I have nothing better to do today. I am quite certain that everyone is calm and in good spirits and even excited for the opportunity to host what will probably be the house party of the season."

Richard ushered her into the chaotic sitting room, chuckling. Such a warm, welcoming laugh he had. "It will be a memorable one, at least. I cannot imagine how all the staff dragons and guard dragons are going to keep themselves from sight. And if they manage the task, it will hardly seem like Pemberley without them."

With the table half-cleared and the small wooden chairs around it gone, the room became a sad empty shell. Two couches piled atop one another edged into the walking space, waiting to be returned to their usual stations. Awkward intruders in a place where they were no longer welcome.

"Just my short time here has reformed my opinions of what a properly managed dragon estate might look like." Lydia dodged around the couches.

"The Darcys do have a way of shaking up one's assumptions about the world, do they not?"

"Living at Longbourn, under Papa's management, I thought change necessarily a bad thing, but I am not so sure of that anymore."

"An open-minded woman! A rare and refined creature indeed." He smiled broadly as he scooped up a large stack from the table.

Merciful heavens, why did he say such things to her when she could not linger and enjoy them?

Lydia found Mr. St. John in the morning room, studying a small handwritten journal as he stuffed large pieces of sausage into his mouth. Perhaps it would not be a wise thing to tell him he ate like a juvenile cockatrice. But it was true.

She chose her chair so that she could avoid looking at him while he ate and poured herself a cup of coffee. "Enjoy the fresh flowers. We have a busy day, today." She nudged Cosette off her shoulder.

Cosette flittered to the windowsill vase of blue hydrangeas, crossing the table a little too close to Mr. St. John's face.

He started, eyebrows raised at the fairy dragon, but quickly returned to his book. Lizzy was right. The man was simply rude.

A quarter of an hour later, with an empty plate and crumbs on his cravat, Mr. St. John turned to her. "When will you be ready to take me to meet the Ring Wyrm?"

"I was waiting for you to exchange pleasantries with me. You know, 'Good day, Miss Bennet.' 'The weather is fine today, Miss Bennet.' 'Might I pour you a cup of coffee, Miss Bennet.'" She flashed her brows and shrugged her shoulders.

He started again—touchy, touchy man—and stared at her bug-eyed. Who knew that his squinty little eyes could get so large and round? "I … I … I am not accustomed to warm-blooded company in the morning room."

"I have always been taught to be attentive to those around me. It is the foundation of all good manners."

His narrow lips opened and closed like a fish out of water. "I shall endeavor to keep that in mind."

Gracious, had he really never been taught? "I should think Cosette and I shall be ready in ten minutes. Might I recommend you return to your chambers and remove the crumbs from your cravat and the sausage from your fingers. Meeting a dragon whilst one smells like food is hardly a good idea."

"Indeed? I have never—"

"It is not the sort of thing that one should have to read in a book somewhere. Greeting a large predator while wearing a meat-fragranced perfume is hardly good sense, is it?" She nibbled her toast delicately, just to make her point.

"When put that way, I suppose I can see the wisdom of it." He stood and bowed from his shoulders. "I will return in ten minutes."

What a strange man. Did all his rudeness stem from ignorance? Who could possibly be that ignorant, though? Especially an officer of the Order. But there were some people who just never seemed to truly embrace the social graces. Was he one of those?

Mr. Darcy could be that way at times, but, according to Lizzy, he had worked hard to learn how to behave properly and disciplined himself to do so. Perhaps Mr. St. John was the sort of person who eschewed such discipline and embraced small-minded opinions. Something to consider later.

"Are you ready, Cosette?" She extended her hand as a perch.

"I do not like that man."

"I know, but you do like Ring, yes? If Mr. St. John must be introduced to him, then as Ring's friend, you should be there to see to his comfort."

"Does that mean I can nip the disagreeable one's ears if he is awful?" Cosette landed on Lydia's hand and preened her glossy black shoulder feather-scales.

"No, it does not. And you know it."

"But April does it."

"We have discussed this before. You may not emulate your brood mother. Ah, Mr. St. John, we are ready for you."

Mr. St. John stood in the doorway, brow furrowed. How much of the conversation had he overheard?

Oh well, if he was uncomfortable, it was his fault for eavesdropping.

The walk to the cart barn proceeded in silence. Was that because of what he had heard, or was he unable to make small talk? Lydia had been told that it did not come easily to everyone. It was not difficult to imagine that Mr. St. John was one of those. Still, it was itchy-prickly that he should prefer the uncomfortable silent air between them to an agreeable, if empty, chat.

At least the morning air was agreeable. Bright and just warm enough to forgo her shawl. Who could object to a morning stroll in such lovely surroundings? One might even consider it a privilege to amble across a beautiful estate.

The guard cockatrice atop the thatched-roof stone barn "cawed" and flapped his wings at them.

"We are expected." Lydia waved broadly at the guard.

The dusty brown guard bobbed his entire body and pointed at the open door with his wing.

A knot of stripey barn tatzelwurms peeked around the doorframe and stared at them with big eyes. They were young ones, still with the oversized ears, eyes, and paws that they would eventually grow into. She curtsied to them. "Good morning, we are here to call upon Ring."

They rose up on their tails so she could scratch under their chins as she passed. Mr. St. John remained at arm's length from them. Perhaps he did not favor furry creatures. That was actually not uncommon among Friends of dragons with leathery hides rather than fur or feather-scales. Or at least that was what Mrs. Fieldings said.

"Good morning, Ring." She dipped in a low curtsey that Ring was happy to accept instead of the proper greeting that would have gotten straw and dust all over her gown. "May I present—"

"Was there to be an introduction this morning?" Ring's eyes twinkled from atop his perch of canvas-covered straw. "I recall no such thing."

"But, I …" Mr. St. John sputtered.

The tips of Ring's undersized wings fluttered. "No, no such thing at all. I do not know if I am in the mood for an introduction today."

Such a tease! "Well, if that is how you feel about it, I shall introduce Mr. St. John to the faithful cockatrice messengers and tatzelwurms, who share your quarters. I know they shall appreciate the acquaintance." She beckoned Mr. St. John to the other side of the barn, where the wounded cockatrice convalesced. His face had turned an unhealthy color—was it maroon or puce?—as he sputtered under his breath.

"Good day, good messengers." She curtsied to the prone cockatrice. Bother. She did not actually know their names.

Bruised and bandaged, lying stretched out on a heap of clean straw, neither wounded cockatrice had been able to stay awake long enough for a conversation the last time she visited. The dark grey one moved his head and opened his eyes. The brown one followed suit.

"Good day," the grey one croaked in a voice more frog than cockatrice.

The brown one groaned and blinked.

"You are awake!" She crouched down beside them.

"Messages? Our messages?" The grey one tried to lift his head but fell back.

"The Sage said they remain in our hands, so all is well. Surely you are hungry now? There is forced meat and broth waiting for you in the kitchen, should you wish it."

"Meat good." The brown one murmured as he caught her gaze.

"I will have it sent immediately. Can you tell me, though, the attack—"

"Wild. They were wild. Angry."

"Not imprinted … on warm-bloods."

Yes! That was the information they needed! Her eyes should not be prickling over that, but they were.

Lydia turned to the tatzelwurms. "Go to the house, and send Dale to me. Tell the kitchen to send meat to the barn. Yes, you shall have a share if you deliver both messages properly. Now go on, the lot of you."

The furry mass of wyrmlings spring-hopped away. Nothing motivated a tatzelwurm like the promise of a full belly. Hopefully Dale or Mrs. Reynolds would be able to sort out the message well enough.

The cockatrice closed their eyes and snored softly. They would waken easily enough when they smelled food.

"Eh-hem. I should like to have my share in the conversation." Ring tapped his tail softly against the floor.

"Should you, now?" She turned back to Ring. "But that would require an introduction that you said you were not—"

"Well, I have changed my mind. It is the prerogative of a dragon to change course as he will. You may introduce the one who smells like sausage now."

Had Mr. St. John ignored her instructions or just done a remarkably bad job of it? If Ring's nose was sensitive, then it might be difficult to banish a strong scent like sausage.

Ah well, nothing to do for it now. She led the bemused Mr. St. John back to Ring. "May I present Undersecretary of the Order, the Honorable Mr. St. John."

Mr. St. John stepped forward and bowed. "I am honored by your acquaintance."

Ring sniffed. "You smell like sausage."

"I … ah … I, that is, I ate them for breakfast."

"And you did not bring any to share? How rude!"

"I … I had no idea you would want any. My late Friend, Rottenstone, did not have a taste for cured meats. I thought that was a general sentiment among dragons."

"Did you? Interesting. I have never tried such a thing, but they smell very nice."

"Then shall I bring you some? I can go right now. I am sure the kitchen can provide."

"That would be an excellent gesture, a most agreeable offering to a new acquaintance."

"I shall return anon." Mr. St. John trundled quickly for the house.

"Did you expect him to do that?" Lydia pulled an old stool close and sat beside Ring. The abraded patches on his hide had covered over with sturdy scabs, and his feet were no longer bandaged. He still drooled a bit, though, through the empty spot in his jaw where a fang should have been.

Ring chuckled his watery laugh. "No, I did not."

"I am not sure what to make of it."

"He is the one the household dragons call the 'disagreeable one', no? Perhaps they reflect the attitudes of their Friends and have judged him too soon. He seems rather solicitous toward dragons."

Lydia squeezed her eyes shut, trying not to laugh.

"But I suppose my opinion of him might change over a plate of sausages. In any case, I have been giving some thought to the plans for the new moon." Ring crossed his front feet in rather a business-like posture.

"Lizzy is most anxious to know what you think."

"To be honest, I find the plans a bit problematical."

"How so? Do you feel endangered in any way? We tried so hard—"

"No, and I think that is the problem."

"I do not understand."

Ring flicked his tail against the canvas-covered hay. "You have only asked me to watch for trespass. I do not think that is aggressive enough. I well know these are dangerous men and waiting for them to reveal themselves is not sufficient. A trap is in order."

"What do you propose?"

"I shall return to my pond, feigning more disability than is real. The fairy dragons can spread the word of easy prey in the pond, to draw the poachers in."

"You would bait a trap with yourself?" Lizzy was not going to like this idea at all.

"A good trap must be well baited, and since we already know they want me, what is better?"

"But the danger to you …"

"That is my choice. I insist. You will tell the Pendragon Knights to see me today? Or should I go to the manor myself and tell the butler that I am there to call upon them in the drawing room?"

"I think the Grand Drawing room would accommodate you nicely …"

"If you insist—"

"But the maids are busy fitting it up for the house party, so perhaps it will be best for them to call upon you here."

.

28
Chapter

July 4, 1815

"IT IS A shame we did not come to know Ring whilst we were boys." Richard turned his horse down the path toward the manor, late-morning sun beating down on the back of his neck.

Ring, now comfortable in his home pond, remained adamant in his intent to bait the poachers into action, but Darcy had insisted on one last visit just to be certain.

"I am not so sure. It may have been a good thing. Can you imagine the escapades he might have encouraged us into?" Darcy drew his horse alongside Richard's.

"I think you could have used a few more escapades in your youth."

"To distract from the scrapes you found yourself in, no doubt?"

"You must agree, it was excellent practice for learning how to think on one's feet." Richard guffawed. Darcy would never admit his childhood had been too straitlaced.

"As you say. You may have my share of it. I did not like it then, and I do not like it any better now."

"As much as I dislike it, Ring's plan is a good one."

"It still leaves him open to too much risk." Darcy glanced over his shoulder toward the pond.

"It is fully his choice."

"And if something happens to him—"

"If the worst happens, the Order will no longer be able to ignore what is taking place. I will see to that." Richard glanced back at Darcy. "But between Walker, Earl, Brutus, and Axel, I am confident the worst will not occur, especially now that we are certain the wild cockatrice were not involved."

"That is one thing in our favor. The cockatrice will still have to be dealt with—"

"Many things remain to be dealt with, but you cannot afford to dwell upon them. Focus upon today's troubles for now. I know it is not your way. You want to have everything planned and ordered. Sometimes, though, that will only paralyze you from dealing with what you must."

"I admire your ability to do that."

Richard swallowed hard. Darcy had never said such a thing before. "We will get through this. Elizabeth and Anne will be safe." And Miss Lydia as well.

"I trust you. I wish I could say the same for our guests, though. Bingley is good-hearted, but can be rather—"

"Look, it seems they have arrived in our absence." Richard pointed to the carriage in front of the manor, and the horses and wagon nearby.

Darcy muttered under his breath and urged his horse into a trot.

A quarter of an hour later, they handed their horses off to grooms at the front door and hurried to the lesser drawing room, their steps matched in almost military precision.

Darcy stopped just before the doorway and cocked his head, obviously trying to listen to gain a sense of the room before he barged in. Not a bad strategy, all told.

"So, you are an acquaintance of my husband, Mr. St. John?" There was no mistaking Mrs. Bennet's nasal whine. "A member of his club, Blue's, is it?"

"Yes, madam." It was not difficult to imagine St. John sweating and fingering his cravat.

"Is it true he takes a sedan chair to the club? That he has such difficulty walking now?"

Darcy clutched his forehead.

Mortifying. That woman was simply mortifying.

St. John cleared his throat. "From what I have seen of him, yes, that appears to be the case."

"Really, now?" she drawled. Pendragon's bones! What was she going to demand now?

Richard plunged into the eggshell-blue drawing room. "Pray, Lady Darcy, forgive our delayed return."

All eyes turned to him. Lydia and Elizabeth shared an expression of profound relief. Clearly the refreshments set out for the guests had not been nearly enough distraction.

Elizabeth stood. "Think nothing of it. Had you a good ride?"

"There is nothing quite so satisfying as a morning ride." Richard bowed at the room as three Bingleys, two Bennets, and Mothman rose to bow and curtsy in return.

Miss Bingley's fashionable gown showed only the faintest traces of road dust, but the other ladies seemed more taxed by the journey, especially Mrs. Bingley, who just might be near the time when she should not wander far from home. Bingley and Mothman appeared in good spirits, though. Perhaps they had ridden their horses alongside the coach.

"I say, I had forgotten just how lovely Pemberley was this time of year," Bingley said. "You really must give us the grand tour, Darcy."

Darcy glanced at Richard with an upraised brow.

Yes, that was a good idea.

"With your permission, of course," Darcy nodded at Elizabeth, "I can think of no better time than now to show you gentlemen about the estate. I am certain the ladies would appreciate an opportunity to rest and refresh themselves after the rigors of travel."

"Charles! How could you?" The edge on Miss Bingley's voice would set a cockatrice to flight. "We only just arrived. Now is not the time to go gallivanting about."

Elizabeth shook her head and raised an open hand. "I think it a splendid notion. Would you ladies like a tour of the house whilst they are off?"

"Would we like a tour? Of course we would like a tour. How could you think anything else?" Mrs. Bennet gesticulated wildly. "I cannot believe you have kept us waiting so long to show us your home."

"I think we have been dismissed." Bingley led Mothman toward the doorway.

"I shall order the horses readied." Darcy bowed and stepped out.

Though meant to appear spontaneous, largely for Bingley's benefit, this jaunt had been carefully laid out days ago. Even to the script St. John would follow to engage the guests as they rode. That had been Lydia's suggestion, based on her recent observations of the man. The strangest thing was that St. John actually seemed to appreciate the direction, improving his attitude overall. Very odd.

From the manor house, the plan was to tour "Darcy's favorite boyhood places." Bingley thought it a splendid notion, wonderfully sentimental, which only showed how little he really knew Darcy at all. Rather a shame, that; but it worked in their favor.

They began at Ring Pond, where they dismounted and explored around the picturesque deep pool, surrounded by rocks and shrubs. Richard told a rather embellished story of falling in as a boy and nearly drowning, only to have Andrew, his brother, tease him that it must have been a dragon living at the bottom of the pond who saved him.

It had been Andrew who had fallen in.

Ring, who watched from the shadows, well away from the men, sent ripples along the pond's surface at the mention of a dragon. The dragon aspect of the story had been his idea, naturally. It was unsubtle, but with the new moon rapidly approaching, they had little time for delicacy.

St. John snorted at the idea of a dragon in the pond—the stuff of small minds and superstitions. Bingley declared it a charming story, the sort common in Derbyshire, while Mothman wondered aloud if there were any other dragon stories related to Pemberley.

That raised the hair on the back of Richard's neck.

For a man who was not particularly spontaneous, Darcy did an excellent job picking up the cue. He explained there were actually five different dragon stories set on Pemberley and offered to include them on the morning's ride. Though not part of his script, St. John agreed. A bit stiff and awkward, to be sure, but enough to set the tone for Bingley and Mothman to approve the plan.

From Ring Pond, they rode to the Blackwoods, admired Broken Tooth Rock, and told the tale of a mysterious rock dragon that hunted in the region. Richard thought he caught a brief whiff of dragon musk—basilisk. Blackwood learning the guests' scent, no doubt. Similarly, Grove watched them from underneath a pile of fallen branches and leaves as they toured Darcy's prize orchard and learnt a version of how Richard and Darcy had fallen from the trees as boys, scared by what they had thought was a dragon hiding among the trees.

Derwent, water wyrm of River Derwent, watched from around a deeply shaded bend in the river as Darcy waxed long—at least for him—on his favorite trout fishing spot, where the fish hid from the local water dragon. He invited both Bingley and Mothman to borrow tackle and take the opportunity for sport whilst they visited. Interesting how Mothman studied the area.

But with what manner of eye did he look? A sportsman's or a criminal's? The man was far too difficult to discern, which was sufficient reason not to trust him. Unlike Bingley, Richard was not apt to offer the benefit of the doubt.

"Gates Meadow will be our last destination before we return to the manor." Darcy guided his horse away from the river.

"What an interesting name. Why is it called that?" Bingley asked.

"There is a farmhouse nearby that is surrounded by a fence with six gates. An old man, who once held the lease, had a fascination with gates and surrounded himself with them," Darcy said. "He did no harm, so my father allowed him to indulge his peculiar interest. The farmer said the gates were to keep the dragon of the meadow away."

That was mostly true. The "old man" with the penchant for gates was actually the drake who called the meadow his territory, a Friend to the old farmer there. Not surprisingly, the dragon was called Gates and, along with protecting his meadow, he kept the gates in working order. He even had permission to approach the local blacksmith with anything needed for the upkeep of his gates. Odd fellow, but pleasant enough. After his Friend passed, Gates remained on Pemberley, in the territory he knew and loved.

"What an odd thing to be fascinated with, gates," Bingley muttered, "but I suppose each has their own oddities."

"And what of the dragon of the meadow?" Mothman asked.

"That is a matter of some curiosity. Have you heard of the dragon of the Chesterfield moors?" Darcy asked.

"The one the priest climbed Winlatter Rock to stop?" St. John guided his horse in a little closer.

"Just that one, yes. Well, the common myth says that the priest chased off the dragon to the Blue John cavern, to the northeast of Chesterfield. But an alternate story suggests that the dragon took up residence here, in Gates meadow, and lives to this day on Pemberley grounds."

"What a fanciful story. All of them, really." Mothman looked back over his shoulder. "But good tales, the things people enjoy hearing. Have you many visitors, who have heard those tales, coming to Pemberley? Interested in seeing those sites?"

"Only occasionally." Hopefully only Richard could detect the strain in Darcy's voice. "But for the most part, those are family stories. Few who are not related know them."

"One does wonder if you would attract more visitors if they were widely known. One never knows exactly what the public will be drawn to."

"I would just as soon not find out. We are private people, and prefer that our visitors be invited guests."

"It would be an interesting strategy, though, to make something of the local dragons to increase notice of a business, do you not think so? A sign with dragons, or a broadsheet, like the one used for the lyrics of ballads, only with a story that might then be tied to the shop. I will have to give it some thought. It is interesting."

No, it was vulgar. And quite possibly dangerous for the actual dragons living in the vicinity.

"You have such unique ideas," Bingley said. "One never knows what you might say or do. I like that in a man."

Bingley might, but the tension in Darcy's shoulders clearly revealed he did not. And Richard was apt to agree.

"Is there not also a legend of the Lambton Wyrm?" Bingley asked.

"Yes, there is." Richard brought his horse alongside Bingley's. "It is an old tale."

"Yet another dragon for Pemberley's collection! Leave it to you, Darcy, to collect something so remarkable as dragons." If only Bingley knew of what he spoke.

"You keep fine horses here at Pemberley." Sweat trickled down the side of St. John's face. Was he that anxious to change the topic of conversation? Hard to tell.

"If you wish to ride the estate whilst you are here, you may certainly take one of the riding horses out."

And be watched carefully by all the guard and estate dragon. But Bingley and Mothman did not need to be made aware of that detail.

"Most generous of you, sir," Mothman said. "I hope it is not an imposition, but my man and I rode my horses here—the carriage was quite full, you know."

"Four ladies do fill a coach rather completely." Bingley laughed heartily, though it was clear he left several thoughts unspoken.

"There is plenty of room in the stables, not to worry. My grooms will see to their needs."

"If it is all the same to you," Mothman said, "my man, Caney, will see to that. My animals are rather high-strung and apt to mischief with handlers they do not know. Will it be a problem for him to ride them out twice a day?"

Unusual. His valet painted signs and tended horses. Strange.

"That reminds me of the idea you were recently telling me about, Buzby," Bingley said. "Tell Darcy about your notions for the stables."

"There will be time for that later. I would much rather hear more about these dragon legends."

.

Chapter 29

July 6, 1815

"I DO NOT know what you have done, Lizzy, but Lydia is quite a different person altogether." Kitty flopped down inelegantly on the chair nearest the window in Elizabeth's office. "It must have been that finishing school you and Darcy—excuse me, Sir Fitzwilliam—sent her to."

The narrow, paneled room, wonderfully perfumed by old books, suddenly became too small for the unspoken words—most likely complaints—hovering around Kitty like a harem of wild fairy dragons, twittering and threatening to nip at ears.

"I like to think Lydia is much happier now." Elizabeth sat near her, barely perching on the soft chair. The need to feel ready to pounce, or flee, threatened to overwhelm her.

"I am sure you would." Kitty tossed her head, chin held high. "Lydia is not herself anymore. Dull and boring. I hardly know her."

And Elizabeth hardly knew this Kitty. Best she keep that observation to herself, though. "I am sorry to hear that."

"Really? You are?"

"What is that supposed to mean?"

"It has been quite some time since you have seemed to care about any of us. Since you secured your own position here at Pemberley, what have you done for Jane or me? You have helped Lydia, and she tells me you have helped Mary—was she not presented to Blue's as well?"

Where had she heard that? Granted, it was true, but …

"Ah, I see that I am right! Mary wrote to me about her trip to London to attend an event. It was the same one you and Lydia attended, was it not? And if Mary was there, she had to have been presented to that company as well. You see, I am not stupid."

It was a rather clever deduction.

"Why, Lizzy? Why? I do not understand why you are so determined to help half your sisters, but the other half you ignore. What have we done to so offend you that you should cast us aside? Lydia—who I know has been a source of embarrassment to you — she lives here with you at Pemberley, while Jane, Mama, and I have never even secured an invitation to visit you until now. You have invited the Gardiners, but not us! Have you any idea how you have hurt Jane by your neglect? I cannot tell you how often she has wondered what she has done to earn your contempt."

"My contempt? That is a very strong word."

"A strong word for strong feelings." Kitty folded her arms over her chest, satisfaction in her eyes. "Yes, Jane is actually capable of those when sufficiently provoked."

"I had no idea. She seemed out of sorts when we were at Ingleside, but I thought it due to her condition. A woman increasing—"

"Poor Jane. You hold your success there over us, too. That you were the first to have a child. At least it was not a boy or we would never hear the end of it."

Hold it over them? Where had that idea come from? She had never mentioned Anne in their company. "You sound like Mama. Was it she who gave you such notions?"

"I know she is loud in her complaints, but she only says what the rest of us think. First Papa neglects us, sending us away from London society in a rush, as though we were an embarrassment to him, and now you continue the neglect. What are we to think?"

"I had no idea you felt this way."

"Well, now you know." Kitty tilted her head with such an air of superiority, Elizabeth nearly succumbed to her urge to assert dominance. "The question is do you care, and if so, what will you do about it?"

"What exactly do you want?"

"You are worried I want Mr. Darcy's money?"

"I said no such thing! Do not put words in my mouth. What do you want from me?" Elizabeth flared her elbows and sat straight, hands clenched tight.

"Is it too much to ask to be treated the same as the sisters you apparently like? The ones you have supported in society? The ones you have introduced among your connections? The ones on whom you bestow what favors are in your power to give? I know none of us expected that you would be the one in a position to help the rest of us—that was to have been Jane—but you are. Have you forgotten how we used to promise to help one another, in whatever ways we had available, to succeed in society?"

That had been so long ago, almost in another lifetime, one uncomplicated by the demands of the Blue Order. How could she explain the apparent prejudice against the dragon-deaf members of the family when Kitty was essentially correct in many of her observations?

"Have you no friends in Derbyshire to whom you can introduce us? Can you not invite us to the dinners and parties you hold at Pemberley?"

"We have only just returned from London. You are the first party we have invited. Does that not count for something?"

"A very little, and very late. Does this mean you are reforming your ways or are you merely offering a few crumbs to your poor relations?"

"I have never considered any of our family poor relations."

"Then why do you keep us at such distance? Why do you continue to ignore Mr. Mothman's application? I know Lydia brought Papa's letter to you. Is that not enough?"

Naturally, it would get back to the betrothal. "The letter seems irregular. Or did you not notice?"

"What is irregular about it? That Papa would actually be paying attention to me, not foisting the responsibility off on someone else?"

"I did not say that."

"But you certainly imply it. He approves of Mr. Mothman. What more need be said?"

Elizabeth's pulse pounded in her temples. "If that is sufficient for you, then what more do you want from me?"

"Your support. Your approval. I know you wish to be divorced from the stain of trade, but like our uncles, Mr. Mothman and I shall not be. The patronage of a family like the Darcys could mean everything to his business and my future."

"I understand that. I promise you, Mr. Darcy has been looking into—"

"What is there to look into? You have supported Mr. Collins! Is Mr. Mothman less?" Kitty's shrill tones sounded exactly like Mama's.

How could she compare the two men, as similar as dragons and horses? "It is what Mr. Darcy insists upon, and he will not be moved."

"And that is all you have to say on the matter?" Kitty leaned forward, gripping the chair's arms.

"What more do you want me to say? I am not Mama. I cannot badger and bully my husband into acquiescence." And even if she could have, she would not.

"You will not help me, then?"

"You have a letter with Papa's approval. What more do you need?"

"I see what you are trying to do, Lizzy, and it will not work. Even if you cast the letter into doubt, have you forgotten that my birthday, my twenty-first birthday, is next month? You cannot stop us from marrying then. How do you like that? There will be no escaping your connection from him!" Kitty stood and tried to tower over her.

Elizabeth sprang to her feet, to tiptoes, quelling the instinct to jump atop the footstool. "Then why do you continue to badger me?"

"You are too cruel! How can I call you my sister any longer? I will not spend another moment in this awful place. I will insist to Jane that we leave right now!" Kitty stormed out.

Merciful heavens—what just happened?

Elizabeth grabbed the back of her chair and sucked in several ragged breaths.

"Lady Sage!" Mrs. Reynolds darted in, pale and wide-eyed. "Forgive the intrusion, Lady Sage, but you must come to the nursery immediately. May says she has detected the scent of a strange dragon."

Elizabeth sprang to her feet and ran up the stairs, nearly knocking Kitty aside at the first landing. She did not breathe until she burst into the bright-white-and-sunshine nursery and scooped Anne into her arms. "What happened? Someone tell me what happened!"

Little Anne pushed against her, whining at Elizabeth's abruptness.

"Pray, Lady Sage, sit down." Mrs. Sharp dragged the rocking chair toward her and encouraged her to sit. "We are all well. According to Axel and the cockatrice outside the window, there is no immediate danger."

Elizabeth bit back the urge to insist that she would be the one to determine the immediacy of the danger. "Tell me what has happened!"

Tatzelwurm May slither-stepped out of her basket and approached, head held very low. "It is my fault, Lady Sage. The drakes insisted that anything out of the ordinary be reported. I have neither seen nor heard anything …"

"But you smelled something, someone?"

"Yes, I did. At least I think I did." She tasted the air with her long, forked tongue. "I know tatzelwurms are not to be relied upon—"

Elizabeth shifted Anne to one side, and scooped May into her lap. "I do not know who has told you such a thing, but if I find out, I shall box their ears soundly. Those words are never to be spoken in my home and never to any of the Pemberley dragons. Do you understand me? A tatzelwurm nose is arguably the most sensitive in all of dragonkind. If a tatzelwurm tells me she smells something, then I believe her. Understood? I believe you. You do not have to guard your words with me. Now, tell me what you smelled."

"I told you she would say that." Mrs. Sharp stepped close to stroke the glossy black fur on the back of May's head.

May purred and curled comfortably in Elizabeth's lap. "All was well this morning until the maid Agnes brought up the tray for breakfast. Something smelled odd then, but I thought perhaps it was just a peculiar smell on the tray from the kitchen. But when she came back to collect the tray, I took the time to smell her. She had the scent of a strange dragon, particularly about her shoes."

"Could she have picked up the scent in the garden, from a wild wyrm perhaps?" Elizabeth asked.

"It is possible. I should have thought. You should not have been bothered …"

"No, May. You were alarmed, and I want to—no, I need, to know why."

"It did not smell like Pemberley, Lady Sage. There is a smell to the gardens here, to everything here. All the dragons carry it, even the wild ones. I think somehow it comes from the estate dragon, a way of marking even the resident dragons as part of the territory."

"I have never heard of such a thing."

"I know it sounds daft—"

"No, it does not. It actually makes a great deal of sense as a way for a major dragon to quickly identify trespassers within their territory. Fascinating. Later I will ask you to tell me more of this, and we will test it with Pemberley. This could be important, May. You have done well." Elizabeth scratched under May's chin. "So, this scent was not a Pemberley dragon?"

"No, not a house dragon, a yard dragon, or even a wild one. It was a strange one. One I've never smelt before."

"You think it was in the house?"

"The smell was not mixed with garden dirt scent. I am quite certain of it."

Elizabeth drew a deep breath. Then another, and a third before she could hear over her thundering heart. "We must act immediately. Walker will be informed and—"

The nursery door flew open and slammed against the wall behind it. "Finally, I have found you! I must see my granddaughter. Finally!" Mama, in her morning gown and cap, surged forward toward the rocking chair. "How pleasing it is to see you in the nursery with your dear—" A shrill scream that would have made a cockatrice proud sliced through the nursery. "Snakes!"

Anne wailed to match, fighting against Elizabeth's grasp and shoving May off Elizabeth's lap.

Mama jumped back and pointed at Truth and Mercy in the basket near the fireplace, then at May near Elizabeth's feet. She ran to the fireplace tools and grabbed a poker. "Get back with the baby, Elizabeth."

"No, madam! No!" Mrs. Sharp ran toward Mama.

"Do not tell me how to act!" Mama swung the poker at the basket.

Mercy and Truth leapt, fangs bared, and latched onto Mama, one on her arm, the other her ankle. May twined around her ankles, fast and hard, knocking Mama off balance.

"I am bit! I am bit! It burns! They have poisoned me! Surely, they have killed me!" Mama staggered back and fell on her backside.

Mrs. Sharp plucked the zaltys off Mama and scurried them into her chambers.

"Snakes! Lizzy, there were snakes in the baby's room!"

"No snakes, you saw no snakes. There was a cat guarding the baby from snakes. She had a ball of green string. Not snakes, string. You saw string." May's raspy persuasive voice made Anne cry even louder.

Mama stared at May, blinking as though trying to focus her eyes. "Cats cannot talk. I am sure there were snakes."

"No snakes. A knot of green string. It was string."

"I feel so odd, Lizzy." Mama grabbed for Elizabeth's arm as she slowly slumped to the floor.

30
Chapter

DARCY PINCHED HIS temples. Having a breakfast tray sent up to their private sitting room had definitely been the right choice this morning. Otherwise, this conversation would surely have begun in the morning room rather than Darcy's office. And so would have Darcy's headache. At least Mothman had waited a whole day from his arrival to bombard Darcy with his business proposals.

Mothman sat across Father's broad desk, staring at Darcy, bold as brass. He laid out sheet after sheet after sheet of foolscap, scribbled with what purported to be a business plan, disturbing the office's calm order and offending Darcy's intelligence—a feat few had ever accomplished simultaneously.

Perhaps Darcy should have been impressed that Mothman had taken the care and time to produce such copious notes. On the other hand, brevity was the soul of wit, was it not? And if that was the case, long-windedness must be the lifeblood of stupidity.

No, that was not entirely fair. There were some genuinely interesting ideas hidden amidst the tide of less viable—and a few ridiculous—notions.

"So, you can see, sir, I have the long run in mind." Mothman pointed at what seemed to be a timeline for the new ventures. "I will begin with the Buzby's Shoppe for Ladies in Sheffield. In five years, I will have acquired enough capital to launch an equivalent shop for gentlemen."

"And you have ascertained the demand for such a shop? I would venture to say—"

"No need to concern yourself with such things. I know my business."

"And the livery stables? Where do they fit into these notions?"

Mothman smiled and rubbed his hands together. So sure of himself. "Yes, you will appreciate this. The livery stable, which I hope to establish in three years' time, will help me to manage the transport costs of goods for both shops."

"You are aware that that is not the typical model for a livery stable?"

"I will, of course, board horses and keep a few for hire. But, and this is the brilliance of my plan, the stables will also serve as a base for a small transport company. I will hire out to transport goods for others. My own wares will be transported along with the paid cargo, essentially allowing me to be paid for the process of transporting my own goods. Thus, my costs are diminished and profits increased." Mothman pointed to a row of numbers that supposedly made his case.

"It is an interesting notion, I grant you. However, I cannot help but notice that you supply almost nothing in the way of evidence to support the viability of the livery stables, or either of the shops."

"You can see it right here." Mothman shoved a page of numbers at him.

"I see numbers and calculations, but how am I to know what they represent? Any man can craft such a list, add, subtract and multiply it to his heart's content, and claim it means whatever they want. But what do these numbers represent? And more importantly, how exactly were they derived?"

"I will have to call my man, Caney, in to explain. He was the one who put them together for me."

"Your valet also handles your business plans, along with your horses and your signs?" Pendragon's bones! What chance Mrs. Reynolds had already brewed a pot of willow bark tea?

"He is a man of many talents, and I am pleased to make use of them all."

"I grant you that he might be. But that does not release you from the obligation of verifying the information he gives you."

"Then what point in having paid him to do it in the first place?"

"You do understand the risks involved with such an unorthodox plan? Are you really willing to take them on without—"

Mothman huffed and dragged his hand down his face. "Yes, yes. You wish to lecture me on the matter of diligence again? I heard you on the matter yesterday. I am not stupid and do not care to hear it again. We can return to these ideas later, when Caney can give you the information you crave."

Insolent, disrespectful, condescending …

"In the meantime, though, what think you of using dragons as a draw to the shop? Change the sign from a moth to a dragon? Print up broadsheets with the stories and the lyrics to ballads, arrange for a community sing or the like. Hire some actors, mummers perhaps to play St. George and the Dragon. Work with local shops, maybe peddlers to provide food in the street, make a real fete of it to celebrate the opening of the new Shoppe for Ladies."

Disgusting, vulgar, and opportunistic were just the first words that came to mind. Surely, Mothman did not want to hear the rest. "Have you considered the expenditure necessary against the returns, both in the long and short term—" A first pounded the door. Who would have the audacity— "Come in!"

The door flew open and Kitty plunged in, eyes blazing, feathers ruffled, so much her mother's daughter. "At last, I found you!"

Mothman jumped to his feet. "My dear, what is wrong?"

"Everything! Everything is wrong!" Tears flowed down her florid cheeks. "My sister is horrid! Mr. Darcy is horrid! This place is horrid!"

"Whatever do you mean?"

The woman was bordering on hysterical. Did Mothman really think he was going to get a coherent answer?

"Have you not already noticed that you will get no help from him? The Darcys have turned against us! Cast us away, poor relations not worthy of their notice. I want to leave."

"She is right."

Darcy bolted from his seat. Who was that? That voice—completely unfamiliar. Certainly not one of the Pemberley Dragons.

"Perhaps you are right, my dear." Mothman extended his hand toward Kitty.

"Make your case another time."

"Perhaps Mr. Darcy is not ready for my level of innovation. Another time, perhaps?"

"Not now! Not ever! I will not be treated in such a manner. I insist we leave immediately." Kitty sounded exactly like Mrs. Bennet.

"Are you sure? It seems rather hasty—"

Elizabeth, Mrs. Reynolds and April in their wake, burst in.

"Yes, yes, you should go immediately. Make haste! Make haste." April called, far more loudly than the other voice.

"Mama has taken ill, and Jane is unwell, too. We cannot risk any contagion affecting little Anne. It is best that you go now. As soon as possible. Mrs. Reynolds and her staff will assist you." Something about the look on Elizabeth's face …

Darcy hurried toward her. "If the ladies are unwell, I will have the traveling coach readied for them. Their journey should be as comfortable as possible."

"Yes. Yes! That is an excellent notion! Go now and make ready." Elizabeth took Kitty's arm and propelled her out of the office. Mr. Mothman followed.

"Make haste! Make haste! You want to leave quickly." April flew after them, with Mrs. Reynolds trailing behind.

Elizabeth closed the door and leaned heavily against it. "You cannot imagine what has just happened."

He took her hand. "Has it to do with a strange dragon?"

"You saw it?"

"No, I believe I heard it persuading Mothman and your sister. Did you see—"

"No, May reported that she smelled a strange dragon on the maid's shoes. Then, in the middle of that, Mama burst into the nursery and saw Mercy and Truth. She went after them with the fireplace poker!"

"Are they injured?"

"No, they defended themselves—they bit her. Did you know zaltys have poison?"

"Pendragon's bones! Your mother?" What sort of sick joke was this?

"The poor dears were utterly distraught. They assured me they moderated their bite so she will only be mostly paralyzed until it wears off. But the Ingleside party cannot be allowed to remain here, even with the new moon upon us! I have already deployed the fairy dragons to persuade the entire party they are unwell and want to leave. We will have to find some other way—"

He grasped her shoulders. "The discovery of this dragon changes everything. Have Walker and Brutus—"

"Yes, yes, they have been informed. Every dragon of the security team and all the staff not involved in persuasion are searching. I have sent for the barnwurms to come and smell for the intruder. They can fit in the smallest of spaces."

"Excellent. Who shall we send with Alister Salt and his team to Ingleside?"

"Fern, definitely Fern. She is sensible and steady. And one of the fairy dragons, too. Perhaps they can ride in the sword case, since it will be unused. That will give them good access to listen to what is said within and craft the necessary persuasions."

"Better they are persuaded before they arrive back at Ingleside." He pulled her close and held her through three long breaths. "Was there any evidence that the intruder made it to the nursery?"

"No. I had May and the zaltys check. The only trace was the scent on the maid's shoes."

A little bit of the tension holding him together faded.

"I do not want Anne so far away, not with the house having been compromised. I want the nursery moved to the family wing." Elizabeth hugged her shoulders.

"Of course. You could even begin the process now, telling all that the nursery needs to be properly aired against any contagion. It might even be helpful for the persuasion for the Ingleside party to hear that."

Chapter 31

HOW ODD, AND even unsettling, the guest sitting room seemed without all the detritus—as Sir Fitzwilliam called it—of their planning efforts. Lydia had come to think of the character and intensity of the space as very different to that which it demonstrated now. Today it was a genteel lady in her visiting clothes, making polite small talk with neighborhood matrons. She liked it better as an intense, brooding officer, wrestling over the details of a mission. A place Jane and Bingley would never understand.

Jane perched, as proper as a woman in her condition might, on the couch nearest the windows, pillows propped behind her to make her as comfortable as might be, given her generally uncomfortable state. Bingley sat next to her, doting and attentive, so much so, Lydia suspected he was trying to avoid other company, probably that of his sister.

"How do you find life here at Pemberley? Do Lizzy and Darcy treat you well?" Jane asked.

"Pemberley is so much more than a fine house and extensive grounds, all of which are wonderful, do not misunderstand. I feel welcome here, at home. I am grateful for their hospitality." Lydia blinked rapidly and swallowed back the growing knot in her throat.

"You will forgive me for asking, I hope. But I did wonder how you and Lizzy would get along."

"Quite well, thank you. I find her way of running a household quite to my liking."

"You are most fortunate." Bingley brushed invisible dust from his knee.

"You have sisters from both the Bingley and the Bennet sides of the family living with you. How do you find that?" If Jane could hint at uncomfortable topics, so could she.

"It has been interesting." Bingley refused to make eye contact. "They have entirely different tastes and personalities."

"They are both dear creatures, to be sure," Jane cut in. "But yes, they are quite different."

"Is that to say that they do not always see eye to eye?" Yes, it was a foregone conclusion that it was the case, but it would be interesting to see how Bingley or Jane would choose to describe it.

Bingley ran a finger around his shirt collar. "That has indeed taken place from time to time."

"I do not remember Kitty having such strong opinions before. From whence do you think they come now?" It probably was not kind to continue pressing, but it felt important. That, and Lydia was just a little annoyed at what they implied about Lizzy and herself.

"That is an interesting question. Do you not think so, Jane?"

"Sometimes she seems much like Mama." Jane shrugged.

"Except when Mrs. Bennet and Mr. Mothman disagree. Then, Kitty sounds like Buzby, without a doubt."

That was worth keeping in mind. It could be nothing, but then again, it might not. "Have you enjoyed Mama's stay with you? I know she was so pleased to finally be able to see your new home after having talked about it for months."

"She does seem pleased to be with us." Jane sounded so hesitant.

"Although she also talks often of the pleasures of London. And wanting to visit Pemberley as well, of course." Bingley's puppy-dog eyes almost pleaded.

"Do you consider Mama content at Ingleside?"

"I am not certain I have ever seen Mama truly content, except at the marriage of one of her daughters." Jane turned her face aside, her cheeks coloring.

So polite, so subtle. So perfectly unable to offer a useful answer. "And you, are you content with the residents of your household?"

Jane cast a pleading look at Bingley, whose ears turned red as beads of sweat appeared on his forehead. "Since you ask, and mind you, I have nothing but good will toward our company, do not mistake me. But it seems to me as though a woman's confinement should be a quiet and peaceful time …"

"And you fear that it might not be?" How she wanted to shake a straight answer out of just one of them!

"When differing personalities live together, then I think it is inevitable that some kerfuffle or another will come of it."

"I always thought a woman would want her mother nearby at such a time." Lydia looked directly at Jane.

Jane raised open hands and leaned back. "It is selfish of me to insist upon it after what we have heard about Papa's condition. Clearly, he is in greater need of her than I am."

"It seems as though you might like me to speak to Papa on the matter?"

"Only if you think it a good idea," Jane said.

Lydia just might run screaming out of a room with so much niceness.

"You are feeling most unwell."

Cosette?

Lydia scanned the room—there, peeking out, just behind the curtain of the far window, near the ceiling. Why was she persuading?

"You have the beginning of a sick headache."

Jane pressed her temples. "Gracious, forgive me, but I suddenly feel quite unwell."

"Good heavens, what is that?" Bingley jumped to his feet, peering through the doorway.

"I will not stay here another moment! Not another moment!" What was Kitty shouting about?

"If you are certain, we shall leave." Mr. Mothman followed closely behind.

"Mama!" Kitty shrieked.

Lydia dashed into the hall, Jane and Bingley not far behind.

Two footmen carried Mama onto the landing from the stairs leading to the attics.

"Mama! Mama! What has happened to her?" Kitty ran to Mrs. Reynolds who stood just behind the footmen.

"She is most unwell. She swooned in the nursery whilst seeing Anne." Lizzy declared as she joined them from the grand stairs. "Mrs. Sharp fears it is something contagious."

"Contagious! Is there a danger to Anne?" Lydia asked.

"Mrs. Sharp is concerned. Mr. Darcy has made arrangements for Mama to return to Ingleside by the traveling coach."

Cold prickles covered Lydia's cheeks. Alister Salt taking the dragon-deaf home? Something was desperately wrong.

"Returning to Ingleside is an excellent idea. It will be best for Jane." What did Cosette have to do with this? *"Miss Bingley feels ill, too, and wishes to return."*

Lydia drew a deep breath. Though she wanted answers, now was not the time to demand them. Elizabeth's wide-eyed glance confirmed her suspicions. Whatever was going on must be very important, and she should not jeopardize it.

"I think perhaps we should return as Jane feels unwell, too. I will see to my sister. You will forgive us, Elizabeth, for being such poor company?" Bingley took Jane on his arm.

"Certainly! You can leave as soon as the coaches are ready—Mr. Darcy has already ordered them. You can wait in the drawing room downstairs. Mrs. Reynolds will see that everything is packed and the luggage cart returned this afternoon."

"Yes, very good, very considerate, thank you." Bingley, a bit glassy-eyed, escorted Jane toward the guest wing, most likely to gather hats, reticules, and Miss Bingley before heading to the drawing room. Cosette had done her part well.

"We are coming with you!" Kitty and Mr. Mothman trotted after them.

"Lizzy, are you well?" Clearly, she was not; pale, face drawn, and, yes, her hands were trembling. Lydia took Elizabeth's arm and led her into the family sitting room, closing the door firmly behind her. "Pray tell me what is going on."

"I hardly know where to begin." Elizabeth sank into the nearest chair, face in her hands.

Lydia knelt in front of the chair and grasped Elizabeth's hands. "What can I do? How can I help?"

"May smelt a strange dragon, and Darcy heard it in his office, persuading Mr. Mothman."

"Dragon's fire! How is that possible? Where could it have come from?"

"We do not know. As I spoke with May, Mama burst into the nursery and attacked Truth and Mercy, thinking they were snakes. They bit her, accounting for her current stupor."

No, she must not laugh, it was not actually funny. At least not today. Someday, though, it would be very amusing.

"Something strange is going on at Ingleside, and it is best to have them away from Pemberley immediately. I instructed Cosette and April to make the necessary persuasions."

"She did a credible job of it with Jane and Bingley."

"I had no doubts she would. We will have to regroup, as it were, after they leave, try to make sense of all this. But the first step is to remove the nursery to the family wing."

"Yes, yes, of course! Little Anne needs to be close at hand." Lydia breathed deep to loosen her pinching chest. "She and Mrs. Sharp can use my chambers. No one will be able to think straight if we are worried for her safety. There is plenty of space in the guest wing for me."

"Oh, Lydia!" Lizzy squeezed her hands until they hurt. "You are too generous. But no, your place is in the family wing. Anne can use Georgiana's chambers; she hardly needs them now. I need you close by as well."

Now was not the time for tears, but later, when all was settled and normal again, Lydia would have a good solid think over this moment, and probably a good cry to boot.

32
Chapter

RICHARD FINISHED RIDING a circuit around Ring Pond. Fair weather and idyllic, pastoral surroundings did nothing to change the fact he was making one last check. If anything, they only made the dichotomy of the situation worse.

In the meantime, St. John confirmed their plans with the Ring Wyrm himself. Those two had connected in an uncanny way. Was it Ring's sense of humor, or perhaps not having lived with a Friend gave him low expectations of warm-bloods in the first place? Either way, who was Richard to judge a dragon's taste in warm-bloods? Especially when it rendered St. John far easier to deal with.

The local wyrms and fairy dragons were in place, ready to alert the security teams if necessary. Provided they remembered what they were to be about and whom they were supposed to contact. Elizabeth had much greater faith in their ability to carry out their assignments than he. But what choice was there? The dependable dragons, cockatrice and drakes, were spread thin as it was. Pemberley was simply too big to cover with the limited dragon-power they had.

Damn it all! Catching dragon-poachers on Pemberley had never been part of their plans. If only— No, stop. Such thinking did nothing but muddy the waters.

A shriek overhead!

Richard stopped his horse and shaded his eyes to peer into the bright blue sky.

Earl?

"A strange dragon is loose at Pemberley! You are needed at the house!" Earl circled overhead.

Bloody hell and damnation! Richard urged his horse into a canter, then a gallop.

Darcy met him just inside the front door.

"Tell me everything." Richard followed Darcy to his office.

"May smelled a strange dragon on the maid's shoes. Every dragon with a halfway decent sense of smell has been deployed to find it. The Ingleside party has departed, under extensive persuasion. The luggage cart with the servants departed not a quarter of an hour ago, half an hour behind the coaches. The nursery zaltys bit Mrs. Bennet—which is another matter entirely—providing a ready means around which to craft the necessary persuasions."

By Jove! "The trespassing dragon has been in the house?"

"I believe I heard it persuading Mothman, here in my office." If Darcy lost any more color in his face, he might well pass for dead.

"Cheeky little bastard!"

"Incredibly bold move, or perhaps an incredibly stupid one, given we are hardly a dragon-deaf household."

"Wyrms are the only type of dragon I have known to be that reckless." Richard glanced about the room. Where might a wyrm hide?

"Mrrow!" A tatzelwurm, one of the grey tabby-striped barnwurms, poked its head through the partially opened green baize servants' door behind Darcy's desk. "You want to see this."

"Elizabeth called for the barnwurms to help search the house." Darcy opened the door enough to admit them both.

Barnwurms? Really? "She's the only one who would have thought of such a thing, but I confess, it was a good idea."

Darcy and Richard followed the tatzelwurm into the narrow, undecorated servants' corridor. The tatzelwurm looked over her shoulder and spring-hopped along what would be the wall behind Darcy's desk.

"Look there." Pointing with her grey tabby-striped serpentine tail, she revealed a hole, chewed through the plaster and the lath behind it.

Motioning for Darcy to get out of the way, Richard knelt, then lay, on the floor. There was something odd. Yes! The tooth marks! "Those are not made by a mouse or rat." He pushed up and dusted his hands against his riding breeches. "Those were made by some kind of wyrm."

Darcy's string of invectives was impressive. Surprising he even knew such language.

"Can you tell—is the scent strong enough that the wyrm might still be there?" Richard asked.

The tatzelwurm, whom he would now think of as Tabby, poked her head into the hole, mouth open, fangs exposed, tongue flicking the air. She slipped in a little farther.

How bloody long could it take to smell out the space?

She hissed and jumped back. "Not there now. Was there, not long ago. But not now. Definitely wyrm." Tabby shook her head and smacked her jaw.

"Could you tell what sort of wyrm?" Richard stroked his jaw, teeth clenched.

"What are you thinking—oh!" Another string of Darcy's newly discovered epithets followed.

"Not a tatzelwurm," she cocked her head so far that her oversized ear faced the ground. "Not a Pemberley wyrm, not water wyrm."

"That is all you could tell?"

She bobbed her furry head vigorously.

"You have done well for us. Go to Brutus for direction, now." Darcy stroked her head, and they returned to the office while Tabby spring-hopped down the servants' passage.

"We need someone who is familiar with the azure forest wyrm scent." Richard drummed his fingers across his chin.

"Definitely. Who might know? I doubt April or Cosette would be able to help. Their sense of smell is not so refined. Do you think May might be able to help? She is so young …"

"If not her, then Earl or Walker. Brutus and Axel were in London with you, but drakes are not nearly so accurate. I will go up and get May."

"We have moved the nursery to the family wing."

"Much better for defense. Good." Richard trotted out. The sooner they knew what they were dealing with, the better.

He reached the top of the stairs and stepped into a well-ordered frenzy of activity, with Mrs. Reynolds in the center of it, directing the traffic from near the attic stairs.

"You want the nursery?" she asked. "In Miss Georgiana's old chambers."

Richard nodded and hurried away, dodging maids and footmen loaded with bundles and furniture.

Georgiana's door stood open, with sunlight pouring out. He had not been in those rooms since he and Darcy were boys. They had sneaked in through the servants' door to put a pair of unsuspecting frogs under her counterpane. Georgiana had not found it amusing. Nor had Uncle Darcy.

Richard peeked through the doorway, just in time to jump aside for a pair of scurrying maids and a little red puck proudly following behind them.

"Sir Richard!" Lydia cried from across the room. She was a sight. A bit dusty and frazzled, curls escaping their pins.

What profound relief that spread through his chest. "You are well?"

"As much as one might be, all things considered. Later, we must plan to sit down and have a good laugh over today's absurdities." Bless her ready sense of humor.

"I cannot tell you how much I will look forward to that."

"Tell me, what news?" Lydia asked.

"I have just returned from Ring, who is well and sounds almost excited about the possibilities for tonight. A barnwurm discovered a hole in the wall in Darcy's office, behind his desk, chewed by a wyrm."

"Dragon's blood!" She pressed her hands to her mouth. "The audacity!"

"Indeed. We are trying to find out more about the wyrm."

"If you need Lizzy, she is in her quarters with Anne. She is most distraught."

"With good reason, especially if we discover what I suspect to be true. If Pemberley was visited by an azure forest wyrm …" He shrugged. "Do you know where May is? I hope she might be able to better identify the scent."

"Upstairs, searching for further traces of the intruder. I will bring her down to Sir Fitzwilliam's office for you, if you like."

Less than ten minutes later, Lydia arrived with May in her arms. The poor little tatzelwurm, wide eyes, pouffed fur, tail flicking wildly. She was hardly more than a wyrmling herself. Lydia stroked under her chin, and she purred loudly.

Darcy sat at his desk, wearing his severe mask of calm, shoulders so stiff he might have broken in a strong breeze. "Thank you for bringing May, and thank you for your efforts, May." What his tone lacked in warmth was made up for by the sincerity in his eyes.

"Mrrrooow." May pouffed even bigger.

"Do you recall Lapis and Indigo, Joshua Gardiner's Friends in London?"

"I do."

"We need to know if the intruder is of the same type of wyrm, an azure forest wyrm. Do you think you can recall the scent well enough to do that?"

"Not Lapis or Indigo, but their kind, yes? The ones with the poison blue skin?" May's tail slowed to a thoughtful flick.

"Yes. Are you willing to try?"

"They have a funny smell to them, their poison skin, I think. Very distinct. I will try."

"Come, we will show you the space." Richard opened the green baize door and guided May and Lydia to the freshly chewed hole in the wall.

May approached the hole with an odd mix of predator and prey in her body language. It was the sort of place a tatzelwurm would hunt their dinner, but it could also conceal the larger wyrms that made tatzelwurms their prey. Like Tabby, she opened her mouth, fangs exposed, tongue flicking, and pushed the front half of her body into the wall.

Hissing and growling, May scrabbled backward, pulling clumps of plaster with her, and spring-hopped into Lydia's ready arms. She pulled herself eye to eye with Darcy, breathing heavily. "I am sure. No doubt. There was a blue wyrm in that hole."

!

33
Chapter

ELIZABETH SURVEYED THE guest sitting room. After the Ingleside party's departure, Mrs. Reynolds had ordered it reconfigured back into a planning room. She even included a pallet for little Anne to sleep upon near the unlit fireplace and a large basket for the nursery dragons. Heavens above, that woman all but read minds!

Elizabeth laid Anne on the pallet and pulled up the little nursery quilt. May, Mercy, and Truth slithered into the basket, weaving themselves into a formidable knot of dragons. It was tempting to seek out a larger drake or cockatrice to be Anne's personal guard, but the little dragons had proved their mettle today, even if it was Elizabeth's mother who had been bitten.

Merciful heavens! If—and that was still a question—they ever had dragon-deaf guests again, the door to the nursery would have to be kept locked at all times! Pray that the persuasions would make Mama forget entirely about snakes in the nursery!

One day she would have to share the story with Lady Dressler and Lady Astrid. They would find the humor in it. Aunt—Lady— Gardiner would laugh, no doubt, but only to conceal her horror. Not that Elizabeth would blame her for that. It was in equal parts horrible and hilarious.

Anne sighed and seemed to smile as her breath became deep and regular with sleep. With one last pat, Elizabeth picked up the candle from the mantel and lit more around the room. The last rays of sunset were quickly fading, and dinner trays would be arriving, along with hungry, anxious, weary denizens of Pemberley.

As Elizabeth lit the final candle on the long table, Mrs. Reynolds and the maid arrived to set out the dinner things. Definitely not the dinner any of them were expecting to be served when they rose this morning.

Lydia, still wearing her dusty apron, dragged in and fell into her usual spot, near the dragon perch Earl favored. "What, we are not to be served in the dining room? I cannot believe it, Lizzy. I dressed especially for the occasion."

This was hardly the time for a joke, but Elizabeth giggled, then laughed until she held her sides, tears running down her cheeks. "Well, perhaps ... perhaps... you should go back to your room ... and find something more ... more suitable to wear.... You are ... terribly underdressed."

"Underdressed, you say?" Richard strode in, still in his riding breeches and boots, covered in road dust and bits of plaster. "I will have you know, I am assured this is the latest fashion in dinner wear. I cannot believe you would be so unaware of the *ton's* latest trends." He dropped into the chair beside Lydia.

"Perhaps that is one of the dangers of living out in the wilds of the Peak District." Lydia barely got the words out for giggling.

"But the demands of fashion here are far more relaxed," Darcy murmured as he shuffled in, St. John at his heels. "I am sure the mistress of the house will find the grace to excuse any faux pax in dress."

Elizabeth gawked at him. Just what could have driven Darcy to jest?

He sat beside her. "Everything is in readiness."

"No, no, not another word until everyone has a plate and is eating. Whatever needs to be said can wait that long. Going hungry will not make any of us wiser or stronger." Elizabeth rallied her weary company into filling their plates from the trays.

"I do not know how Cook took plans for a full dinner and made them into a cold supper that tastes like this!" Lydia bit into a slab of pigeon pie.

"Everything tastes better sauced with hunger and exhaustion," Richard murmured over an equally large bite of cold pork with mayonnaise.

"No. Everything tastes better with honey and jam." Cosette buzzed across the table and landed near Lydia's plate.

"She is right." April flittered to the edge of Elizabeth's glass and tasted her wine.

"Be careful, we need our wits about us tonight." Elizabeth opened a nearby honey pot and placed it near her glass.

"What were you able to learn?" Darcy handed a pot of jam to Lydia.

"None of the household dragons or the garden wyrms saw the intruder, and only the tatzelwurms were sensitive enough to have even smelt it." Cosette said through slurps of red berry jam.

"I wish that surprised me, but wyrms are particularly good at remaining undetected, since they are preyed upon by so many other dragons." Richard frowned and shuddered a little.

"The tatzelwurm you have been calling Tabby found traces of the smell in the servants' quarters," April said. "I never liked the notion of having the Ingleside warm-bloods here in the first place."

"That does not mean the wyrm was associated with them, though. We know Mama and Kitty are dragon-deaf. The Bingleys as well. And Cosette was certain that she persuaded Mr. Mothman whilst we were in Sheffield."

"He definitely cannot hear dragons." Cosette fluttered her wings for emphasis.

"Has anyone considered the servants?" Mr. St. John asked without looking up from his sausage and potatoes.

"But there are no resident dragons at Ingleside, even among the servants. At least that is what the wild dragons told Earl when we visited."

"That does not rule out a dragon working independently." Darcy stabbed a pickled cauliflower with his fork.

"But it is a wyrm! We met the blue wyrms in London. While they are good enough fellows, to be sure, they are like other wyrms, preferring the company of their own kind to that of warm-bloods. Why would one—and correct me if I am wrong, but I understood that May only smelled one—be working alone among warm-bloods? Two together, perhaps, but just one? It does not make any sense." Richard took a long draw from his beer. "Were there any hearers among the servants?"

"Not among those we met," April paused and cocked her head, the way she did when she was thinking hard. "But I do not think we met them all."

"So, really, we know nothing more about the intruder than we did this afternoon." Darcy popped a bit of bread into his mouth as though to keep from saying more.

"That is not a loss, just a failure to gain ground. There is a meaningful difference between the two," Richard said.

Awkward silence descended as everyone attended their plates.

"The Ring Wyrm assures me all is in readiness in his territory," St. John managed to sputter through his full mouth.

"Derwent sent word that the river is secure. Blackwood says the same of Broken Tooth." Richard broke a piece of bread, sending a shower of crumbs across the table.

Cosette and April dove for the crumbs. Had that been an intentional provision for the fairy dragons? Richard was the sort to think of that sort of kindness.

"Grove and Gates have also indicated their readiness." Darcy wrapped his hands around his wineglass and stared into it.

"What precisely are we ready for? With the Ingleside party returned to their home, what can we reasonably expect?" Lydia asked.

"That is an excellent question. I am not sure anything is reasonable right now." Elizabeth pushed a pickle around her plate, her third so far. They were particularly tasty tonight.

A dark shadow swooped across the near window. Elizabeth tensed, ready to spring to Anne's side.

"Earl!" Richard waved her down as he threw open the window.

Of course, he was due back now. She should have known better.

Earl flapped to the dragon perch and landed with far less elegance than Walker. But this time he did not come close to knocking the perch over, so he was improving. He was so much grown, it was easy to forget he was still a youngster.

"You have news?" Lydia asked as she handed him a slab of pork straight from the serving dish.

"Important news." Earl tore off a large shred and gulped it down in a single bite. "Juniper and Fern remain at Ingleside to ensure no further persuasion is necessary. The warm-bloods seem ready to believe something they ate at Pemberley did not agree with them, and the ladies have all taken to their beds. The old, shrieky one recovers from the poison." He gulped down another large bite.

"And the trespassing dragon?" Darcy asked.

"No sign. But—" The third bite finished Earl's meat. "There is more. The furry one—"

"You mean Mothman?" Richard asked.

"Cosette calls him the furry one," Earl muttered. "Yes, him. He did not return to Ingleside with the rest."

"Where is he? He did not remain on Pemberley?" Elizabeth asked.

"No, no. But I heard him say he had business in Lambton. He took a room at the Black Bull in the village."

"Could he have been persuaded to do so?" Darcy asked.

"I cannot be sure. I heard nothing, but his horse carried saddle bags. If the wyrm was secreted in one, its voice would not have been loud enough for me to hear."

"Would a horse accept a dragon literally on its back?" Lydia asked.

"It would be unusual," Richard said. "But Pemberley trains its horses to tolerate dragons, so I suppose it could be done."

"Mothman did not want the Pemberley grooms exercising his horses." Darcy said. "I do not know what to make of that, but surely it cannot be anything good."

Elizabeth shuddered. That was simply a polite way of saying it was indeed bad.

"So then, we will proceed as planned tonight?" Richard asked.

"I see no alternative." Darcy took a deep draw from his wine.

!

Chapter 34

IMMEDIATELY AFTER DINNER, Darcy, Richard, and St. John made their way through the moonless night to the cart barn. Still, quiet air blanketed the landscape in anticipation so thick Darcy nearly gasped for breath. Saddled horses nickered softly, acknowledging their arrival. Whether or not they were ridden tonight remained to be seen.

They would wait here, in the blanket of darkness, for any word from of the security teams of trespassers on the grounds. What action would follow depended on so many things. Exactly the sort of plan Darcy despised. Having to wait for the privilege of acting on it—or not—might just drive him out of his skin.

What was worse? Having something to act on, or waiting all night for nothing? Reason suggested one thing, but his thundering heart and twitching reflexes demanded something else altogether.

"Have you gotten this close to their activities during your investigations, St. John?" Richard's voice came from the dark corner nearest Darcy.

"No. I have never had the opportunity." It sounded as though the admission might pain him. "Clearly, there are advantages to working together."

Richard shifted and seemed to lift a hand. "Wait. I hear something."

Wings flapped through open windows. Darcy's breath caught. Talons scrabbled on the hard-packed dirt.

"Trespassers have been spotted!" Earl hissed, a frightening shadow in the darkness. "Heading toward Ring Pond."

They jumped to their feet. Richard pushed open the door, and they mounted.

Merciful heavens, let the house be safe!

Earl led them through the murky landscape, the horses uncertain in the moonless night. Step, step, step. Bloody creatures—so damn slow! The interlopers would be gone by the time they got there.

The shadowy figure of the manor disappeared behind the rise. Perhaps a third of the way there. Pray Ring could hold them off …

Step. Step. Step. Step.

A clearing on the right. Halfway.

"Wait! Stop!" Walker shrieked overhead. "The Blackwoods! Intruders in the Blackwoods!"

Dragon bloody bones and fire!

"I will go to Ring!" St. John declared and urged his horse faster in Earl's wake.

Richard wheeled his horse toward Darcy. "Where—"

"With him, to Ring. Go." St. John might have the desire and enthusiasm, but those qualities did not make up for the experience and training he lacked.

Darcy directed his horse to follow Walker.

"Three men, converging on basilisk Blackwood. I could not tell if there were any more. She is in the open, near Broken Tooth as agreed."

He pressed his heels into the horse's sides with little change in pace. "Damn!"

"There is time. The darkness is to her advantage. Remember, she insisted on baiting the trap herself, but that does not mean she has a death wish."

"The offer came only after learning of Ring's intentions, suggesting—"

"A basilisk could hardly permit a greater show of bravery from a lowly knucker, could she?" Walker snorted.

"It is always dominance with you dragons, is it not?"

"Always." Walker snorted. "Why else do you think Derwent and Gates are doing the same? As for Grove, a knucker will always be more dominant than a forest wyrm, but pride keeps Grove from showing her throat without a fight. Both you and Pemberley must understand these things if a little dragon is to manage the territory."

They would have to come back to that later.

Time crawled by, a tortoise on a cold winter's night, until they reached the road that would take them to the Blackwoods. The horse broke into a canter.

Richard glanced over his shoulder. St. John remained half a horse length behind, but kept up the quick pace though the open clover field.

"Two men were detected, their paths converging on Ring Pond." Earl circled low overhead.

Odd. That did not seem enough manpower to take on a dragon, even one of Ring's size. Unless they were heavily armed and intended to kill him outright.

Not an unlikely possibility.

"Can Earl go on ahead to assist Ring if needed?" Tension pitched St. John's voice high and tight.

He did realize that Earl was supposed to keep them from being ambushed on the way, did he not? Oh, bloody hell! "Yes, go, see to Ring."

Earl squawked and flapped off, cutting through the dark sky like a mythical creature of lore. Which, in truth, he was.

"We have no way of knowing how heavily armed they are. It is too dark for projectiles, which is to our advantage. Ring's best defense is to remain underwater. Remember, your role is to distract the poachers and allow his escape. Understood? Shout, run, keep moving. For the love of Pendragon, keep out of their reach. Leave intercepting them to Earl and me. We will coordinate efforts with the rest of the team that should be converging on the site." By Jove, he hated working with untrained men. All told, it would be enough if St. John did not hamper efforts.

"If that is the way to protect him, then I will do that."

Surprising, but not unwelcome. If the man could follow orders, he might yet prove himself useful.

Not far now. The edge of the pond should be in view soon. Yes, there. That dark-on-dark patch, with the darker silhouette rising from the surface.

Richard hooted something resembling an owl's call. Ring slapped the water with his tail.

All was well—for now.

Richard waved St. John toward a clump of shrubbery—his agreed-upon cover near the water's edge.

Earl warbled a bird-like sound. Good, he had perched in the tall trees just beyond Ring Pond.

Richard dismounted and walked the horse to a group of shrubs and tied it. From here he could watch and wait.

Where was the bloody turn-off to Broken Tooth? Easy enough to miss in the daylight, locating it in the dark was simply not going to happen with Darcy's limited, warm-blooded vision.

Walker swooped close, somewhere to the right. "There. Leave the horse, and follow me."

Darcy tied the horse and removed a wooden club from his saddle bag. He picked his way through the encompassing shadows, barely making out Walker's deeper black form.

A scream echoed off the hillside, piercing the Blackwoods with the sound of soul-crushing dread. But was it man or dragon?

"Go. I will make it through on my own."

Walker cut through the trees, nearly silent, death on wings.

Darcy picked up his pace, but he might as well have been slogging through the deepest mud as he struggled not to trip over deadfall and debris.

Another scream, louder, closer. Men's voices. Not close enough to make out words.

Almost there.

He paused where the trees thinned into a clearing, squinting, forcing his eyes to make sense of the black shapes before him.

Blackwood stood atop Broken Tooth, precariously balanced on two of the stones. The most defensible position, but a dangerous one. Two men, no, it was three, circled the stones, just out of her reach.

The basilisk hissed, tail lashing, her body swelled. Front paws swiped at the nearest foe.

Wait, what?

One of the men stopped circling and unslung a bag from his shoulder, dumping a long wriggling form to the ground.

Darcy shivered away the prickles dancing on the back of his neck. Dragon's fire! No!

The dark form disappeared against the rocks. Blackwood reared up on back legs, hissing and growling, snapping at something Darcy could not see.

A smaller growl answered and a blob of shadow shot through the darkness at Blackwood's throat.

She tumbled back off Broken Tooth toward Darcy, pawing at her face, screaming as she thudded to the ground.

Her head seemed misshapen—no, wait, something clung to her. A wyrm, it had to be that blue wyrm, attacking her with its skin-borne venom.

That sounded like the attack Ring had described against himself. Damn it all, they had tried this same sort of assault before.

"There! It's down. Make haste!" The nearest man waved to the others, and they descended on the flailing Blackwood, her movements weakening, coordination failing.

Richard slipped between two large peony bushes and crouched among the leaves and flowers, settling in to wait and watch.

Earl called again, a shrill piercing tone. Intruders approached.

Ring slipped down into the pond, only his eyes and the top of his head visible above the surface. Nearly impossible to discern under the moonless sky.

Richard forced himself to breathe, quick shallow breaths, muscles taut as a bow string.

There, just out of the cover of the trees, a figure in a greatcoat, carrying a tied, lumpy bundle. He cupped his hands around his mouth and hooted three times.

Ring dipped completely below the pond's surface.

The intruder stopped and scanned right, left, and right again, then scurried to a wooden bench near the edge of the pond. "Cri-cri-cri."

Frog song?

"Purreek. Pureek. Pur-pur-pureek." Where did that come from?

"Cri-cri-creeek!" Greatcoat tucked the bundle under the bench, then removed three more parcels from within his coat and placed them with the bundle. "Waaaa-wraaa-wreeep."

"Rummm-ruuum. Gunk!" There, that came from the stand of trees.

Greatcoat cast about and scurried into the darkness.

Earl screamed a call reminiscent of a hunting hawk. The guard drakes would be following Greatcoat and hopefully subdue him before he left the estate. The first prize of the night, but hopefully not the only one.

There was someone—Frog Man—still out there, ready to take possession of those packages. Surely, he would make his appearance soon.

Richard settled back amongst the peonies to wait. Surely, it would not be long.

Walker's screech echoed off the rocks, becoming a cacophony of cockatrice screams, amplifying the terror-inducing power. Darcy's knees weakened, and his gut trembled, threatening to turn to jelly. Breathing hard in time with his racing heart, Darcy ran toward Blackwood's attackers.

Where were Brutus and his team?

Walker dove at the nearest man, talons reaching. The target ducked away, but a second turned directly into Walker's swoop. Screaming, he clutched his face and staggered away.

"What was that?"

"Owl? Hawk?"

"No, dragon!" That was a dragon voice. The wyrm? Yes. A wyrm voice. "Cockatrice. Woods is full of them."

"There's one that lives at the house. Maybe more than one." That voice was familiar. Just barely, but familiar. "What the hell is it doing here?"

Walker screamed again and dove for the voice.

Three more shadowy figures emerged from around the hillsides. Shouting and pointing, sticks— no, clubs—in hand.

Six now. How were they to take on six?

Thwack!

Wood landing on flesh. Walker screamed, careening into Broken Tooth Rock. A man shouted; wings rustled and flapped.

Thwack!

Blackwood howled.

"Leave her alone!" Darcy shouted, plunging into the fray, club swinging.

Blackwood swept one man off his feet with her tail as two more descended on Darcy. His club hit something soft.

A man grunted and staggered back.

A second blow landed hard, a head perhaps, and a shadow-figure fell to his knees.

"Who is that?"

"Came out of the woods!"

"Cobalt! On point!"

A long shade flew out of the darkness toward Darcy's face. He swung his club but lost his balance as it swung through empty air.

Growling, a heavy, cold body wrapped around his shoulders, his neck, writhing, rubbing.

Darcy's mouth went numb, then his face. The darkness lost focus, and he sank to his knees.

"Come on, Frog Man, show your ugly face," Richard muttered under his breath. Had the guard drakes apprehended Greatcoat?

He rubbed his arms, hair standing on end. What was in those damn packages? Deep breath. He would know soon enough. By dawn he would know.

Waiting.

That was the worst. Just waiting. Anticipating, not knowing. Thinking, considering, what might be. What could be. But that was never how it happened. Always something one never expected.

In the dark. The still, heavy air. Heavy with possibility, terrible possibility, weighing down, thick and suffocating.

"Skree!"

Richard jumped, nearly leaving his skin behind.

Earl!

Someone approached.

There, from the trees opposite the way Greatcoat had gone. Looking left, looking right.

Fool never looked up.

Creeping carefully. Looking again, hesitating. Faster now, toward the bench.

"Caw-ca-caw!"

Richard bolted from the peony bushes, sprinting for the bench.

Frog Man snatched the packages, turned to see Richard. Shouting, he ran, straight toward St. John's hiding place.

Above, Earl swooped toward them.

A dark blur—St. John—plunged into Frog Man's path.

A tangle of bodies. Shouts. Frog Man ran again.

Earl dove, grabbed the shoulders of Frog Man's coat. Richard dove and swept him to the ground. Again.

Blows landed, but Richard's heart beat too loud to feel them. His own fists landed: ribs, shoulder, face. Knees on chest, he forced Frog Man back.

"Can't breathe! Can't breathe! I surrender!"

Richard eased back, just enough. "St. John, get the rope."

"You're not going to hang me! No, you can't!" That voice, familiar.

"A judge will decide that. I'm just going to make sure you see one."

St. John skidded to a stop beside him and handed him the rope.

A scream like nothing Darcy had ever heard cut through the darkness, sharp and rasping against his skin. Walker answered in kind.

A man shrieked even as Darcy heard more than felt a club glancing off his own ribs. His arms would not cooperate, his legs like lead, heavy and still.

Must stand, must fight. Protect Elizabeth, Anne. Protect Pemberley.

Cannot succumb.

He pushed himself to hands and knees, panting, straining. The world whirled about him, taunting. Promising to make sense, then dancing just out of reach.

A large, winged darkness filled the darkness with screaming men, scrambling, crying.

Hissing and growling. A light!

A flame, there, close enough to reach as a leathery blanket enfolded him, sheltering. And the trumpet, so loud, vibrating his bones, every part of his being, drowning out the screams, the terror.

Embraced like a caterpillar in a cocoon, the world rocked with a thrumming that was nearly a purr. Comforting, secure, sanctuary.

His ears cleared, grounding to the muffled sounds of the night.

So long. How long?

Itching, prickly nettles across his skin faded into vague uneasiness, and he forced open his eyes.

The leathery blanket peeled back.

"Keeper? You well now?"

Pemberley?

Pemberley!

He brought his head up so sharply it nearly struck Pemberley's chin. She unfolded her wings and set him on his knees with her front paws.

Pressing his hands on the ground, he gulped air until the world stopped spinning. "What are you do-ing here?"

"It new moon. Rosings and Chudleigh say practice fly on new moon. I practice like they say. Matlock say must survey territory at new moon. I survey. Then saw you." Her tone dropped deeper, growly. "What going on?"

"Poachers were attacking, Vicontes." Blackwood shambled toward them. "We were trying to capture them."

"And I not told? This my territory." She stomped and rumbled, a tiny spurt of flame at her muzzle. "Why you not tell me? Keeper? This not good."

Dragon thunder! "You are right. We did not realize. You should have been consulted. It was a serious oversight, and it will not happen again."

"You right. Not happen again. When you well, we talk."

One of the men on the ground groaned and stirred. Pemberley whirled on him, growling and flaming. Screams of pain—or was that fear? Sounds of men scrabbling back.

"The wyrm? There was a blue wyrm here. Poisoned me." Darcy blinked and shook his head. Perhaps that would cast away the remaining fog.

"I have it." Walker cawed from somewhere high. "Richard comes with a barrel to cage it."

"Does it live?"

"Yes. I have it by the throat—it cannot speak."

Lights appeared in the woods, bobbing, growing brighter. Lanterns, those must be lanterns.

Richard!

"Bloody dragon's fire!" Yes, that was Richard. "Pemberley, did you manage this?"

"My territory. I protect. Blackwood good help." Pemberley opened her wings and lifted her head high in the lantern light.

"Bind them up and get them in the cart. Load the bodies first." How many men did Richard have with him?

Richard walked toward Broken Tooth and the poachers. "You? Oh, bloody hell! Darcy, come quickly!"

Hands—he was not entirely sure whose— helped Darcy to his feet, and he trudged toward Richard's voice and the light near it.

"This man," Richard tied the man's hands, "is Caney, Mothman's manservant. If I do not miss my guess, the leader of this vile band."

"You don't think it was that idiot Mothman?" Caney snarled, testing his bonds. "Dragon-deaf and dumb as a stump. Cobalt is smarter than 'im.'"

Was that a greater insult to the blue wyrm or to Mothman?

"Get that barrel fastened securely and load it with the bodies. Tie the ones that can walk behind the cart—double the ropes. And get them to Matlock." Richard clapped Darcy's shoulder. "Stay here. You are in no shape to be walking about. I will be back in a moment."

Pemberley strode up to him, proud and dominant. "I could guard here, but Matlock taking trespassers. He keep them away Little Keeper."

"Absolutely, you could. I can see that now." He reached to scratch under her chin, nearly losing his balance.

"I angry that wyrm. He hurt you. He lucky Walker got him first."

"I will recover, do not worry."

"Of course he will." Richard sauntered back. "I sent Walker to the house with the news. Time to get you back as well." He pulled Darcy's arm over his shoulders. "Pemberley, Grove, Gates, and Derwent are still on alert. I think the danger has passed for to-night. How do you wish to inform them?"

"I fly. I see them. Ring, too. Tell them what happened. They all good help me." Pemberley waddled off, extended her wings fully, and launched.

Chills raced down Darcy's back. A firedrake in flight, even not full-grown, made a fearsome image, even when he could barely make her out.

"Ring Pond?" Darcy struggled to form words. "What happened?"

"Not nearly as exciting as here. We found Mothman skulking about. For all his bluster about not dealing in smuggled goods, he arranged a drop point with a free trader to pick up a load of lace, silk, and the like."

"No danger to Ring?"

"No, Mothman seemed oblivious to the dragon. Had him taken to the cart barn. Little chance of seeing him prosecuted for buying such goods, unfortunately. The free trader got away, but there was little chance of prosecuting him, either."

"Mothman. Was he involved in the poaching?"

"Not likely. Caney is right. He is an idiot. Earl is quite certain the wyrm was persuading him of a great deal."

"Just how far did those persuasions go?"

"We will find out, but first you need to get home."

35
Chapter

July 7, 1815

LYDIA SHOULD HAVE slept soundly, knowing the danger had passed, and the men were little worse for the wear. Should have, but did not. How could anyone with a mind and a heart simply drop into slumber after hours of pacing the floor and peering into the darkness hoping for some sign of good news?

Thankfully, dawn, and a reason to be up and about, were only a few hours off when she had been banished to her chambers with: "No dragons were injured and Sir Richard had gone on to Matlock with the prisoners, so there was nothing for her to do." Or so Lizzy had insisted.

While technically correct, Lizzy's pronouncement had nearly pushed her to forget all Mrs. Fieldings' teaching, stamp her feet, and throw a fit that would have put Mama to shame. But she did not. She went to her chambers like the good girl she did not feel like being.

Still, that did not mean she could not be up at dawn, waiting in the morning room for someone to rise and answer her questions.

So many questions.

Cosette, still exhausted and snoring in a fluffy heap in a basket of "soft", remained behind as Lydia made her way to the morning room. She ought to have Betsey lay out a pot of jam for Cosette so she would not have to search for food when she woke up, famished. For all their small size, fairy dragons ate an astonishing amount.

An odd stillness pervaded the corridors as Lydia slipped downstairs. As if a silent lingering tension had faded away, leaving the house to rest properly for the first time since they had arrived. Hopefully, someone had managed to enjoy such a rest.

She peeked into the peach-colored morning room that basked in a rosy sunrise glow.

Strange. Sir Fitzwilliam never took breakfast in the morning room.

He glanced up from his newspaper. "Good morning."

"Am I disturbing you?" She hesitated at the doorway despite the welcoming fragrances of coffee and breads inviting her in.

"Not at all. The coffee is still hot. Would you care for some?"

"Sir Richard has revealed my darkest secret." She sat at the round table, leaving an empty chair between them.

"It is a risk associated with being in his company, I think. I fix the blame on him for having developed a taste for the stuff myself." He poured a cup and passed it to her.

"I am surprised you are up so early this morning."

"Blue wyrm venom is not conducive to sound sleep. Elizabeth assures me that the violent dreams will pass in a day or so."

She might have teased him but for the dark circles under his eyes. "Has there been word from Matlock?"

"Earl reported that Richard and Cownt Matlock have everything in order. The prisoners are to be taken to London, directly to the Blue Order offices. This is not a matter to be handled at a local level. Richard will be accompany the prisoners and make a full report to the Council."

"Oh." Cold lead poured through her veins. He would remove from Pemberley, and their joint efforts would be over. She should have realized that would be the outcome. It was obvious, really. Foolish, foolish girl to ignore what had always been on the horizon.

"He will be coming back this morning before he takes his leave, though." Darcy's tone seemed a bit apologetic, almost an acknowledgement of feelings she could barely admit herself. "I do not think he had anticipated the trip himself. It is on the cownt's orders. I hope I am not too forward in suggesting that he might not be pleased with the assignment."

"You are very kind." She swallowed hard. Darcy really was. A trait that was too often overlooked in his character, hidden by the somber structure he tended to impose, a golden, sympathetic thread that ran through everything he touched.

Lizzy was a fortunate woman.

She cradled the hot coffee cup in both hands and stared into its dark, warm depths. "What of Mr. Mothman?"

Darcy stifled a groan in a sip of coffee. "Indeed, what of him? It is a conundrum, and I am not certain how to rectify it. I would ask for Elizabeth's input, but I refuse to wake her from a sound sleep for the likes of him."

"Perhaps I might help?"

He turned to stare out the window as though considering, then nodded. "I am of mixed minds with regards to him. On the one hand, he has clearly been duped by his man, Caney, and Cobalt, the blue wyrm. Persuaded, quite illegally, for their purposes. I cannot in good conscience hold him responsible for being susceptible to that level of persuasion."

"True, but the ease of the persuasion does suggest something about the strength of his character, his resolve. Or so I understand."

"Quite. And there is no ignoring the fact that he arranged to pick up smuggled goods on my estate." Low, rugged notes crept into Darcy's tone. "That was no spur-of-the-moment decision but required planning and intent. It is difficult for me to blame that merely on persuasion. Worse, the crime is nearly impossible to prosecute—he claims he did not know the goods were smuggled—"

"Liar."

"Or an imbecile, or both. He did not know the name of the courier, and in all likelihood did not even have the true name of the seller. So, there is no legal course to follow there, either."

"Which is worse, feeling used by him or Pemberley's pollution by the free traders?"

"The Order would say the latter. All members, but especially Keepers, are enjoined to keep as much distance as possible from anything questionable, especially the grey areas at the borders of the law. The secrecy of the Order cannot risk compromise."

"And how many actually follow that advice?"

"It does not matter. I will." Of course he would. Duty and honor were Darcy's lifeblood.

"I see. So you cannot allow yourself to be connected to the man. If Kitty marries him, you must cut off all ties to that part of the family, but that is at odds with your duty to your family."

His eyes grew wide.

"What else but that obligation could account for your taking me on to live with you? I have been the fortunate recipient of your sense of duty, and I will not forget that." She looked away again. "I cannot imagine what it must be like to be torn between two opposing obligations."

"Quite that, exactly. I have wondered if Mothman was persuaded to like your sister, or it was his real inclination that drew him to her, and I do not know how to find out. If it was persuasion, then it must be undone somehow. If not, it would be unethical, even illegal, to interfere with his affection through persuasion."

"It is not exactly the sort of thing one comes right out and asks, is it?" She chuckled under her breath. "I believe Cosette might be able to help, though. One of the dragons studying to be a companion at Mrs. Fieldings' told her that she had heard of persuasions being used to manipulate young ladies into marriage. It was that dragon's belief that a young lady could be persuaded to identify her own feelings and listen to them, if a persuasive dragon approached the matter correctly. Cosette is most persuasive. Perhaps she might be able to encourage Mr. Mothman to confess his true feelings for Kitty."

"I have never heard of such a thing. Does Elizabeth know about this?"

"I just assumed she would. It never occurred to me to mention it. I will have Cosette discuss it with her, if you like."

"Yes, you definitely should. But the longer we confine Mr. Mothman, the more difficult things become. Would you and Cosette be willing to speak with him out in the barn? If you can just find out his true state of mind toward your sister, Elizabeth and I will know how to act."

"I will go to Cosette right now."

An hour later, with Cosette full up on jam, they made their way to the cart barn. Still early, the heat of the day had already cut through the morning freshness, promising a scalding afternoon. Definitely best to get this over with now.

But then what would she do? How strange it would be without the purpose that had defined her last month in Derbyshire. Perhaps she could find some way to assist Elizabeth, who always seemed to have too much to do.

The cart barn rose up ahead. The wounded messengers had been removed to another barn for their recovery, and Ring was back in his pond. From a makeshift hospital to a makeshift prison, what a strange little building the thatched-roof stone barn had become.

She knocked on the door. "Mr. Darcy has sent me."

Brutus' long black nose nudged the door open. "For what purpose?"

"To gain a better understanding of Mr. Mothman's frame of mind." She peeked past the huge guard drake into the dimly-lit barn.

Mothman sat, utterly disheveled, back against the wall, arms around his knees, head down. Miserable. He looked up at her, relief blooming on his face. "Miss Lydia!"

Brutus stepped aside to allow her in.

"The boarhound listens to you! How marvelous! Sir Richard forced me here last night and set his dog on me. I have not the faintest notion why."

"Is that so?" She pulled an old stool near Mr. Mothman and sat down. "I find that difficult to believe." She shrugged her right shoulder. Cosette flittered to the roof and clung to a rafter, nearly upside down.

"Excuse me? Who are you to question me? I was the one assaulted in the middle of the night and held here as a prisoner."

"What exactly were you doing on another man's land in the middle of the night? Men of honest intent do not go skulking about under cover of the new moon."

"Skulking? You were not even there. Do not cast judgement where you have no information."

"What else would you call it?"

"I was receiving goods I had duly purchased."

Lydia closed her eyes and pinched her temples. "And you see nothing wrong with the manner in which that took place?"

"I must manage my business as I see fit. Acquiring goods for the best prices is part of that."

"And you are happy with that manner of doing business?" Lydia glanced up at Cosette.

"She wants to know how you really feel. Are you happy as a haberdasher? Do you miss being an apothecary? Are you satisfied with business as it is?"

It was strange hearing questions in a persuasive voice. So different from the usual business of fairy dragons.

"It is different to what I was accustomed to." Mr. Mothman scratched his head, rather like a dog scratching at fleas.

"How so?"

"Why did you change your trade?"

"I was an apothecary, you know. A good one, I think."

"And did you like it?"

"I did. The mixing and brewing. The sorting out what each customer needed. Most satisfying." He wrapped his arms around his knees, rocking slightly as he stared at a shuttered window.

"Why did you leave it?"

"I am not sure. It seemed a good idea at the time. One of those thoughts that flies in and will not leave you alone. I rather miss it, though. Your sister, she thought it dull. Never wanted to hear about what I used to do. Only about the haberdashery and the new shop."

"Do you truly wish to marry Miss Bennet? Do you like her very well? Enough to propose marriage?"

Mr. Mothman's forehead wrinkled, and his eyes lost focus as though he were thinking deeply. Very deeply. Deeply enough that he might do himself an injury.

Lydia waited until her skin prickled, and she could no longer sit still. "Did it bother you that she thought your former trade so dull?"

He blinked again, then his eyes widened. "Yes, yes, it did, to be perfectly honest. I felt it most deeply. Just because she thought it dry and unrewarding did not make it so."

"I can imagine. I do not enjoy conversing with those who do not approve of my own interests."

"It was difficult. But she did love to hear about the new laces and ribbons and buttons I discovered."

"I can imagine. I like those well myself."

"I saw that when you visited. There is something pleasing in seeing a customer's eyes light up the way yours did. The same used to happen in my apothecary shop. When I prepared something to improve a customer's health. Most gratifying."

"I imagine, though, there were many other gratifying aspects of your friendship with Kitty."

"Do you like Kitty very well?"

He scratched his head again. "I expect that there are, there were. Forgive me for saying this, but I am having a difficult time recalling them."

"She is a pretty girl."

"Indeed, very attractive."

"I am sure you had many pleasant conversations together."

"I suppose? It is difficult to recall a single one."

"Surely you enjoyed spending time together. She is a pleasing companion, yes?"

"I once thought so."

"I do not understand. You wrote to my father, insisting you should be permitted to marry her. Carried the letter to London yourself, and brought back his response."

He squeezed his eyes shut and shook his head. "That was Caney's idea. He thought it appropriate. I recall dictating a letter to him, but barely remember what it said. I saw Bennet's response, but thought it odd that it was in Caney's handwriting. But Caney told me that Bennet's secretary was unavailable, so he took the dictation himself. Now that I think about it, it does seem uncomfortably odd. He was so certain that Miss Bennet would make a suitable wife."

"Forgive my forwardness, but you do not seem so certain."

"No, I suppose I am not. I fear that sounds rather bad. I am not the type of man who vacillates on such a thing."

"Perhaps not, but it seems a rather important consideration to work out before one is betrothed. Yes?"

"It does. And the more I think about it, the less certain I become. The more certain I am that it might not be the good idea I once thought it. Do you think she will be distraught? I hate the thought of that." He scowled and ran his knuckles along his fuzzy muttonchops.

"Any young woman would be made unhappy, to be sure. But my friends and I will see to it that she will make a good recovery, should it be necessary."

"That would be most kind of you. I suppose I should tell Sir Fitzwilliam of my change of heart. How well do you think he will receive it?"

"I am certain he will appreciate your integrity in preventing what might bring great unhappiness to so many. Shall I let him know you wish to speak to him?"

"Yes, please do. And, do you think I could have something to eat? I find I am quite peckish."

"Of course." Lydia stood and curtsied. "I will attend to that right now."

Brutus followed her to the door. "You and Cosette were brilliant. I have never seen such a persuasion before."

She scratched under his chin as Cosette landed on her shoulder. "Do not scare him too badly while I go for Mr. Darcy."

He yipped with a backward glance toward Mr. Mothman, then closed the door behind her.

"This is a good thing?" Cosette cuddled against her cheek.

"Mr. Darcy had no desire to see him connected to our family."

"But you are not happy."

"Kitty will be sad. Mama will be furious, might even insist they marry anyway, and Jane will be distraught from all the tension." Sad how that sounded typical for the Bennet family.

"Perhaps for a bit, but it would not surprise me if that wyrm meddled with your mother and Kitty, too. If so, we can make things better for them and, if they are happy, then Jane will be also."

"And if Cobalt did not?"

"I am sure an acceptable persuasion can be found to assuage their bruised feelings. They were illegally meddled with by a dragon, even if only the furry one was persuaded. In that case, it is appropriate that dragons should set the matter right."

"That does seem in keeping with the spirit, if not the letter, of Blue Order Law." Lydia should probably check with Darcy or Lizzy first, but with their approval, it would be nice to be able to make Ingleside less melancholy, even if they would never credit her for the favor she had done them.

"Oh! Look there!" Cosette hovered in front of her face and pointed toward a sleek figure in the sky. "Earl and Sir Richard come!"

36
Chapter

RICHARD GLANCED OVER his shoulder, catching the bright morning sun in his face. At last, Matlock was out of sight. Though it was almost always a relief to leave there, rarely did he feel it quite as strongly as today.

Two dead poachers had already been boxed up and sent along to London, to see what could be learnt from their remains. One of the injured men, bitten by Blackwood, would probably not make it through the day. Basilisk venom was a terrible way to die, but it was difficult to gather much sympathy for him. The tragedy was of his own making.

The other three, along with Cobalt, now confined to a proper cage, would be loaded onto a coach for London as soon as Cownt Matlock concluded his business with St. John. A day or two at most.

So little time left to spend at Pemberley.

With Miss Lydia Bennet.

This was not the way he had planned for it all to come to a close. Not remotely. But he had his orders.

Damn it all.

"Look," Earl called from overhead. "Cosette and her Friend."

Lovely. And now all the things he needed to say would come bumbling out of his mouth, and he would sound like an idiot.

And his ribs still burned where Mothman had kicked him. Sweat trickled down the side of his face, leaving a muddy smear on his sleeve as he tried to rub it away.

Just bloody fantastic.

A handful of minutes later, Lydia waved at him as Earl and Cosette flew twittering circles overhead. Did Earl not realize how stupid a twittering cockatrice sounded? How was it the little fairy dragon had convinced him to try? Such an odd pair they were.

"Good morning, Sir Richard," Lydia curtsied. The lines around her eyes told of a sleepless night. "How fare you after last night?"

He rubbed at sweat along the back of his neck. "Bruised and tired, but I have known much worse. Good work was done last night. It was worth it."

"I am certain it was, and I hope to have added a bit to that good work this morning." Her lips quirked in a dear hint of a smile.

"Indeed? How is that?"

"It seems that Mr. Mothman's interest in my sister has not weathered the latest storm. His affections for her, rather like his entire fancy for Buzby's Shoppe for Ladies, seem to have been rather wyrm-ridden, as it were." She lifted eyebrows over sparkling eyes.

Truly? She had just said that? He laughed until his bruised ribs ached and tears threatened to flow.

"You have not had a great deal of sleep, have you?"

"None at all to speak of." He dragged his sleeve across his eyes. "Something I hope to remedy before I am forced back to London."

"Sir Fitzwilliam mentioned that you would have to depart soon."

"I am at Cownt Matlock's beck and call. He is anxious to have the filth removed from his lair."

"Who could blame him? Was it Mr. Mothman's servant at the center of it all?"

"We certainly have not got to the bottom of it all, but it seems Caney is a key force in coordinating dragon poachers and connecting them with customers interested in those goods. I am sure we will learn more from him in London, but it will not be pretty. I hope not to be involved with it."

"I am glad to hear it. You have done enough for King and Keep already." By Jove, she had a lovely smile.

He offered his arm, and she took it, leaning warm and soft against him.

"Do you anticipate another assignment with the Order?" The tiniest pearl of dread permeated her voice.

"Not immediately. I cannot, I should not."

"Should not?"

"I have been away from Netherford, Keep and dragon, for quite some time. Disagreeable as he may be, St. John has made me aware of aspects of my own estate that have not been adequately managed. Netherford and I need to attend to our own business."

"So, you will be returning to Derbyshire?"

"That is my intention."

They walked on in silence that grew less and less comfortable by the moment.

Earl squawked and Cosette scolded as they circled above.

Bloody interfering dragons. "I heard you. That is enough." He waved them off.

Such a look she gave him!

"I am afraid our Friends are rather insistent."

"On what? I do not understand."

"Truly? You do not? Perhaps I have underestimated you, Miss Bennet."

"Sir Richard, if you have aught to say to me, then perhaps you should do me the honor of saying it directly, or if it is not important enough to say in such a manner, then let no more be spoken of it." She scolded like a fairy dragon!

He stopped and stared at her. "You are unlike any woman I have ever known."

"Am I to believe that is a good thing or not?" Oh, but the look in her eyes was too serious. Truly? Did she not understand?

"It is a very good thing." He rolled his eyes and shook his head. "One would think such things would be easier to say."

"If they are so difficult, do you even wish to try?" Her eyebrow arched just so, the spitting image of Elizabeth.

"I must. I would never forgive myself if I did not. And Earl would be insufferable!"

"Then for his sake alone, you have my full attention."

"Our time together has been too brief, Miss Bennet. Far too brief. In just this short month, I have come to enjoy your company, to rely on your insights and opinions in ways I had never expected."

The corners of her lips turned up. Thank heavens!

Now if only his words would continue to cooperate. "I would like to speak with Darcy about … to ask his permission … that is to say, it is too soon, I think, for anything more formal, but, with a bit more time, perhaps you might consider a quiet courtship? There is but one thing that gives me pause, though, and it is only right I am open and clear with you on the matter."

She broke eye contact and gazed into the distance. "Of course you must be. I would have nothing less. What is your concern?"

"You have mentioned it yourself, so it will come as no surprise, I am sure." Pray let it not be.

"Perhaps it will not when you finally deign to tell me?" She crossed her arms and tapped her fingers along her shoulder.

"Not long ago, I was raised from my lot as 'spare to the heir' into a Keepership and estate of my own because of Netherford. I do not take this responsibility lightly. Establishing a new estate is taxing, and St. John has made me aware of even more challenges ahead. I do not hold it against you that you and Netherford have had some … difficult experiences between you. Truly, I do not hold that against you. But our position, our relationship, Netherford's and mine, it is fragile. I cannot afford to do anything to jeopardize it. I cannot consider any courtship without Netherford's approval."

"Is that all?" Now she was rolling her eyes.

"Is it not enough?"

"I have already told you, I hold no grudge against him for what happened in Hertfordshire. I well understand how foolish I was and how Wickham …"

"The less said about that scoundrel, the better."

"I am certain I already told you, I would like the opportunity to make amends with Netherford, if he will permit it. While I would just as soon not dwell upon those times, I well understand the need to make things right."

"And you do not resent that all must be contingent upon that reconciliation?"

"I am not so reformed as to claim that level of virtue." She laughed, with just a tinge of sadness. "So let us just say, I do not resent the need for it. I would not wish to live with a cranky dragon like Longbourn ever again. I do not envy Mr. Collins' life for that."

"Then, may I speak to Darcy before I leave?"

"Absolutely."

"You will come to Netherford, then?" He blinked back the head-swimming dizziness that threatened.

"As soon as proper means might be arranged."

"A house party, then. I will invite the Darcys to come. Lord knows I need their help in bringing the Keep up to standards. And you will join them? As soon as may be managed?"

"I would like nothing better."

Earl squawked his approval and Cosette, adorably but unsuccessfully, attempted to mimic the sound.

Chapter 37

July 8, 1815

"I AM SO glad you helped Keeper, but why did you not tell me you were practicing your flying?" Elizabeth dodged out of Pemberley's way as she stalked along the long wall of the cellar lair.

Slivers of light, angling through the narrow windows along the ceiling, captured floating dust motes in their path, and cast long dragon-shaped shadows on the floor. The narrow slices of sun, though, did nothing to dispel the musty cellar odor, punctuated with smokey dragon musk.

"Why I not tell you? Think what you not tell me! That is problem. I is dragon. I has wings. You know Chudleigh and Rosings teach me fly. You think I not practice?"

"I had no idea you could fly so well—"

"I practice since Bolsover. Practice much. Understand dragon need fly!" Pemberley slapped her tail against the stone floor.

"Certainly, but you should have told us what you intended to do."

"But you not tell me what doing. That not right! I angry. Very angry." Angry enough for wispy tendrils of smoke to rise from her nostrils.

"What we were doing was dangerous, not something for—"

"A baby?" Pemberley pounced and landed at Elizabeth's feet, pressing her face into Elizabeth's.

Elizabeth barely contained her gasp as she edged back.

"I dragon! I dangerous! No secrets!"

"You are so young, we only thought—"

"You wrong! Matlock say I must be strong. Only keep territory if I strong. You not make me strong."

But she was only a baby—

"It way of dragons. Every dragon must hold territory or not have it. If Keepers hold for me, then I weak. Not good dragon. I will be good dragon." Pemberley's talons raked along the floor stones, screeching, raising the hair on the back of Elizabeth's neck.

"Of course, you will. You already are. We, Keeper and I, the whole Order, it seems, have much to learn about young firedrakes and territory. I am sorry we did not fully understand."

Pemberley bumped her head under Elizabeth's hand for a scratch. "Not like be angry. Need you understand."

"We are trying, dearling. We will sort this out."

"Soon meet with big minor dragons. Cownt Matlock say they help manage territory. It their duty help me so no big dragon takes territory and makes them go. You and Keeper help all understand how do that?"

"That is a good plan. We will begin as soon as possible." Interesting that Cownt Matlock would have come up with that suggestion, considering his notions of hierarchy among dragons. She and Darcy had come to a similar conclusion, but all things considered, it was probably best Pemberley hear it from Matlock right now.

"I go Matlock now. You and Keeper be there, yes?"

"The coach is being readied. We will bring Mr. St. John as well."

"I still no like him, but he knows things. And I need know things." Pemberley huffed as she turned for the dragon tunnel, tail sweeping broad strokes along the floor. "Cownt need know things, too."

What had Pemberley done?

Alister Salt stopped the carriage at the edge of Matlock estate's ominous dragon woods, near the barely visible path that led to the dragon lair. The silence in the coach had been oddly companionable the whole journey. Perhaps Lydia's advice to Mr. St. John was making a difference. He was almost tolerable company today.

Almost.

Brutus, Axel, and Kingsley escorted them to Cownt Matlock's lair, while Sergeant guarded the coach. Walker and Earl soared overhead. Elizabeth sighed. Would there ever again be a day when their every move did not have to be under the watchful eyes of guard drakes and cockatrice? Best not dwell on that now.

Or that April had stayed behind in anticipation of Matlock's temper.

Darcy offered his arm as they made their way to the lair. He had endured his own tongue-lashing from Pemberley with grace and humility, reserving the expression of his frustration for their private sitting room. Raising and managing a baby firedrake in possession of one of the finest territories in the country was proving to be far more complex than any of them had imagined.

Chisholm scurried to meet them as the lair came into view. "The cownt and viscount await you. The cownt has instructed the junior Keeper as to his comportment during this meeting." That her secretary had managed to say that with a straight face was a testimony to the sleek black drake's professionalism.

"You are prepared to record the proceedings?" Elizabeth asked.

"And to make copies for the earl, viscount and undersecretary as well." Chisholm chirruped, a mite cheekily, and bounded into the lair, presumably to announce their arrival.

Had Lady Astrid known of Chisholm's sense of humor when recommending her for the position?

"Approach." Cownt Matlock's deep tones resonated off the lair's rocky walls, reverberating in her bones. A most fitting testimony to his rank and status.

And a little too reminiscent of Longbourn in a temper, though. She shook the tension out of her arms. Pulling her shoulders back and lifting her head high, they entered the dragon's lair.

Little Pemberley stood at Matlock's side, a bright red against his deep blue-green hide, so proud, so serious. How much she had grown, even since leaving London. Gracious!

They made their formal greetings and were duly acknowledged by both major dragons. Now, the challenge.

She curtsied deeply. "The Dragon Sage and Undersecretary of the Order bring the local Keepers together that we may present our concerns to Cownt Matlock, the leading dragon of Derbyshire." This was the way the problem should have been approached in the first place.

Beside her, St. John bowed.

"Your petition to present has been accepted." Matlock looked from the viscount to Darcy and back.

Darcy bowed. "This Keeper welcomes your attention."

Andrew, the viscount, leaned forward just enough to mimic a bow and mouthed along with Darcy.

Matlock's upper lip peeled back in a growl.

Andrew jumped. "This Keeper welcomes your attention."

In the shadows, Chisholm scribbled in her notebook. It would be interesting to see how she recorded that incident.

"Present concerns," Pemberley said, head held high.

St. John stepped forward, adjusting his cravat. Pray he kept to the language they had agreed upon earlier. After his earlier missteps, he would have only one chance to make his case.

"The poachers captured last night on Pemberley grounds have revealed serious defects in the Dragon Keeping at both Matlock and Pemberley Keeps."

Andrew muttered under his breath, something about Richard making a power grab for the estate. Richard had been right; it was best he not attend this meeting.

Mr. St. John cleared his throat. "As is set forth in the Accords, in such a situation, it is the prerogative of the estate Dragon to file a formal complaint against the Keepers in error, or go so far as to demand the replacement of the Keeper with one who will better manage their responsibilities to Keep and Dragon."

Andrew muttered something about the failure of certain dragons to manage their territory properly.

Matlock growled.

Foolish, stupid man! Elizabeth held herself rigid and clenched her fists. A dragon with Matlock's status would never, never admit his failings before anyone of lesser standing, which in his case meant anyone lower than Brenin Buckingham himself. Even then, the subject would be approached sideways rather than head-on.

With dragons, it was always about dominance, even at such a time as this. Failure to declare shortcomings was not the same as failure to acknowledge them. Even St. John understood, once he deigned to listen to her explanation. As long as dominance was preserved, matters could be successfully addressed, and that required a certain delicacy, one challenging for warm-bloods who thought themselves dominant.

Matlock nudged Pemberley forward with his wing. She waddled two steps toward Darcy. "I review errors with Keeper. Am satisfiered … satisfactioned … believing Keeper and Sage will do right. I not need formal actions. But expect reports about all the things on new moons."

Darcy bowed. "Keeper is grateful for Vicontes Pemberley's understanding. The Keep will be managed to her satisfaction."

"Undersecretary …" —Pemberley looked at Mr. St. John in such a way as to suggest she meant 'disagreeable one'— "will stay near until I satisfactioned all problems knowed."

"As you will, Vicontes." Mr. St. John bowed, deep and slow. "I am honored to serve King and Keep."

Pemberley nodded at him and waddled regally back to her place.

Perfectly, she had managed her role perfectly! Elizabeth exhaled the breath she had forgotten she was holding.

Matlock rounded on Andrew with a predatory swiftness that had them all jumping back. "As for you, junior Keeper," —he emphasized 'junior' with a growl—"your muttering makes it clear. I am neither satisfied nor convinced that you understand the problems, much less have any intention to remedy them."

Andrew stammered, open hands held between him and Matlock.

"I have lost faith in you, junior Keeper. You are lazy, selfish, and arrogant. Your failures are many and your strengths are few, if any. You do not deserve the title of even junior Keeper. I will personally make your failures known to the Keeper of Matlock. Undersecretary, you will assist me in filing a formal complaint to be heard by the Minister of the Court and the Minister of Keeps. I understand an audit will follow."

Andrew staggered back.

"Do you wish to see the junior Keeper removed?" Mr. St. John asked, carefully not looking at Andrew.

"Were not Matlock's Pendragon Knight already Keeper to Netherford, I would have him installed as junior Keeper."

Andrew gasped and grabbed for the rock wall behind him, whispering something about being the legal heir to the estate.

"But Netherford is content with his Keeper, and I will honor his request to maintain his current Keeper. So, for now," Matlock huffed a smoky breath toward Andrew, "I insist on a proper steward to manage the estate and adequately train the junior Keeper in his duties."

"I will make it so, Cownt." Mr. St. John bowed again.

"But understand," Matlock pressed his face close enough for Andrew to feel the heat of his breath, "I will have no further patience for your excuses and failures. The steward will report to me, and any, and I mean any, account of resistance from you, and I will insist that Netherford release his Keeper to me."

"I knew Richard was behind this—"

Matlock roared, filling the vast cavern with palpable sound, a force that rattled bones and threatened to rip insides asunder.

"Sir Richard has insisted, repeatedly, he does not want Matlock estate. Even threatened to move to France to avoid it." Mr. St. John managed to keep a somber expression as he stammered through his statement.

Anyone who knew Richard, and his feelings about France, would understand the seriousness of the threat.

Andrew probably had no idea.

"There are other Pendragon Knights I can call upon. Upon my orders, the estate can be declared in irretrievable debt and sold off to Darcy for his next whelp to inherit." Matlock nudged Elizabeth with his wing.

"His what?" Elizabeth pressed her hands to her belly, every inch of her skin crawling with cold nettle-prickles. A tiny flutter tickled under her hand. "Pendragon's bones!" She sagged back into Darcy's arms.

"A new little Keeper?" Pemberley flapped her wings and danced her front feet.

"Is it so?" Darcy held her tightly, eyes huge with astonishment.

"I had no idea. The last few months have been so chaotic … I never thought … but yes … yes, it is possible. The cownt must be right." Oh, merciful heavens! That explained a very great deal.

"Of course, I am right. It will hatch near the last new moon of the year."

"How do you know?" Darcy asked.

"Every whelp on Matlock has been presented to me prior to their hatching. After several hundred years, one learns the signs." Matlock crossed his front feet, arrogant and self-satisfied. He snorted at Andrew again.

"But my sons …"

"With your example, they are no doubt as worthless as you. If I will not have you, then they will not do for me, either."

"We are ruined!"

Darcy released Elizabeth, stormed to Andrew, and shook him by the shoulders. "You would rather surrender your inheritance than humble yourself and submit to the Blue Order law? What kind of man are you? You are a disgrace to your house."

"The lizards are impossible to please. There is no hope!"

Darcy looked as though he would slap his cousin, but Mr. St. John stepped in. "That is what the Ministry of Keeps is for. And on behalf of the Secretary's office, I will assist as well. We have no interest in seeing such irregularities take place as would garner the notice of the dragon-deaf. Like the sale of a significant estate. If a dragon-deaf man like Mr. Collins can adequately manage a Keep, then a viscount is surely not without hope."

Playing to the man's pride was not inappropriate, but did he have to do it at the expense of the Bennet family?

Probably. There were no other dragon-deaf Keepers in the kingdom. Still, it did nothing to ease Elizabeth's dislike of either man.

"Resign your Keep now, or commit to the work." Matlock growled until the ground vibrated. "Choose!"

"I ... I can do ... do no less than a dragon-deaf commoner," Andrew muttered, defeat sloughing off him in sheets.

"I will accept your miserable excuse for a commitment, warm-blood. For now. Do not forget you can easily be replaced. I will not hesitate." Matlock snorted a puff of smoke. "You are all dismissed. Pemberley, attend me." Matlock turned tail, forcing the warm-bloods to dodge and nearly knocking Andrew off his feet. Pemberley waddled behind, with a backward glance—and was that a wink?—at Darcy and Elizabeth.

"Shall I assist the viscount back to the manor?" Mr. St. John asked. "We have much work to do."

"Yes, do. I will have a horse sent to Matlock so you may return to Pemberley at your leisure." Darcy escorted Elizabeth away from the entryway.

Would Andrew live up to his commitments or would he lose the estate? She pressed her hands to her middle once again. Though it was tempting to want that for her child, the trouble it would bring within the Order and beyond was simply not worth it.

"Do you wish your happy news to be a part of the official records, Lady Sage?" Chisholm appeared at her elbow, grinning as only a dragon could.

"I think I will have to decide that later. After we become accustomed to it ourselves."

Epilogue

July 8, 1815

DARCY LEANED BACK and took a deep draw from his tankard. Pemberley's cider certainly had to be the best in Derbyshire.

Although still in its guise as a planning room, the guest sitting room seemed the right place to gather on the eve of Richard's departure for London. The fading colors of sunset through open windows painted the room in deep golds that blended into the candlelight, emphasizing the new tranquility that had settled over the space.

"Is it true, we have Pemberley to thank for Cownt Matlock's new-found attention to his territory?" Richard leaned back and laughed as he handed Earl a bowl of cider.

"She takes after Elizabeth, taking matters into her own talons." Darcy chuckled.

"Full of righteous indignation, she marched herself to Matlock under guise of seeking his advice—which she did as well, mind you. As told by those who overheard, she crafted her questions on territory management in such a way as to shame him into behaving the way a proper dominant dragon ought to conduct himself." Elizabeth's face glowed as only a woman increasing could. "I could not be more proud of her."

"Perhaps that is why the cownt pre-empted your good news the way he did. A bit of payback for the experience?" Richard winked.

"Perhaps, but do not forget he threatened to have Matlock estate sold off to me." Darcy raised his tankard slightly.

"Did Cownt Matlock really say that?"

"Indeed, he did. You can read Chisholm's faithful records on the matter before I seal them into the packet for London," Elizabeth said.

"I will take you up on the offer. Netherford will want an exact account of that conversation. Matlock had once approached him to suggest his Keeper might be commandeered in service of the Grand Dug."

"I can only imagine he was not happy about the prospect." Lydia sat next to Richard, her color high.

Richard's announcement had not come as a surprise, not exactly, certainly not as much as Elizabeth's news—at least Richard had been able to share it himself, rather than hearing it from the Dragon Chancellor of the Order. But it was still going to take some time to become accustomed to Richard's interest in Lydia as reality, rather than attribute it to the delusions of wyrm venom.

If Uncle Matlock was not utterly beside himself over the situation with Andrew and the threat to put Matlock in Darcy's hands, Richard's choice in courtship would certainly send him over the edge. Dragon's bones, things were going to become interesting.

"Understanding the precariousness of his position makes Netherford rather hesitant to argue with the Grand Dug of the Order, but no, he was not at all happy about it. He will be pleased to know Matlock is considering other alternatives. But those are problems for another day. Let us dwell on happier things." Richard raised his tankard. "I offer a toast to your happy news and to the cow-pawed dragon who delivered it."

What a way to have learnt of their coming blessing! The sort of thing that only happened when one was married to the Dragon Sage!

"Perhaps you should not say such things about the cownt. They do have a way of getting back to him." Elizabeth glanced at the fairy dragons daintily perched around their own teacup of cider.

"None in this company would dare." Walker shrieked a warning at any other dragons in earshot. "Would they?"

Juniper and Fern peeked through the servants' door and squeaked, "No, sir."

"And I certainly tell only proper tales." Storyteller Raven, the lesser cockatrix, landed on the sill of the open window and extended her wings in greeting to Walker, then turned to Elizabeth. "Your good news, though, has taken wing, quite literally."

"I should not be surprised. You will tell Papa for us, Richard, before the dragons do?" Elizabeth said.

"As soon as I arrive in London."

Dragons' bones! Ingleside would have to be told as well. Darcy rubbed the back of his neck. What new turmoil would that bring?

"I thought to offer a story in honor of the news." Raven glided to the edge of the table.

"I love a good story." Lydia leaned forward, hands wrapped around her tankard.

"Naturally, you have heard of St. Margaret, the patron saint of ladies in your favored condition." Raven bowed to Elizabeth with a flourish found only in the best of storytellers.

"We have, indeed."

"You will have heard, then, of how she was swallowed by a dragon, but escaped unscathed." Raven spread her wings and crept in a small circle to face each of her audience in turn. "But it will come as no surprise that is not the real story of Margaret and the Dragon, just a convenient myth to cover the details that only the Blue Order might know. The truth of the matter—"

A screaming fairy dragon streaked through the open window, a blur in the candlelit room. Raven dodged the fairy dragon's inelegant landing in a dirty heap on the table.

"Pax! That is Pax!" Lydia leapt to her feet and scooped up the disoriented fairy dragon. "Jam, hand me the jam. She must eat quickly."

Richard all but threw the jam pot to Lydia, who steadied Pax as she gulped sustenance.

Cosette and April converged on Pax, preening her, supporting her, twittering to help settle her nerves.

What was Pax doing here? Darcy's heart thundered in his throat, stalling his words.

"Blood! She is bleeding!" Lydia cried, turning to Elizabeth. "May, yes? May can help?"

"I will get her." Earl sped out the door before Elizabeth could speak.

Elizabeth crowded in close. "How were you injured? What happened?"

"Cockatrice," Pax blurbled through a mouth full of jam. "On Pemberley."

"I have had enough of those flying lizards." Walker hissed. "Vicontes Pemberley gave me leave to manage them as I saw fit. They will be out of the territory tomorrow."

"I will help you!" Earl landed on the table, May following close behind.

Lydia backed away as May approached, purring and whispering soft, soothing reassurances, and asking permission to tend Pax's wounds.

Mrs. Reynolds appeared—how did she always know when she would be needed and in what way?—with a basket lined with warm stones from the kitchen fire, cotton wool, and a soft blanket.

Fed, warm, and bandaged, Pax huddled in the basket, twittering softly.

Perhaps now Darcy might find command of his words once again. "What happened? Georgiana, is she with you?"

A shudder coursed from Pax's jam-stained beak down her dingy-white, bedraggled feather-scales, ending at her tail. "No, she is not. I could not help her, so I came … I came for help....Terrible! Terrible! Terrible danger!"

"Where? What?" Richard demanded.

"She is in terrible danger! You must come! You must come!"

For more dragon lore check out:
**Elizabeth's Commonplace
Book of Dragons**
and
Dragon Myths of England
At RandomBitofFascination.com

Acknowledgments

So many people have helped me along the journey
taking this from an idea to a reality.
Debbie, Diana, Megan, Linda, Maureen, and Ruth,
thank you so much for cold reading, proofreading and
being honest!
My dear friend Cathy, my biggest cheerleader, you
have kept me from chickening out more than once!
And my sweet sister Gerri who believed in even those
first attempts that now live in the file drawer!
Thank you!

Other Books by Maria Grace

Jane Austen's Dragons Series:
Pemberley: Mr. Darcy's Dragon
Longbourn: Dragon Entail
Netherfield:Rogue Dragon
A Proper Introduction to Dragons
The Dragons of Kellynch
Kellynch:Dragon Persuasion
Dragons Beyond the Pale
Dragon Keepers' Cotillion
The Turnspit Dragon
Dragons of Pemberley

Remember the Past
The Darcy Brothers
Fine Eyes and Pert Opinions

A Jane Austen Regency Life Series:
A Jane Austen Christmas: Regency Christmas Traditions
Courtship and Marriage in Jane Austen's World
How Jane Austen Kept her Cool: An A to Z History of Georgian Ice Cream

The Queen of Rosings Park Series:
Mistaking Her Character
The Trouble to Check Her
A Less Agreeable Man

Sweet Tea Stories:
A Spot of Sweet Tea: Hopes and Beginnings
Snowbound at Hartfield
A Most Affecionate Mother

Inspriation

Darcy Family Christmas Series:
Darcy and Elizabeth: Christmas 1811
The Darcy's First Christmas
From Admiration to Love

Given Good Principles Series:
Darcy's Decision
The Future Mrs. Darcy
All the Appearance of Goodness
Twelfth Night at Longbourn

Behind the Scene Anthologies (with Austen Variations):
Pride and Prejudice: Behind the Scenes
Persuasion: Behind the Scenes

Non-fiction Anthologies
Castles, Customs, and Kings Vol. 1
Castles, Customs, and Kings Vol. 2
Putting the Science in Fiction

Available in e-book, audiobook and paperback

Available in paperback, e-book, and audiobook format at all online bookstores.

On Line Exclusives at:

www.http//RandomBitsofFascination.com

Bonus and deleted scenes
Natural History of Dragons
The Blue Order World

Free e-books:

Rising Waters: Hurricane Harvey Memoirs
Lady Catherine's Cat
A Gift from Rosings Park
Bits of Bobbin Lace
Half Agony, Half Hope: New Reflections on Persuasion
Four Days in April

About the Author

Six-time BRAG Medallion Honoree, #1 Best-selling Historical Fantasy author Maria Grace has her PhD in Educational Psychology and is a 16-year veteran of the university classroom where she taught courses in human growth and development, learning, test development and counseling. None of which have anything to do with her undergraduate studies in economics/sociology/managerial studies/behavior sciences. She pretends to be a mild-mannered writer/cat-lady, but most of her vacations require helmets and waivers or historical costumes, usually not at the same time.

She writes Gaslamp fantasy, historical romance and non-fiction to help justify her research addiction.

She can be contacted at:

author.MariaGrace@gmail.com

Facebook:
http://facebook.com/AuthorMariaGrace

On Amazon.com:
http://amazon.com/author/mariagrace

Random Bits of Fascination
(http://RandomBitsofFascination.com)

White Soup Press (http://whitesouppress.com/)

On Twitter @WriteMariaGrace

On Pinterest: http://pinterest.com/mariagrace423/

.

Made in United States
North Haven, CT
11 June 2022

20108847R00269